CAROL J. NELSON
AUDRA
DYING for LIFE

Book One

BookBaby Publishing

Pennsauken, New Jersey

Audra Dying for Life

© 2020 Carol J. Nelson

www.caroljnelson@gmail.com

First edition

ISBN: 978-1-09830-360-0

In loving memory of my husband, Larry Nelson. He not only encouraged me to write, he appreciated my stories. After a courageous battle with Parkinson's disease, he went home to be with the Lord before they were published.

ACKNOWLEDGEMENTS

Heartfelt thanks to Dr. William K. Summers MD for taking time to suggest and clarify medical conditions for the characters in this book.

Special thanks to my editor, Deirdre Lockhart. Working with her was like taking a class in Fiction Writing 101. She reminded me of basics and taught me skills I wasn't even aware I lacked. She corrected my errors with humor, patience, and grace, and pushed me when she knew I could do better. Without her guidance, this book may never have been published. She's proven to be not only my editor but also a friend and sister in the Lord.

TABLE OF CONTENTS

CHAPTER ONE

A LIFE CHANGER

AUDRA KNIGHT PAUSED ON THE SIDEWALK BEFORE CHANDLER'S Grove Medical Center. Despite the sun heating her face, she shivered, and it wasn't from the air conditioning in the doctor's office. The icy hand of fear had grabbed her by the throat the moment Dr. Rhonda said she needed to do a biopsy.

Dr. Rhonda smiled when she reassured her it probably wasn't cancer, but fear wasn't rational. It shuddered down Audra's spine and callously whispered, "Remember what happened to your mother. Remember your grandmother."

Her stomach contracted into a rigid ball that nearly nauseated her as her heels clacked across the parking lot. She slid behind the wheel of her Ford Focus and closed her eyes. This couldn't be happening. Fumbling the phone from her purse, her fingers trembled as she tapped her sister's name on her cell. "Do–do you have a minute?" she asked Laney when she answered.

"Well, I *am* kind of busy right now. Is it important?"

Of course, it's important! she wanted to yell into the phone. She shook her head. "It can wait. I'll call you back later," she murmured. She slid her phone into her purse and backed out. *She never has time. I wonder if she even realizes how much I still need her.* She pulled onto Fifth Avenue. She'd stop at Tamina's instead.

In less than ten minutes, Audra rapped on Tamina York's first-floor apartment door. Her eyes were stinging from held-back tears when the familiar blue door with a crooked number two swung open.

Tamina's usually easygoing smile faded, and she just stood there while her black mascara-enhanced lashes blinked. "Girlfriend! What's wrong? She thrust her hand forward. "You look like you're in shock."

"I am, and I'm scared." Audra grasped Tamina's offered hand and lurched into the apartment. "I just came from Dr. Rhonda's—I think something bad's going to happen."

Tamina didn't say anything but opened her arms, and Audra sagged into her comforting embrace. A tear slid down her cheek as she rested her head on Tamina's shoulder. She couldn't say anything else yet, either.

"You're trembling! Come on and sit down." Tamina perched on the edge of the white faux-leather couch and faced Audra at the other end. "If you saw Dr. Rhonda, it has to be a female problem. Before I left on vacation, you told me you'd finally started your period after four months. What happened?"

Audra crossed her arms around herself and faced blankly ahead. "It never stopped. After two weeks, I called Dr. Rhonda, but it took another week before I could get in—and it's still going." She blinked back tears as she stared into Tamina's warm-brown face. "Dr. Rhonda wants to do a biopsy as soon as possible, and that's just turned me to jelly."

"Are you afraid it'll be like your mother?"

"Well, yeah. I was only twelve when she told me she had cancer, and I vividly remember standing beside her hospital bed. She looked so terribly ill… It was hard to comprehend that was really my mother. Her image will be engraved in my memory forever." Her hands fell limply into her lap and she leaned her head against the back of the couch. "The same thing happened to my grandmother, but I don't remember it. For over twenty years, I've been living knowing I'm at risk and suddenly the Big C could become a reality. To tell you the truth, I'm terrified."

"Have you told your sister?"

"I called, but she was too busy to talk."

Tamina reached over and squeezed Audra's hand. "I wish she would have had time. I don't even want to think of something bad happening to you."

Audra jerked herself upright. "You don't understand—it *could*! And I have all these what ifs. We go back to work in two days, and school starts next Wednesday. What if I get too sick to teach? What if I have to quit? My mother and grandmother both had husbands to support them when they got ill. I don't. And what if something happens to me, what will happen to little Rosa? Her great-grandmother's old, and what if something happens to *her*? Who will be there to help Rosa grow up?"

Tamina squeezed Audra's knee. "Whoa, slow down! I know this has given you a jolt, but, number one, you haven't had the biopsy done yet. It may not be as bad as you fear. Number two, medicine has advanced a long way since your mother and grandmother went through it. Number three, no matter what happens to you, I'll be here to stand with you through it. And number four, I promise that, if anything really bad should happen, I'll look after Rosa myself."

Audra's head fell to the back of the couch, again, and she closed her eyes. "Thank you, Dr. Tamina. As usual, you're right on target." She let out a long sigh. "Getting hysterical won't help the situation, but I guess a biopsy to look for possible cancer was just too up-close and personal—I'm not handling it very well, am I?" She leaned forward and propped her elbows on her knees. "I don't have a choice. It's gotta be done, ready or not, but I can't bear to talk about it anymore. It's too depressing."

Audra twisted toward her friend. She'd been so focused on herself she hadn't noticed Tamina's freshly cut pixie hairdo, the brush of apricot blush across her smooth-as-silk brown cheekbones, or the glow of her largest hoop earrings. Audra eyed her white leggings and black, bronze, and white cold-shoulder tunic. Her platform sandals lay on the turquoise rug beneath the glass and chrome coffee table. A paper plate of cookie crumbs and an open magazine occupied the glass-topped end table.

"You're looking good. Been out shopping?"

Tamina rolled her eyes. "No. I had to go downtown and pick my dad up and take him home. He spent overnight in jail for disorderly conduct. He looked awful — so thin. I don't think he's eating. Still chain-smoking, though. He complained of a pain in his stomach, too."

Audra's eyebrows knit. "What landed him in jail?"

Tamina grimaced. "He got in a scuffle downtown, and a policeman just happened to be nearby. If he'd kept his mouth shut, he wouldn't have been in trouble — but he had to mouth off to the officer. I tell you I've never seen anyone so stubborn."

"Oh? My father would have been right up there tied for first place."

"Yeah, but your dad's dead. You don't have to deal with it."

"Touché." Audra planted her elbows back on her knees and rested her chin in her hands. "Yuck. Speaking of him brings up memories nearly as bad as my mother's cancer, and just as depressing."

"Well, aren't we a pair? Come on into the kitchen. I cooked a chicken breast and boiled a couple of eggs. Let's build salads and drown our troubles with a glass of chocolate milk."

After they ate, Audra went home. She closed her living-room drapes and flopped onto the couch on her stomach. Tamina always made her laugh, but today her humor had merely been a Band-Aid. She was exhausted from the emotional upheaval. She closed her eyes and was on the verge of drifting into sleep when a picture formed in her mind like a surreal painting. The Big C had shattered her, and disjointed fragments of her body were scattered across a bizarre, jagged background of her mother in a hospital bed and her father wearing his perpetual frown. Slashing right through the middle was a giant, black question mark. She jolted up, jerking away from the unsettling mental image. Life had suddenly changed, and the only thing she knew was that fear was going to be her biggest enemy.

She pushed up from the couch and went to the kitchen. She gritted her teeth as she punched in her sister's phone number. *I wish I hadn't told her I'd call her back.* She forced a smile when Laney answered—a smile Laney couldn't see. "Oh, hi, are you still busy?"

Laney let out a long breath. "I've gone from busy to fuming. Amanda told me she was going shopping but spent the whole day with this kid named Ross. Andy and I have been uncomfortable since she met him, and we've told her that." She sucked in a fresh breath as if to give herself courage to continue.

"Andy told her she can't see him anymore because he's afraid he's going to get her in trouble, and for the first time, Amanda threw it in his face that he isn't her father and she didn't have to listen to him." Silence captured the line for a moment. "Well, I blew up and got in her face. Now she's not speaking to either one of us." She fell quiet again, and all Audra heard were her faint whispers of breath. "I'm scared for her, Audie. She's only sixteen, and I'm afraid she's going to make the same mistakes I did, and I can't bear to think of it."

Audra blinked at Laney's outburst. "Oh, Laney, don't even *say* that! It reminds me too much of you and Father. It's like stirring up muddy water," she blurted out, and resentment against her father rose up so suddenly she felt choked. She had to wait a moment before she could speak. "I'm sorry. I shouldn't have said that, but things could have been so different if he hadn't gotten bitter — "

"I know, but I don't want to talk about it," Laney said in a voice so low Audra barely heard her.

Audra continued holding the phone to her ear but remained silent. Her sister wouldn't talk, and once again, she felt pushed aside and out of her sister's life. *She probably won't want to talk about my doctor visit, either, but I guess it can wait.* "Well, I'd better let you go."

She hung up and went into the next room and sat at her piano. She played Handel's "Largo" because that's what was open, but it left her feeling lonely. That had been her mother's favorite piece to play, and hearing it brought her to the verge of tears again. Her fingers stilled before the last notes, and she lowered her face into her hands. *I don't want to face cancer. I don't want to deal with a dysfunctional family. I want everything to be like when Mom was with us.*

CHAPTER TWO

BACK TO WORK

AUDRA'S EMOTIONS CALMED DOWN BY WEDNESDAY, THE FIRST workday of the new school year. The August New Mexico sun was baking the tan brick of Chandler's Grove Academy as she and Tamina entered, making the cool air in the hallways a welcome relief. Their heels clicked on the tile floor as they walked down West Hall to the gym.

They grabbed cups of coffee from the paper-covered table at the back, then chose seats in the last row of chairs. Audra smiled at Tamina. "In spite of my possible crisis, I'm glad to be back at work. I always do look forward to watching your little fifth graders graduate to my mid-school English class."

Tamina tipped her head toward Audra. "And I'm glad to see you smile."

Sheldon Bentley, the middle-school principal, stood to address the assembled staff. Tall, with receding black hair, there was a distinguished air about him in his white dress shirt and blue tie. The room quieted when he cleared his throat. "Good morning and welcome back to Chandler's Grove Academy where our motto remains Your Child's Potential Is Our Only Concern. I trust each of you had a restful summer and are anticipating another successful year here. I'm looking forward to working with all of you for the good of the students and…"

Audra sipped her coffee. *This is the eighth time I've heard this pep talk. Sheldon's a proficient principal, but he never varies his speech much. I wonder if a biopsy's painful.*

She glanced over at short, plump Margo Wilson, Sheldon's counterpart on the elementary side of the school. *She still has her hair permed into a ball of frizz—pay attention to Sheldon.*

"This year we have the pleasure of adding three new teachers to our staff, and for their benefit, I'd like to mention that a brief history of how Chandler's Grove Academy evolved from the work of Josiah Chandler and his friend Sgt. Kirkwood is available on the side tables with the rest of the handouts." His eyes moved across his assembled teachers and office workers. "And for you veterans, I'll add that through the ongoing support of ACT, our founder Jeremy Chandler's company, our new cafeteria kitchen and twin lunchrooms will be up and running next week."

A ripple of applause rose from the group. Sheldon waited for quiet to return and then gestured toward the front row. "We have three new teachers this year—two in our middle school and one in our elementary program—and if they will please stand, I'd like to introduce them."

As two men and a woman stood and faced the audience, Audra and Tamina shifted to get a better view.

"Dann Day joins us from the Chicago school districts where he gained experience with elementary and middle school music programs. He will be our new band and orchestra teacher."

Tamina leaned closer to Audra. "Oh wow! Hunk doesn't even begin to describe him."

Audra glanced toward the front, swallowed, and decided to ignore her friend's remark.

"Sure hope he does better than Gordon Blackwell did the last three years. We don't need another disaster in the music program," she whispered behind her hand.

"Heather Easton hails from Minnesota," Sheldon resumed. "As our new sixth-grade math teacher, she's beginning her third year of teaching. And finally, Vern Gilbert comes to us from Montana and will be teaching fourth grade over on the elementary side." He began clapping as he added, "Let's give them a warm welcome!" The staff of teachers, aides, and office workers applauded as he shook hands with each of the new faculty members.

Audra's gaze traveled back to Dann Day. *He is good looking but just forget it, girl. Your future is too unsettled to let such thoughts enter your head.*

After Margo Wilson's welcome speech and instructions to pick up the handouts on the side tables, Tamina and Audra parted. Audra picked up her papers at the same time Jerold Altman, the seventh-grade science teacher, stepped up to the table with Dann Day in tow.

"Audra, I'd like you to meet an old college buddy of mine. I can assure you there's going to be some big changes in the music department with Dann in charge. Dann, this is Audra Knight, our sixth-grade English teacher." He turned back to Audra. "I'll be spending the rest of today showing him the ropes."

Dann's hands came out of his pockets as he smiled and shook her hand. But before either of them could utter a word, Jerold caught another teacher arriving at the table by the arm. "Hey, Carl, I'd like you to meet Dann Day."

As Dann shook hands with Carl Muller, Audra moved on. She'd felt the flush on her cheeks at Dann's smile, but she chose to ignore it. With an eager spring to her step, she crossed the room to meet Heather, the new sixth-grade teacher. *She's pretty, but she looks so young! She makes thirty-three feel old. I wonder if she's Scandinavian with that long blond hair and coming from Minnesota? Does she even realize all the single male teachers are gathered around her?*

Waiting to introduce herself, Audra noticed Heather's full attention wasn't on the individuals shaking her hand. She followed Heather's line of sight to Jerold Altman, Dann Day, and Vern Gilbert off to the side. Jerold was gesturing with his hands while enlightening Dann and Vern about something. Jerold's wedding ring was evident even at that distance. Heather wasn't taking him in.

Well over six feet tall and loose-limbed, Vern hunched forward to catch Jerold's words. His stubble of black hair blended into his five-o-clock shadow, highlighting angular features. In contrast, Dann stood several inches shorter than Vern. Well-groomed brown hair complemented his gray eyes and even facial features. She was willing to bet Heather was looking at Dann.

She shrugged, walked forward, and held out her hand. "Hi, Heather. I'm Audra Knight—sixth-grade English. Your room will be just down the hall from mine."

"I'm glad to meet you." Shaking Audra's hand, Heather gave her a half-smile before her eyes darted back to the trio.

Audra tried again. "The Southwest must be quite different from Minnesota. Are you having any problem adjusting?"

Heather dragged her eyes back again. "Yes, I can't get used to a brown landscape, and my skin is having a hard time getting accustomed to the dryness." Once more, her eyes shifted.

Audra glanced at her watch. She wanted to stop by her room before she went home, and Heather didn't seem too interested in conversing. "I have to run, but I'm sure we'll get better acquainted. I'll see you later, Heather."

Heather dismissed her with a nod. Audra walked a few steps away before looking back. Heather was already headed for the group of men. Audra chuckled. *Looks like she's staking her claim right out of the starting gate.*

CHAPTER THREE

NO DOUBT HOW THINGS STAND

DANN DAY SCOWLED AT THE BAND MUSIC LYING IN A JUMBLE ON the floor next to the music cabinet. "Whoever filed this did nothing but make a mess," he grumbled. He needed a cup of coffee to see him through this sorting and filing job. The teachers' lounge was just down the hall where West Hall intersected South Hall. He'd only be gone a minute.

He wrinkled his nose as he filled a foam cup with coffee to take back to his room. It smelled burned. Turning from the coffee urn, he nearly bumped into Heather Easton and rocked back on his heels to keep from spilling the hot liquid. He'd heard the door open but hadn't noticed her crossing the room. Now, she was standing next to him — too close for comfort, with an eager smile.

She'd approached him the same way the day before in the gym — just appeared next to him out of nowhere. She didn't say anything, just stood close to him, listening. He'd felt so uncomfortable he'd excused himself. Maybe she was just trying to be friendly but having her so close felt claustrophobic.

"So," she moved in front of him, her smile still in place, "how do you like living in this godforsaken place? Nothing but cactus and rocks in every direction and a river that's no more than a weed-filled ditch—it must seem like a one-horse burg after living in Chicago."

He cringed at the teasing quality of her voice and backed into the coffee bar. "No, I like it. I think all the mesas and rock formations are quite distinctive. The town's an oasis in the desert, and that 'weed-filled ditch' is an arroyo. I imagine when it rains in that canyon to the east the water comes roaring through at a pretty good clip."

Heather rolled her eyes. "Whatever."

Dann's forehead furrowed at her indifferent answer. "I don't think it can be a one-horse burg, either, to support a school like this."

"Well, possibly not, but I'm not used to school starting in August." She flipped her long hair away from her face.

He sipped the acrid coffee, and his face screwed up in a shocked grimace. "Yuck! That pot must have been sitting there over summer." He dumped the coffee in the sink. "Excuse me, I have to get rid of this cup."

Heather barely moved, and her honey-blond hair tickled his arm as he pushed past her. He pitched the cup, and it dropped with a plunk into the wastebasket five feet away.

"Nice shot," a feminine voice complimented him.

Dann turned. *It's her! Oh wow, what gorgeous brown eyes.* His heart rate increased as he crossed to the couch. He jammed his hands into his pockets and rocked up on his toes. "Good to see you again. I wanted to talk to you more in the gym on Wednesday, but when I turned, you were gone."

Her full, pink lips parted in a pleasant smile. "It looked like Jerold was keeping you occupied. Welcome to the Grove. I hope you enjoy working with our music students."

"Thanks." He nodded toward the cup in her hand. "How can you tolerate that coffee?"

Her laugh rippled. "I cut it with hot water from the tap. It's pretty putrid otherwise. So, are you Dan for Daniel?"

He shook his head and chuckled. "No, I'm Dann with a double *N*."

Her eyebrows rose. "A rather unique spelling. Is there a story behind it?"

His chest swelled with elation that she should ask. "A very short one. My parents wanted to combine my father's name, David, and my mother's name, Janna. A boy would be Dann, or a girl would be Danna. When they found out they had twins, I got Dann, and my sister got Davene."

He removed his hands from his pockets and crossed his arms. "What about Audra? I've never known an Audra."

"No?" She straightened the papers she held. "My mother seemed to have a penchant for unique — at least for girls' names. My brother is Evan Christopher after our father — nothing unusual. My sister is Loretha Elaine, after our great-grand-mother. However, when Evan was small, he couldn't handle it. He called her Laney, and much to my mother's chagrin, it stuck. When I came along, I was named Audra Marlene after a former student of my mother's."

Dann grinned. Her cheeks were turning pink. "Do you enjoy teaching at the academy?"

She creased her handouts in half. "I do. I went to school here when I was a youngster, and when I was offered the chance to come back to teach, I snatched it."

"Ahh, a local girl. You must know a lot about this town."

"I suppose so." She checked her watch. "I need to get back."

As she started to stand, her dark-brown hair flipped on the ends and stroked her shoulders as she moved. He reached to help her up.

Halfway to the door, Heather stepped forward and flashed a smile. "I know new teachers shouldn't be spending their whole day in the lounge, but if you have another minute, Dann, I'd like to ask you something."

Audra glanced at him. "I'm going on."

As he moved forward to open the door for her, he caught a partial view of Heather's face. He swallowed hard at the strange chill shivering down his spine. She was looking directly at Audra. Her lips contorted into a rigid line, and her eyes narrowed into a threatening glare. The look lasted only a second, but he knew Audra saw it. She recoiled a step before she fled.

Heather swooped her long blond hair off her shoulders and let it fall back again like a golden wave. Her lips relaxed into a smile. "Did you find an apartment yet?"

Dann stared at her, trying to comprehend what had just happened. She obviously had no idea he'd seen her expression, but he didn't want to answer her stupid question. He wanted to run down the hall and tell Audra he didn't like what Heather just did. His jaw tightened. It wouldn't be wise to say what he was thinking. "Yes. Why do you ask?"

She turned the curves of her body into prominent view. "Just curious. Mine's nearly downtown, but I think it's too pricey. I was wondering if there are less expensive places in your neighborhood. What part of town are you in?"

His eyebrows knit. *I'm not about to let you know where I live.* "I'm not anywhere near downtown, but I have a lot of work to finish today. I have to get back."

"Oh, sure. Well, I'll just walk along with you. I have to get back, too."

He stepped into the hallway. Audra was nowhere in sight. He took long strides toward West Hall, and Heather kept up with him. They were nearing the band room when she altered her voice. "What do you still have to do to your room to be ready for students next week?"

Oh, stop trying to be coy. "Way too much to be wasting time out here in the hall," he grumbled. Yes, he was being rude, but she was being… He didn't want to *think* about what she was being. He opened the door to the band room. "Bye. Have a good day." He closed the door with a bang, crossed the room, and stood in front of the chaotic pile of music on the floor.

I just moved fifteen hundred miles to get away from a designing woman. He kicked the side of the file cabinet, leaving a small dent.

After Audra got home, she stomped to the backyard and yanked weeds for twenty minutes. Back inside, she played two songs at the piano and stopped. She paced from the kitchen door to the fireplace and back and paused beside the telephone. The agitation churning her insides was not abating. She called Tamina.

"Do you have a minute, girlfriend?"

"A few. What's up?"

"This was the most bizarre day." She explained Heather's reaction in the lounge and then huffed. "I'm glad looks can't kill—I would have died on the spot. Three days and she's claimed him as her private property."

"Uh-oh, does the little blond have a jealous streak?"

"Maybe." She dragged out a chair and plopped down at the table. "What really ticked me off was I felt the same as when I was a kid and my father got angry. Even when I hadn't done anything, his anger always left me feeling insignificant and worthless."

"Ouch. Sounds like she was acting like a cat with her claws out." Tamina giggled.

"Or some adolescent flirt." Audra gave a short laugh. "I guess if I can separate how she made me feel from what she actually did, I can find it amusing. Dann and I had a short generic conversation about family names—how was that making a pass at him? If she'd asked, I could have told her I have no intention of pursuing him. But, if Heather's hot for him, it's none of my business. So, what are you doing?"

"I'm ready to walk out the door for my tutoring class."

"I forgot—Well, thanks for letting me vent. I do feel better. I'll talk to you later."

She drummed her fingers on the table. Her short conversation with Dann *had* made her feel better than she had in days, and she rather liked the little tingle when his hand touched hers. *Okay, girl, knock it off! You've got one big health problem facing you, so don't go getting any romantic notions — even if he is the best-looking male to hit town since who knows when.*

After she ate dinner, she returned to the piano for a more relaxed time of playing. However, uninvited thoughts of Dann darted in and out like a needle pulling a thread through the fabric of her mind. She sighed. *A good-looking guy like Dann probably has a gorgeous girlfriend in Chicago, so why should I even dare to think he'd be interested in me?*

CHAPTER FOUR

SISTERS

ON THE FOLLOWING MORNING, AUDRA PUSHED HER EMPTY CEREAL bowl aside on the table and propped her chin in the heel of her hand. Dr. Rhonda had her biopsy scheduled for Monday, and she was supposed to have somebody drive her. Tamina had a teachers' meeting, leaving Laney as her only option. Her lips pulled to one side. *I really wish I didn't have to call her.*

She forced cheer into her voice. "Hi! What's going on with you at eight o'clock on Saturday morning?"

"Oh, hi." Laney's flat voice cut through the line. "The boys have only been out of bed an hour, and they're already driving me nuts. Tease, tease, tease—I'm glad school's about to start."

"How's Amanda?"

"Umm—kind of moody. She came out of her room long enough to eat breakfast, and now she's back in there. Did you need something?"

"Sort of. I need a ride to Dr. Rhonda's on Monday morning…" Letting her voice trail away, she waited.

A long silence elapsed before Laney asked, "Why?"

"She's going to do a biopsy—but I don't think it's anything serious."

Another long silence. "Of course, I can take you, but why didn't you tell me sooner?"

Audra's teeth clamped together. "I tried. You were busy."

"Oh, I guess I've had too much on my plate lately. What time do you need to be there?"

Her voice went soft. "Ten."

"Will nine forty be early enough to pick you up?"

"Yes."

Nothing but Laney's soft breath came through the line until a long exhale reverberated in Audra's ear. "You're sure it's not serious?"

She caught her lip between her teeth. "Probably not. I'm meeting Tamina in a bit, and we're taking Rosa and Kayla to buy school clothes."

"Okay. I'll see you Monday."

Feeling hollow, she dropped the phone into its cradle and stared off into space. *She didn't even ask me why I need a biopsy.* The biopsy could lead to a hysterectomy, but it wouldn't be like having her appendix or her gallbladder removed—it would be her womanhood that was taken away. She was single with no prospects for marriage, but everything in her wanted to hold on to what made her a woman. Still, a hysterectomy would be better than dying like her mother and grandmother. Both had their families before they got sick, but it could be she'd never have that chance.

Hollow hurt.

Audra picked up eight-year-old Rosa Espinosa, and they met Tamina and Kayla, Tamina's nine-year-old charge from the Buddy Program, at Hudson's Department store. The squeals of delight as the girls chose jeans, skirts, tops, underwear, and socks lifted Audra's spirits, but she couldn't completely shake the hollow feeling. As they walked toward the children's shoe department, Tamina nudged her arm. "Hey, girlfriend, you seem preoccupied. You still worrying?"

"Not about the biopsy. I talked to Laney, and I feel so–so frustrated. We used to be close, but now she seems so distant. I think it must have something to do with Father, but I don't know if she's as angry at him as I am or not."

Shifting the stack of jeans to her left arm, Tamina stopped walking. When the girls ran ahead to check out tennis shoes on little plastic pedestals, she gave Audra a quick hug. "Have you tried talking to her about it?"

"Our conversations never seem to go anywhere."

Rosa spied a pair of pink, lavender, and blue flowered tennies, and Audra's smile returned when the child cried out, "Oh, Miss Audra, these are just what I've been dreaming about!"

Audra touched Tamina's arm. "Okay, no more self-pity. This is the girls' day. Let's make it memorable."

The shopping finished, Audra headed for the parking lot with Rosa hugging her Hudson's bag like a treasure. The girl bounced along beside her. "Oh, Miss Audra, thank you soooo much. I can't wait to wear my new clothes to school—but oh, this is heavy."

Audra's heart swelled as she took the bag from Rosa. If she ever had a daughter, she doubted she'd love her any more than this precious little girl who'd been part of her life for two years. But a daughter of her own was a concept too remote to consider.

They picked up hamburgers, fries, and shakes at Burger Basket before returning to Rosa's great-grandmother's deteriorating house. Cracks ran across the tan stucco like spider veins, and white paint had flaked-off, leaving patches of naked wood on the trim. Thorny goathead weeds claimed the bare-dirt front yard, and dead branches poked through the leaves of a tired elm like skeleton arms. The whole Kirkwood neighborhood on the edge of downtown looked the same.

Mrs. Espinosa remained seated in her dark-green easy chair when Audra and Rosa entered the dim living room. Rosa tossed her bag on the creaky brown couch with a thump and began pulling out colorful knit tops.

"Grandma, you just have to see the new clothes Miss Audra bought me." She piled jeans and shirts on the old woman's lap.

"Maybe we should eat first," Audra called over her shoulder as she set the take-out bags on the Formica table with shaky chrome legs.

"Oh please, Miss Audra, just one more minute." Rosa dug deeper in the bag. "Look, Grandma, my new shoes have flowers all over them. Aren't they beautiful?"

"Oh my, yes." Mrs. Espinosa lifted her head and sniffed. The aroma of hamburger, pickles, and onions drifted in from the kitchen. "But I think Miss Audra's right. I think we should eat right away." She motioned Audra to help her stand, and tears glistened in her eyes. "How can I ever thank you?"

Audra put her arm around her. "It just makes me happy to see you and Rosa happy." *She is a happy child, and she has no concept that they are almost destitute.*

She set a junior burger in front of Rosa and slid the super-sized one to Mrs. Espinosa. It was probably the first meat they'd had in days. After peeling back the paper on her conventional burger, Audra pressed her lips tightly. *Should I tell her about the biopsy? It will probably cause her as much sorrow as the day she showed me Lorraine's photo. I'll never forget her anguished expression when she explained her granddaughter died of cancer and there was nobody to care for Rosa but her.* The tang of pickles and sauce converging with the grilled meat was delicious, but her forehead furrowed as she chewed and swallowed. *What will happen to them if I end up with cancer, too? How will it affect Rosa if she loses two people she's loved to that–that disease? I'll wait till I get the results.*

The hollow sensation engulfed her again.

CHAPTER FIVE

STUDENTS RETURN

ACADEMY STUDENTS RETURNED TO CLASS ON THE THIRD Wednesday of August. The biopsy had been performed on Monday, giving Audra Tuesday to rest, and today she was getting acquainted with her new sixth graders. She relaxed and smiled as she stood near her classroom door greeting her second-period students the same as she had for first. The children moving up from elementary school to middle school straggled in, some timid and unsure, others full of confidence as if having six new teachers and changing classes every hour was no big deal. The boy with the unruly brown hair was one of the latter.

Audra introduced herself when he entered the room.

The boy shook her outstretched hand. "I'm Taylor Bailey." He looked about. "Cool room. I like your bulletin board. Do we have assigned seats, or can we sit where we want?"

"You may sit wherever you like." She wouldn't have any trouble remembering this boy's name.

He headed to a seat farthest from her desk. Before he sat, he beat his chest Tarzan-style and flexed nonexistent muscles saying, "Me Taylor. This Taylor's desk."

Students who had come in before him muffled giggles.

Audra kept her eyes on his progress across the room. *He's cute but a little small for his age. I'll bet he makes up for it by clowning around.*

Several minutes after the bell rang, the door opened again. She stopped addressing the class and approached the girl with mousy-brown hair tucked behind her ears. "Are you looking for sixth-grade English class?"

"Yeah," the girl mumbled, sullen face downcast.

Audra studied her. "What's your name?"

"Maddie."

Audra couldn't get a clue why she seemed so gloomy. "Does Maddie have a last name?"

"Lester."

"I believe the only seat left is in the back next to Taylor Bailey, if you would please sit down."

Taylor waved his hand until Maddie noticed him. She edged her way to the back, clunked her notebook on the desk, and slouched in the chair.

"We were just getting started, Maddie," Audra said. "I've asked the class to write two paragraphs about what they did over summer. When you're finished, please bring it to my desk."

Audra returned to her desk. She penciled Maddie Lester's name on her seating chart next to Taylor's and letting her gaze roam across a room full of bright new clothes, fresh haircuts, and brand-new pencils, she began the task of matching names and faces. She would learn a lot about each child personally and academically in these two paragraphs. Maddie only wrote for a few seconds before sitting back in her seat, pouting and silent. She handed in her paper last, and it only took Audra a glance to read it. *I didn't do anything.*

It would take a few days for her students to shake summer cobwebs from their brains, but she doubted that was Maddie's problem. By the end of the day, Audra decided second period would be the most interesting and challenging.

Dann Day sank back in his desk chair at the end of classes and locked his fingers behind his head. Working with his intermediate and advanced bands and orchestras confirmed what he suspected last week—the academy's music program was dead. He'd spent hours scrutinizing the music library and inspecting the school-owned instruments. No wonder the music program crashed. His eye caught the glint of the baritone horn lying on his worktable, its valves so sticky he hadn't been able to assign it to a student today—like a couple of other essential instruments. Worse, students were unmotivated, and most hadn't touched their instruments over summer. But he didn't blame them. They had lacked leadership for two years and were struggling with uninspiring music. *Will I have enough time in the school year to get these kids back on track?*

He studied the list on the desk in front of him:

1. Baritone horn has sticky valves

2. There is no oboe

3. Bass drumhead is split

4. String bass and bow need restringing

5. Piano needs to be tuned

6. Need ten more music stands

7. Need all new music folders (Could use 128)

8. Need new music (How much is budgeted for music?)

He shook his head. Getting the bands and orchestras ready for winter concerts would be difficult. They certainly wouldn't measure up to the young musicians he'd taught in Chicago, but he'd give it his best shot.

A knock at the door preceded Heather.

"Hi." She waved airily.

"Hi." His voice went flat. *Trapped.*

She advanced without invitation. "How was your first day?"

"All right. It will take time to get acquainted with all the students." *Don't just barge in like that.*

She strode to the center of the room. "I was curious to know what your band room looks like." Pivoting so her figure was in full view, she scanned the semicircle of chairs and four glassed-in practice rooms along the left side. "How many kids you got this year?"

He exhaled a breath. *Just be polite.* "I have two mid-school bands and two orchestras until I get the elementary beginning band and orchestra started."

"That's six classes." She sidled closer to his desk, keeping her eyes on him. "So, you won't have a free period?"

He shrugged. "Oh, I will." *Would you even understand elementary band and orchestra sharing a period?*

She positioned her hands on the edge of his desk and leaned over. "Do you drive a maroon Jeep Cherokee?" She smiled as her mane of hair cascaded forward over her shoulders.

He cleared his throat and rolled his chair back a foot. "Yes." *You're too close, and you know what I drive. You saw me getting out of it this morning.*

"You didn't say where you live, but would you be interested in carpooling? It shouldn't be too hard to figure something out to save on gas."

There it was — the bombshell. His mouth turned dry. *Would she tackle me if I tried to run out the door?* He ran his hands over his thighs. "No, I don't think that will work. I'm–I'm going to start riding my bike to school." He gave his watch a quick glance and stood up. "I've got to get going. I have to catch Sheldon before he leaves."

"Really? I'll walk to the office with you. I haven't checked my mailbox yet."

Frowning, he ushered her into the hall and locked his door. *You're harder to get rid of than gum on the bottom of your shoe.*

Imitating his long strides down West Hall, Heather followed him into the administration office. While she veered left to the mailbox wall, he stopped at the counter separating the secretary's area.

"Mr. Bentley still here?" he called out to the office workroom where a light was on.

"No, he just left a few minutes ago," somebody answered back. It sounded like Georgia.

"I'll catch him tomorrow. See you later, Heather."

He scrambled out the door before she could catch up and jogged to his car. He drove to Jake's Bike Shop for a bicycle. He *would* be riding to school now.

On Saturday after school started, Audra's first piano student returned from summer vacation. Just as she finished playing "Moonlight Sonata," the familiar *clack-clack* of Kevin Miller's skateboard rattled up her front sidewalk.

The freckled redhead half-smiled as she let him in the house, his new Vans squeaking on her hardwood floors. He dumped his music books out of his backpack onto the piano bench and propped them on the piano before slouching onto the bench.

She stood at the end of the piano with her head cocked to one side. "You don't look like you're ready to get back to lessons."

He gave a little shrug. "Mom says I gotta." He rearranged

his three books on the shiny grand piano.

She perched on the pecan occasional chair. Getting a boy to love music was even more enjoyable than teaching him English. Sometimes she wondered why she'd caved in to her father's angst that she wouldn't be able to support herself with piano lessons as her only source of income.

"So, what did you do over the summer?"

His face broke into a grin. "I got to go to soccer camp—it was so cool. I can hardly wait for practice to start. And then we went to Kansas to see my grandma and grandpa. They're getting kind of old, but my grandpa's still tough enough to throw a baseball." He squinted one eye and screwed up his face. "Oh yeah, then my cousins came from Texas, and we got to go swimming every day."

She laughed. "Well, that was quite a summer. It doesn't sound like you had much time to practice the piano."

"Mom made me play a few times. She made me play for my aunt and my cousins, and they said I play very well."

"Well, you do."

A sudden grimace pulled at the corner of his mouth. "I've kind of been thinking of quitting."

She sat straighter on the chair. "Why?"

He shoved his hands under his legs and turned his face down. "Oh, there's these guys I play soccer with—they've been teasing me…" He looked at her out of the corner of his eye. "They say playing the piano is sissy stuff, and it's for girls."

"I see." She leaned forward. "And do you think it's sissy?"

"I don't know."

"What do those boys do when they're not playing soccer?"

"Computer games—all the time."

"Do you like computer games?"

He lifted his head. "Sometimes, but I get bored with them."

"Kevin, there will come a time when those boys will get bored with them, too, and they won't have anything else to do. You have a God-given talent, and if you continue, you will always have your music to enjoy." She stood and rested her arm on the edge of the piano. "Some of the greatest pianists are men. They are respected for their music, and people are touched when they listen to them."

His eyes fastened on hers as he listened.

"I'll bet some of those men were teased at first, too, but they must have decided playing the piano was worthwhile. They had to be courageous when they were made fun of."

He sighed and pulled his hands out from under his legs. "I guess you want me to be courageous, too, huh?"

She smiled. "I don't see why you can't be a soccer hero *and* a pianist, but only you can make that decision. But right now, review a song and play it like a concert for me." She shoved back in the occasional chair and listened as he gracefully fingered the keys. There was a difference in his playing. He was feeling the music, proving he really did like to play.

After the lesson, she stood at the door as Kevin's skateboard *clack-clacked* across the cracks in the sidewalk. *How I wish I hadn't let Father talk me out of becoming a piano teacher.*

Without warning, resentment toward her father rose up and choked her. Her throat closed the same as when she'd talked with Laney. She swung the door shut as if hiding her anger from unseen observers and covered her face with her hands. *This anger isn't good — but what am I going to do?*

CHAPTER SIX

REPRIEVE

Audra slipped onto a gray upholstered chair in the consulting room. A computer monitor occupied the desk in front of her. The only other thing in the room to attract her attention was the portrait of Dr. Rhonda, her husband, and two teenage children on a cabinet next to a vase of mauve silk flowers.

Dr. Rhonda entered with a quiet, "Hello, Audra." At her desk, she rotated her chair to face the computer screen and sat silent while Audra's file loaded.

Audra held her breath, focusing on Dr. Rhonda's attractively styled auburn hair.

Still silent, Dr. Rhonda scanned the report, pressed back in her swivel chair, and gazed over her half-glasses. "Complex hyperplasia with atypia."

Anxiety hit Audra like a sucker punch. As she clutched her chair arms, her brain felt paralyzed. *Complex whatever it is doesn't sound like a good thing.*

Dr. Rhonda took off her glasses. "The condition occurs when the lining of the uterus grows too much or thickens. It can happen when a woman produces estrogen without enough progesterone. Women who have a history of missed periods or who never get pregnant are at higher risk. And, of course, family history plays a part, also."

Audra's eyebrows shot up. "I guess I'm batting a thousand, then, aren't I?"

Dr. Rhonda just continued in her usual soft voice. "Atypical means there are abnormal cells. The abnormal cells aren't cancerous, now," she stressed. "However, with this type of hyperplasia the risk is high that they will eventually progress to cancer, and we absolutely don't want that to happen. You're still young, and occasionally, this clears up with treatment. But with your family history, I don't want to take any chances. You've been on a low dose of progesterone, but now I'm going to put you on a high-dose regimen of progestin to see if you will shed those cells. I'll do an injection today, and we'll do another biopsy in December. We may have to do another injection then, depending on where you're at, and we'll do a final biopsy next April."

Audra whooshed out a breath so pronounced that Dr. Rhonda glanced up and smiled. Audra closed her eyes. *Thank God, it's not cancer — I have another chance!* She blinked back relieved tears.

She left the doctor's office with hope and thanked God, again, for the reprieve. She couldn't remember the last time she'd said a prayer. When she got home, she called Laney, then her sister-in-law, Marsha, and finally Tamina. After telling it three times, she flopped on the couch, every ounce of energy drained from her.

Audra went to work the next morning with a glorious sense of freedom. The millstone of anxiety had vanished. Her classroom was quiet as she surveyed her second-period students hunched over their worksheets identifying adjectives and adverbs. Satisfied they were all at work, she twirled her chair to face the whiteboard and closed her eyes. She could feel the tension that had kept her in knots for so many weeks ebbing away. She wanted to savor the return of a calm spirit.

Closing her eyes shut out the classroom, but she couldn't turn off her ears. She was aware of feet shuffling beneath a desk, she heard a sigh, and then a faint rustle as an eraser wrinkled someone's paper. There was the hum of the air conditioner in the background. A long sniff followed a sneeze at the back of the room. And a giggle. She spun her chair back and observed her class. It was Maddie. She wasn't working—she was poking Taylor Bailey with her pencil. Taylor grinned but kept working. So much for relishing her moment of calm.

"Maddie, please get back to work," Audra called from her desk. She began grading the stack of first-period worksheets but glanced up at Maddie every few seconds.

Maddie jabbed Taylor a second time, and he tried to suppress a giggle. The third time, he snatched the end of the pencil and pulled. He grinned as their tug-of-war nearly dragged Maddie from her seat.

Audra started for the back of the room. *Maddie's pushing the envelope today.* Taylor's cheeks reddened as she approached. He twisted back to his work, deliberating over an answer. She leaned over Maddie. The girl's face turned blank, and her mousy hair smelled sweaty from first-period PE.

"Maddie! You haven't even started your worksheet. You need to know this material before we start writing our stories. Come up to the front table and get going. You only have five minutes to finish." Audra shook her head. *Racking up another F! Her parents are not going to be impressed with her papers at open house. If she doesn't improve, I'll have to talk to them.* She pivoted and looked back at Taylor. His face was pulled into a crestfallen frown as Maddie walked away.

After the second-period students emptied the room, Audra retrieved Maddie's paper from the pile. The girl had completed six of the fifteen sentences correctly in five minutes. Audra grimaced. *She could be a straight-A student — why the refusal to complete her work?*

Taylor's dejected face came to mind. Her face screwed up in thought before she tipped her head and laughed. "Of course. I should have seen it last week. Taylor's crushing on Maddie."

It took another two weeks of reviewing grammar before the short stories were written. Audra had spent hours drawing out her students' imaginations and demonstrating ways to create pictures with words. Today was the final day for the assignment to be turned in, and she still hadn't seen anything from Maddie.

Audra faced her students. "Okay, guys, it's time for our spelling game, so line up in your teams."

The youngsters scrambled to form three lines in front of the board.

"You know the rules. When I say a word, the person at the head of the line writes it on the board. If it's misspelled, the person behind him must correct it before spelling the next word. Your team loses a point for every mistake, but if *I* have to catch the mistake, you lose two points. Team One has held the trophy for two weeks now, so come on teams two and three — go for a win."

Three whiteboard markers squeaked as the students wrote their spelling words, sending the pungent odor of marker fluid wafting across the room. Maddie moved up to the head of her line, and Audra chose a word from the extra credit list. Without hesitating, Maddie marched forward and wrote *disparagement* under her team's column. Her face beamed when she turned around. Team Two would win with that word. "Way to go, Maddie," her teammates cheered.

Audra smiled at her. This was the only group exercise Maddie participated in with any enthusiasm, but Audra didn't understand. Maddie never missed a word at the board, but she always misspelled at least three words on the final spelling test.

The game finished, Audra went to her desk and started reading a story that had been handed in while the class silently read their library books. A loud smack startled her. Maddie slapped her story onto her desk and stood waiting for her to look up. As soon as Audra glanced into Maddie's face, the girl retreated behind her stony mask and sauntered back to her chair.

Audra picked up the stapled papers. A curly fringe edged the left side where it had been torn from a spiral notebook. She read three pages, caught her breath, and looked back at Maddie. She had demanded her attention, but now she was slouched in her chair reading—ignoring Audra. She finished the story, look-ing back at the girl twice. *Is this made-up or is it real?*

Maddie had captured the pathos of a girl whose dog was dying as the result of her unsympathetic father's unreasonable-ness. In the end, the dog lived, and all seemed to turn out well. *But, what prompted such a story?* Maddie certainly knew how to portray an indifferent, unfeeling father. Was it really made up, or was an element of Maddie's real life incorporated into it? At any rate, it would be the only good grade in her Open House folder.

She walked back and stood next to the girl's desk. "I read this, Maddie. It's a wonderful story."

Maddie shrugged. "Thanks. I like to write stories." She resumed her reading.

Audra returned to her desk. *Now that I'm feeling better, I hope I can reach her.*

The annual open house was held on the third Wednesday

of September. Audra always enjoyed her first chance to meet her students' parents. Tonight, moms and dads were following an abbreviated schedule of their child's day in order to meet each teacher, and when the passing bell sounded, she scooped up three unclaimed folders from first period and fanned out the second-period stack. She pulled Maddie's folder out of alphabetical order and set it to the far right of the table. She pressed a sticky note to the first page that said, *Please see me after the period is finished.* Of all the parents, she especially wanted to meet Mr. and Mrs. Lester.

She immediately recognized Mr. Bailey, a heavyset man with the same unruly brown hair as his son. Despite the disparity in their size, the Bailey men boasted a remarkable resemblance. He wore a gray work shirt with *Allen* embroidered on a white patch. After a quick glance around the room, he tried to stuff himself into the chair of a nearby desk. "I don't remember desks being this small when I was in school!" He laughed, courting the other parents' attention.

His wife found Taylor's folder on the table and approached Audra, extending her hand. "I'm Joyce Bailey, Taylor's mom, and my husband, Allen." She nodded toward the man trying to fit into the too-small chair. Tall and thin, with her black hair pulled back severely, she looked tired.

Audra accepted the woman's hand and introduced herself. "I enjoy having Taylor in my class."

"Does he give you any trouble?" Mrs. Bailey thumbed the edge of her son's folder.

"Not trouble—I just have to remind him to pay attention once in a while. He does good work, though."

Mrs. Bailey's shoulders sagged a bit, and the softest smile twitched her thin lips. "Oh, I'm glad to hear that." As she went to sit beside her husband, Audra wondered how much they sacrificed to send Taylor to the academy.

Other parents came into the room, found folders, and sat down. Audra kept glancing at Maddie Lester's folder to glimpse who picked it up. He was the last to arrive. She had been on the verge of starting her speech, but she waited and watched him.

Appearing to be in his forties, he wore a finely tailored gray suit and a red tie. His conservatively cut dark hair complemented a narrow mustache. He sat at a desk closest to the door and placed Maddie's folder in front of him.

"Welcome to second-period English class." As she explained her expectations for her sixth-grade English students, she found herself speaking toward Mr. Lester most of the time. He was preoccupied.

"Are there any questions?" she asked when she finished. Mr. Lester opened Maddie's folder and skimmed each sheet of paper, then closed it again. His jaw tightened. When the passing bell rang, he stood and left the room without giving her a chance to introduce herself. *Will he even read the story?*

At the end of the sixth period, Audra joined parents and teachers in the new cafeteria for cookies and punch. She scanned the room but didn't see Mr. Lester. *Did he see my note, or did he ignore it?* Allen Bailey was speaking to several men. When he paused, they all laughed. Joyce Bailey was standing alone drinking punch. Several parents, recognizing Audra, asked questions about their children they wouldn't voice in the classroom.

When the room began to empty, she headed toward the refreshment table to find only crumbs on empty plates remained. As she surveyed them, Tamina burst through the double doors from the cafeteria's elementary side.

"Any punch left over here?"

Audra waited for her to cross the room. "Punch, but no

cookies. What's up? I thought you would have been long gone by now."

"A couple of sets of parents needed extra time to talk, and by the time I got my room straightened, they were cleaning up our lunchroom. But you know me. I talked too much, I didn't get anything to drink, and now I'm thirsty." Tamina laughed at herself.

"Did you have Taylor Bailey in your room last year?"

"I did. He's a good kid. He craves attention, and he shows off. But he's smart and needs to be challenged."

Audra nodded. "I came to the same conclusion. What about Maddie Lester?"

"Hmm, I don't recognize the name. Are you sure she was in elementary here?"

"No, I'm not." She caught a whiff of spicy aftershave and glanced over her shoulder.

Dann Day selected a cup of punch, chugged without stopping, tossed it in the trash, and grabbed a second one. He eyed both her and Tamina over the rim of the cup. "It's getting late — why are you still hanging around?"

"I'm about ready to go," Audra answered. "Dann, have you met Tamina York? She teaches fifth grade on the other side."

"No, I guess I haven't." He extended his hand and added, "Dann Day."

"Tamina's another hometown girl who came back to teach straight from college."

"So, you've known each other for years?" he asked, focusing on Audra.

"No," Tamina cut in with a laugh. "I lived on the wrong side of the tracks to know her back then. We didn't meet until I landed the job here. Audra took me under her wing, showed me the ropes, and has been an encouragement ever since."

Then, like an undetected stealth plane, Heather arrived. She executed a touch and go at the table, snagging the last punch, and made a precision landing in front of Dann.

Dann's eyebrows shot up as he lurched a step back.

"How did your evening go?" Heather directed toward Dann, her gaze excluding Audra and Tamina.

His smile vanished as he jerked his head away from her scrutiny. When he managed to recover a half-smile, he held Audra's eyes for a long moment before he joked, "I *pleaded* with the parents to make their kids practice their instruments." He finished his punch and tossed his cup into the trashcan. "I'll see you later. I've got to get going."

"I'll walk with you." Heather dropped her full cup of punch into the trash. "I don't like to walk across the dark parking lot alone." When he didn't wait for her, she had to run a couple of steps to catch up.

The corner of Audra's mouth pulled. "I don't like to walk in the dark," she mimicked in a condescending falsetto, then tossed her empty cup into the trash. "Oh, sure!"

Tamina rolled her dark eyes and giggled. "Adolescent flirt sums it up. Dann sure lost his smile when she showed up."

"It's so juvenile. If she'd quit getting in his face, maybe he'd notice her. She's pretty enough." Audra paused, and her eyes narrowed. "I'll have to admit, though, I really don't like her." She turned on her heel and started toward the exit.

"Hey, girl." Tamina moved up beside her. "Didn't you even notice? You were the one he was looking at—not Heather."

Audra cast a sidelong glance at her friend. Of course, she noticed, and something deep inside had responded. But her reprieve was too tenuous to be thinking of Dann Day. "So?"

"So, give her a run for the money."

She shook her head and kept walking.

CHAPTER SEVEN

EVAN'S PERSPECTIVE

LOUNGING ON HER PATIO ON SATURDAY, AUDRA POLISHED OFF her sandwich, closed her eyes, and lifted her face to the warm autumn sunshine. Flowers were waning, and the normally raucous house finches had relinquished their summer song for peaceful quiet. Too quiet. All she could hear was Tamina's words advising her to give Heather a run for the money. Those words had been teasing at the corners of her mind for days. *Why can't I turn them off?*

Like the stirring of a gentle breeze, a picture drifted into her mind. It didn't completely surprise her; it was the second time the image had floated into her consciousness, unbidden, strangely pleasant, and a bit unsettling.

She could see Dann Day standing in front of her at the open house, smiling and captivating her with sparkling gray eyes. Sighing, she opened her eyes, and the recollection disappeared. *No, I can't pursue him. My health risks hold too much potential for heartbreak.*

An indefinable sensation coiled through her insides— almost as if something had roused her from a deep sleep.

The side gate rattled, and she hopped from her chaise as

Evan walked into the backyard. With the sunshine glinting on his straw-colored hair and casting a shadow along his short, straight nose, he resembled their father.

"Ready for your new storm door?" Setting his toolbox down, he snugged his arm around her shoulder. "What's this about you having a biopsy? Everything's okay, isn't it?"

She slipped her arm around his waist. "For now, yes. The doctor will keep close tabs. Mind if I watch? It's been so long since we've talked — how's the restaurant doing?"

He selected a screwdriver and began loosening the hinges on her worn-out screen door. "We've been so busy this is my first day off in two weeks."

"And you're here instead of at home? Ev, why didn't you protest when I asked you if you could help me?"

He grinned. "You promised me a root beer float, and you know what a sucker I am for those."

"The last I heard, you were going to start catering. How's that working out?" She wadded up the plastic wrap he stripped from the new door.

"We'll have to hire more help quite soon. Sometimes I wish Father could have lived long enough to see it a success. He never believed Marsha and I could do anything with that wreck of a place."

Her eyebrows shot up. "Sounds like you have some resentment toward him."

Evan shoved the door into the frame with a grunt. "Not so much now. He never could understand why I wanted to be a chef, but it turns out the business major he insisted I get has been a big asset running the restaurant."

Dropping back onto the lawn chair, she tucked her knees to her chest. "Did Father help you out when you went to culinary school?"

"Are you kidding?" He glanced at her sideways. "No. He said paying for one degree was enough. He never was happy I became a chef, and I suppose if he were still around, he'd tell me I wasted the twenty grand he left me by investing in the restaurant." He marked new holes to drill.

She rested her chin against her knees and stared at the ground while he drilled but looked up when it grew quiet. "Ev, Father tried to control your career, and it was obvious how he tried to run Laney's life—do you think Laney is holding resentment, too?"

He sat back on his heels. "Why are you dredging up all this old stuff?"

"I guess I still have a lot of anger toward him. I hated the way he treated Laney and Amanda. And did you know he never once put his arm around me to comfort me after Mom died or let me go back to Sunday school after she was gone?" She bit back the bitterness tightening her voice.

"The only thing Laney ever told me was that, after she came back pregnant with Amanda, Father refused to give her a dime."

Her chest tightened. *I always thought she didn't want to ask him for money. I used most of my savings to help her get back on her feet, and he refused to help?* A fresh wave of resentment burned like bile in her throat. She sucked in a deep breath. "I'm glad Laney got her twenty grand the same as we did, but I guess I begrudge him that, too. Twenty grand for his kids and three-quarters of a million to his charities."

He nodded. "I don't think he wanted us to be *too* comfortable. He was always trying to make sure we could stand on our own two feet."

"Yeah." Her voice turned hard. "Like he was saying 'I made mine—you make yours.' I guess I never felt it was given out of love."

He dropped to his knees to adjust the bottom plate. Moments passed before he tipped his head her way. "Audie, you were just a kid when Mom died, and I left right after. From a few things Laney has said, I know it was rough for both of you. But you must admit—Father was successful and so was his father. I think his greatest concern was having his children be successful, too. I think that's why he had a problem with Laney. In his eyes, she wasn't doing as well as he expected her to."

He stood and tossed his screwdriver into his toolbox. "He didn't know how to show affection, yet, in his own way, I think he loved us. But yeah, occasionally, I still have hard feelings over the way he pressured me to do things his way—I mostly just stuff it. Come on, let's have those floats." He held the storm door open for her.

From the landing, Audra scooted up the steps to the kitchen, plopped ice cream into two tall glasses, and set out two cans of root beer. She plunked onto a chair and braced her elbows on the table. "Well, he pressured me, too. I wanted to teach music, not English—but he had his way. Still, he didn't say anything when I wanted to work for my master's in music before I started teaching—even though I doubted I'd ever have a career in music."

She twirled her spoon in the melting ice cream. "When Laney told me how rebellious Amanda has gotten, all the resentment I've harbored just bubbled to the surface." She slouched back on her chair. "But I'll admit the fear over this stupid biopsy business has gotten me edgy, too."

"Do you feel angry at that situation?"

Her face screwed up. "I'm not sure if I'm more scared or angry."

Leaning her chin in one hand, she bobbed the ice cream in her float. She'd been able to buy a house her father built and furnish it the way she wanted because her job paid better than any public-school system. Her inheritance had bought a grand piano she never could have owned otherwise. *Father wasn't all bad. He gave me an education that's allowed me to live a good life... But why did he have to be so mean? Why did he have to get so bitter and make life so miserable? Why can't I just let it go?*

She didn't have the answers. She didn't know what else to do except stuff it again the same as her brother.

CHAPTER EIGHT

AUTUMN LEAVES

OCTOBER BROUGHT NOTICEABLE CHANGES IN THE WEATHER ON the high desert. An early frost ushered in pleasantly warm Indian-summer afternoons, but chilly nights turned the huge cottonwoods in Audra's yard into a blaze of gold before some of the leaves fell. Since Kevin wouldn't be coming until two p.m., she grabbed a rake to tidy her yard.

Wearing blue jeans and a blue zip-up hoodie sweatshirt, and with her hair secured in a ponytail, she raked leaves from the gutter and the driveway into a pile. The squeak of bicycle brakes caught her attention as Dann Day, matching her in blue jeans and a navy sweatshirt instead of his usual tan chinos, skidded to a stop at the curb.

"Hey, I didn't know you lived on Bend Avenue."

She walked over to the sidewalk, holding her rake. "I've lived in this house going on six years."

He eyed the older ranch-style house. Mortared red brick halfway up the front was set off by white siding and gray trim. "I ride past here all the time. I live the other side of Main on Lincoln. I get on Bend and come right by here to get the bridge across the arroyo to the school."

With a little cock of her head, she propped the rake against the plastic bag-lined trashcan. "Were you at the school on a Saturday morning?"

"No. I rode past the school out to Lake Patterson and back again just to ride under all those golden cottonwoods. I didn't realize they put on such a fantastic show."

"Aren't they great? I think our school grounds are the prettiest spot in town this time of year. Just seeing them when I walk to class in the mornings is a treat." She raked a couple of stray leaves toward her pile.

He grinned at the pile of leaves. "You know, I don't think I've raked leaves since I was in high school." He breathed deeply. "I love that woodsy autumn smell. Would you care to have some help?"

"I never turn down help." She laughed. After he parked his bike in the driveway, she handed him the rake and pulled the trashcan closer. "You can rake. I'll bag." Picking up the dustpan from the grass, she scooped a heap into the bag.

He raked half the grass before he stopped and faced her. "What made you decide to become a teacher?"

She straightened and studied him as he casually leaned on the rake, looking at her. "My mother was a second-grade teacher at the academy. She went back to work when I was six, but she died when I was twelve. I made up my mind right then I was going to be a teacher." She stooped for one more scoop and rested the dustpan on the edge of the trashcan. "What made you decided to move to the Grove?"

He shrugged. "I ran away from home." He turned his back on her and jabbed leaves out from under the evergreens along the foundation of the house.

So, that topic's off limits.

A gust of wind blustered across the yard, propelling leaves out of the mound and back across the grass. As they laughed, she corralled the errant leaves back to the pile, and the awkwardness disappeared.

Moving to the backyard, he raked a pile large enough for her to start tossing and then paused. "I've been riding my bike around quite a bit trying to get acquainted with the town. I've seen the Josiah Chandler Bank Building downtown dated 1895, and I know it's where the old money came from. But what drives the economy now? Mr. Bentley's handout said Josiah Chandler's great-great-grandson, Jeremy, infused a lot of money into the town, but I haven't seen any indication of where it comes from. I've seen some really neglected neighborhoods north and east of downtown, but I've also seen some pretty elaborate homes farther west."

She smashed the leaves down in the trashcan. "It's Applied Ceramics Technologies—we call it ACT. Jeremy Chandler graduated from MIT in 1941, and in the sixties, he started the company so far south of town they had to look out for rattlesnakes. The town's almost grown out to it now." She picked up another dustpan of leaves and dumped them into the can. "When he founded the academy, he stipulated that a percentage of ACT profits would always go to the school, but other parts of town never received one benefit from his philanthropy."

When curiosity arched his brows, she shrugged. "People who worked for Josiah started the town, and I've always heard he took good care of them. But I've often wondered why the Chandler family settled in the cool of the trees on the east side of the arroyo and Phineas Kirkwood and his camp of cowboys were relegated to the desert side. Even back then, it appears there was a dividing line nobody dared to cross."

He gave an understanding nod, and then returned to giving long sweeps with the rake through the leaves gathered along the patio.

After scooping the last of the leaves, she tied the final bag and set it with the others at the side of the garage. "You look warm." She retrieved the rake from him and set it inside the garage. "Would you care for something to drink?"

"Sounds good. What do you have?"

She gave a slight cock of her head. "Root beer, coffee, or water." Then she opened the back door and skipped up the steps to the kitchen door.

He raised his eyebrows as he followed her. "Root beer? Sounds good. I haven't had one in years."

The stove clock said twelve thirty. "Well, actually it's lunchtime. Can I offer you a sandwich with your soda?"

Slipping into a chair and bracing his arms on the kitchen table, he continued to watch her face. "Sure."

She deposited a can of soda in front of him and another on the counter for herself. "I don't usually keep root beer on hand, but I paid my brother a float a few weeks back when he installed my storm door." She removed her hoodie covering a pink tee and hung it on the back of the chair across from him.

Dann popped the tab on his soda and fixed his eyes on her trim figure while she made tuna sandwiches. *Nice. I like her hair up like that — bet being in her English class is a ball.* He tore his gaze away and examined the room. The cupboards and table and chairs were matching white, but the pale-yellow walls and accents of dark green gave zing to the décor. He twisted in his chair. Three narrow windows overlooked the backyard, while the opposite side formed a *U* with one window over the sink. *Good taste. I can imagine her friends gathered in a comfortable room like this.*

When Audra set baby carrots and a plate of cookies on the table, he looked into her dark eyes. She only held his eyes a moment before she averted hers. *Shy? Maybe there's a boyfriend involved? I never considered that. Oh boy.* When she returned to the counter, he stood and moved to the doorway to the next room and crossed his arms. *Maybe I'd better back off...*

Suddenly, his eyes widened, and his hands dropped to his sides. A glossy midsize grand piano created an elegant, black island against the simplicity of white walls and hardwood floors. He whipped back around and met her fetching two sandwiches to the table.

"That's one awesome piano."

"Thank you." Her cheeks flushed pink, and she looked down, fiddling with the gold-rimmed edge of her plate. When she lifted her face again, a soft smile parted her lips. "Did you always live in Chicago?"

He had to swallow the lump in his throat. "In the suburbs—Skokie. My family moved into a small, redbrick bungalow when I was seven, and the folks are still there."

He couldn't keep his gaze from reexamining her face as they ate, but after finishing his second cookie, he wiped his fingers on his napkin and pushed his chair back. He didn't want to let that amazing piano just sit there without hearing it. "Would you play something for me?"

Pure delight flashed in her eyes. "Sure, let me wash my hands."

Enjoying her enthusiasm, he followed her into the next room. A pecan occasional chair with a splash of red-orange in its upholstery cozied near the piano. Dozens of neatly cataloged music books crammed a bookcase, and a table with a silk plant seemed to sun itself under the front window.

His eyes tracked the hardwood running the length of the room. A couch in tones of caramel and cream, a pair of pecan occasional chairs, matching the one by the piano, as well as a wheat-colored side chair completed a three-sided conversation area before a redbrick fireplace. The area was compact, simple, and striking, leaving the artistic focus on the piano.

She chose a book as he went to the chair by the piano. She began playing Chopin's "Etude In E," and he relaxed into the musical flow. Next, she moved into Chopin's "Raindrop," and then her slender fingers nimbly scampered through "Butterfly." When she finished, he stood up and moved closer to the piano. "I'd say you're a real Chopin fan—I enjoyed that."

She laughed. "I love the challenge of Chopin's fast runs. But I got lazy over summer, and I'm having to work to get the edge back."

"Seems you accomplished it." He sat back down.

A smile played at the corners of her mouth. "But it's not always Chopin," she added as she fingered the opening two-note melody of Beethoven's "Für Elise." Finally, the sentimental strains of "Moon River" and "Misty" rippled through the room, soft and wistful.

When she finished, he stared at her. "What are you doing teaching English instead of music?"

When their eyes met, she couldn't look away, and she swallowed hard. His gray eyes were sparkling, and a pleasant sensation, like an internal feather, fluttered deep inside. "Actually, I do both."

Propping his elbows on his knees, he planted his chin in his hands, still holding her gaze. "How many piano students do you have?"

"Five. They're all I can handle and keep up at the academy. Two are in high school, and one wants to major in music in college. Two are in middle school, and Patty is in elementary." She glanced at her watch. "Kevin will be here in a bit. His heart is still divided between sports and music, and I have to work around his soccer games. Sometimes he comes on Saturday morning, sometimes in the afternoon. So, what do you play?"

When he leaned back in the chair, she shifted on the bench to see him easier. "Violin and flute. My sister and I started violin when we were in fourth grade. My father played violin — well, he still does, he plays in a community orchestra. He taught us more advanced music at home in addition to what we were playing at school, and he gave me a love for classical music." He stretched his legs out straight and locked his hands behind his head.

"In eighth grade, I decided I wanted to play in marching band when I got to high school. Dad was willing for me to join the band on one condition — that I didn't give up violin. He said if I wanted a flute, I'd have to work for it. So, I worked after school at my uncle's grocery store and bought a used one. I practiced hours every night that summer, and when school started, I was last chair in the freshman band. Davene stayed with orchestra in high school, so I played all her violin music with her."

"Do you play much for your own enjoyment?"

Before he could answer, the doorbell rang. After a quick introduction to Kevin, Dann left.

She stopped in the middle of the room. Warm prickles were attacking her all over. *He thinks I should teach music! How big a compliment is that? He sat there all relaxed like he's been here a hundred times — and his look melted me like…like…* She raised her eyes to the ceiling. *Oh, stupid female problems!*

Kevin was staring at her. She had no idea what he'd just said to her.

Dann pedaled away. *She's definitely a different sort of woman. She probably plays every day for her own enjoyment, and how long has it been for me? Months? Admit it, guy, you've been too busy having a*

pity party, and it's time to make a change.

That evening, Audra tucked the phone under her chin when Tamina called. Her smooth voice flowed over the line.

"Hey, girlfriend, what've you been up to all day?"

"Right now, I'm in the kitchen folding a load of laundry that's been waiting for me because I had company this morning."

"Oh yeah — who?"

Audra chewed her lip and pulled a crisp white blouse out of the laundry basket. *How much do I tell her?* "Dann. I was out in front raking leaves, and he saw me and stopped."

"Dann as in Dann Day?"

"Yeah. He helped me rake and I offered him a root beer and we ended up having a sandwich and we talked and he asked me to play the piano." *Boy, was that a run-on sentence.* "You know, when Heather's not on the scene, he talks a lot — and he smiles, too. He was still here when Kevin came at two. Not my typical Saturday."

Tamina laughed. "Well, I wouldn't mind having a Saturday like that."

"Please don't go making something out of it. It was just a friendly chat." Audra bit her lip. *And friendly chats make you do flip-flops on the inside? Remember what you're facing. Romantic notions are out of the question. Forget it.*

"Oh hey," Tamina said. "I called to see if we're going to do the usual pizza and movie on Halloween. By Tuesday, I'll have had enough of witches and goblins at school. I'll be ready for a break."

Audra glanced at her kitchen calendar. "Tuesday? Pick me up at five thirty. Kelli always leaves promptly after her lesson."

"Cool. See you then."

After they hung up, Audra scowled at the blouse she was still holding. Why did Dann have to walk into her life now? No way could she get involved with him. Not with cancer still a distinct possibility. But what about her thoughts? If she wasn't going to let him into her life, she had no business wondering what it might feel like with his arms around her or wishing he'd look into her eyes again. She'd never felt that way over any other man, so why was she finding it so difficult to quash those nagging impulses that kept flashing through her mind?

CHAPTER NINE

A DIRTY TRICK

On Tuesday night, Audra and Tamina ate pizza at Canyon Road House before they drove to Cinema Four where they chose the animated cartoon. Anxiety over her future was beginning to clutch at Audra again, and she welcomed the humor. They were still chuckling over the movie when Tamina braked in Audra's driveway, but as the headlights flashed onto the front of the house, Audra's demeanor suddenly changed.

"What's that?" She pressed her forehead to the side window, straining to see the front door as it dimmed with shadows again.

"What's what?"

"It looked like something was written on the front of the house—like graffiti." She jogged across the dry grass with Tamina following. Three-inch-high letters in black marker printed A. K. + D. D. on the siding next to the door. She gawked before blurting, "What *is* this, some kind of joke?" Her heart banged against her ribs, each beat feeling like it lurched into her throat.

Tamina moved to Audra's side. "A. K. plus D. D.! Uh-uh, girlfriend, you holding out on me?" She giggled.

Audra jabbed her with her elbow then jammed her fists

against her hips. "No way. It's not funny."

"I'm sorry." Tamina grew serious. "I'm still in a silly mood."

"This *has* to be some sort of prank, but who? I've got to wash it off." She unlocked the front door, ran through to the kitchen, and returned with a spray bottle of cleaner and paper towels. She sprayed soapy cleaner onto the black letters causing a trickle of inky suds to run down the siding.

"Halloween prank, you think?"

"I wonder." Audra stabbed at the stain with a paper towel and then repeated the process a second time. "Thank goodness, it wasn't permanent ink. Come on inside."

With the bottle of cleaner still in her hand, she slumped onto the couch. "Can you think of anyone else besides Dann Day that D. D. could possibly mean?"

"No." Tamina perched on the edge of the side chair and shook her head, sending her hoops bouncing against her neck.

Audra frowned. "Me, either, but it doesn't make sense. That's the kind of prank kids would pull, but how would any students at school know I'm even acquainted with Dann? He's never spoken two words to me outside of the teachers' lounge."

"But isn't that what makes it a prank? Choose two people's initials just to see what sort of a rise you can get? Or see if they get embarrassed?"

"Maybe. But as far as I know, there aren't any kids from school in this neighborhood."

Tamina pulled a wry face. "Maybe it's not kids."

A grimace twinged over Audra's lips. "Why would an adult do such a stupid thing?" For a fleeting moment, Heather's face bombarded her mind. *Oh, that's too absurd even to consider.* "It makes me angry, but I suppose, it could just be a prank." She sat motionless for a moment and then crossed her arms over her body. "No, it makes me feel vulnerable — like I'm being spied on." She rested her elbows on her knees and dropped her chin into her hands.

"You didn't give out treats, so maybe it's just some kid's trick."

A deeper grimace twisted Audra's lips.

Tamina raised an eyebrow. "Come on, girlfriend, it's not like you to get so upset over something like this... Or is it something else?" Tamina tipped her head and squinted one eye at Audra. "Is it somebody writing on the house that's bothering you, or is it more about whose initials they are?"

Audra didn't move.

"How long did you spend with Dann on Saturday? It sounded like you kind of enjoyed it. Is there by any chance a crush you don't want to admit?"

Audra sucked in a quick breath and let her shoulders sag, remembering the hours spent with Dann. "It's not a crush—no, maybe it is. It's just, well, A. K. plus D. D. is a fantasy I can't indulge in. He's a really nice guy, and he makes me feel things I haven't experienced in a long time. But I can't let it happen. My future's too uncertain, and I wouldn't put a man through that."

Audra looked up. Beneath her cute pixie haircut, Tamina's gaze was boring into her. Audra squirmed. "Okay, for a split second those initials panicked me for fear somebody knows a secret about me that I certainly don't want known, and at the same time, they were tantalizing and something I can't have."

Tamina scooted back on the couch. "Ouch. Here you are struggling with something and all I do is get flippant. Forgive me?"

"Of course." Audra stood up. "I overreacted—again. Lately, my anger button is getting pushed way too easily. But we need to cut this short—still work tomorrow."

After she saw Tamina to the door, Audra took the bottle of cleaner to the kitchen. *I have to stop thinking about Dann. Was I that transparent? Tamina saw right through me. Why was I so concerned somebody might think I have a secret? Because… Because…* She couldn't translate it into words, but despite the ten-ton weight on her shoulders starting with a capital C, something deep inside her was struggling to be free.

CHAPTER TEN

WHO'S GUILTY?

AUDRA SLEPT FITFULLY AS SPECULATIONS ABOUT THE INITIALS' ORI-gin knocked around her brain without providing an answer. She awakened with a start. *Those initials can't be a coincidence. It has to be somebody who knows me. But who?* A north wind rustled tree-bound leaves against her bedroom window as a harbinger of winter. She tugged her blanket around her shoulders. *I don't want to go to work today. I want to stay and hide. Too bad, girl, that's not an option.* She willed herself out of bed with a vague sense of impending disaster. She plodded to the bathroom, fear eroding what little peace she'd gained.

Everything seemed completely normal at school. During each class, she studied faces for furtive or guilty looks passing between students. Nothing. Even Taylor and Maddie got along. Taylor gave Maddie a candy bar, probably from his Halloween stash, and for once, the girl didn't break the rules and open it in class.

Arriving home, Audra saw Lucy Sanders, her neighbor across the street, unloading groceries from her trunk. Lucy always knew everything happening in the neighborhood.

"Hey, Lucy, can you wait a second?" Audra called out as the woman started carrying a bag toward her front door. "Did you by any chance see anybody hanging around my house last night?"

Lucy's dyed-red hair bobbed as she shook her head. "No, I had the door open off and on all evening giving out candy, but I didn't see anything over at your house. Your kitchen light was the only one on, so I knew you were gone. Why?" She shifted the bag in her grip. "Did something happen?"

Audra hesitated. Geraldine Dodge, her neighbor on her left, had cattily referred to her as Lucy Loose Lips. Audra smiled at her. "Oh, just a little prank—nothing serious. Well, I have to get back. I'll see you."

There was no hint on Thursday, either. She went home after school confident the incident could be forgotten.

On Friday, she arrived at school eager for her classes to finish the unit they were studying so she could send them home with no homework for the weekend. Keys in hand, she approached her classroom ready to unlock the door, and there it was again—A. K.+ D. D. in black marker on the window of her classroom door. Her hands began shaking. *Someone right here at school did it!*

Her face heated as she scanned the empty hall. She pulled a tissue from her purse, wet it at the drinking fountain across the hall, and wiped the initials off.

She entered her room and sat at her desk. How many teachers had walked by? How many students on their way to their lockers saw it and laughed? Any number of persons could have seen it before she'd scrubbed it off. What if *Dann* saw it?

She closed her eyes. She hadn't talked to him since they raked leaves, but what if he *did* see it? She pressed her fingers to her tingling cheeks. *He'd think I'm on the same juvenile level as Heather, chasing him—begging him to throw her a bone of recognition.* She hid her face in her hands and groaned. *I knew this was going to turn into a disaster.*

As students entered the room each period, she busied herself with papers on her desk. The day dragged, and she had to force her mind to stay focused. By the time school was over, she had a massive headache. She went home, and while ten-year-old Patty played her piano lesson, Audra sat in the pecan chair and rubbed her temples. After Patty left, she called Tamina.

"Incredible!" Tamina said. "Did you report it to Mr. Bentley?"

"No." She rotated her head to relieve the viselike grip tension had on her neck. "I thought about it after I'd already wiped it off — but, actually, just thinking about telling him embarrassed me."

"Girl, he needs to know."

"I'm just hoping it doesn't happen again."

"Don't count on it."

CHAPTER ELEVEN

ALFRED YORK

Two hours later, the kitchen phone jangling jolted Audra—*Oh, I must have fallen asleep with the ice pack on my neck.* She gingerly hobbled from the couch to answer.

"Aud? I need help." Tamina's voice shook. "I'm in the emergency room. I took some leftover soup to my dad and found him on the bathroom floor. He was throwing up blood, and he was so weak I had to get an ambulance. Can you come?"

"Of course." Audra forgot about her headache. "I'm on my way."

A nurse was checking Alfred York's vitals when Audra walked into the Kirkwood Memorial Hospital room. Tamina rushed into her arms and clung to her.

"Do they know what's wrong?" Audra asked.

"Not yet. They have to run tests." Mr. York moaned, and Tamina leaned over the side rail. "Dad, it's Tamina. I'm here."

A rose-colored cotton blanket was pulled up to his chin, and his face, his dark skin sagging around bony features, contrasted the crisp white pillowcase. Tamina brushed her hand over his graying black hair. "It's Tamina," she repeated.

"I heard you," he acknowledged with his eyes still closed.

Tamina took her father's hand. "Dad, how long have you been throwing up blood?"

"I want you to get me home."

"Dad, you can't go home. They need to find out what's wrong."

"Don't you tell me what I can't do." His voice sharpened. "I want you to get me home." He tried to lift his head and sank back into the pillow. "I don't want to die here in this hospital."

Tamina's fingers jerked back from his. "Don't say that, Dad. You need help. You're not going to die—but you can't go home." Tamina smoothed her hand across his forehead. "They're going to run some tests in a little bit. You need to cooperate."

He opened his eyes and glared. "And don't you go sassin' me, you hear? If you won't take me home, then I'll get William." His head sank back on the pillow again.

"Quit being so stubborn," Tamina shot back. "There's no way Uncle William will take you home."

Audra backed away from the confrontation. She couldn't listen to it. The quarrel sounded too much like her father yelling at Laney, and she found herself shrinking inside as she had all those years ago. *Will I ever be free of him and the power he still has over my emotions?* She stepped outside the curtained cubicle. The bickering continued. A knot formed in her stomach, and her head pounded to her heartbeat.

Tamina left the cubicle and joined Audra at the nurses' station. "He's as obstinate as ever. Totally exasperating." She shook her head, then frowned. "What?"

Audra couldn't look at Tamina and let her gaze fall. "My father died at his desk from a heart attack, and I never had a chance to talk to him—to say all the things that should have been said. It was shockingly final, and it left a hole. I hope you won't let—"

Tamina dug her fingers into Audra's arm as alarm distorted

her face. "Do you think he'll die?"

"I don't know, but I think there's something seriously wrong. Did you notice how yellow his eyes are?"

Tamina nodded. Then her whole body sagged. Audra pulled her friend to herself and held her. After a moment, Tamina edged back into her father's cubicle. Audra could hear her softly speaking, but she couldn't understand her words.

At midnight, the doctor motioned them out to the hallway. "From the first results, it appears he has cancer somewhere in his body." When Tamina shrank back and sucked in a gasp of air, he furrowed his brow. "Were you not aware of this?"

Tamina clutched Audra's wrist. "No. He told me his stomach was hurting, but he was too stubborn to go to the doctor."

"From what he's presenting, I'd say it's stomach cancer. I've ordered a PET scan first thing in the morning. I suggest you go home and sleep. There's nothing more they can do tonight."

Tamina turned to Audra. "You go on. I'm going to stay."

Audra put her arms around her friend. "I'll come back tomorrow as soon as Kevin's finished with his lesson."

Kevin left at eleven, and Audra choked down a sandwich before she headed for the hospital. Concerns over what Tamina might be facing had her stomach knotted. It was too similar to her own situation. When she arrived at Mr. York's room, Tamina sat hunched in the beige vinyl chair. They were still doing the scan.

When they wheeled Mr. York back into his room, he looked worse than the evening before. An hour later, Tamina was called into a consultation room, and Audra accompanied her. A different doctor pulled up a chair and sat in front of Tamina.

"I'm very sorry, but it doesn't look good. When he came

in, he was presenting several symptoms—pain in his stomach, vomiting blood, yellow eyes, and swollen lymph glands. That raised suspicion, and the PET scan confirmed it as stomach cancer. Did he know he had cancer?"

Tamina hugged her arms around herself. "He complained his stomach hurt and he was having a hard time eating, but he's so stubborn—he refused to see a doctor. If he suspected what it was, he never let on."

"It has metastasized. Nearly all his internal organs are full of cancer, but there's another complication. His blood pressure dropped dramatically early this morning, and his respiratory rate is elevated. That would suggest sepsis. The scan showed he has a bowel obstruction. Apparently, it's already leaking toxins into his bloodstream. We've started him on antibiotics, but his body is so compromised, I doubt we can stop it."

Tamina gripped the armrests. "I think he knew he was dying, but he never let on... He just never let me know what was going on. How–how long will he have?"

"Not long. Sepsis will probably take him quickly. All we can do is keep him comfortable. I'm sorry."

Audra put her arms around Tamina to comfort her as the doctor left. Audra held her friend while she silently sobbed, but she felt like she was suffocating. Her stomach and her throat were so tight she couldn't speak. *Cancer's no respecter of persons – my grandmother, my mother, Rosa's mother – and now Tamina's father. Am I next?*

Fear was like a fierce hand gripping her throat. She wanted to cry to relieve her own pain. She wanted to run away—just leave. But she couldn't. She had to be strong. She held Tamina all the tighter.

When they walked back into Mr. York's room, two people were standing by the bed. Mr. York was sleeping.

Without greeting them, Tamina grasped Audra's wrist.

"Audra, this is my Uncle William—Dad's brother—and Aunt Alva."

Audra offered her hand to the man who, although heavier, bore a strong resemblance to Alfred York.

Uncle William shook her hand and shifted back to the bed. Aunt Alva nodded and moved closer to the window. Tamina gripped Audra's wrist again.

"So, what have they said?" Uncle William asked.

"It's stomach cancer—but he also has sepsis." Strain blunted Tamina's voice. "Everything's too far advanced."

William stared at his brother. "He's not going to make it. Our old man looked just like this before he died. Your aunt and I were going up to Farmington to see Leroy and Cora Mae, but I guess we'd better postpone so I'll be here to make arrangements."

Tamina straightened her shoulders, and her voice grew cool. "If that time comes, I'll make arrangements."

"Who will do the funeral?"

Tamina's lively eyes grew blank. "I really haven't been thinking about those things. Would your pastor do it?"

William's face pulled into a frown. "Well, I guess we'll have to postpone the trip for sure. It will take some real arm twisting to get him to preach for a backslider like Alfred."

Feeling like she was intruding in a private family matter, Audra loosened Tamina's hand and returned to the hallway. The conversation between Tamina and her uncle petered out, and they left after another ten minutes.

Audra rejoined Tamina at her father's bedside. Mr. York's eyes were sunken, and Audra couldn't stop staring at him as his breathing, the only sound in the room, labored on. *He's going to meet God shortly. Is he ready? Am I?* Clamping her teeth together, she fisted her hands. She didn't want to think about that. She desperately wanted somebody to hold her and tell her it was all going to go away. With a deep breath, she loosened her clenched grip and nudged her hand along the bedrail close to Tamina's, and Tamina closed her fingers around hers.

"I'm glad Uncle William and Aunt Alva left. I was afraid he was going to get himself cranked up to give me one of his lectures."

"About what?"

"It's always the same. I never should have taken a job at the academy. It's my duty to teach in Kirkwood Addition and take care of our own. Never mind how I mentor Kayla and tutor down there two afternoons a week — and if it isn't that, it's about what I should be doing to keep Dad from drinking."

Audra lifted her arm around her shoulder, and they stood silently next to each other. At dinnertime, she brought sandwiches, boxed cherry pie, and cartons of milk from the cafeteria. They kept their vigil into the night. Nurses came in at closer and closer intervals as the sepsis gained control. Alfred York died at 1:56 a.m. Sunday morning with Tamina holding his hand and Audra standing beside her with her arm around her.

"At least I got to tell him I loved him." Tamina rested her head on Audra's shoulder.

Audra released a sigh of relief.

Audra spent Sunday afternoon at the funeral home while Tamina arranged details for the funeral. She was tired on Monday, and by her fifth-period free time, she just wanted to go to the teachers' lounge and close her eyes. Her hand was already on the doorknob when she saw the initials written in the corner of the door's window in the same black marker — too large to miss.

Anger flashed first, followed by humiliation and an expletive. Cringing, she peeked around the empty hall to see if anyone had heard. She didn't need this after everything with Tamina. She narrowed her eyes at the offensive initials. *I can't believe it! Have those stupid things been there all day?* Every teacher who visited the lounge had to have seen them. Did they guess who the initials stood for? She withdrew her hand from the doorknob and marched to Sheldon's office. Tamina was right. He had to know.

Sheldon Bentley was in a conference and couldn't be disturbed. Audra stopped at the West Hall water fountain, wet another tissue, and strode back to the lounge. She wiped the glass clean and hesitated before the door. She couldn't go in. She'd die of embarrassment if other teachers were in there on break. *Why didn't one of them just wipe it off?* She returned to her room. She'd have to find time to talk to Sheldon.

Mr. York's funeral was on Thursday, November 8, at eleven o'clock. Uncle William's pastor consented to do the service but refused to hold it in his church.

Audra, Margo Wilson, and three other elementary teachers sat together near the back of the chapel at Bell And Lucas Funeral Home. A bouquet of flowers on a white wire stand flanked each end of the plain, russet-colored, closed casket. The academy had sent one of the bouquets. Tamina, wearing her black sheath and a gold chain necklace, already occupied the front row when they took their seats. She wore no hat like the other women in the family did, but her gold hoop earrings gleamed prominently. Besides Uncle William and Aunt Alva, maybe twenty other people — probably more family, attended, but Audra couldn't identify them.

A portly gentleman in a tight black suit entered by a side door and stood before the casket. He said a short prayer and began to speak. She expected words of comfort, but instead, he issued a warning against backsliding and evolved into an exhortation against alcohol. Locking her eyes on the back of Tamina's head, Audra ached for her as her mind drifted to her own father's funeral.

His funeral was stark like this one. Since her family hadn't gone to church in such a long time, they didn't even know a minister anymore. It wasn't like her mom's funeral at all. Two men, who had worked for her father, told stories of how he was so charitable, but they sounded like they were talking about some stranger. Funerals should bring comfort, especially if the person who died left you angry and confused.

The man in the black suit stopped talking. Someone on the funeral home staff instructed those who were going to the cemetery to line up behind the hearse. Margo Wilson and the other teachers said they had to get back to school and left after giving their condolences to Tamina. Audra waited and pulled her red Focus into the very end of the line.

The interment lasted no more than ten minutes. The grave was in a far corner of the cemetery. Alone off to the side, Audra shivered in the cold wind rattling the bare branches above his grave. As soon as the family laid their roses, one by one, on the casket, Tamina edged up to her.

"Will you please go with me to Uncle William's?" She gripped Audra's wrist. "The whole family's going. Uncle William picked me up this morning, and without a car, I'll get stuck over there all day. I don't think I can face it."

Uncle William's house was large and comfortable. Larger than her own. As the relatives came in, men removed suitcoats and ties and, along with the women, laid hats, coats, and ties on a bed down the hall. Audra found a place to sit in the living room, staying present, but not part of the camaraderie. The family's laughter and teasing and the stories they told on one another drifted over her as they worked to get food on the table. Soon a buffet of ham, chicken, breads, three salads, baked beans, three cakes, and two pies resembled an all-you-can-eat restaurant.

Tamina wasn't really part of it, either. She moved in and out among aunts and uncles and cousins but didn't join the banter. As soon as they ate, Tamina approached Audra. "I'm ready to go home." Their exit barely created a stir.

In the car, Tamina's fingers trembled removing her father's memorial folder from her purse. She stared at his picture, touching his face before slipping it back in. "Thanks so much for going with me. I don't know if you know it, but you were my shield."

"Oh?" Audra's eyebrow shot up as Tamina looked across the front seat.

"Uncle William made some comments on the way to the funeral home, and the longer the morning drew on, the closer I felt to panic. I didn't want there to be a big row, but if I went alone, they would have all let me have it." She tugged at the hoop in one ear before releasing a long breath. "Uncle William and Aunt Alva stopped by on Sunday night. He said the whole family thinks I should have made Dad live with me and taken care of him. They probably never knew I suggested it once, and, boy, did he ever set me straight. I never brought it up again. But…they obviously think it's my fault he died. I can usually shrug off Uncle William's remarks, but I'm more stressed than I realized."

They drove in silence for several blocks before Tamina shifted to face Audra, her head leaning back on the headrest. "That funeral sounded just like Uncle William. I didn't find much comfort in it."

Audra kept her eyes on the road. "Do you believe in heaven?"

Tamina appeared to think about it for several seconds. "Uh-huh, I do."

"Do you think your dad went there?"

"I want to think he did. When I was a little girl, he took Mama and me to church, but after she ran off and he started drinking, we didn't go anymore. That fat old preacher talked like there's no chance to go to heaven if you drink, but I don't know if I agree. I always thought you went to heaven because you believed in Jesus."

Audra shot a glance across the front seat and caught a little quiver on her lips.

Tamina's gaze drifted toward the side window, and her voice softened. "I didn't like it when he drank, but as far as I know, he never got drunk — he just liked to have a nip now and then with his friends down at Pappy's Tavern. We argued, but he was still my father. I loved him despite it, and now I'm going to miss him." She leaned forward and looked into Audra's face. "Do you think your father went to heaven?"

Audra tapped her fingers on the steering wheel, thinking. "You know, I really only thought about it once, right after the funeral. The two men who gave eulogies talked about how fair he'd been and how he'd given to so many charities, but neither of them said they loved him or would miss him. He never had time for God or spiritual matters as far as I could ever see. I guess I concluded that, if I were God, I wouldn't let him in. It's a good thing I'm not God."

CHAPTER TWELVE

AN EMBARRASSING DAY

THE SUN WAS BRIGHT, BUT THE WIND WAS STRONG AND SHARP, whipping Audra's hair into her face. She snugged her jacket closer around her as she quickened her pace across the parking lot. *Definitely Thanksgiving weather.* She spotted Georgia's car already parked in her reserved spot by the front entrance. *Good. I'll have plenty of time to ask her to run off the invitations to our Thanksgiving potluck.* Reaching the sidewalk, her heels clicked a staccato beat. *I'm glad Tamina feels sufficiently recovered from her dad's funeral to help me with the dinner.* Then a gloomy reflection twitched her lips: *What is there about a funeral that leaves you melancholy? It must be the reality check on your own mortality.*

Then the staccato beat ceased. Riveting her gaze ahead, she clenched her briefcase handle and her breath chuffed. *No, no. It can't be…*

Her heart pounded as she sprinted toward the trashcan near the entrance. The A. K. + D. D. scrawled on its side flashed like a neon beacon. Darting up the steps, she jerked the door open, *Please, please don't let there be any inside.* But there they were— scribbled on the side of a locker at the corner of North Hall.

She marched into the sixth-grade hall where more initials vandalized the computer lab window, the drinking fountain, the library door, and every classroom down the hallway. This time the initials slanted sloppily as if the writer had been rushed.

Audra came to an abrupt halt in the middle of the hall. Anger built like a pressure cooker about to explode in her chest. There would be no hiding the graffiti today. There was no way she could clean it all off. Everybody was going to see it. She pivoted around and marched back to West Hall and yanked open the office door just as she noticed it written on their window.

"Georgia, is Mr. Bentley here yet? I have to see him." Her voice blared too loudly. She swallowed twice to subdue the storm inside her.

"Is there something wrong, Audra?"

"Didn't you see those initials?"

"Yes. And I saw it outside, too. I was just getting ready to clean my window. These kids."

"Do you know whose initials they are?" Her voice was still too loud.

"To tell you the truth, I didn't even notice."

"A. K. and D. D."

Georgia's hand covered her mouth. "Oh dear! Yours?"

"And?"

"D. D. Hmmm, I can't think who that could be."

Well, maybe not everyone has it figured out. Audra lowered her voice. "Dann Day, maybe?" She wasn't sure if the look on Georgia's face was shock or disbelief.

"Oh no! Oh, Audra, I'm so sorry. I'll clean it off right away."

"Thanks, but it's all over North Hall — plus on the trashcan outside. I do need to talk to Mr. Bentley."

She barely had time to breathe deeply, compose herself, and let the anger dissipate before she poured out the story to Sheldon Bentley and apologized for not coming to him when it first happened. As she talked, he pulled out a black file box and flipped through cards. When she finished, he shut the box. "There aren't any students with those same initials, so I guess you could be right." He leaned back in his chair. "I'm going to walk the halls to see what I can see. I'll take care of it."

Just before first period ended, Sheldon Bentley's calm voice interrupted class. "Attention all students, this is Mr. Bentley. I have just completed a walk around the campus, and I found numerous graffiti markings on school property. I am disappointed that one of our students has done this, and it will not be tolerated. As a warning, anyone caught writing on school property will be suspended, and if any student sees another student marking, they should report it to the office or a teacher immediately. This is an act of disrespect to our school and to every student and teacher. I desire that every student take pride in our school. Thank you and have a good day."

She busied herself at her desk when the announcement came, but she couldn't resist sneaking a peek. Suppressed smiles crinkled almost every face. So, the students all knew what it meant.

At lunchtime, she went back to the office to make her forgotten copies. After school, she took copies to Margo Wilson for the elementary side. Everywhere she went, she was certain someone was laughing.

CHAPTER THIRTEEN

THANKSGIVING

THANKSGIVING DAY DAWNED CRISP AND CLEAR. STARTING EARLY, Audra and Tamina chopped onion, celery, and giblets for the stuffing and put the turkey in the oven to roast. They had the potatoes mashed, gravy thickened, and the turkey carved shortly before one. When the guests began to arrive, each one commented on the tantalizing aroma.

Sheila, the flamboyant art teacher, and her husband, Steven, brought sweet potatoes with marshmallows on top and two cans of cranberry sauce. Ellen, the middle-aged widow from elementary carried in cooked carrots and cauliflower in cheese sauce. Vern Gilbert had two dozen dinner rolls and a tub of margarine. Heather brought two store-bought pumpkin pies and whipped cream in a squirt can. A veggie plate, dip, and two bottles of wine, one red, one white came with Greg and Russ, and finally, store-bought lemon-pineapple-cream gelatin salad came with Carl.

The men drifted to the living room to wait for the women to arrange the bounty, and Heather followed them. Audra stood at the end of the kitchen table, placing dinner rolls in a towel-lined basket when Heather asked, "Anybody know what Dann Day's doing today?"

Audra strained to hear an answer. The consensus among the men seemed to be that nobody knew. *So, Heather came hoping Dann would be here, too.* Audra had to admit she'd wondered if he would come, but she hadn't even seen him in a month.

She'd rearranged the living room with a folding table from school and a card table at one end so they could all sit together. Lively conversation touched on the weather, sports, the most difficult class this year, and Christmas-break plans.

When there was a pause, Ellen bent forward, seeking a view of everyone's face. "I heard a rumor the school was hit by graffiti. Does anyone know what happened? I didn't see anything on the elementary side."

A long silence answered her before Heather ventured to lean in. "I saw it. It seems somebody was trying to fabricate a little romance." An innocent tone accompanied her wide eyes.

Immediately voices tumbled on top of voices — Tamina, Carl, Sheila, and Greg.

"Oh, it was nothing."

"It's been taken care of."

"Mr. Bentley nipped it in the bud."

"It was just something that got out of hand."

Then an uncomfortable silence permeated the room.

Even though she knew her cheeks were red, Audra lifted her head. *So, everybody does know. They've been kind enough to keep it to themselves, but rumors always grow the fastest when the truth isn't known.* So, as calmly as she could, she shifted her gaze to Ellen. "I'm afraid I was the butt of a rather embarrassing prank, but it's been taken care of."

Ellen covered her mouth with her hand, her face blushing red. "Oh, I'm so sorry. I didn't know."

Easing her gaze along the table, Audra fixed her eyes on Heather. She was sitting there with her elbows on the table, her chin braced on the backs of her hands, and—she was smiling! Gloating!

You're actually enjoying this! Audra swallowed hard, then caught her lip between her teeth to fight down the anger rising in her throat. *You're purposely trying to embarrass me.* She stood and pivoted her body away from Heather, holding back the words she wanted to blurt out. She addressed the opposite end of the table. "More coffee anyone?" *At least my voice didn't catch.*

Everyone declined, but they were quick to say they'd eaten too much, and a chorus of groans arose because they hadn't even eaten pie yet.

"Hey, Audra, let's clear the table and sing old songs like we did last year," Greg suggested.

"Yeah, that was fun," Carl added.

Relieved, Audra escaped from the table to hide her embarrassment. The men carried dishes to the kitchen while the women loaded the dishwasher and washed up the guests' serving dishes. She sloshed hot, soapy water into the greasy turkey roaster and set it out on the patio to tackle later.

Heather avoided her as she dried Ellen's casserole dish and the pot the potatoes had cooked in and then found her way back to the men in the living room.

As soon as the kitchen was finished, Audra settled at the piano. She introduced "In The Good Old Summer Time," and everyone pressed closely together to see the words. She followed with "Let Me Call You Sweetheart" and "My Wild Irish Rose" and then glanced up.

Heather was watching her, her mouth tight, her face set in a hard scowl.

Audra moved on to "By The Light Of The Silvery Moon" which prompted some good harmony and "Frankie And Johnny." The group moved from one song to the next in a comfortable congeniality, except for Heather. She refused to join in.

Vern tired of singing first. "Does anybody play cards?"

"Hey, let's play poker!" Heather pushed her way out from behind the piano. Her face cleared like a mask falling off. "Do you have cards?"

Audra slid from the piano bench. "I can probably dig up an old deck."

Ellen, Sheila, and Steven said they needed to go. They were still too full for pie — and no, they wouldn't take any with them. Carl turned on football, leaving six around the school table.

The penny-ante game lasted an hour and a half. Heather took everyone's money, flirted with the men, and taunted and teased Audra and Tamina if they lost even a penny to her. The pie was eaten, and finally, everyone went home except Tamina.

"Oh, I ate too much, and I'm tired to the bone." Audra stretched out on her stomach on the couch. "So, girlfriend, what did you think about the day?"

"The food was fantastic." Tamina collapsed into the wheat-colored chair, stretching her denim-legging clad legs in front of her. Looking girlish the way her hair fell across her forehead, she scrunched her eyebrows into high arches. "But the rest of the day? I was sorry Ellen brought up the initials."

Audra shrugged. "Well, everybody else knew what they meant, so I couldn't very well deny it." Audra's mouth pulled into a grimace. "But did you notice how much Heather enjoyed my embarrassment?"

"Couldn't miss *that*. I've been dying to ask how you felt about it."

"Well, if the whipped topping had been sitting there, I would have been tempted to give her a cream facial."

Tamina's teeth flashed white, and Audra waited for her to stop laughing.

"Honestly? She pushed my anger button, and I reacted way too quickly. I let her get to me. But luckily, I managed to curb the urge. She's a ditz."

"What was with her when we were singing?"

"I don't know." Audra shoved herself upright and lifted her dark hair off her shoulders. "Sort of reminded me of the look she gave me in the lounge that day." She pulled her fingers through her hair and let it fall back into place. "Did you feel put down when we were playing poker?"

"Well, duh." Tamina rolled her dark eyes. "She didn't have a complimentary thing to say about either of us the whole time. But you know what? I still think she's competing with you in her own mind. Something about you playing the piano really ticked her off—maybe because she wasn't getting any attention. But, boy, did she crow when she was winning at poker."

"I'm not in competition with Heather—for anything." Audra stood and headed for the kitchen. "But I dislike her more and more."

CHAPTER FOURTEEN

AFTER THE FEAST

AT NOON THE NEXT DAY, AUDRA TOOK A PLATE OF TURKEY LEFT-overs to Mrs. Espinosa for lunch and brought Rosa home with her. Opening the back door, Rosa bounced across the landing and up the steps to the kitchen, unzipping her jacket on her way. "Can I play the piano, Miss Audra?"

"Sure, sweetie, but please put your coat where it belongs."

Rosa picked up her jacket from the kitchen floor and ran to the spare bedroom with it. Audra was still shaking her head when the doorbell rang.

Dann stood at the door with a serious look on his face. Her face froze. *He must have come to talk about our initials scrawled all over the school. Oh, I should never have procrastinated telling Sheldon — and I shouldn't have tried to hide it from Dann, either.*

His face remained expressionless. "Ma'am, seeing as how yesterday was Thanksgiving and all, and most people ate tur-key — would it be tacky if this poor, lonesome fellow asked if you could spare a sandwich? I could work for it." He affected sad-puppy eyes and drew down the corners of his mouth. When he lowered his chin and directed a woebegone gaze at her, a small grin began tugging at his lips.

She couldn't help but throw her head back and laugh off her relief. He hadn't come in anger.

"Well, I do have a messy turkey roaster I forgot about. Come on in." She held the door open to him. "You couldn't have timed it better. I was about to get the turkey out of the fridge."

He followed her through the living room and stood beside her when she paused at the piano.

"Hey, Rosa. I want you to meet somebody."

The one-fingered "Mary Had A Little Lamb" faded, and the bright-eyed little girl with twin black braids peered up at them.

"Rosa, this is my friend, Mr. Dann. He teaches at the same school I do." Turning to Dann, she nodded. "Dann, this is my very special friend, Rosa Espinosa."

He shook the child's hand. "I'm glad to meet you, Rosa Espinosa. So, do you enjoy playing the piano?"

She beamed. "Oh yes. Miss Audra is teaching me." Then a frown drew her mouth downward. "But I hardly ever get to practice."

"Okay, you can work some more while I fix lunch." Audra gave the girl's shoulders a squeeze before she continued to the kitchen.

Dann followed, his face serious again. "Am I interrupting anything?"

Audra glanced over her shoulder. "No, I spend a day with her whenever I can, and it's been a while. Coffee with your turkey sandwich?"

"Coffee's fine." He slid into the chair on the backside of the table and watched her. "How'd it go yesterday?"

So, he is aware there was a dinner. "It was nice. There were ten of us. I wondered if you might join us, but nobody seemed to know where you were." She didn't look at him but busied herself measuring coffee and water into the coffeemaker.

He cleared his throat. "I wanted to be here."

She cocked her head toward him and raised an eyebrow. But rather than expand on that, he cleared his throat again.

Audra got the turkey, Miracle Whip, and Heather's leftover pumpkin pie from the refrigerator. When she faced Dann again, he was scowling at his hands clasped in front of him. *Something's bothering him. It just has to be the initials.*

He didn't look up. "I hope you don't mind how I invited myself for lunch. I could almost taste a turkey sandwich, but I really came because I need to talk to you."

Her heart started beating faster. *I knew it. He's upset about the initials.*

His face remained sober. "I need to apologize for something."

Averting her eyes, she slathered Miracle Whip onto the bread slices. *Why does he need to apologize? I need to apologize.*

Rosa bounded into the kitchen. "I'm finished, Miss Audra. Is lunch ready?"

Audra's gaze met Dann's across the kitchen. Silence snuffed their conversation.

He shifted. "I should have waited to tell you," he mumbled toward the table.

A perplexed twist tightened her mouth, and she licked a blob of Miracle Whip from her thumb.

He stood and grinned at Rosa. "Well, Miss Rosa Espinosa, I'll bet lunch will get on the table a whole lot quicker if we give Miss Audra a hand. If you know where everything is, let's set the table."

Dann appeared to relax while they ate. Drawing Rosa into their conversation, he seemed to enjoy interacting with her. He laughed at her knock-knock joke, which made no sense at all, and his eyes sparkled when they met Audra's across the table. *Well, he's not angry. I wonder if he actually is lonely.*

After they shared the pumpkin pie, he rubbed his hands together, "Okay, where's your turkey roaster needing to be cleaned?"

"Are you serious?" She shoved back from the table. "I was joking. You don't need—"

"Hey, I said I'd work for food, so bring it on."

When she retrieved the roaster from the patio, he attacked the pan with a steel wool pad and soapy water. "Who all came yesterday?"

After she named them off, he commented, "Sounds like fun." He made no mention of why he hadn't come. He rinsed the roaster and handed it to her. Then, apparently in no hurry to leave, he leaned against the counter while she dried it.

"I'll take this to the basement later." She set the roaster on the counter and chewed her lip. She'd committed her afternoon to Rosa, but if he still felt a need to apologize, she didn't want to rush him off. She hesitated before confessing, "I promised Rosa I'd take her out to Lake Patterson to feed the ducks since I have a bit of stale bread and a few rolls left over from yesterday. Would you care to go with us and get some fresh air?" If he decided to go along, it certainly wasn't going to change her mind about not getting involved with him.

His eyes lit up. "Yeah, I think I'd like that."

The way he smiled and his eyes sparkled…she couldn't ignore the little zing pulsating through her. No, it still wasn't going to change her mind.

Lake Patterson wasn't a lake at all, but a pond of placid water about fifty yards across formed by an underground spring only a dozen yards beyond Chandler's Grove Academy. Academy Circle Drive provided public access to the walking and biking trails around the pond.

Audra pulled into the parking area and smiled to herself. Rosa certainly had attached herself to Dann. She'd chattered nonstop the whole way—about her school, her scraped knees, her lack of pets, and, lastly, her best friend, Sadie, who had a very large dog named Doofus.

Dann seemed to enjoy it as much as her lunchtime joke.

After scrambling from the back seat, Rosa took two rolls from Audra. "Here, Mr. Dann, you can throw some, too."

Five mallards and two Canada geese swam close and fought for the hunks of bread tossed to them. They stood on the bank and laughed when the birds snatched the final bit and then paddled away as if they'd never been tempted to act so silly.

After the birds retreated, Dann skipped a flat rock across the surface.

"Oh, Mr. Dann, show me how to do that!" Rosa clapped, hopping from foot to foot, and then giggled as her attempts plopped into the pond with a *sploosh*. Audra fared a little better by getting two skips from the rocks she pitched side-armed as he instructed.

They walked the path along the narrow creek meandering westerly from the pond to the arroyo. Rosa alternated between running ahead and walking hand-in-hand with Audra until the fence surrounding Josiah Chandler's historic mansion stopped them.

Audra not only felt entirely comfortable walking under the nearly bare cottonwoods with Dann beside her, but she also sensed layers of anxiety being peeled away from her. If only there were some way to package this peace and take it home.

By four, it began cooling off, and a chilly breeze kicked up as they quickened their pace back to the car. "I need to make a stop on the way back." She shivered as she slid into the driver's side. "When I have Rosa out for the day, I always stop and pick up burgers and fries at Burger Basket and take them back to eat with her and her grandmother as a little treat. I can drop you off to pick up your bike... Or, if you'd like, you can go with us."

Rosa hung over the front seat, looking into Dann's face. "Oh, come with us, Mr. Dann. Pleeeease!"

He grinned at her. "Pleeeease!" he mimicked. "Well, I guess I could, but on one condition. I get to buy the hamburgers. Get your seatbelt on."

They carried the bags of hamburgers, french fries, and chocolate shakes into Mrs. Espinosa's house and placed them on the worn Formica table with shaky chrome legs. Mrs. Espinosa, a petite woman, perched in her dark-green easy chair occupying one corner of the tidy living room. She had confessed to Audra that she'd turned eighty-five this year. Still, her black hair wound back in a tight bun didn't show a strand of gray as it framed a wrinkled face pierced by jet-black eyes.

After Audra made the introductions, Dann shook the frail woman's hand. Mrs. Espinosa seemed short of breath today as Audra helped her out of her chair before they all moved to the kitchen. Dann pulled food from the bags and passed it around. His eyebrows raised in wonder at the way Mrs. Espinosa devoured a simple hamburger and some fries.

When he stood and started gathering up the wrappers and greasy french fry containers, Rosa's grandmother raised an eyebrow to Rosa. The child stopped drinking her milkshake, scooted behind Audra, and coiled thin arms around her neck. "Thank you, Miss Audra, for lunch and the ducks and the walk and—" She spun to Dann, and after hesitating a moment, she put her arms around his waist. Her head barely reached above his belt. "Thank you, Mr. Dann, for the hamburgers and for showing me how to skip rocks." She smiled at him, and then, with a little bounce, she was back at the table making long slurping noises with her straw, getting the last of the milkshake.

Audra moved behind the table and kissed Mrs. Espinosa

on the cheek. The elderly woman held on to her hand. "Thank you. You're so good to us."

Dann reached over and took Mrs. Espinosa's free hand. "I am so glad I got to meet you."

Audra had barely eased away from the curb when Dann asked, "How did you get acquainted with Mrs. Espinosa and Rosa?"

"Rosa's mother, Lorraine, died three years ago of cancer. Lorraine was Mrs. Espinosa's granddaughter. Rosa calls Mrs. Espinosa Grandma, but she's actually her great-granddaughter. All I know is Mrs. Espinosa raised Lorraine, and now Rosa. I think there was another granddaughter, but she never talks about it."

She glanced over at him before she turned onto Main Street. She gulped. He hadn't moved his gaze from her. "A teacher at school, Juanita Gonzales, was Lorraine's best friend. She helped Mrs. Espinosa with Rosa until her husband was transferred and they moved. Before she left, she introduced me to Rosa. She was six by then, and that little girl stole my heart."

"I don't wonder. I think she's stolen mine, too. I sort of gathered they're low income."

She shot a look at him. "More like destitute."

"Oh." He crossed his arms and seemed thoughtful. "Are you really giving her music lessons?"

She sighed as she clicked her blinker and changed lanes. "No. I've taught her several one-fingered melodies, and you heard her whole repertoire at lunchtime. I wish I could teach her and a whole lot of other disadvantaged children, but if there's no piano at home to practice on, we'd all end up pretty frustrated."

"I've had the same desire sometimes." He stared out his side window and rode in silence for half a block. "I haven't forgotten what I wanted to tell you this noon. I shouldn't have said anything then. I didn't want to continue in front of Rosa, but thanks for asking me to go along with you. It turned out to be a delightful day."

"I'm glad you enjoyed it." Out of the corner of her eye, she caught him rubbing his hand over the side of his face and chin.

"Remember the Saturday we were raking leaves? You asked me why I moved here, and I said I ran away?"

"Yes."

"It's pretty much the truth, but I must have sounded like a jerk." His jaw clamped. "I need to apologize for not telling you the whole truth." He took a deep breath and exhaled it. "I've been married, and I'm divorced."

Her shoulder jerked against her seatbelt, but she kept her eyes trained on the road ahead. She was stunned—not because he was divorced, but because he had chosen to tell her. She never would have expected him to share that—he hardly knew her. She tried to imagine him with a wife, but it just wouldn't compute. She gave him a quick glance before concentrating on the road again. She had to pry her tongue from the roof of her mouth before she could ask, "Did you want to talk about it?"

"No, not really. Her name was Gail, and it was a big mistake. My dad tried to tell me so. She was a model, and I didn't figure out until too late she wanted a career more than a marriage. For her, life was parties—wine, music, beautiful women, and beautiful men—no babies, no family." He sighed. "I wanted a family." He locked his hands in his lap. "One day she handed me divorce papers, walked away, and went to New York looking for her big break."

Even with no idea why he was telling her all this, she hurt for him. She parked in her driveway and shut off the motor. The car was dark, but the lone light from the kitchen window high-lighted his profile. "I'm sorry to hear that, Dann," she whispered.

He shrugged and unfastened his seatbelt. "But that isn't what made me run. For the first year I was a workaholic, but desperately lonely the next year. I joined a singles' club and met Jasmine. I'm not sure that was even her real name—she's what made me run. I don't want to slam her, so all I'll say is she had plans to remodel my life, and she wouldn't take no for an answer."

Audra ducked her head. *And now there's Heather.* Heather's dirty look in the teachers' lounge popped into mind. Anger welled up in her chest and compressed her lips. *And she's not going to take no for an answer, either. Poor Dann.*

He clasped his hands behind his head. "By the time school let out this past spring, I had to get away. I stopped here to see Jerold on my way to California, and he told me the academy was looking for a band and orchestra teacher. Sheldon hired me on the spot. I suppose it was a bit cowardly, but leaving Chicago seemed like the perfect solution. I visited my sister, rushed back to Chicago, cleaned out my apartment, and returned a week before school started. *That's* how I got here."

She pressed herself into the corner of her seat. She'd spent the afternoon enjoying his company, being comfortable in his presence, admiring the way he related to Rosa. She didn't want to be grappling with anger at Heather and puzzling out why he'd tell her this.

He rubbed his hands over his thighs, then faced her. They stared at each other across the front seat for several moments. "Are you wondering why I'm telling you this?"

"Yes." She swallowed. "Because I have no idea why."

A small smile curved his lips, and he kept looking into her eyes. "Because I felt like a phony. I should have told you the truth when you first asked, but I chickened out. Then I decided it would be better if you didn't hear it on the grapevine." He leaned his head back on the seat and closed his eyes. "The thing is, it's all connected to why I didn't come to the potluck. I don't know if you've noticed, but Heather's been coming on strong to me since we started working—shades of Jasmine. Vern said she was going to be at the potluck, and I couldn't face a whole day in her company."

Opening his eyes, he looked at her long enough to induce that little tingle deep inside again. She gulped, striving to keep her voice from sounding neither hard from her anger at Heather nor giddy from the inner stirring. "What you've told me isn't at all what I was expecting to hear. But I'm not shocked—things happen. However, you apologized to me, and now I need to apologize to *you*. You see, I thought you came to talk about our initials being smeared all over the school—"

"What are you talking about?" Dann shifted as his face registered surprise.

Her face went hot. "You didn't see A. K. plus D. D. written on the lounge window—or your window—or the office window?"

"You plus me?" He shook his head. "I guess I must have seen it on my window once, but it didn't dawn on me what it meant. I just spit on my hand, wiped it off, and chalked it up to mid-school mentality. So, why do you have to apologize to me?"

She leaned toward him. "Because I didn't go to Mr. Bentley immediately, so it could be stopped. Someone wrote it on the front of my house on Halloween, but when it showed up at school, I was too humiliated to tell him. I thought it would stop on its own, but it didn't. By the time it got out of hand,

I was mortified you had seen it and were offended — or worse, that it would turn into a rumor about us. A rumor would be a lot harder to stop." She drew back and lowered her eyes. "I'm so embarrassed."

Dann exhaled a long breath. "Is that the graffiti Mr. Bentley was referring to?"

"Yes."

"Do you have any idea who the culprit is?"

"Only suspicion, but no proof."

"If it happens again, will you please call and tell me?" He smiled when she glanced up.

"I don't have your number." She reached for her purse perched on the console and wrote his number in her check register.

"Are you in the phone book?"

"My landline is. I seldom use my cell."

He gave a short laugh. "I don't give my number to just anybody, you know, but just so you know, that phone number is there if you ever need to talk about something."

His words struck a place deep within her — a secret place — as if Dann had offered to let her cry on his shoulder. *Yeah right. I'll just call him up and say, "Hey, Dann, I think I might get cancer — you want to talk about it?"*

She winced. That wasn't fair. He had no way of knowing how much she really needed someone to lean on.

When she tilted her head, their eyes met and held. She felt like he was looking into her soul. That was uncomfortable. She sure wasn't ready for that.

"I-I need to get going," she managed to say. "But if you throw your bike in the trunk, I'll drive you home."

CHAPTER FIFTEEN

SORTING OUT THE EMOTIONS

As SOON AS AUDRA AWOKE, THOUGHTS OF THE DAY BEFORE BOM-barded her. She sat up, plumped her pillow behind her, and hugged her knees to her chest.

Dann was different from any man she had ever known—unlike any of the men in Chandler's Grove, for certain. The last date she'd had was with Marty Preston four years ago. Three weeks later, he and Sherlene Taylor left town and got married in Vegas. The only bachelors she was acquainted with, now, were the three who had come for dinner on Thursday.

Carl, the eighth-grade science teacher, was in his fifties and already paunchy. Russ, the shop teacher, was probably seven years younger than herself, and Greg, the seventh-grade math teacher, reminded her of Laney's second disaster, Darryl. She'd rather stay single than date any of them.

She sighed. By her own choice, she generally paid no atten-tion to men. Her father influenced a large part of that, but her sister played a part also. She ran her hands through her hair. She didn't want to think about that. It would only make her angry. She wanted to sort out how she felt about Dann.

He's the most honest, forthright man I've ever met. He's

divorced — so? That hadn't changed her perception of him as a kind, sensitive, nice guy. *He's fun to be with.*

How long had it been since she'd had just a simple day of fun? *But what if he wants to see me again — what if he asks me out?* Her heart lurched. *Oh-h-h boy.* She pressed back into her pillow and closed her eyes.

Yesterday with Dann satisfied something inside her more than she could explain. *But I can't get involved with him — I just can't. I could get the word I have cancer at any time. I could die. Wouldn't it be better for nothing to start between us than to have him face heartbreak and grief?*

Tears welled up in her eyes. Her heart wanted something entirely different from what her mind was trying to convince her of. Her body collapsed over onto the mattress. Then she buried her face in her blanket and moaned. "Oh, God, I don't want to go through this. I'm scared and so alone. And why did I have to meet Dann when I can't have any kind of relationship?" Sobs shuddered through her until she remembered that, even though it was a holiday weekend, Kevin was coming for a make-up piano lesson. She forced herself to get up and shower.

The day was cold and blustery, but Kevin's skateboard sounded on the sidewalk right on time. Audra let him in, and he dropped his backpack on the couch before unzipping his hoodie.

"Don't you freeze riding your skateboard on a day like this?"

"Aw, it's not so cold." He grinned. "Besides, I didn't even wear a jacket when I played soccer." He methodically arranged his music on the piano, and she eased onto the occasional chair to the side. Recovered from her emotional lapse, she was glad for a music lesson to occupy her thoughts. She gave him three gold stars for songs he played perfectly, and when it was time to assign him new songs, they traded places.

"You are playing very well, Kevin. I'll assign you two new songs out of your regular books. For your third song, I want you to pick something you like and would like to learn just because it's fun. I found a book I think you might enjoy, and it has songs right at your level. I'm going to play a few, so tell me if there's one you like."

After the first two selections she played, he wrinkled up his nose and turned his thumbs down. Next, she began the strains of "Londonderry Air," and after two lines, he leaned forward. "Hey, I know that song. My grandpa played it on a CD when we were there this summer. He said it was called 'Danny Boy.' "

"He was right. A long time ago, an Irishman wrote the music, and it was known as 'Londonderry Air.' Years later, another man wrote words to the music, and it became famous as 'Danny Boy.' Would you be interested in learning how to play it for your grandpa?"

"Sure. I really like it."

"I'll write the name of the book down so your mother can buy it for you." With a smile, she reached for the notepad. He'd work hard, she knew.

Minutes after he left, her thoughts returned to Dann walking along the creek trail beside her and those pleasant stirrings when he smiled and held his eyes on hers.

CHAPTER SIXTEEN

CHRISTMAS IS COMING

AUDRA DROPPED HER BRIEFCASE ON THE KITCHEN TABLE AND PIV-
oted toward the calendar hanging on the end of the cupboard.
The fifth of December already. She stared at the telephone. The next
biopsy loomed before her, and stress already knotted her stomach. *What if those abnormal cells have changed? What if I do have to
go through what my mother went through?* Dread seemed to cling to
her. She'd never pictured herself actually facing this nightmare.
She wanted it to go away—but it wasn't going to, and suddenly
denial shifted to anger. "It's not fair!" she yelled at the empty
room. Then she dialed Dr. Rhonda's office and made an appointment for the eighteenth—the first day of Christmas break so she
wouldn't have to take time off work.

She sank onto a kitchen chair and forced herself to grade
book reports. She had planned to go to Dann's band concert
in the gym but was in no mood to pretend she was happy. She
scribbled a B+ on Taylor Bailey's report, then pondered. He'd
asked if she would be at the concert, and she'd assured him she
would. She sighed. She couldn't change her situation and supporting her students' participation in the music program was
important. Like it or not, she'd put on a smile and try to enjoy
the evening. As if nothing was wrong.

After the concert, Audra remained in her seat while parents, grandparents, and siblings emptied the bleachers. She felt calmer than earlier. Watching Dann direct his three bands fascinated her. Although he had inherited a dying program, he acted as if these kids were the best band in town. Maybe they weren't the best musicians yet, but they *were* beginning to respond to Dann's leadership. From where she sat looking down upon the gym floor, the cleanup almost looked like he had choreographed it. One group of girls collected music, another group of students moved music stands back to the band room, and the rest of the junior musicians carted chairs off the gym floor so PE could be held tomorrow. *He has them working together – that's great!*

Her back straightened as Heather crossed the wooden floor. From Heather's expression and gestures, she must be gushing on over the concert. Dann kept shaking his head, communicating disagreement. Audra stood and, carrying her coat, descended to the gym floor.

Dann moved away from Heather to meet her. "Well, what do you think?"

"Good job. I can already tell a big improvement in the midschool bands over last year." She glanced at Heather before turning her back on her. "I heard some mistakes, so you're right, they need to be practicing more at home. But your beginning band is off to a good start. They should be an outstanding concert band in three years."

"Thanks." Leaning closer, he added under his breath, "That was a more honest evaluation than the one I just heard. Are you coming to the orchestra concert tomorrow night?"

"I'm planning on it." She started to put her coat on. Dann took it from her and held it. When she turned to slide her arm into the sleeve, Heather was glaring at her. *Heather's jealous, and she doesn't even know I can't be anything more than friends with Dann.*

Audra said goodnight and strode toward the exit, smiling. Jealousy was the only thing Heather would ever get out of her pursuit of Dann and knowing that made Audra feel the best she'd felt all day.

On Friday, Audra was approaching the teachers' lunchroom when Russ Carlson, the shop teacher, waved a paper and motioned her over. When she detoured to him, he handed her the sheet of notebook paper folded in half. She opened it and froze at the black-marker words: *A. K. thinks he's Danndy.*

"I found this tacked up on the bulletin board." He pointed to the wall near the teachers' lunchroom door.

She folded the paper again. Angry heat surged through her chest. "Thanks for taking it down, Russ." Her voice hardened. "This is getting way too personal." After Russ walked off, she reopened the paper. Had a childish mid-school student truly thought up such a play on words? Who? She wadded the paper and threw it in the trashcan.

After the orchestra concert the night before, she'd decided to go straight home and was already in the stream of people heading for the exit when Dann waved. She gave him a thumbs-up, he grinned back at her, and she went on. Only when she saw Heather on the sidelines did Audra shiver a little, knowing she'd seen the exchange. Is it possible *she* wrote this pointed little barb and tacked it up where teachers were bound to see it? Heather enjoyed her embarrassment at the Thanksgiving dinner, but would she go this far to humiliate her?

Audra moved into the serving line. She'd lost her appetite.

That evening she paced the living room, balking at the idea of calling Dann. It took her ten minutes before edging to the kitchen phone and punching in his number. *Absolutely, the only reason I'm calling him is because he asked me to.*

"You asked me to tell you if any more graffiti showed up."

He sighed. "Where was it?"

"A sheet of paper tacked to the lunchroom bulletin board, so technically, it wasn't written on school property. Whoever did it got a little personal and tried to be clever."

"How?"

She related it and spelled Danndy for him. "I'm grateful Russ took it down."

Dann groaned, and then came a long silence. "Did you show it to Mr. Bentley?"

She winced. "I hate to admit it, but I was so angry I threw it away. I do need to tell him, though."

Another silence. "I'll leave it up to you, but after Christmas break, I think I'll start roaming the halls before and after school and see what I can find."

"Maybe that's the only way the culprit will get caught."

He paused a second before adding, "Actually, I was going to call you in a little bit. I was wondering—do you give Rosa a Christmas present?"

"Yes. I get something for her grandma, also."

"I'd like to get something for them, too. I'm going home for Christmas, and I only have this weekend to get something, and so I was wondering—well, would you go with me to help me find something suitable?"

Every inch of her body suddenly felt prickly, and the voice in her head was screaming, "Say no. Say no."

But he's asking for a favor. How can I refuse to help him with that? He's not asking for a date.

The voice in her head shut up.

"I can't tomorrow. I have Kevin's piano lesson in the morning, and then Tamina and I are going to help Rosa and Kayla bake Christmas cookies. Then, if I have time, I'm going to take Rosa to buy something for her grandmother. Would Sunday work?"

"That'll work."

Just one problem with the whole scenario: she knew she'd enjoy it.

Audra grabbed her coat when Dann arrived at her house promptly at one. Backing his Cherokee out of the driveway, he asked, "So, how did it go with the girls yesterday?"

She laughed. "Other than flour from one end of the kitchen to the other, it was great. I had to scrub the floor this morning."

"Sounds like fun."

Is he joking? She peeked across the console at his steady gaze out the windshield. *Not joking. He would have enjoyed it.* She focused on his profile.

"When I took Rosa shopping, she knew exactly what she wanted to get her grandmother. She said she needed new fuzzy slippers because her feet get cold, and she picked lavender ones. She really touched me—she saw a poinsettia plant and asked if we could buy one to make their house look pretty."

"Did you do hamburgers, too?"

"Oh, sure. I think Mrs. Espinosa would be more disappointed if we didn't do it than Rosa would!"

"I've been thinking. When we were there, I noticed most of their dishes are chipped and don't match. Would dishes be a suitable gift for Mrs. Espinosa?"

Audra suppressed a gasp. He wasn't thinking of a box-of-candy or pair-of-gloves kind of gift. She pondered it a few seconds. "I think she'd be overjoyed. I was thinking of getting her a warm sweater. Hers is getting pretty thin and worn."

At Northgate Mall, he opened her door and swept a gallant hand forward, his lips twisting into a lopsided grin. "Lead on. I have no idea where to look for dishes."

She led him to the second floor of Hudson's Department Store, and he looked at every bit of tableware on display. Passing by the formal china, he paused only briefly at plain white sets and shook his head at a set with plates shaped like green grape leaves. He stopped at a table of stoneware and lifted one plate from the place setting. "What do you think of this set?" He turned it toward her. A rose band edged the cream-colored plate, and a rose on a green stem embellished the center. The mugs, cereal bowls, and serving bowl were cream on the inside and rose on the outside.

"I think you have very good taste. I'm sure she'd like them."

After stowing the box in the back of his Cherokee, they reentered the mall. She strolled alongside him. "Do you know what you're going to get Rosa?"

"I've been thinking about it, and I don't have a clue for her. Would you like to look for a sweater for Mrs. Espinosa first?"

She found a delicate blue sweater in Hudson's women's department. In the girls' department, she bought a navy corduroy jumper with a white knit turtleneck embellished with rosebuds, and a pair of white tights. She watched him out of the corner of her eye more than once. Not once did a bored look cross his face.

"Yesterday, Rosa told Kayla she wants a Barbie doll, and I thought I'd get her that, too. Would you care to browse a toy store?" she asked.

He took the bags from her and carried them.

His face rapt, he sauntered the length of the doll aisle. Big dolls, little dolls, cloth dolls, a dozen kinds of baby dolls, cute dolls, ugly dolls, doll families, and then the Barbie dolls. "How does a little girl know what kind she wants?" He laughed.

"Oh, little girls just seem to have that in their genes." She waved her hand. "There's one for every interest, I think."

"Oh, look at this one with the long black hair! Doesn't she look Hispanic?" He eased a box from the shelf. "And look at the outfit she's wearing—a real hipster."

"You like that one?"

"Yeah, but it's your present, you choose."

"Actually, I like it. I think it will be a hit with Rosa, too. Do you want to walk around a bit to see if you get any ideas?"

As they walked up and down every aisle, his gaze roamed back and forth. Nothing attracted his attention until they reached the bicycles at the back of the store. She smiled to herself. He looked over the girls' bikes the same way he had inspected stoneware—intently comparing features while "Santa Claus Is Coming To Town" played in the background.

He paused and stared down at the bikes lost in thought. "No, wait. Those Christmas carols give me a better idea. Pay for the doll and come on."

With the transaction at the cash register finished, he took her by the elbow, escorted her into the mall, guided her through the sea of shoppers, and into the music store. Inside, he took a quick look around and then led her to the back. He stopped in front of the electronic keyboards.

"Dann, you've got to be kidding—those are expensive."

"The plain vanilla ones don't cost too much. Do you think she'd like it?"

"Oh my, yes!"

"Could you, or would you, start her on music lessons if she could practice on something like this?"

"Well, I suppose I could. The touch would be totally

different from playing on my piano, but, on the other hand, it will probably be years before she'll have a piano of her own — if ever. I'd have to teach her at her house, but it could work." She shook her head. "It's still a lot of money even for the smaller ones."

He touched her arm. "Quit worrying about it. I saved up money for a plane ticket, and then my folks got me a ticket. I want to do this for Rosa," he said with a grin.

Audra gawked at him. Someday he was going to make some little kid a wonderful dad.

His exuberance was infectious. They returned to his Cherokee laden with bags of gifts and sacks of Christmas wrap and ribbon. They drove to the rear of the music store where an employee loaded the keyboard. She couldn't remember ever having this much fun Christmas shopping.

At her house, they moved the coffee table out of the way, sat on the living room floor with scissors and tape, and transformed each box into a mysterious, beribboned secret. Still sitting on the floor, she leaned back against the couch. "When were you thinking of delivering all this?"

"Could we do it tomorrow or Tuesday? I have to drive into Albuquerque and catch my flight out of there on Wednesday, and I really want to see Rosa's face when she opens all this."

"Tuesday will be better. I have an appointment tomorrow." She checked her watch. She was overstepping the bounds of just doing a favor, but... "If I thawed some ground beef in the microwave, I could make a pot of chili. Would you care to stay and eat?"

Between bites of chili and crackers topped with cheddar cheese slices, he said, "I'll get to Skokie on Wednesday, and then on Thursday, I'll drive Mom and Dad to Milwaukee. Davene and her family are flying from California, and they'll arrive in Milwaukee on Thursday, too. We'll all spend Christmas there with my grandparents on my mom's side. They still have their huge old house in the country."

"That sounds wonderful. My family never did anything like that. Is Davene staying long?"

"No, they're flying home again on Tuesday. I'm going back to Skokie with the folks. After all these years, my dad decided to take up a new hobby. He wants to try his hand at woodturning, so he wants us to close in a workshop and build a workbench in their basement. I don't know if we'll get it all done before I have to leave or not, but I'll be back here New Year's Eve."

After he left, she sat on the couch admiring the stack of presents and anticipating Rosa's and Mrs. Espinosa's response. An uneasy thought wiggled into her brain and reminded her that Laney had agreed to drive her for her biopsy in the morning. Then there'd be the agonizing wait to hear the outcome. *Don't want to dwell on that.* She sprang from the couch and called Mrs. Espinosa to let her know they would be coming on Tuesday.

Audra and Dann, their arms laden with Christmas presents, grinned at Rosa's wide-eyed expression when she opened the door. Stepping back from the doorway, she was unable to contain her excitement. She hopped up and down, first on one foot and then the other.

Audra crossed the living room and arranged her presents beside the poinsettia plant — the closest thing they had to a Christmas tree. Two presents already nestled beside it — one present was the box concealing the fuzzy purple slippers, and the other was probably a gift Mrs. Espinosa had gotten for Rosa. He placed the box with the dishes on the other side of the plant.

"We've got one more, sweetie." Audra gave Rosa's arm a little squeeze.

Watching from the open door as Audra and Dann lifted the

box out of the back of the Cherokee, Rosa squealed, "Grandma, come see the enormous box—oh, come quick."

They carried it between them into the house and set it on the floor, letting it lean against the wall next to an oak straight-back chair.

Mrs. Espinosa, standing by then, already had tears running down her cheeks. "Oh, bless the Lord, what is all this?"

Audra hugged her. "Sit down. There's no sense waiting another minute to open everything."

Rosa held the jumper in front of herself and twirled around the center of the living room. She ran to her grandmother, cuddling the Barbie doll. "Oh, Grandma, it's *just* what I wanted."

Mrs. Espinosa pressed her cheek into the blue sweater. "Thank you, thank you," she repeated over and over. She held her hands over her face and wept when she opened the set of dishes.

Finally, only the box sitting beside the chair remained. Rosa's eyes were sparkling as she studied it, still not sure it could possibly be for her.

"What does the tag say?" he whispered.

Rosa bent over the box. "It says To Rosa From Mr. Dann." She lifted her gaze to him. "It's really for me?"

"Yes, it is. Go ahead—open it."

The girl began ripping paper and pulling off bows until the top of the box was bare. She stared. "What is it?"

"What does it look like?"

"Well, the picture looks like a piano, but a piano is too big for a box."

He knelt on one knee. "See the keys? It's called a keyboard. You play it like a piano, and it sounds almost like a piano. But it's small enough to fit right here in your own house."

Rosa gaped from him to Audra, to her grandmother, then

back to him. "Help me open the box," she shrieked, jumping up and down again. Soon foam packing, unattached legs, a bag of hardware, and instruction manuals littered the floor.

While he set about to attach the legs, Mrs. Espinosa proposed serving them coffee in her new cups. Audra carried the box to the kitchen and washed the dishes while Mrs. Espinosa set a dented metal coffeepot on the stove to percolate and arranged the rest of the cookies Rosa had baked.

As they worked in the kitchen, Mrs. Espinosa nodded toward the living room. "He's a wonderful man, Audra. Don't let him go."

Audra smiled at her elderly friend but didn't respond. *If only it were so easy.*

CHAPTER SEVENTEEN

THE REST OF THE HOLIDAY

CHRISTMAS EVE, AUDRA SAT ON HER COUCH IN FRONT OF THE coffee table and studied the unexpected Christmas bouquet delivered minutes earlier. Equally unexpected was the skipped heartbeat when she read: *Thanks for taking the time to shop with me. Have a wonderful Christmas, and I'll see you when I get back, Dann.* She inhaled the aroma of spicy carnations and fingered the ruffly edge of a blossom. *He shouldn't have, but...*

She hadn't put up a Christmas tree just for herself. And even though she knew she couldn't allow a relationship with Dann, the arrangement made the room cheery, and its surprise lifted her spirits.

Red and white carnations interspersed sprigs of holly while a bright red cardinal perched on a dry twig flocked with artificial snow. Sinking her nose in the flowers, she recaptured the awe-filled look on Mrs. Espinosa's face, Rosa's uncontained glee, and Dann's enthusiasm. She'd been close to tears watching Rosa's excitement when he plugged the keyboard in and she played her one-fingered "Mary Had A Little Lamb."

Audra sank back on the couch. *I wonder what he's doing with his family right now. He's probably having more fun than I'll have tomorrow at Laney's.* A wave of loneliness washed over her. Five envelopes stood at attention on her dresser, each containing fifty bucks for her niece and four nephews. Unimaginative gifts, but she wasn't close enough to any of them to know what they'd like for Christmas, and she doubted they'd be as delighted when she arrived at Laney's tomorrow for dinner as Rosa and Mrs. Espinosa had been.

She checked the water level on the bouquet. *It doesn't feel like Christmas Eve. I wonder what church Tamina's going to tonight? She's never done that before, but I don't know why I didn't go with her. It would have been better than sitting here all alone.*

She got up from the couch and wandered to the kitchen, recalling going to church on Christmas Eve years before. *Yes, I wore that burgundy velvet dress. And one year I was an angel in the pageant.* She made a cup of instant coffee and curled up in the wheat-colored chair with her partly-finished novel. Words escaped comprehension, and the coffee grew cold.

At four thirty, she sat at the piano, but she didn't even know what she wanted to play. Her heart wasn't in what she liked to do the most. She perused her collection of music books until she spied a Christmas carol book.

She began by playing the most familiar songs and soon was singing along. When she reached the end of the book, she carried the book to the couch, switched on another light, and began to read. She read every verse of every song. She had sung the carols as a child but had heard them with a child's ears. Today, the shepherds, the angels, Mary, Joseph, and the Baby Jesus were all there in the songs, but words were jumping off the page.

There, in "Silent Night," — "Son of God, love's pure light." She'd never noticed the contraction mark before. It didn't mean the Son of God *loves* pure light as she'd always sung it. It meant the Son of God *is* the pure light of love.

And there, in "Hark! The Herald Angels Sing" — words she certainly hadn't comprehended as a child and was only beginning to now: "God and sinners reconciled." She continued:

"Veiled in flesh the God-head see, Hail the incarnate Deity. Born that man no more may die. Born to give them second birth."

She flipped the page and read "What Child Is This?" There, in the second verse—"Nails, spear, shall pierce Him through, The Cross be borne, for me, for you." Yes, she'd heard in Sunday school how Jesus Christ died on the Cross but had she ever really contemplated how the Baby Jesus in a manger came with the explicit mission of dying on the Cross?

She read on. "God Rest You Merry, Gentlemen" – Oh, it didn't mean merry gentlemen as she'd always thought. God wanted them to be merry because Jesus had been born—"To save us all from Satan's pow'r when we were gone astray."

She dropped the book into her lap. When her mother died, her father said they didn't need God and didn't allow her to go back to Sunday school. That had hurt deeply, a hurt that never went away. *But why didn't I start going to church again when I was old enough to go on my own?* The music said it: she had gone astray. That was her fault, and guilt pressed in on her. She picked up the book again. She'd never heard of the next carol, an old Italian hymn.

Oh! Infant Jesus, Thee I love;

Kindle a flame within my breast,

Let Thy spirit divine dwell there-in

So I will never more be distress'd.

With hearts that overflow with love,

We worship Thee, King of heav'n above.

She closed the book, and tears welled up in her eyes. "Oh, God," she moaned. "Oh, God." Salty tears ran down her cheeks until she retrieved a box of tissues. She blew her nose, and tears kept coming. "Oh, God, how do I get back?" She leaned her head against the couch.

When she finally looked at her watch, it was seven. It had been dark for two hours, and she hadn't noticed. Wet, wadded-up tissues surrounded the bottom of the Christmas bouquet like a mound of white snow. She gathered them up and threw them into the kitchen trash and washed her hands. Her face felt dry and stretched where she had wiped off her makeup, but her heart felt peaceful. She got two eggs out of the refrigerator, scrambled them, and ate them with toast and hot tea. *I wonder if Dann attended church with his family?*

The next day, Audra set her towel-wrapped casserole of potatoes au gratin on the counter. *Isn't it funny that after all these years we still fix ham and au gratin potatoes for Christmas like Mom always did? I wish she could be here with us.* She studied her sister. With her eyebrows knit together, she looked harried from all the holiday prep. *The older she gets, the more she looks like Father.* "Merry Christmas, Laney. Mmm, the ham smells good."

Laney looked up from carving and brushed a tendril of escaping light-brown hair toward the hairclip at the base of her neck.

"Hi. Just a sec and I'll wash my hands."

Voices drifted into the kitchen as Andy greeted Evan and Marsha. Audra pressed herself against the refrigerator when her brother and sister-in-law carried three kinds of dessert from the restaurant into the cramped kitchen.

"Hey, Laney. Room in the fridge for these or in the garage?"

"In the garage, Ev, it's cold enough." Laney stepped over to Audra and touched her cheek against her sister's. "Why don't you pop your potatoes in the oven to keep them warm?" She passed on and held the door open for her brother and sister-in-law.

Returning from the garage, Marsha held Laney at arm's length. "Your outfit's gorgeous. Christmas present?"

"Yes, from Andy."

Audra's sister and sister-in-law hugged closely.

"Let me take my coat off, and I'll be back to help." Marsha squeezed Audra's arm on her way by.

Audra's stomach twisted into a hard knot. *Calm down. You had such wonderful peace last night – don't lose it. I'm sure they didn't mean to slight you – it was just a hug.* Just a hug, but loneliness draped itself around her like a clingy dress.

As soon as the kitchen was cleaned after the noon meal, she motioned to Amanda. "Do you know where the boys are? I'd like to give you your presents."

When Audra peeked into the bedroom, she found her four nephews whizzing miniature cars around a new Christmas race-track. "Santa came again. Meet me at the Christmas tree."

The boys streaked past and sprinted to the den. When she caught up to them and sat cross-legged on the floor with them, they craned forward with excitement.

"Jonah, you're first." She studied the boy as he ripped open his envelope. *Sure can tell he's Laney's son. He looks like pictures of Father when he was young. I wonder if Father was a happy child?* "Do you know what you want to buy with your money?"

The six-year-old beamed. "Uh-huh. I saw this firetruck at the Toy Box." He stretched his arms wide. "It's this big, and it has a ladder that cranks up and a real hose."

She laughed at his exuberance. "Okay. Jon, what plans do you have for your money?"

Jonah's eight-year-old brother looked thoughtful. "I want a Lego Batman set. Mom says it might be too hard for me to put together, but I think I can do it."

"And, Patrick, what do you want?" she asked Evan's nine-year-old son.

"Grandma and Grandpa gave me money, too, so I'm going

to put it all together and buy a bike 'cause mine's too little now."

Audra smiled at him. *A businessman like his dad.*

She turned toward Steven, Evan and Marsha's eleven-year-old. It was like looking into the face of one of her students. "You're last, Steven, but what ideas do you have?"

Steven's black brows drew into a serious line over his flashing eyes. "I was looking online, and I found this neat kit to build a computer. It teaches you all kinds of stuff."

Suddenly, Jonah bounded out of the circle, plopped on his knees in front of her, and threw his bony arms around her neck. "Thank you, Auntie Audra. Can we go play with our race-track now?"

Audra chuckled and hugged him to herself before he raced off. *Such delightful kids.* The other boys were fidgeting. After they acknowledged their gifts and sped off, she uncoiled her legs and settled herself on the couch next to Amanda. *She and I used to be so close — how did we drift?*

"So, let me guess—you're going to buy clothes with your gift."

"You're *so* right. Hudson's will have a big sale, and I can't wait to see what I can find."

"Hmm, I might have to look myself — so, what else is going on in your life?"

Amanda twirled a lock of blond hair and shifted her gaze to the Christmas tree. "Oh… I have a steady babysitting job now. And I have a new boyfriend. His name is Tim. I think Mom and Dad like him better."

Audra's tight stomach loosened while she talked with Amanda, but when Amanda received a text from Tim and excused herself to her room, the loneliness crept in again. She felt empty. *I didn't even know Laney had gotten new den furniture. I'm in my sister's house, and I feel like a stranger.*

Sighing, she stood in front of her sister's large Christmas

tree. Dozens of colored balls glinted with points of reflected light, but she hunted a specific one. *There it is.* A clear amber-glass ornament with tinsel inside hung near the star crowning the tree. The family heirloom had come from Germany. She'd always asked if she could hang it on the tree. It had passed from her grandmother to her mother and then to Laney as the eldest daughter. Amanda would inherit it someday. A lump formed in Audra's throat. *Oh, Amanda, I hope you cherish it as much as I always did.*

Will I ever have a family and a Christmas tree?

She didn't hear the whisper-soft steps on the carpet, but she was aware of the delicate scent of lilac just as Laney's strong arm slipped across her back and her fingers pressed against her shoulder. "Did you find it, Audie? It's up at the top as usual."

Audra's voice turned soft. "I found it." She wanted to turn and throw her arms around her sister. She wanted to murmur, "I love you, sis," in her ear. But her mind rebelled. She stood para-lyzed. *Why don't you hug me tight the way you did Marsha?*

Laney dropped her hand and motioned Audra toward the couch. "Come on and sit down. I didn't want to say anything at the table, but have you gotten the biopsy results yet?"

"Not yet." Audra perched on the new couch with its kid-proof brown fabric. "I absolutely hate the waiting. My mind is never completely free of it, and sometimes it's exhausting."

"Oh, Audie, I'm sorry. I didn't mean to distress you," Laney said without getting up from her chair. "You've always been conscientious about getting your yearly checkups. I just feel everything will be all right."

Marsha reached over and patted Audra's hand from the other end of the couch. "Will you please let us know as soon as you hear the results?"

"I will."

Laney glanced over her shoulder as if to make sure someone

was out of earshot. "Amanda has a new boyfriend," she whispered. "He seems like a nice kid, and she doesn't seem quite as rebellious."

"She was telling me about him." Audra offered a weak smile, but the feeling of being distant and alone grew stronger. Laney had her family, and her life revolved around them, as it should. But with the biopsy's uncertainty hanging over Audra, there was a good chance married life and a family could totally pass her by. She gazed at the amber ornament. *I've spent half my life in denial. I'm not content being single like I keep telling myself. I do want a husband and a family.* There was that strange feeling, again, like something boxed up inside her was trying to get out.

By four o'clock, she had enough of feeling like she was on the outside looking in. She fixed two plates of leftovers for Rosa and Mrs. Espinosa, and a smaller one for herself and spent the evening with them. Mrs. Espinosa was acquainted with loneliness, too. Her only other family, another granddaughter, lived miles away in Chicago.

Two days after Christmas, Audra sat across from Dr. Rhonda as she absentmindedly tapped her pen on the desk. When Dr. Rhonda looked up from her computer, something clouded her blue-gray eyes, and Audra stiffened. *She doesn't want to tell me.* She swallowed hard.

"Audra, the progestin therapy isn't working as quickly or as decisively as I'd hoped. The progestin has caused you to shed some of the concerning cells, but not enough to assume this will clear up by itself. Abnormal cells are still present. I'm going to give you another injection, which will take you to March, and then I'll do a final biopsy in April. I ordered this one just to be certain nothing is escalating."

She turned a straightforward look on Audra. "You're still

young enough to have a child, and I certainly want to give you every opportunity to have a family if that's what you want. I'm concerned, naturally—and I know you are, too—but I don't want you to panic. It just may be things *will* turn around in the next few months." She tapped her pen on the desk again. "Do you have any questions?"

Questions? With her mouth so dry? She studied the picture of Dr. Rhonda and her smiling family on the cabinet. She was a striking woman, probably in her mid-fifties, with a handsome husband and three beautiful children. She didn't look like she'd ever had female problems.

Audra shook her head and stared at her lap. *I don't even know what to ask.*

She couldn't shake the fear this time. She drove to Laney's, but Amanda said she had taken the boys to a movie. She stopped at Tamina's, and she was gone, too. At home, she flopped across her bed. She had never felt so alone.

CHAPTER EIGHTEEN

PARTY TIME

THE NEXT AFTERNOON, AUDRA WAS CURLED UP IN THE WHEAT-COL-
ored chair, attempting to finish her novel when the phone rang.
"Audra? Vern Gilbert here. Greg and Russ are over here talking
about New Year's Eve. We were wondering if it would be possible to get those of us who played poker on Thanksgiving
together for a party at your house—you have the most room."

She closed her eyes. Depression was still nagging at her,
and all she could envision was sitting across from Heather and
listening to her put-downs. Not fun.

When she didn't answer, Vern asked, "Is there a problem?
We'll all bring something again."

She remained silent. Dann's card said he'd see her, but
it didn't say he'd see her on New Year's Eve. Perhaps a party
would help her get her mind off him. She shouldn't be thinking
about him, anyway. It might clear her emotions of Dr. Rhonda's
news, too.

"Audra? You there?"

She sighed. "Yes. I guess that could work." *I'd say don't call
Heather, but it would sound tacky.* "I'll tell Tamina. Have everybody bring snack stuff, and if you feel you need to drink, bring

your own. Come around eight." She hung up and mentally kicked herself. *Why didn't I just decline?*

The poker game was in full swing around the kitchen table on Saturday night when the phone rang. Audra's heart lurched. She had a certain feeling it was Dann. And there was Heather only an arm's length from the phone. She stared at her newly dealt hand. *Full house, aces high! It's bound to be a winner — but what if that's Dann?* The phone jangled again, and she stood. *First chance at a pot in an hour, but...* She folded the cards and laid them face down. "I have to get the phone. I'll fold." She squeezed behind Vern and grabbed the phone on the third ring.

"Hello." She stepped into the piano area and stretched the cord as far as it would go and turned her back. *I hope Heather can't hear me.*

"Hi, I'm back," Dann greeted her.

She chewed on her lip. *I never should have agreed to this get-together.* "Did you have a good trip?" She tried to keep her voice from betraying her delight over his call.

"The flight was bumpy, and I had to fight the wind driving in from Albuquerque. What's going on? Sounds like a party."

Audra took a deep breath. "Vern got together the poker players from Thanksgiving." She chewed her lip again in the following silence. "I didn't know what time you were getting in — would you care to join us?"

Dann stayed quiet for a moment. "Heather there?"

"Yes."

Another long pause. "Okay, I'll come for a while."

When the doorbell rang ten minutes later, Vern jerked his head toward Audra. "I thought everyone was here. Who's that?"

She flopped her cards facedown. "Bye me." She scraped her chair back and darted for the front door without answering.

Dann stepped in and unzipped his jacket. "I feel a bit like I'm intruding."

"You're not." Her pulse quickened as he shrugged out of the jacket. *He's here, and I wish I could walk out to the kitchen and tell the rest of them the party's over.* She could feel the blood rising to her cheeks as she put her hand out for his coat. "I'll put this in the spare bedroom and get you a folding chair."

Vern glanced up as Dann entered the kitchen. "Hey, man, I wasn't expecting *you*." He raked in the pot. "I'm on a roll. Ante up and give me some fresh money to win."

Heather's face perked up. Obviously pleased to see Dann, she patted the end of the table. "Pull up a chair and sit by me."

Dann snagged a plate of chips, dip, and a Coke from the counter and pushed in on the opposite end of the table between Tamina and Greg where Audra set his chair. Heather's lips set in a pout. He won two pots in a row, nearly bankrupting Heather. A grimace etched her face and remained there.

At five minutes till twelve, Vern raked in another pot, then tossed his cards to the middle of the table. "Hey, Audra, it's almost midnight—play 'Auld Lang Syne' for us."

At the end of the song, Vern checked his watch and started counting down from ten until he shouted, "Happy New Year!" Grabbing Heather's upper arms, he pulled her close and kissed her. She rolled her eyes and stepped away from him. Then he turned to Russ, standing on the other side of him, clapped him on the back, and shook his hand before he hugged Tamina and began pumping Greg's hand. The rest of the men began gripping each other's hands with New Year's greetings and hugging Tamina and Heather.

With the congestion around the piano, Audra stayed seated on the bench. Vern kissed her cheek as he stopped behind her, and Greg and Russ hugged her shoulders. Looking up, she spied Dann cornered behind the piano with Tamina and Greg on one side of him and Heather pressing forward on the other. A combination of panic and dismay overtook Dann's face as Heather stretched up to kiss him. He caught her upper arms, but she still managed a quick brush across his lips.

"Happy New Year, Dann." With a laugh, she flipped her long blond hair over her shoulder. He escaped to the kitchen, and Heather retreated to the living room, grinning.

After the rest of the group drifted into the living room and started talking, Audra shifted on the bench with her back to the piano. She listened as Dann tossed empty soda cans, beer bottles, and dip containers into the trash. Dishes clinked as he put them in the sink. He was irritated, and she couldn't blame him. She shouldn't have had the party. She shouldn't have invited him. She *should* open the front door and usher Heather out.

Several minutes later, he dropped onto the piano bench without saying anything. Audra couldn't see Heather, but the feeling that her eyes were on them was palpable.

Audra nudged his shoulder with hers. "I feel like I just fed you to the lions."

He tipped his head to her ear. "It wasn't a lion—it was a lioness, and she was on the hunt."

She couldn't suppress the smile that tugged at her lips. "But I should have begged off on 'Auld Lang Syne.' That's what started it all."

"Hah! That wouldn't have made any difference. Vern's been trying to get Heather to notice him for months, and she won't give him a tumble. If it hadn't been the song, he would have thought up something else. She just took advantage of the situation."

Audra scarcely stopped from asking why Vern would bother. She gave a little shrug, dismissing the topic. "Thank you for sending me flowers."

Everything in her wanted to tell him she'd thought of him every time she'd looked at them. "Did you see them in the other room?"

He smiled. "First thing when I walked in. I thought about you all week. Despite Heather, I'm glad I came tonight, but I really need to get going. It's been a long day." He offered his hand for her to stand and, still holding it, locked his gaze onto hers. "There's something I've been thinking about. I'll give you a call." He gave her hand a slight squeeze, and after retrieving his jacket from the bedroom, he left.

Only Tamina stayed to help clean up. Audra cleared the kitchen table and loaded the dishwasher. Tamina wiped the countertops. "You're awfully quiet, girlfriend."

"I know." Audra busied herself tying up the trash bag and putting a new liner in the wastebasket. She should be resisting thoughts about Dann, willing herself to say no to them, and not letting her heart race because he'd thought about her, or being curious about what he had on his mind.

"I kept looking at the flowers on the coffee table, and when you and Dann were sitting on the piano bench, it clicked. He sent them to you?"

She lifted her face. Tamina steadily peered back. She should have told her. "Right before Christmas."

An impish smile tugged at Tamina's lips. "Something happening?"

Audra took the trash bag down and set it on the landing before coming back up and plunking on a kitchen chair. She rubbed her temples. "Can I just say I'm fighting an inner struggle and leave it at that?"

Arms folded, Tamina leaned against the counter. "Sure, and I won't press you. But did you see Heather when you and Dann were talking?"

"I was pretty certain she was watching us."

"*Watching* you?" Tamina blurted. "Girl, she got really tight-lipped and couldn't stop staring. I think you really pushed her button."

"I'm afraid I've pushed Heather's button more than once lately — but then she's pushed mine, too."

CHAPTER NINETEEN

THE START OF A NEW YEAR

AUDRA SLID HER LESSON PLANS TO THE CENTER OF THE KITCHEN table and moved to a narrow window. The pungent aroma of sauerkraut and pork ribs simmering on the stove permeated the house. *I wonder if either Laney or Evan recall how Mom cooked this menu every New Year's Day. They always grumbled about it, but I loved it.* The window was too clouded with condensation to see out, but the wind-driven snow pelting against the glass sounded like sand. She startled when the phone rang.

"Hi, are you busy?" Dann asked when she answered.

She leaned against the doorjamb. "Just gathering momentum to get back to work tomorrow."

"Remember last night when I said I'd been thinking about something? I'd like to run it by you. Do you recall at the band concert when you said the kids really need to practice more at home?"

"Yes?" She loosened her shoulders and rubbed the back of her neck. It seemed he'd been thinking something safe and impersonal.

"I've been racking my brain for a way to motivate these kids. I realize not every kid in middle-school band and orchestra is going to become a lifelong musician, but I'd like my students to experience what can be achieved with serious practice."

"And you have an idea?"

"Call me crazy, but it keeps rattling around in my brain." A long breath whispered through the line. "The only problem is I haven't figured how to work it logistically... Because it involves you."

"Me?" Her spine straightened against the doorframe as she clutched the phone cord. *Well, so much for being impersonal.*

He chuckled. "Yes, you. I'm hoping you'll play some duets with me. You know? Piano and flute for the band students and piano and violin for the orchestra."

Audra plopped on the kitchen chair she vacated earlier. "You want to do this during class time?" She planted her hand on top of her head. The concept was overwhelming.

"I don't know when else it could be done. I'd like it to be as soon as possible to give the kids some time to work before the spring competitions."

"But we're teaching at the same time."

"That's the part I haven't figured out. First, I wanted to see if you think it is too farfetched or if it might be workable."

She stood and paced the length of the phone cord. Her heart was already banging against her ribs. Accompanying Dann would be...exhilarating.

Back off, girl. You're forgetting your decision. Don't get drawn into something you'll regret. She swallowed hard, rested her head against the doorjamb, and stared at the ceiling. *Calm down. He's asking for another favor. He needs your music, so it's not personal. Act professional.*

She cleared her throat. "How do you think our playing together would influence these kids to practice more? I mean, just a flute with a piano isn't going to sound much like a band."

"I know. … The thing is, my concert students here are just now playing what my intermediate kids in Chicago were playing. I'm thinking if I—or we—could present some live music to show them adults and teachers still practice and enjoy making music, we might generate new enthusiasm, and if they practiced more, I could get them playing more interesting music."

She filled her lungs then let air spill past her teeth. "I can see what you're trying to do, but, well, frankly, there's been a lot of mischief with our initials being linked. I don't want to add fuel to unintentionally give someone the impression there *is* something going on between us."

Phew! Her voice stayed steady, and he couldn't see how red her face was turning.

Dann's end of the line turned silent. "Oh," he finally said. "I didn't give that a thought. Maybe you'd rather not do it."

She could feel disappointment dulling his former enthusiasm, and she sat and cupped her chin in her hand. "I didn't mean to throw cold water on your idea. It has merit, but have you talked to Sheldon? He may be the deciding factor."

"I wanted to find out your reaction first."

"My honest reaction? It sounds like an awesome idea, but before I commit myself, I'd like to know how he feels. If he has any hesitation while the graffiti is still a problem, I'll have to decline."

"I'll talk to him sometime this week."

Audra hung up and slumped down in the chair. His smile the night before flashed in her mind. *How on earth can I do this favor without getting entangled in my own emotions? Maybe I should have flat out said no.* She recalled their initials, like black blemishes, tagging the sixth-grade hallway. *Oh, I'm sure Sheldon will say no.*

By the following week, Christmas break seemed to be out of everyone's systems. On Tuesday, Dann knocked on Audra's classroom door after school. He stood to the side and hooked his thumbs in his pockets while she was writing on the whiteboard.

"I'm sorry it took so long to get back to you." He cleared his throat. "Sheldon didn't have much time last week. He said my idea was rather unorthodox and he couldn't see a way for you to be in two classes at once."

She finished writing the assignment on the board before she put the marker down and faced him.

He shrugged. "He didn't say no, so I asked him to think about it and made an appointment to talk about it again." Her eyebrow went up questioningly, but when she didn't interrupt, he took a step closer. "The more I thought about it the more I decided to take a different tack. We had a long meeting yesterday. I explained my motive and why I'm asking for your help, and I laid out your concerns. I told him I'd like him to give a pep talk to the students on how beneficial music will be throughout their lives and how the bands and orchestras represent Chandler's, and with more practice, they could give the public middle schools some real competition."

"What did he say?"

Dann laughed. "When I said his presence would give it more weight, he was hooked. He said if we don't take more than half the class time for each session, we can do it. He'll get a teacher aide to sit in your class, but if you take over for the rest of the class time, he won't need to get a substitute for the whole day."

Staring at Dann, Audra drew back a step. *Sheldon agreed to this? I can't believe it – I was so certain he'd have qualms.* "Sheldon wasn't concerned about us doing this together with the graffiti?" Her voice almost squeaked.

Dann grinned. "The only thing he cautioned was, 'If you take this on, I'm certain I can trust you to be aboveboard and circumspect. If it creates another problem, we'll deal with it then.' "

She continued staring. *I don't dare get involved with him, so why shouldn't it be circumspect?* Her cheeks heating, she let her gaze fall to the floor. *Dann wants this for the good of his students. If I say yes, I'll just have to concentrate on helping him accomplish his goal.*

Suddenly, she shivered. Crazy, but she felt like her father was standing next to him looking—no, scowling—at her. The impression was so real that, when she looked up, she almost expected him to be there. She took a deep breath and swallowed hard before she smiled at Dann. "All right, I'll do it."

He let out a huff as if he'd been holding his breath. "You know it's going to mean a lot of running back and forth for you?"

"I'll wear my track shoes!" She raised one eyebrow and glanced sideways at him before she realized how close that had been to a flirt.

Dann rocked up on his toes and continued grinning. "We'll have to look for music."

CHAPTER TWENTY

PRESSURE ON ALL SIDES

LATER THAT WEEK, AUDRA APPROACHED A KNOT OF TEACHERS gathered at the lunchroom bulletin board. Her stomach tightened. A pinned sheet of notebook paper fluttered there. The words *Will Knight turn into Day?* blazed like a flaming billboard.

Her eyes narrowed. "That makes me sick!" Her lips compressed, and her hands began to shake. This was the boldest message yet. She shoved through the group and ripped the sheet off the board, sending the pushpins flying. Paper in hand, she suddenly felt naked, encircled by her coworkers. All eyes were on her. She crumpled the paper into a tight wad. "I'm sorry, but I *am* angry. Please excuse me."

When the group split to allow her through, she slammed the offensive ball into a trashcan near the entrance.

"We were just discussing what should be done to stop this," Doris Stevens said to her back.

Audra stopped but didn't turn.

"I think someone better get serious about catching this delinquent," Jerold Altman added.

Without responding, she moved into the serving line. She picked up a tray and banged it onto the rail. She was angry at the note—angry her ire erupted in front of the other teachers. She gave her tray a push to start it through the line, then inhaled a pleasant fragrance hanging in the air. *I've smelled that recently. New Year's Eve.* "Angel" *Tamina called the perfume.* Her body tensed. *Heather's right behind me.*

Heather leaned forward and whispered into her ear, "Is it starting to get under your skin?"

Audra whipped around. "Yeah, and just to let you know, you are at the top of my lists of suspects."

Heather tossed her long hair over her shoulder and chortled. Teachers, both ahead of them and behind, craned their necks. "Oh, that's rich." Blue eyes sparked above a smug turn of her lips, "I think little Miss A. K. is having a meltdown."

Humiliation and anger choked Audra's throat, causing her breath to come in ragged gulps. She raised her hand, but in disgust at the awful thing she was about to do, she abandoned her tray on the rail, avoided everyone's eyes, and ran out of the lunchroom. She was trembling when she reached her classroom. She hated Heather. Absolutely hated her.

She collapsed onto her desk chair and hid her hot face in her shaking hands. *I almost slapped her. I let her get to me. I've never been so ashamed. Did they realize I almost hit her?* She rubbed her throbbing temples with her fingertips. The headache was only going to get worse by skipping lunch. *But I can't go back to the lunchroom.*

She crossed her arms on her desk and rested her forehead on them. *I judged Father as weak and mean-spirited for his anger, and I don't have the faintest idea how to get rid of my own. Can you inherit anger? Oh, God, where are you?*

At a knock on her door, she straightened up and guardedly crossed and cracked it open enough to see Doris Stevens. She opened it for her.

The older woman looked over her shoulder before she

entered. "Are you okay?"

Audra shrugged, her throat still tight. "I–I'm not sure. Please forgive me for behaving badly." She couldn't look Doris in the eye.

"Oh, Audra, what she said to you was terrible. I can't imagine how embarrassing this has become for you, but I hope you don't think any of the other teachers are making fun of you."

Audra shook her head. "I hope not. I've just been having a little bit of trouble with Heather."

"Is there anything I can do?"

"No—yes! Could you please get me a sandwich and a carton of milk if there's anything left? I didn't get any lunch."

Audra's head was still touchy from yesterday's stress when she took two aspirin with lunch and headed to the teachers' lounge. *Just ten minutes on the couch should get me through the afternoon.* Her hand froze on the doorknob, and her breath refused to leave her chest. Several teachers huddled in a group—were they looking at another graffiti note? Her heart started beating faster. She couldn't ask.

When the group opened enough for her to move closer, she relaxed. They were looking at the newspaper. "Did something happen?"

With the paper turned her way, she skimmed the headline: Boy Killed By Speeding Car. A picture of the boy dominated the sidebar. She jolted and pulled the paper closer.

She felt like she was going to be sick.

"Kevin? Oh, no, it can't be!" She glanced at the beginning of the story. Kevin Miller, son of Mr. and Mrs. Leonard Miller... "No, not Kevin." She shoved the paper away.

"Do you know him?" somebody asked.

"He's... he was one of my piano students."

"Oh my goodness, Audra! I'm so sorry to hear that." Doris Stevens laid a hand on Audra's shoulder.

Audra recognized Doris's voice, but she went numb. She couldn't bear to read the story. Someone slid a chair behind her, and she sagged into it. "What happened?" she finally managed.

Doris took her hand.

Someone else explained, "Witnesses at the scene said he was waiting at the corner of Fifth and Main for the light to change. He was watching the light, and when it turned, he put his skateboard down and started across. Apparently, he didn't see some punk speeding through the red light. After he hit Kevin, he crashed onto the median, and another driver and two pedestrians held him until the police came."

Audra covered her face with her hands. The first bell rang. Students would be returning from lunch, but she didn't move.

Another voice said, "We've got to get to class. Somebody go get Sheldon."

The door opened and closed.

She dropped her hands into her lap. "Go on to your classes. I'll be all right." One by one, the teachers left the lounge, leaving her alone in the empty room. She closed her eyes and tried to calm her racing thoughts until Sheldon entered.

"Russ Carlson told me what happened. Are you going to be all right?"

"I think so. I'm sorry. It was just so sudden—"

"I can certainly understand. Are you able to go back to class?"

"Yes." Her head was pounding, and when she stood up, her legs wobbled like rubber. Sheldon opened the door for her and walked beside her down West Hall to her room. Without a teacher in the room, the kids were noisily talking and laughing, but when she stepped in with Sheldon, the din ceased. He stood by the door as she crossed the room to her desk. She paused next to it for something to lean on. *Don't cry — not in front of the students.*

"I've just gotten some very sad news, and I'm a little shaken up." She scanned her wide-eyed class. "I'll be all right, but please start the period reading your library books."

They obediently pulled out their books and began to read. Sheldon slipped out and closed the door.

The afternoon dragged on interminably. As soon as the last class cleared her room, she locked her door and drove home. She retrieved the book where she had found "Londonderry Air" and sat at the piano. She played it once, and then a second time, singing and half crying, "Oh, Danny boy, the pipes, the pipes are calling." When she got to: "It's you must go and I must bide," she broke down and sobbed. She ran to the bedroom and fell across the bed. "Why, God? Why Kevin?" she cried, burying her face in her pillow. It was almost time for Patty to arrive for her lesson before Audra sat up. *Maybe Heather's right. Maybe I am having a breakdown.*

Kevin's funeral was held on January 17. Audra entered the sanctuary and was ushered to a seat halfway down. The pews were nearly filled with quiet, somber-faced people, but she didn't recognize any of them. A boy about the same age as Kevin sat in front of her. She caught a glimpse of red, swollen eyes when his mother passed tissue to him, and he wiped his eyes before leaning his head on her shoulder. *A classmate? Best bud? Cousin? No, a cousin would sit in front with the family.*

Audra slipped a tissue from her purse. She was going to need it.

A sea of white and blue flowers drowned the small, blue casket, while baskets of multicolored flowers huddled together in front of the casket, creating the sense of a quiet garden.

The softly playing organ stopped, and the pastor walked forward holding a Bible. He said a prayer and read several Scripture verses before asking everyone to join in singing two verses of a hymn in the bulletin. Following along, she lifted her voice with the others, letting unfamiliar words wash over her.

I know that my Redeemer lives,

What comfort this sweet sentence gives.

He lives, He lives, who once was dead;

He lives, my ever-living head.

He lives and grants me daily breath;

He lives, and I shall conquer death;

He lives my mansion to prepare;

He lives to bring me safely there.

The pastor stood facing Kevin's parents. "Kevin's with Jesus now. He was a wonderful boy, and we all loved him. He had things to do and places to go, but it only took one split second of misjudgment on a young driver's part to have him taken from us.

"I talked with Kevin not too long ago about heaven and asked if he thought he'd go there. He kept his eyes on me, and with all confidence said, 'Sure, Pastor, Jesus died on the Cross for me to forgive my sins so I can go to heaven.' So, today, even though our hearts are heavy with grief, we celebrate because we are confident Kevin is with his Lord."

She dabbed her eyes with the tissue. Yes, these were words of comfort. This was the comfort that was so lacking in her father's and Mr. York's funerals — the comfort she desperately longed for.

"...and I pray you will be able to find it in your hearts to forgive the young man whose terrible lapse of judgment caused a death."

She looked up, dumbstruck. *How can Kevin's family ever forgive in such a situation?* She gazed at the pastor. His earnest expression portrayed a belief that they would be able to forgive. She wiped her eyes again. *Where would you find that kind of fortitude?*

Following the service, Mr. and Mrs. Miller stood in front of their pew and received each person one by one, with a hug, a kind word, a thank you. Audra watched from her pew. Although their faces were somber, strength emanated from them. Their voices were clear. They weren't overwhelmed or defeated. Somehow, they had joy in the midst of their grief. Their calm peace consoled her heart. She allowed other people to go forward until she was the last one in line.

She walked forward, stopped in front of Kevin's parents, and grasped their hands in hers.

"Thank you for coming, Audra." Mrs. Miller tightened her grip.

"I'm going to miss Kevin very much." Audra squeezed back. "He told me you visited his grandparents last summer. May I ask which of your parents that was?"

"We were at my parents' home." Mrs. Miller nodded toward the end of the pew where a gray-haired couple stood side by side with Kevin's little sister.

"May I speak to all of you a moment?" Audra said.

Mrs. Miller's dark eyes widened. It took her a moment to comprehend what Audra had requested before she motioned her parents to join them.

"This is Audra Knight, Kevin's piano teacher," Mrs. Miller said. "My parents, George and Selma Phillips."

Audra laid her hand on the older man's arm. "I just wanted to tell Kevin's grandfather that Kevin was learning to play

'Danny Boy' just for him. He worked harder on that song than any other. He almost had it memorized because he knew his grandfather loved it and played it on a CD for him." As Audra shifted her gaze from parents to grandparents, tears filled the eyes of each one.

"Thank you for telling me." Mr. Phillips clasped her hand in his, and Audra hugged each of the older couple.

Mrs. Miller reached for her and threw her arms around her tightly. "I'm glad you told us. I didn't know Kevin was practicing for his grandpa."

Audra had to leave. Tears were streaming down her face. Not only tears of sadness but tears of joy over being able to give the family a memory of their son and grandson they would treasure forever.

When she eased into her driveway, Dann exited his car at the front curb and, without a word, followed her around to the back door. "Tough time?" he asked when they stopped in the kitchen.

She grabbed a tissue from the counter and blew her nose with a nod.

He studied her face. "All afternoon I was thinking how much you must be hurting, so I ducked out of my free sixth period early. I had a feeling it was going to be hard for you."

She threw the tissue into the garbage before turning toward him, still keeping her eyes down. "Thanks."

He hesitated, but then he took a step closer and brushed her arm. She didn't look up, but she didn't resist. He slid his arms around her, so she laid her head on his chest. There were no more tears, just silent, cleansing sobs shaking her whole body. They weren't for Kevin, though. They were for the twelve-year-old girl who had sought so long for comfort after her mother died. Dann continued to hold her, even after she grew quiet. When she stepped back, she looked up at him, losing all focus but his gentle gray eyes.

"Thanks. I really needed that—more than you'll ever know."

He stood in front of her with his hands at his sides as if he didn't know what to do next. "Is there anything else you need?"

She shook her head. "No, I'll be okay. Your being here was—it was a tremendous help."

He gave a deep sigh, and his voice grew soft. "I guess I'd better get going then."

She watched his back as he descended the steps. *I wish I could ask you to stay and have dinner with me — spend some time with me — hold me one more time.*

CHAPTER TWENTY-ONE

THE WHEELS COME OFF

THE DAYS AFTER THE FUNERAL DRAGGED. HOWEVER, THE LONG evenings when Audra was alone with her thoughts were an even bigger problem. *And here I am again. Friday night in my pajamas, sitting in the middle of my bed, brushing my hair, struggling with the same thoughts that have bugged me ever since the funeral.*

Disturbing thoughts were already launching their evening invasion. *Will I develop cancer?* That was the big one. *The doctor says it isn't cancer, just abnormal cells, but somewhere along the way, Mom and Grandma must have started out with abnormal cells.*

Why couldn't she merely tell herself not to worry? Couldn't it ever be that easy? She flung the brush into the bedside drawer and slammed it shut, then scowled at the force she'd used.

I pray you will find it in your hearts to forgive. The words from the funeral echoed in her brain.

If the Millers can forgive a man who took the life of their child, what am I going to do about the people who have hurt me in lesser ways? Like my father. Laney. Heather.

What if another graffiti paper shows up? What if my temper gets out of control and I really do slap Heather? What if I lose my job because of it? She didn't have a shred of proof Heather had anything to do with the graffiti, but she'd allowed Heather's antagonism to provoke her into an accusation.

Then there was Dann. He held her close on Tuesday in a simple gesture of sympathy, and it was still having an effect on her. Standing with his arms around her, she knew there was a hole in her life. A hole she wished he could fill. She enjoyed having him around—she missed him when he wasn't there. *He's fun to be with, generous, sensitive, and honest, but I'm not sure his wounds are healed. What if we fell in love, and I did develop cancer? No! For the hundredth time, I can't inflict such pain on him.*

She gave a little shrug. It probably was a moot question, anyway. He held her close on Tuesday, but she hadn't heard a thing from him since.

The mental conversation was still playing in her head when the phone rang. She walked barefoot to the kitchen to answer it. "Miss Audra?" Rosa's voice trembled. "Grandma's sick. Her head is really hot, and I don't know what to do."

The whirlwind of frightful scenarios in her mind was replaced by a trip to the emergency room with Mrs. Espinosa.

Waiting was boring. Audra read the poster with all the warning signs of a heart attack three times while listening to doctors and nurses rustling about in the next cubicle with a man who came in with chest pains. She empathized with the baby crying incessantly in another curtained-off section. She kept watch over Mrs. Espinosa lying motionless on the bed, eyes closed, skin gray.

"How much longer, Miss Audra? It's stinky in here," Rosa whined and flopped herself over on Audra's lap.

Audra blinked scratchy eyes. Her body ached from sharing the lone turquoise chair with Rosa for three hours.

Finally, the curtains grated on their track, and the doctor stood in front of Audra. "Her X-rays show pneumonia. I'm going to admit her so we can get her on antibiotics and watch her. Is the girl your daughter?"

She nodded toward Mrs. Espinosa. "She's her great-granddaughter. She'll go home with me." She struggled to extricate herself from the chair.

The doctor leaned over Mrs. Espinosa. "Is that where you want the girl to go?"

Mrs. Espinosa nodded and added a weary yes.

Audra took the old woman's hand. "I'll keep Rosa with me as long as necessary, so don't worry—Oh, I'll need some clothes for her, may I take your house key?" Mrs. Espinosa only lifted a finger in affirmation.

She roused Rosa. "Come on, sweetie. You're coming home with me tonight. Can you tell Grandma goodnight?" She groped around in Mrs. Espinosa's floppy black purse until she grasped a key on a string. She had to hold on to Rosa to keep her walking in a straight line to the car.

When Audra awoke in the morning, things felt out of order. Rosa was asleep in the spare bedroom in the twin-size bed that had been her own when she was a child. She hadn't had to get up and fix breakfast for a little girl since Amanda was small. Also, it was the first Saturday that Kevin wouldn't be coming. That was going to take some adjustment. She got up to take her shower before the litany of thoughts started in again.

When she returned to the bedroom, Rosa was sitting on her bed with her knees pulled up inside the white sweatshirt Audra had given her to sleep in, the long sleeves swallowing her hands.

"What's wrong with Grandma?"

"Pneumonia, sweetie. She must stay in the hospital so they can give her some medicine to make her better. How about if we have some breakfast and go over to your house to get you some clean clothes? Then we can go to the hospital and see how she's doing."

Rosa's face brightened. "Okay. Can I bring my Barbie doll over here, too?"

"You bet." Audra squeezed her shoulders.

There were no clean clothes. Everything the girl and Mrs. Espinosa owned appeared to be in the overflowing wicker hamper in the cramped little bathroom. Audra went to the kitchen to get a trash bag to take the laundry home to wash and halted at the disaster spread before her. An empty bread wrapper, two empty, dried-out soup cans, a crusty saucepan, crumbs, and a table knife smeared with peanut butter littered the counter next to the stove. The odor of days-old rotting chicken packaging wafted from a trash bag under the sink.

Rosa's hand slipped into Audra's. "Grandma couldn't cook, so I made some soup."

"I see that." Audra momentarily closed her eyes. *Oh, I hope Tamina was serious about caring for Rosa if something bad should happen to both me and Mrs. Espinosa.* She started cleaning up the kitchen.

They didn't stay long at the hospital. Although Mrs. Espinosa's skin was still gray and she didn't say more than a whispered "hello," she looked better than the night before.

Rosa patted her grandmother's wrinkled hand. "Why does she have all those tubes, Miss Audra?"

As Audra explained the IV and oxygen, Rosa moved closer to her and wrapped her arms around her waist. Audra draped her arm around the girl's shoulders. "She's going to be all right, sweetie, but I think we'd better let her rest some more. We'll come back tomorrow." She bent over Mrs. Espinosa. "I'm going to take Rosa back to my house again. You rest and get better and don't worry about anything, all right?"

Mrs. Espinosa nodded and gave a weak smile. She reached over and squeezed Rosa's hand.

Back home again, Audra started the laundry and played games with Rosa. After the fourth game of Go Fish, she felt impatient with childish games and weary of her thoughts. Irritated with herself, she excused herself and went into the bathroom, locked the door, and backed against it with her eyes closed. *Where did the easygoing, go-with-the-flow girl I used to be go?* She came out of the bathroom and asked Rosa to go play with her Barbie doll while she made a phone call. She punched in Tamina's number who answered with, "Hey, girlfriend, what's up?"

Audra smiled in spite of herself. "I need a shoulder to cry on."

"Want me to come over?"

"Yes, but I can't talk yet. Rosa's here. She called me late last night, and I had to take Mrs. Espinosa to the emergency room. It looks like I'll have her for several days, anyway. Suddenly I feel like a ton of bricks fell on me."

Tamina paused before asking, "Feel like going out for pizza?"

"It might do me good."

"Let's go out and pass some time until Rosa goes to bed, and then we can talk."

Audra, Rosa, and Tamina went back to Audra's after pizza at Canyon Road House. Sometime past nine, they finally sat at the kitchen table with cups of decaf coffee. Audra had forgotten how many excuses kids could think up to forestall bedtime. Rosa wanted to be in on whatever Audra and Tamina were about to do until Audra finally told her they were going to do big people stuff and please stay in bed. Rosa had crawled under the puffy pink comforter and fallen asleep at last.

"What's bothering you, girlfriend?" Tamina stirred milk into her coffee.

Audra fiddled with the cup handle. "Where to start? My last biopsy still showed abnormal cells. Dr. Rhonda told me not to panic, but it's impossible not to worry. I keep getting scared that I'm going to be next in my family."

"Girl, I can't imagine what you must be going through. Is there anything I can do to help?"

"If you know how to pray—pray."

Tamina smiled across the table.

Audra wrapped her hands around her hot cup. "Something else happened… I guess it happened the day before Kevin was killed. With all that went on with him, it just fell out of my head. I haven't even told Dann. Somebody pinned another graffiti note to the bulletin board by the cafeteria. It said, 'Will Knight turn into Day?' "

"Whoa! That turned things up a notch, didn't it?"

Nodding, she sipped her coffee, letting warmth calm the anxiety rising in her throat as she shared. "Big time. I just don't see how one of the kids at school is thinking this stuff up. A bunch of teachers were standing around the bulletin board discussing the note, and when I saw it, I got really angry. I grabbed the paper and threw it away. I was going to go ahead and go through the lunch line, but…" She shared what Heather did. "I lost it, Tamina. I just lost it."

Audra hugged her cup between her hands, again. Trembling on the inside, she lifted her head and looked at Tamina's smooth brown face. Her dark eyes were wide. "I was so filled with anger…it scared me."

"That's not like you at all."

"Maybe it is. It seems to be my new normal. Thinking I am capable of losing my temper to the point I would hit somebody over some graffiti makes me nervous."

"Oh come on, girl."

"No, I'm serious. Well, then I went to Kevin's funeral — and there really is such a thing as a good funeral, by the way." She related what the pastor said and her own belief that the Millers truly could forgive his killer. "And where does that leave me? I've got all this anger inside me for Heather and my father, and I don't *want* to forgive them."

Tamina placed her hand over Audra's. "Hey, I know you've had issues with your father, but I've never seen you this upset. What's wrong?"

"I don't know." Audra shook her head. "I've been angry for a long, long time, but lately, every little thing triggers an angry response. I'm angry because I could get cancer. I'm angry about all the graffiti nonsense. I'm angry at Heather. I'm angry at myself for losing my temper, and I'm angry because I can't control my anger."

She turned her hand over and gripped Tamina's tightly. "All of a sudden, I feel like this has exploded into something really ugly. My anger has burst out of some secret closet, and I can't get it back in because it's grown fat and ugly and it won't fit anymore. Oh, girl, I'm miserable."

Letting go of Tamina's hand, Audra traced her finger along the crack in the center of the table. No need to say anything about Dann, but it was pressing on her as much as the other things. She swallowed another sip of coffee, set it back down, and sighed. "Dann's got me all befuddled, too." Her finger exerted added pressure on the crack. She couldn't look up. "After the funeral, he was waiting for me when I got home. It had been emotional for me, and he knew that. He held me, well, really close."

She had never confided something so personal, not even

to Tamina. She rushed on, "It touched a place in me hurting and lonely ever since my mother died. But now I feel guilty because I can't stop thinking about him. I haven't heard from him all week, and I feel like I'm being torn in two different directions."

She tipped her head toward the other room. "Then this happened with Mrs. Espinosa, and I'm worried about her, too. She's not a strong woman... What if she...?" She couldn't finish her sentence. "I love Rosa dearly, and I'll care for her as long as necessary. But this afternoon I felt like the wheels fell off. My father always told me I'm in control of my life and I have to take care of myself, but I guess I feel totally inadequate and my life is spinning out of control."

She paused. That was what she hadn't been able to put her finger on all week.

Tamina lowered her chin and glanced up, her eyebrow raised. "Do you think you're really the one in control of your life? I think you just preached your own sermon."

A slight laugh escaped Audra's tight throat. "I feel like I just spit something out that was gagging me."

"I've got something I haven't shared with you, too."

"Oh?" She studied Tamina over the rim of her cup as she downed the last of her lukewarm coffee.

"I've started going to church."

The cup jolted, nearly choking Audra on her final swallow. Staring at Tamina, she forced the liquid down her throat. "You're not kidding me? Where?"

"Chapel Of Grace. A little, old church down on Canyon Road where I went on Christmas Eve. I've needed some answers, too." Tamina reached across the table and enclosed Audra's hand in hers. "Look at me, girlfriend."

Audra looked up, their gazes holding until she knew Tamina was in earnest.

"Would you please go to church with me in the morning?"

"But I've got Rosa."

"She can go with us. I'll pick you up at nine forty."

Audra paused at the side of Tamina's car, sorting through a curious mixture of excitement and apprehension. A magnet seemed to be drawing her from the inside, compelling her to come this morning, and yet, there was a drawing back. Inside the church, she was going to be in the presence of God. God, whom she'd relegated to second place for far too long. *Is he angry with me?*

A weather-stained front door stood open, its dark frame contrasting against tan stucco, crumbling here and there. She held Rosa's hand and entered with Tamina.

"Hi, Tamina. Good to see you this morning." Handshakes were offered by a tall, balding man wearing a wide smile. Bulletins were pressed into their hands.

Audra shook hands. *Wow! They already know Tamina by name.*

Still holding Audra's hand, the smiling man peered at her. "A friend of Tamina's? Welcome. My name's Clarence."

"I'm Audra." She couldn't help but return his smile. Her muscles uncoiled as she followed Tamina, and her face stopped feeling like plastic.

Clusters of parishioners visited in the aisles, and Audra and Rosa, shunted from group to group, were introduced in each one—Sheila, Mary, Erna, Les, Connie... *This is like learning a room full of sixth-graders.*

"Let's sit there." Tamina towed Audra toward a row of empty seats.

Even after Rosa settled next to her, people stretched across

Tamina to shake her hand and say hi to Rosa. *Surprisingly, I feel part of the group.*

Audra didn't recognize the songs they sang—they seemed more modern than the hymns she remembered, but the people sang with impressive fervor.

After three songs, Pastor Moorehouse, a graying man, probably nearing sixty, stepped in front of the congregation. He asked everyone to turn in their Bibles to First Peter.

She couldn't remember where it was.

Tamina tipped her head and whispered, "Every Sunday they all read a chapter of the Bible together out loud." She reached for a Bible in the rack mounted to the pew in front of them and flipped to the table of contents. *Tamina must not know where it is, either.*

As they began reading, Audra's heart pondered the words flowing in and over her. *Oh my, the Bible is forceful when you read it out loud.* When they came to "Cast all your anxieties on Him, for He cares for you," she focused on those words.

Pastor Moorehouse used those words as the basis for his sermon. The third time he repeated them, she decided her father had been extremely wrong. He never went to church or read the Bible, so how would he know whether or not God cares for you? A weight dropped from her shoulders. She felt peaceful like she had on Christmas Eve. God had nudged her already back then. *Well, God must care for me. He sent Tamina to get me when I didn't go to him on my own.*

After church, when Tamina pulled into her driveway, Audra reached across the console and hugged her neck. "Thanks, girlfriend. I guess God knew I was going to be there today. He had that sermon planned just for me."

"Oh yeah? I thought it was just for me!" Tamina laughed with her.

Audra opened her door. "Come on, Rosa. We have to grab

a sandwich and get over to the hospital."

They stayed at the hospital about an hour before Mrs. Espinosa was ready to sleep again. The nurse confirmed she was doing better but gave no word on when she might go home. Audra swung Rosa's hand as they exited.

If God cares for me, he also cares for Mrs. Espinosa and Rosa.

CHAPTER TWENTY-TWO

THE MOTH AND THE FLAME

ON THE WAY HOME FROM THE HOSPITAL, AUDRA STOPPED AT Canyon Road Shopping Center. She let Rosa pick out coloring books, crayons, a sticker book, and a three-movie collection DVD containing *The Cat In The Hat*, *Babe*, and *Beethoven*. As much as she loved Rosa, she couldn't sit at her side every moment.

Audra settled the girl in front of the television with *Babe* and punched in Dann's number. "You sound absolutely awful!" she exclaimed when he answered.

"Actually, I'm better." His voice was hoarse and hollow. "A cold knocked me for a loop. I started coming down with it after you went to the funeral, and I missed the rest of the week of school. I had to go to the doctor on Friday as I ended up with an ear infection."

She stood motionless. Then a wave of relief washed over her. He hadn't been ignoring her—he'd been sick. For a second, she remained there, taken aback by how pleasant that knowledge felt.

Enough, girl. Get back to business. "I'm sorry to hear that, so I'll only keep you a minute." She gripped the telephone receiver, trying to keep from sounding happy. "I just wanted to let you know Mrs. Espinosa is in the hospital and —"

"What happened?"

"I took her to ER Friday night. She has pneumonia. They haven't given me any idea when she's going to be able to come home. I'm keeping Rosa, and it might interfere with looking for music."

There was a long pause. "Time's getting away from us. Could you possibly go on Wednesday and take her with us?" he croaked.

"Sure, if it's all right with you. Are you going to feel well enough by then?"

"Oh yeah. I'm staying home yet tomorrow, and I'll go back Tuesday. I'll call you to see if it's going to work for Wednesday."

"Well, you take care of yourself."

"I will." He chuckled. "I'm going to go drink another gallon of hot tea."

She continued to stand by the phone after she hung up. *He wasn't ignoring me. He was sick.* She shouldn't enjoy that so much.

Audra dropped Rosa off at school in the morning, went to work, picked Rosa up after school, hurried to the hospital, spent thirty minutes with Mrs. Espinosa, rushed home, gave a piano lesson, fixed dinner for two, spent time with Rosa until her bedtime, finished grading papers, and finally fell into bed herself. *I don't know how working mothers keep up such a pace.*

When Dann called on Tuesday evening, she told him, "The nurse wasn't certain, but she thinks Mrs. Espinosa will be released on Thursday."

"Do you want to go ahead with our plans to look for music tomorrow?"

"I can meet you at Jorgenson's Music after I pick Rosa up. It's right there by her school."

During sixth period on Wednesday, Audra got a note from the office saying Mrs._Espinosa was going to be discharged at four and needed Audra to drive her home. She collected Rosa at school and met Dann as arranged with a change of plans. His only comment was, "I'll follow you. I'm going with you."

By the time they checked out of the hospital, dropped a prescription at the pharmacy, and got Mrs. Espinosa home, it was nearly five thirty. Audra settled her on the couch cuddled in her warm blue sweater and a blanket. In the kitchen, Audra discovered the refrigerator bare, with not even an egg to scramble.

"There's nothing for them to eat. I wonder if they get this low on food very often," she whispered to Dann when he came into the kitchen.

He glanced at his watch. "Her prescription should be ready, so maybe we should pick up some groceries."

The store was jammed with rush-hour shoppers. Frustration twisted Dann's lips after their cart was filled with essentials. "It's late. Let's grab a roasted chicken and some salad fixings and eat with them."

Her shoulders sagged with gratefulness. "I'm all for that. How about some rolls and maybe an apple pie, too?"

Once they finished eating, Mrs. Espinosa needed to go to bed, and Audra offered her an arm to lean on. Entering the bedroom with the elderly woman, she stifled a groan. "Oh, Mrs. Espinosa, I took all the clothes from your hamper home with me to wash, and they're still there."

Mrs. Espinosa sat on the edge of the bed. "Oh, that was good of you. Just look in the closet, there should be an old housecoat I can wear tonight. I want to keep my sweater on, too."

Inside the door-less closet, a tattered, green duster hung on a hook. When Audra helped Mrs. Espinosa into it, the clothes she took off were in nearly as poor shape.

"I forgot to tell you." Mrs. Espinosa touched her arm as Audra pulled the blankets over her thin body. "My neighbor, Consuelo, called while you and Dann went to the store. She's coming in the morning to help get Rosa off to school."

Audra released a puff of relief. "I still have your key. I'll run home and get your clothes and let myself in when I get back. Is that all right?"

"Yes. Thank you so much for all you've done for us." Mrs. Espinosa reached her hand out to Audra, and Audra bent down and kissed her goodnight.

When she returned to the kitchen, Dann had already washed the dishes and was drying them and setting them in the cupboard. Rosa was sitting at the kitchen table reading her library book out loud to him. Audra slid into the chair at the end of the table. As soon as Rosa reached the end of her chapter, Audra said, "Sweetie, it's time for you to get ready for bed."

The girl frowned but got up obediently.

Audra rummaged through Rosa's small dresser and found a pair of black tights with a hole in the knee and a long-out-grown purple sweatshirt. She explained how she needed to go get their clothes, so if Rosa heard her opening the front door, she shouldn't be frightened.

When they left, Dann walked her out to her car, and when he opened her door, she paused beside him and rested her hand on his forearm. "Thank you for coming with me. I don't know what I would have done without you."

He covered her hand with his and met her eyes. "I'm glad I could help. We still need music, though. Can we look for music Saturday afternoon and then grab something to eat?"

"What time?"

"Four o'clock?"

Audra gently removed her hand from his arm. Doing Dann

a favor was turning into more than she'd bargained for, but they *did* need to get music. His eyes were still on hers. "That will work," she said with a smile.

Gathering up the clean laundry, Audra decided she couldn't let Mrs. Espinosa stay alone all night. She grabbed her pillow and an extra blanket, drove back to the rundown neighborhood bordering on downtown, and spent the night on Mrs. Espinosa's lumpy couch sleeping in her clothes. She fell asleep thinking of Dann's invitation and chastised herself for being like the proverbial moth flying to the flame. She should resist, but she couldn't. Well, maybe it wasn't that she *couldn't* — she didn't want to. Cancer or no cancer, she really didn't want to.

CHAPTER TWENTY-THREE

PLAYING WITH FIRE

AUDRA FINGERED HER GRAY SKIRT WITH THE ROSE PLAID THREAD hanging in her closet, undecided what to wear as she and Dann looked for music. He hadn't told her where they were going to eat afterward. *This skirt, my rose turtleneck sweater, black boots, and gold chain necklace can go to any restaurant in town, but is it too dressy? Maybe I should wear slacks I always wear to school.*

She smoothed her hand across the fine wool. *Am I trying to impress Dann? We're going to be out in public – is there a chance a student from school might see us and tell another – and another? Is that the way the rumor would start? Miss Knight has a boyfriend – or worse, the old maid has a boyfriend. Would they laugh?* Her cheeks felt like flames had touched them.

She unclasped the skirt from its hanger. *No. We're doing this as a professional matter. It's not a date.*

She stepped into the skirt. Either he wasn't disturbed about being seen together, or he'd already forgotten about it. *I should have reminded him on Wednesday when he suggested this – not now when he's made plans. Just stay detached.*

Audra was waiting when Dann arrived, his voice still husky from his cold. They drove to Jorgenson's Music Store on the fringe of downtown where she stood a few feet from him as he checked a row of books in the flute section. He glanced up as his fingers skimmed titles.

"I want to give the students a variety of music — some classical, but some on the lighter side, too." He slid a book out and then nestled it back on the shelf. "The trick will be to find classical pieces short enough for the class time we're allotted."

She eased out a blue volume and opened to its table of contents. "This one's arranged for violin and piano. It says it's wedding songs, but it's just short classics. Look at the wonderful melodies — 'Liebestraum,' Air from Handel's *Water Music*..."

Stepping closer, he read over her shoulder. His breath warmed her cheek with a soft flutter. Sandwiched between him and the bookshelf, she couldn't move. She swallowed hard.

"Mmm," he reached over her shoulder to point at the list, "there's a favorite of mine, too, 'Entrance Of The Queen Of Sheba.' Hang on to that book."

As he drew his arm back, their eyes met. Neither of them looked away, but she felt her eyes widening as she inhaled his spicy aftershave.

"Oh. I'm sorry. I didn't mean..." Abruptly, he turned on his heel, strode to the sheet music drawer, and raked his fingers across file folders of musical compositions.

She stared at his back. Her heart pounded while the fallout from his look filtered from the base of her throat to the pit of her stomach as she'd never experienced before, and she couldn't stop it. She forced herself to breathe deeply and exhale slowly. *No... It can't happen like this. It was just an accident, I'm sure. Did he feel it? Is he too embarrassed to look at me? Do I just ignore it?*

She swallowed twice and edged down the aisle. *Is he looking at music or just hiding?* When she trusted her voice, she stepped behind him. "Remember, this is just a small music store. Maybe you'd have better luck looking online."

He glanced over his shoulder, a sheepish smile tugging at his lips. "Oh, I know I can. I just thought it would be more fun doing this together so you could have a say."

She held her breath before slowly exhaling again. *Just stay detached. Stay professional.*

At the cash register, Mr. Jorgenson put the piano score in one bag and the violin pullout in another. He smiled at her. "I hope you'll enjoy playing these duets, missy."

"Missy?" Dann repeated, opening Audra's door for her.

"Yes. I've bought music from him since I was a little girl."

He grinned. "I forgot—you're the hometown girl. You know everybody and everything about this town." He hopped in the Jeep and started the motor. "My appetite has returned with a vengeance." He laughed. "So, what does the hometown girl know about Knights & Pawns? Jerold says it's one of the nicest restaurants in town."

She chewed her lip. Knights & Pawns was Evan and Marsha's restaurant. *Should I warn him?* "I think Jerold is very discerning. They serve exceptional food, and I love the atmosphere."

"Yeah? What's it like?"

"An old English pub, with chess sets in every conceivable place—you know, for knights and pawns. I think you'll be surprised if we go there."

Her sister-in-law was on duty as hostess this evening. *Well, like it or not, Dann's going to meet the family.* Audra furtively glanced around, and her shoulders loosened when she didn't see any students.

Marsha did a double take but gained her composure before leading them to a table for two in a quiet corner. Dann helped Audra off with her coat and pulled out her chair before he sat. When he noticed the hostess still standing beside their table, he looked up. "Yes?"

Should I go with a formal introduction or lighthearted? She chose the latter. "Dann, I said you'd be surprised if we came here. This is my sister-in-law, Marsha Knight."

His mouth formed an *O*, and his eyebrows shot up as he scraped his chair back and stood.

"Marsha, this is Dann Day, our band and orchestra teacher at school. We're working on a school project together."

He offered his hand to Marsha, and while they exchanged pleasantries, Audra scanned the surrounding tables. She leaned back in her chair. *Nobody I recognize.* She let her shoulders fall and rotated her neck. *It's a good thing he walked off in the music store. Did he have any idea my heart was racing? Thank goodness, he seems as eager as I am to ignore that little incident.* She silently exhaled, relaxing her abdominals. *I'd like to unwind and enjoy this dinner in the spirit he offered — just a thank you for helping him.*

Marsha glanced back to the sitting area. "I'm pleased to meet you, Dann, but please excuse me, I have people to seat. Do enjoy your dinner."

Dann chuckled. "Well, that was a surprise."

Audra shifted. "Actually, I wasn't sure how to handle it. I hope you don't mind."

He shook his head and laughed. "Not at all."

They ordered wine from a waitress dressed as an English barmaid, and he turned slightly, hooking his arm over the back of his chair. "So, how did your family get to the Grove?"

"My grandfather owned a construction company in Albuquerque. He saw a potential housing boom when ACT started up and sent my father to Chandler's Grove when Evan was two."

Their wine was set on the table, but he ignored it. He leaned forward and rested his forearms on the edge of the table.

"Did your father build any of the big homes on the west side?"

"Only one. A gorgeous home for Bradford Chandler when Bradford was mayor, a long time ago now. Besides my own neighborhood, he also started a lower-priced neighborhood north on Main past Canyon Road." A surprising surge of pride for her father's accomplishments burst through her in spite of her problems with him. As she'd been talking, she'd put her elbows on the edge of the table, resting her chin on the backs of her hands. She was looking directly into Dann's eyes. Embarrassed, she sat up straight and sipped her wine. "Tell me about your family."

As they ate wedges of iceberg lettuce drenched in bleu cheese dressing, he talked about growing up in Skokie. They were still talking when filet mignon with shrimp skewers on the side arrived with fluffy, whipped sweet potato for Audra and french fries for Dann.

Halfway through their meal, Evan approached, his white chef's hat standing straight and tall above a fresh, spotless white coat.

Evan gave a slight bow when she introduced him, and then he held out his hand. "I'm very happy to meet you."

Dann gripped it. "My pleasure, to be sure. I'm very impressed with your restaurant. Where did you get all the chess sets?"

"I started collecting them when I was in college. Some are new, but most of them Marsha and I found in antique shops and estate sales. Did Audra tell you how we came up with the name Knights & Pawns?"

"She mentioned that you and Marsha are the knights and your boys are the pawns. I like the play on words." He nodded toward his plate. "I can see why you're such a success—your food is superb."

"Thank you very much. I hope you have a nice evening."

Evan gave a short salute before returning to the kitchen.

After they finished their meals, two dishes of apple crisp with ice cream were set before them. They hadn't ordered them, and when their check arrived, Dann's eyes opened wide. He tipped it to her. *Paid in full, Evan and Marsha* scrawled across the bottom.

"Snow!" Audra laughed and held her hand out to catch a fluffy flake. While they ate, a thin film of snow had painted the sidewalk and parking lot white, except where tire tracks left glistening stripes of black asphalt.

"It must have just started." She lifted her face to the nighttime sky. The snow was invisible until it reached the arc of light from a parking lot lamppost. Illuminated flakes fell noiselessly upon them. "I love to walk in this kind of snow."

"How about walking in it downtown? I discovered a couple of art galleries open on Saturday night down there."

Her breath caught in her throat. This was above and beyond doing him a favor. This wasn't supposed to be a date. Would Sheldon consider it circumspect? She should say no. She should resist. She should go home and not let this advance one iota. But she didn't want to.

"Really?" She giggled. "And it's not even tourist season."

Despite the long look in the music store, everything in her wanted to go with him—or was it because of it? Just this once. Besides, how many academy school kids would be at an art gallery on Saturday night? She flashed him a smile. "All right, let's check it out."

Dann drove downtown and found a parking space a block from the galleries. Walking there, they halted beneath a streetlight. Snow was coming down harder. Ribbons of white outlined branches and stuck to street signs. Feathery snowflakes fell so rapidly they couldn't see beyond the illuminated circle they stood in. They were enveloped in a magical fairyland.

He reached out and squeezed her cold hand. "I really do miss snow once in a while."

Audra tipped her head back, and as flakes hit her face and eyelashes, an unexplainable rush of emotion washed over her — as if she'd been let out of a cage. There was no fear of cancer in this delightful snow-fairy realm. Everything here was clean and full of life and enchanting. She felt her chest would explode with the sensation of freedom, and she didn't want to step out of this mesmerizing bubble of make-believe.

They toured both galleries hand-in-hand. They chuckled at paintings that looked like somebody stepped in paint and slid around on the canvas, but marveled at the realism of others — their kind of art. They favored the second gallery as it gave the illusion of walking through a lovely mansion. The whole building radiated softness and warmth with its cream-colored walls and mauve carpeting.

Paintings hung along the walls and sculptures sat in the middle aisle. They almost returned to the front of the building when Dann stopped and pointed. "I've looked at this one several times, and someday I'd like to own it."

She stepped closer. Encased in its heavy, dark-walnut frame and depicted in the style of an Old Master's still life, it offered a time-honored background of fruit on a table. But the young, fair-haired boy in a pale-blue polo shirt was contemporary. Seated before a music stand, he diligently practiced his violin. "Something about it really grabs me," he added in a hushed whisper.

"It seems to say that, for musicians, practicing never changed over the ages, doesn't it?" she mused. She checked the price tag — 1500. No wonder it was a "someday" dream.

When they arrived at Audra's back door, the snow pelted down, coating their hair and jackets. The fairyland effect increased by the minute, but she forced herself to disregard it.

Dann was standing too close to her. He was looking into her face, but he seemed indecisive. He glanced down, and then back again before edging backward. "I'll start looking for music online right away."

"Good. I'm looking forward to playing together."

"Me, too. Well, I guess I'd better get going."

He hesitated a moment, and she reached out and touched his arm. "Dann, thank you for dinner. I enjoyed the evening."

His face lit up. "So did I."

He paused. There was that indecision again.

"I really must go. 'Night for now."

"'Night."

Audra awoke and was aware she'd overslept because the bedroom was too bright. The urge to turn over and go back to sleep tempted her. Instead, she stretched and checked the clock. She bolted upright. "Nine fifteen! I can't get ready for church in twenty minutes." She threw the blankets back, padded barefoot to the kitchen, and called Tamina.

"Hey, girl, I forgot to set my alarm, and I just woke up. Come on over after church and eat lunch with me."

"You must have been out doing the town. I called several times yesterday afternoon before I decided we weren't going to do anything last night. Then I called twice more before I went to bed to see if you were going to church, and you still didn't answer."

"Yeah, well I'll explain when you get here."

Audra returned to the bedroom, propped her pillows, and sat with her knees pulled up. She rested her forehead on her crossed arms, and thoughts of the night before flooded in. She'd had a wonderful time with Dann—too wonderful. It had been necessary to look for music, but holding hands going through art galleries? That was guy-and-girl stuff, pure and simple.

And Dann's uncertainty standing at her back door as if he were contemplating kissing her goodnight? She straightened her legs, sagged into her pillow, and groaned. *Ohh no—I've been foolish. I can't let that happen.*

She slid down and hid under the blankets up to her chin. *I liked holding hands, and it got in the way of my better judgment. I'm playing with fire! I absolutely can't let myself get caught up any deeper with him.*

At lunchtime, Audra lifted the lid from a can of chicken noodle soup and inhaled the hearty aroma of condensed broth. She was reaching for a pan when Tamina's knock rattled the back door. Skipping down to the landing, she opened the door.

"I'm sorry I missed the service. This church stuff isn't a habit for me yet." Audra hugged Tamina when they entered the kitchen.

"So, you really were out on the town? Who with?"

"Drop your coat, and I'll tell all." Audra dumped the soup into a pan, added a can of water, and waited for Tamina's return. "Dann asked me to play some duets with him for his classes. He had to clear it with Sheldon, and we finally shopped for music yesterday afternoon and then went out for dinner."

Tamina widened her eyes and rounded her lips. "Ooh! A little romantic interlude?"

Audra grimaced. "It wasn't supposed to be, but—oh, girl,

my mind's in a muddle." Spoon in hand, she faced Tamina. "What would you do if a handsome hunk of a guy asked you out and you had the Big C staring you in the face?"

Tamina lifted two soup bowls from the cupboard, set them on the table, and raised her eyebrows at Audra. "Oh boy! I don't know. Are you still havin' an inner struggle?"

"Big time." Audra set bread and peanut butter on the table and retrieved the raspberry jelly from the refrigerator. "The whole purpose of the duets is to motivate his students. I want to, but I feel like I'm playing with fire. Spending time alone with Dann practicing with those stupid initials all over the school…?" She shrugged. "I sure don't want a rumor to get started that the initials are true."

While Audra divided the soup between the two bowls, Tamina folded her arms and braced a hip against the counter. "Do you have any idea how Dann feels about the initials?"

Audra sighed. "I don't think he's overly concerned."

"Maybe I'm being nosy, but how do you think he feels about you?"

She froze. *Yeah, that's nosy. But I did say I'd tell all.* Shyness warmed her cheeks. "I'd say there's a mutual attraction, but I don't want to lead him on. If I *am* playing with fire, I need to turn the sprinklers on before one of us gets burned."

"Huh!" Tamina plopped into a chair. "Or tell him up front what's going on and let him make the next move."

Forcing her movements steady while her heartbeat slammed her chest, Audra began spreading peanut butter on a slice of bread. *Sure, tell him I may have to have a hysterectomy, and the guy who wants a family will make a move — as far away as possible.*

Long after Tamina left, her words stuck. But she couldn't imagine herself saying them to Dann. She'd do her best to help him with the music, but she'd keep her feelings in check.

CHAPTER TWENTY-FOUR

PLANS START COMING TOGETHER

AUDRA OPENED THE FRONT DOOR WITH A "HI" WHEN DANN arrived the following Saturday afternoon. She caught his now-familiar aftershave as she led him to the kitchen. She couldn't help but breathe in the pleasant scent. He dropped a folder of music and a CD onto the table.

"I had to overnight express this, but I think we're in business. There's not a whole lot of music for flute-piano duet outside of classical, but I did find a score for "Let It Go" from *Frozen*. I think most of the kids have seen the movie, so they should recognize it. We could do it with violin, too."

She picked up the books. The James Galway book would be for flute, of course. She shifted it aside, flipping over two pieces of sheet music. Bach's "Badinerie" – she'd heard it before – and "Ashokan Farewell." Her gaze lifted. "Isn't this actually for fiddle?"

He grinned. "Yep."

That would be interesting. The CD was James Galway's *Legends*.

Dann hung his jacket over a kitchen chair. "I've had the CD since it first came out, but I didn't realize there was a flute-piano book for it, too. There's a selection on it I want you to hear."

They spent the next two hours trying out different songs — some flute, some violin. "I feel like I'm at a feast, and I can't quit stuffing myself even though I know there's still dessert coming!" She laughed. "I don't want to stop, but it's dinner time. Should we quit or call out for pizza?"

"Pizza. Can we play the CD while we're waiting?"

She ordered pizza while he put the disk in her changer and chose the song. As she followed the music, she couldn't help but tap her foot to the beat of "Harmonium."

"Oh, wow, that's really high energy, isn't it? It would take some practice for sure, but I think the kids would go crazy for it." She cocked her head to one side. "If Sheldon wants us to do this on the eighth of March, we have just a month to get it all together. Think we can?"

"If we practice twice a week to start with, anyway. Your piano is far better than the one at school, but I'll make sure it's tuned before we play for the students."

They ate the pepperoni, mushroom, and black olive pizza before they played for another hour.

After he left, she stretched out on her stomach on the couch and buried her face in her sweater sleeve. Playing with Dann was indescribably enjoyable, even more than she had anticipated. They'd practice on Saturday afternoons and Wednesdays after school. Had she bitten off more than she could handle? She'd promised Rosa she'd start her music lessons on Saturday mornings, and now there would be church on Sunday mornings.

I don't know when I'll find time to clean house, but I don't want to give this up. She sighed.

Dann certainly spent more than eighty dollars of his own money on music, and the look on his face as he played proved he was totally committed. She couldn't let him down.

Tension started building in the back of her neck. She closed her eyes a moment, and *Give your anxieties to the Lord, for he cares for you* floated into her mind. She flopped over on her back and stared at the ceiling. She had focused on the Lord caring for her, but she'd hardly thought about the give-your-anxieties-to-him part — and, boy, did she have anxieties. She considered each one. "Well, Lord," she said out loud, "I don't know how to give you my anxieties, but since my life is still spinning out of control, I'm going to need your help every step of the way."

On Tuesday morning, Audra sauntered to her room through the empty North Hall, savoring the quiet of having arrived before any students. Still ten steps from her room, she slowed. A small moan escaped her lips. "Oh please, not again." The blank side of a white index card flashed at her from the window of her classroom door. Turning the card over, she found the A. K. + D. D. in the same printing as before. Anger rose quickly, but she forced it down. "There's no sense reacting without even thinking," she muttered.

She stared at the card in her hand. *This card was placed backward as if whoever put it there only wanted me to see it. Why?* She looked up and down the hall but didn't see any other cards. *I wonder...*

Her heels clicked on the tile as she strode down West Hall. A blank card showed conspicuously in Dann's window, but she passed it by and hurried on to the lounge. The lounge was more important. Nothing there. She breathed easier and returned to Dann's door.

His room was still dark. *I'm not going to leave that stupid card for someone else to find before he gets here.* She reached for the card and then stiffened as she recognized a familiar scent. *Heather's perfume — she's been here only moments ago. Where is she?* She spun around to see Heather at the drinking fountain down the hall.

Heather stood straight and, seeing Audra, began walking toward her. Audra clamped her jaw closed and locked her gaze on the ceiling. *I refuse to battle with you. I refuse.*

"Well, what did you find?" Heather purred, her voice low. "Are you curious enough to look at the other side?"

Audra narrowed her eyes. "What makes you think anything's on the other side?" She winced. That had popped out against her better judgment. Her hands balled into fists. *I refuse.*

"I peeked." Heather swung her heavy hair over her shoulder. "Still getting love notes, huh?"

Audra's face felt hot. A few students lingered at their lockers, but as soon as first bell rang, students on their way to first-period classes would flood the hall. She absolutely had to keep control of herself and not create a scene.

"You know, you're kind of cute when you're angry." Heather winked. "It doesn't take much to get your temper up, does it?"

She's baiting me. Audra scowled. She slipped the offending white card out of Dann's window, creased it in half, and clutched her fist around it. "Get lost, Heather. You sound like a playground bully, and it really doesn't become you."

Heather waggled a finger and laughed. "Oh, easy does it! What would Dann think if he saw you now?"

Audra bit her lip. The first bell rang, and students, who had been spending their last free minutes with friends outside the doors, streamed into the halls.

Doris Stevens rounded the corner from the lounge. She stopped behind Heather and gave Audra an inquisitive look before starting down the hall.

"Hey, Doris," Audra called. "Wait up. I'll walk with you." She pushed past Heather and left her standing there.

She marched into her classroom, slammed her purse on her desk, and yanked its zipper open. *Oh, that woman. I should have ignored her — simply walked off. But I didn't. This anger problem is* not *going away.* She jammed the two cards into her purse and sighed. *But at least I didn't slug her.*

When her first student entered, she forced a smile and sat on her desk chair. *If only Pastor Moorehouse would preach about anger. He's so down to earth — I wish I could sit with him and see if he could give me some insight.* She drummed her fingers on her desk. *Well, why can't I? I'll bet any number of people get an appointment with him to discuss problems. Dann will be coming tomorrow — but Thursday, I'll do it Thursday.*

On the following day, Audra practiced with Dann until six o'clock when he laid down his flute. "Would you care to run over to The Yellow Rooster for chicken?"

Turning on the piano bench, she hesitated, and a slight grimace tugged at her lips. "I want to help you do this, but... I don't think we should go out together. It's those initials — I found another card in my window and one in yours yesterday. Heather hassled me. I'm afraid if..." She gave a little shrug and peered up at Dann.

"If you're not comfortable going out, we won't." He swabbed his flute, zipped it in its case, and jammed his hands into his pockets. "Would it be okay if I picked some up and brought it back?"

"Yes, that would be better." She sighed. *Fast food after practice twice a week will get pricey. He shouldn't carry the whole load.* She folded her hands in her lap and stared at them. "Umm... It looks like this project's going to take more than just a couple of weeks, so if I can, I'd like to reciprocate. I'm starting Rosa on her music lessons this coming Saturday, but I should have time to cook dinner Saturday night — if you'd care to do that." When she peeked up, he was grinning at her.

"Well, thank you. I think I'd enjoy that."

From then on, it was take-out or order-in on Wednesdays and home cooking on Saturdays.

When Audra started Rosa on her piano lessons, Mrs. Espinosa whispered behind her hand, "I'm glad you're starting the lessons. I've heard her play 'Mary Had A Little Lamb' at least three hundred and fifty times."

Audra brought a kitchen chair into the living room and sat next to Rosa in front of the keyboard. She worked with her for thirty minutes while Mrs. Espinosa perched on her faded, dark-green easy chair and listened. Rosa remembered the names of all the keys Audra had taught her, and she was enthralled to discover those black notes in her new book told her, like a little roadmap, which keys to press, how long they stayed pressed, and which direction they went. They played and sang the names of the notes together and did the same for the first two songs. Rosa promised to practice every day.

Then, turning to Mrs. Espinosa, Audra flashed a grin. "You've been listening and watching—would you like to learn to play, also?"

Mrs. Espinosa waved Audra off. "Oh no, I'm too old to do that..." But she peered at the keyboard as she spoke, so Audra sank to the floor before her chair, took the old woman's hand, and smiled at her.

"You can do whatever you set your mind to doing. Come and try, and if you don't like it, then you can just listen."

She helped Mrs. Espinosa from her chair. Hesitating a moment, the old woman inched her way to the keyboard, sat down, and stared at the keys.

Audra scooted closer. "Did you hear Rosa singing? It

sounded like the alphabet, didn't it? She was singing the names of the keys. Let me show you." She played, sang, explained, and coached until the elderly woman, voice wavering, joined in singing an octave of notes.

Mrs. Espinosa's wrinkled face beamed as she accomplished the simple three-note tune Rosa had played minutes before. Audra put her arm around her shoulders.

Her fingers still on the now-silent keys, Mrs. Espinosa just sat there. "Do you really think I could learn to play?"

The hope in her voice was more melodious than any music. Audra slid her arm around her waist and laid her head on the older woman's shoulder. "I'll tell you the same thing I tell all my students. Yes, with practice, practice, practice."

They laughed together.

CHAPTER TWENTY-FIVE

FINDING TRUE PEACE

AS ARRANGED, AUDRA DROVE TO CHAPEL OF GRACE TO MEET with Pastor Moorehouse on Thursday. She swallowed her anxiety and rapped on his office door.

"Come in." Settled at his desk, he looked grandfatherly in his black slacks, burgundy-plaid sports shirt, and baggy gray cardigan. His warm gaze and welcoming handshake chased the last bit of fear she felt over the prospect of baring her problem. She settled in the chair he indicated.

He swiveled his chair to face her. "I believe I've seen you in church a few times. What can I do for you?"

She scooted to the edge of her seat. "I've only been to your services three times, but I went years and years without going to church at all. I suppose that's the reason why I'm where I'm at."

Pastor Moorehouse rested back in his chair and laced his fingers in his lap, every bit of his posture giving the impression he was ready to listen. And she was eager to talk.

"I've been having some anger issues lately, and I just need some advice on how to deal with them." *This is going to sound so ugly.* She twisted her hands together before continuing.

"My mother died when I was twelve," she began, and a

litany of hurts, resentments, and anger followed—everything she'd locked up inside her against her father, Laney, and more recently Heather. She expressed her fear over the risk of cancer and, finally, Dann—not because she was angry with him, but because it somehow seemed right for Pastor to know.

Unburdening herself felt so good. When there was nothing more to add, she stopped, certain she'd been honest and hadn't justified her own actions.

"I see." Pastor Moorehouse straightened in his chair, tenting his fingers. "I understand your concern over your anger and your desire to deal with it. But, if I may, I'd like to give you hope for overcoming this problem—not with some sage advice from me or with a how-to book on dealing with anger, but with something infinitely better. May I?"

Audra held her eyes on him intently. It wasn't what she expected him to say. "Yes, of course."

"Since I'm not well acquainted with you, can you tell me if you think you'll go to heaven?"

She bit her lip. "That's hard to answer. I know I did when I was a child, but…" She pondered the years since her mother's death. "Right now, I feel I've failed God so completely… I'm not sure he'd let me into heaven. I feel guilty about all this anger and hatred, and for pushing him out of my life for such a long time—I certainly don't deserve to go to heaven."

Pastor Moorehouse's smile softened his whole face. "There's not one of us who deserves to go to heaven, Audra. The Bible says we're all sinners deserving of death, but because God loves us, he offers us grace instead of death. Jesus was crucified to forgive all our sins, so we are saved from our sentence of eternal death. We receive eternal life with the promise of heaven, and because Jesus was our substitute, not one of us can boast and say, 'I'm going to heaven because I've earned it.' "

At Kevin's funeral weeks earlier, his pastor had spoken of

Kevin's belief that he would go to heaven because Jesus died for him. No wonder it had been comforting to her. God had been speaking to her then. She sat silently, remembering the Christmas carols. When she looked back at Pastor Moorehouse, she confidently leaned forward. "I *do* believe Jesus paid for my sin and gave me eternal life. Yes, I'll go to heaven."

He nodded. "You've already told me you've experienced anger and hatred, unforgiveness, bitterness, resentment, rebellion, rejection, and pride toward the people who have hurt you." He ticked them off on his fingers. "Jesus wants to set you free from those."

She grimaced. Every one of those dreadful things were true, but it sounded so... "I want to be free," she said, grasping for a newfound hope.

"Jesus paid for our sins, so they no longer have the power to hold us in shame and bondage, but he wants us to forgive others the way he forgives us."

He leaned forward in his chair. "Let me tell you what forgiveness is *not*. When you forgive somebody for hurting you, it does not mean you are saying what they did was okay. When you've been the victim of someone else's ill temper and sin, it's not okay. Sometimes it's terrible. Forgiveness means I release that person from my own judgment and desire for revenge, and I allow God to deal with them." He settled back in his chair again, giving her a few moments to think. When he spoke again, his voice grew gentle. "The key to your freedom lies in forgiving the ones who have sinned against you. If you're ready to take that step, then I simply want you to talk to your Heavenly Father and tell him everything you forgive your earthly father for."

"You mean out loud?" she peeped.

"Yes. I don't need to hear it—you do. When your own ears hear it, you will never doubt that you've done it."

Audra closed her eyes and ducked her head. "Heavenly

Father…" Now what? She'd never prayed out loud in front of anyone. It felt strange, but she pressed on. "I…forgive my…" As soon as she uttered "father," the logjam broke. Words tumbled out almost faster than she could think them—all the things her father had done or said that had hurt her—but along with the words came the tears. Pastor Moorehouse was ready with a fistful of tissues as if he anticipated she'd need them, and when she could think of nothing more, she stopped and blew her nose.

"You're halfway through. Now I want you to confess to your Heavenly Father the sin attitudes that have separated you from him—your anger and the unforgiveness you've harbored, the bitterness, the resentment, the pride, and anything else that comes to mind—and ask him to forgive you."

She closed her eyes again. How clearly she could see her own wrong now! And all along she'd felt her father was the only one at fault. She almost shook her head over her blindness.

When she finished, Pastor Moorehouse pointed to his Bible. "Remember, God promises to forgive us if we confess our sins."

She couldn't stop smiling. *I'm forgiven—I truly am.* She was eager to continue when Pastor Moorehouse asked her to go through the same process with both Laney and Heather.

She got home five minutes before Mary Lynn arrived for the piano lesson Audra had postponed until six. Exhausted, she was also exhilarated. She'd never felt this wonderful—or this clean. She had come home a different person. She'd found true peace, and all she could say was, "Thank you, Lord. You're awesome."

Two afternoons later, the tantalizing aroma of slow-cooker beef filled the house as Dann entered the kitchen and watched Audra setting the table for three. As usual, he gulped when she looked up at him, her brown eyes shining and her face dewy like she'd just put on fresh makeup. He couldn't keep his eyes off her, but when she smiled at him, there was something different about her.

She placed the last napkin and repositioned a knife that was out of place. "Thanks for suggesting Tamina come while we practice and then eat with us. Besides not seeing much of her lately, I'm interested to hear her comments on the music."

He craned his neck toward the window. "She just drove up. Shall I let her in?"

"I'm finished. I'll go with you."

Tamina perched on the pecan chair and listened as if she were in a concert hall. Starting with the flute music, they played through "Let it Go," "Pink Panther," "Hoedown," and "Annie's Song" before moving on to "Alley Cat" — to which Dann had improvised a jazz line — and finally to "Badinerie" and "Harmonium." They switched to the violin and worked their way through "Let it Go," once more, then Air from *Water Music*, "Ashokan Farewell," "If I Were a Rich Man," "Entrance of the Queen of Sheba," "Moon River," and Saint-Saens's "The Swan."

Tamina clapped when they finished. "Wow! That was exciting. I can see why you're enjoying this — and I truly hope those kids appreciate the time and effort you're putting into this."

Dann and Audra grinned at each other.

He wiped his flute and tucked it into its case. "Thanks for the input, but I hope Sheldon doesn't put a stopwatch on us. If I say *anything* between songs, we'll go overtime."

After nestling his violin in its case, he sat at the table. The music was still throbbing through him as he watched Audra slicing the beef for french dip sandwiches. *Her hands fascinate me. So graceful. So expressive. She moves up and down the keyboard with such perfection, then comes into the kitchen and wields a knife like a master chef.*

While Tamina layered cheese on top of the meat, Audra

ladled the juices for dipping into three bowls and set one in front of Dann. He swallowed hard when her beautiful eyes rested on his. It was only for a moment, but his mind instantly swept him back to a snowy night when snowflakes had brushed her cheeks and he'd gazed into her eyes. *I made a promise to myself that night, but it's going to be torture keeping it.*

Audra and Tamina joined him at the table, and Tamina dipped the end of her sandwich into her broth. "Mmm… this girl can cook."

"Just as well as she plays the piano," Dann joined in.

Audra lifted her gaze to him, a smile teasing her lips. "Thank you both for the compliments." Her eyes remained on him when she said it.

Even after she looked away, he continued staring at her. *She seems different today — as if she's glowing with a very becoming peace.*

CHAPTER TWENTY-SIX

THE MYSTERY IS SOLVED

PAPERS WERE SCATTERED ACROSS AUDRA'S DESK, AND SHE hunched over them erasing and rearranging lesson plans. She and Dann would be playing their duets on Thursday, and she wanted her aide to have an easy time looking after her class. She hummed "Annie's Song" as she worked, savoring the inner peace that still lingered with her.

Finished, she locked her room, hurried toward the exit, pushed the heavy door open, and paused. *Did I pick up my grade book?* She let the door slam shut again and checked her briefcase, her purse, and her pockets. No grade book. She picked up her briefcase and started the return trip to her room.

As she veered into North Hall, a boy—Taylor Bailey?— stood at the other end of the hall. He placed something in the crack of the window in Heather's door and then hurried on. He hadn't seen her.

She dashed to her door and glanced at the card in her window just long enough to see the familiar initials. "Taylor," she shouted. "Taylor, wait." The exit door at the other end of the hall whined open and crashed shut again. She wouldn't be able to catch him.

Audra pulled the index card out of her window frame. Beside the initials were the words: *They make beautiful music together.* She crossed the hall and plucked a card from the computer lab window, then dashed on down the hall, finding cards in the windows of the library and the rest of the sixth-grade classrooms. She pivoted to her right down East Hall without finding any in the seventh-grade windows. She stopped to catch her breath before swinging into South Hall. Nothing in eighth-grade windows, either. At the teachers' lounge, she found another card as well as one on Dann's door. Eight cards in all.

Her pace slowed walking to West Hall to collect her grade book. *Should I report it to Sheldon or confront Taylor first?* She checked her watch. In only a few minutes, Jason would be waiting for his piano lesson. She'd confront Taylor first. Tomorrow.

Once Jason finished, she heated a frozen turkey TV dinner and cut an apple. She still couldn't believe Taylor was responsible for all the graffiti, but she'd have to think more about it later. She sat at the kitchen table, correcting and grading the sheaf of papers she'd brought home.

Taylor stayed on her mind the whole evening, but strangely, she felt more curious than angry. *I need to talk to him, but I'm not sure what I should say.* She put her feet up on the coffee table next to the Bible Pastor Moorehouse had given her before she'd left his office.

Picking it up, she noticed a bookmark left in it. She opened at the bookmark where someone had underlined part of a verse: "Forgive as the Lord forgave you." Had Pastor Moorehouse underlined it?

She tucked the narrow strip of cardboard back in Colossians so she could find it again. *Suddenly, forgiveness is jumping out at me at every turn.*

She'd felt so clean and wonderful in Pastor Moorehouse's office.

The following morning, Audra kept her eye on Taylor as he entered her classroom. He kept his face down and shuffled to the back. Sitting there, his unruly hair even more awry, he fidgeted in his seat. *Guilt can certainly change a person's countenance!* A few minutes before the bell should ring, she walked back to Taylor's desk.

"Taylor?"

The boy peeked up. At the tip of her head toward her desk, he got up and followed her. He stood in front of her desk with his back to his classmates.

Holding the eight index cards toward him, she said, "I saw you putting these in the hallway windows."

He shifted from one foot to the other. "But I thought I heard you go out the door."

"I forgot something and came back."

Taylor lowered his head and stared at his shoes.

"We need to talk about this, Taylor. I don't want you to be afraid all day — I want you to have a good day — but I want you to report back to me right after school this afternoon."

"Yes, Miss Knight. I understand." Head still down, he shuffled back to his desk and was silent until the bell rang. He probably wasn't going to have a good day.

At the end of third period, she wrote a note, folded it into quarters, and took it with her to the lunchroom. Dann sat in his usual spot, eating with Jerold and Russ. She had never approached him in the lunchroom, but she casually walked over and handed him the note.

He unfolded it and read. Refolding the note, he nodded and placed it into his shirt pocket and then continued talking. Jerold and Russ nodded their greeting to her and went on listening to Dann.

After school, Dann arrived first. She showed him the cards and told him how she had caught Taylor. They waited until Taylor walked through the door. Shock tightened his features when he saw Dann.

"I'm sorry I'm late," the boy said, licking his lips. "My mother picks me up after school, and I had to run out and tell her I have to talk to you." He rubbed his hands against the sides of his jeans.

She motioned him to sit at the table with her and Dann. She kept her tone pleasant. "Taylor, I asked Mr. Day to this meeting because he's involved, too. We would like you to explain how this all happened and why you did it."

Taylor picked at his thumbnail and squirmed in his chair. "Maddie Lester dared me to do it on Halloween—" After a pause, he stuttered, "I–I thought she'd like me if I did it."

"Why did you choose mine and Mr. Day's initials?"

"Maddie came up with the idea for your initials, Miss Knight. She told me she was mad at you because you gave her a bad grade. But using Mr. D's initials was my idea. My cousin lives real close to your house, Miss Knight. And one Saturday, we were riding bikes, and I saw Mr. D raking leaves with you. I asked my mother if I could go trick-or-treating with my cousin, but he didn't have anything to do with it."

Audra sighed. "Didn't you think it was wrong to mark on my house?"

"Well, at first I did." He tugged at his shirt and shoved his hands under his legs. His lips twisted to the side. "Maddie said it would be okay if I used a washable marker. I didn't think it would hurt anything. Did it wash off okay?" His forehead wrinkled in doubt.

"Yes, it finally did wash off, but it left a clean spot on the front of the house."

Dann cleared his throat. "I can understand a Halloween prank, but why did you start doing it at school?"

Taylor fidgeted again. "Maddie thought it was funny, and she dared me to do it again. I didn't get caught, and so it kind of turned into a game. I thought Maddie would like me, but she doesn't."

"Did you know it was wrong?" Dann pressed.

Looking down, Taylor nodded. "Yeah."

She folded her arms. "What does it mean when two peoples' initials are put together with a plus sign?"

"It means they are in love." Taylor grinned, totally unabashed.

"Didn't you stop to think how Miss Knight or myself might feel if people saw our initials together?"

His eyes widened. "No, I didn't. I saw you raking leaves, and I thought you were her boyfriend. That's why I put your initials together."

Dann blew his breath across his lips and then flopped the index cards on the table in front of Taylor. "How do you know we make great music together?"

The boy flashed his grin again. "On Saturday, my cousin and I rode past Miss Knight's house. Your car was in the driveway, and I heard you playing music, even with the door closed. Then I came out of the gym after basketball, and I could hear music coming from the band room. I peeked in and listened, but you didn't see me. I wish I could play that good."

"Play that well," she corrected.

A twinkle sparked in Dann's eyes, and his lips twitched as though he was having a hard time suppressing a smile. He motioned with his head for her to follow him.

"You stay there a minute, Taylor. I want to talk to Miss Knight." They moved to the far side of the room near the windows. "Rather ironic. The one day we practice in the band room instead of your house," Dann said. "So, what do you think?"

She turned her back on Taylor. "I think he's mischievous and a real romantic for a boy, and he doesn't seem to have any discernment when it comes to letting a girl lead him on."

He faced the window, also. "Sounds familiar."

She tipped her head to hide a smile and then fastened her eyes on him. "But I didn't feel he was trying to be malicious, do you?"

"No, not at all."

"Well, I spent a long time thinking about all of it last night. I can't speak for you, but the only thing that was hurt was my pride. I was more afraid what other people would think than anything." She watched Dann's profile. His eyebrows knit as if he were contemplating what she said.

He jammed his hands into his pockets. "That may be true, but he still did wrong."

"And we can't let him get away scot-free, either. Sheldon's going to have to know, and he's going to insist Taylor's parents know." She paused, and then added, "I guess I just don't want there to be an excessive punishment—I don't want to see him kicked out of school. What do you think?"

"I think, Miss Knight, that you have a very soft heart." He turned his back squarely to Taylor and tipped his head toward Audra. "And there's no one else I'd rather have my initials attached to," he whispered. He gave her a sidelong glance. Her lips had parted, and she was staring at him.

We're supposed to be reprimanding this boy, and you're making my heart beat like a bongo drum. She hastily looked at the floor.

He couldn't suppress his smile. "In other words, you want us to intervene on his behalf?"

"What could we do?" She looked over her shoulder at Taylor. He was watching their every move.

Dann crossed his arms and rocked back on his heels. "Well, Sheldon said the consequence would be suspension, but we could suggest an in-school suspension. We could ask to have Taylor work out his suspension by practicing his trumpet for thirty minutes a day after school in the band room for the rest of the year unless he has an excuse from his parents. What do you think?"

"I think, Mr. Day, you are quite sensible, but you have a heart that's pretty soft, too." She focused her gaze out the window. She didn't dare smile at him.

"Well, he did say he wished he could play better music, didn't he? Come on."

They walked to where Taylor sat with his eyes wide. "Come on, Taylor, we're going to go see Mr. Bentley." Dann didn't smile, letting the boy stew a bit.

They met Sheldon walking out of his office. As he glanced at the boy's downcast face, his eyebrow arched as if to say "trouble?" "Is there something I can help you with?"

"Yes." Dann ushered Taylor forward with a hand on his shoulder. "We were just bringing Taylor to your office for a little talk."

Sheldon unlocked his office.

Taylor's face showed far more fear as he confessed to the principal. Sheldon Bentley sat tugging at his lower lip while the boy talked. "I'm sorry I did it, Mr. Bentley. I thought it was a big joke, and it really wasn't," he ended, nearly in tears.

Dann leaned forward. "Mr. Bentley, could Taylor sit in the counselor's office for a minute while Miss Knight and I speak to you?"

"Yes, I guess that would be all right."

Dann opened the door to the adjoining room and flipped on the light. Taylor followed him and sat ramrod straight on a straight-backed chair in front of the counseling table. "It will be just a couple of minutes, Taylor."

Back in Sheldon's office, Dann vouched for the boy's normally good behavior in both of their classes. Then he detailed what they had observed, the conclusions they had reached, and their recommendation for an in-school suspension.

Sheldon Bentley drummed his fingers on his desk. "I will have to speak to his parents—there's no way around that," he finally said. "But I guess if the two of you are satisfied that's enough compensation, I can agree to an in-school suspension." He straightened in his chair. "Bring the boy back in."

White-faced, Taylor stood in front of the principal's desk.

"Taylor, I will have to speak to your parents about this, and I did say whoever was caught writing the graffiti would be suspended. You committed a serious mistake, and so there will be a consequence. However, Miss Knight and Mr. Day have asked that you be given a second chance. They have suggested that, instead of you missing classes while being suspended, I give you an in-school suspension. This means you will have to stay after school every day for thirty minutes the rest of the year, and you will have to report to the band room and practice your trumpet during those thirty minutes. The only way you can miss is to have an excuse from your parents. Do you understand?"

"Yes, sir. When will it start?"

"As soon as I talk with your parents, but if you're ever caught doing it again, you will have to pay the whole consequence— you will be suspended from all classes. Do you understand?"

"Yes, sir. I won't do it again."

"You can go now."

Air whooshed from the boy's lips as his shoulders sagged. Then he spun toward Audra and Dann. "Thank you." He gave a gulp. "I'll practice really hard." And he darted out of the office.

Dann stood and shook Sheldon's hand across his desk. "Thank you, sir, on behalf of both of us, but before we leave,

I'd like to remind you that tomorrow after school we will be having our final practice in the band room before our duets on Thursday. Would you be able to stop in long enough to ensure everything is coordinated and ready?"

Sheldon wrote a reminder on his desk pad. "I'll be there."

Dann and Audra walked to the parking lot together. "It's finally over," he said. "I'm pleased with the way it turned out, but I have a feeling the worst punishment for Taylor was when he had to explain to his mother why he had to stay after."

"You're probably right." She pushed her sleeve back from her watch and sighed. "I'm going to be late for a music lesson again."

CHAPTER TWENTY-SEVEN

DUET DAY

AUDRA ARRIVED AT SCHOOL FIFTEEN MINUTES EARLIER THAN usual on Thursday morning. This was the day to play the duets! She had slept well, her enthusiasm was high, and she could scarcely wait to see how the students reacted. It felt like waiting for Christmas.

She slowed in front of her classroom door with her key in her hand. "Oh my word!" Her hand flew to cover her mouth. A garish red heart decorated her door, surrounding A. K. + D. D. in letters six inches high. A diagonal arrow pierced the middle like an overgrown Valentine.

Disappointment thudded in her chest. They had trusted Taylor not to do it again.

She stood riveted in front of the door before reason returned. This wasn't Taylor's writing, and the heart was huge — stretching all the way to the top of the window. *Could Taylor have reached so high?* No. Unless he brought a stool to school, he was too short. She'd question him, but she seriously doubted he could have done it. But who else? *Heather? Could she actually have done it this time? She's taller than I am.*

When she and Dann were playing their dress rehearsal

in the band room, she'd been arranging her music for the next selection when she caught Heather at the open door with the same angry look she'd seen before. Her immediate assessment had been that Heather was jealous. Dann nodded that he was ready to start the next song, so she'd dismissed it. With his back to the door, he couldn't have seen Heather.

Could this be revenge? A familiar anger began to constrict her throat. If Heather did it, they'd be dealing with a whole different scenario than Taylor. Her cheeks grew hot. *If Heather did it, I'm going to...to... Well, what can I do?* She jabbed her hand into her purse, grabbed a tissue, and stepped toward the drinking fountain across the hall to wet it. Her hand froze midair. *No, I won't wash it off yet. Somebody else is involved, and I don't want Taylor to get unjustly blamed.* She stormed down the hallway to the office.

Georgia sat alone in the outer office.

"Is Mr. Bentley here yet?" Audra asked, breathing harder.

"He just got here. Why?"

"Could you please tell him I need him quickly?"

Georgia pressed the intercom button. "Mr. Bentley, Audra Knight says she needs you quickly."

Within seconds, Sheldon came into the outer office.

"Mr. Bentley, could you please come to my room right away?" Without waiting, she left the office. She was starting toward her hallway when Dann entered.

"Dann, hurry! Come to my room," she called. He accelerated his pace and followed her.

Sheldon arrived right behind them and placed his hands on his hips as he studied the red heart. Dann moved next to him. "Uh-oh..." His tone left no doubt that he felt let down.

She glanced between the two men. She didn't have time for something so annoying on this particular morning. She wanted to be calm and collected when she went to the band room. And both men were obviously already blaming Taylor.

"I thought uh-oh at first, too, but Taylor couldn't have done this."

"Why not?" Sheldon arched a brow across Dann at her.

"Look." She reached to the top of the window. "I can just barely reach the top of the heart. Taylor isn't tall enough."

Sheldon Bentley crossed his arms in front of his chest. "Well, you're probably right. Any ideas?"

"Has to be someone who doesn't know we've caught Taylor."

"You have somebody in mind?" Dann tilted his head.

Pam Gardner, Audra's aid, walked up. Two other teachers strode down the hall whispering over what they saw.

"I'd rather not incriminate anyone—I don't have any proof." Audra unlocked the door. "But I wanted you to see something's still going on, and I don't want it to be blamed on—" She cut her words off. Only the three of them knew about Taylor. The men knew what she meant.

Nodding, they both left.

Audra pushed the door open. "Pam, I have to get going, or I'm not going to reach the band room on time. Would you please look over the instructions on my desk while I wipe this window off?"

The first bell rang as she finished swiping the window and students began filling the hallways. Emotions in turmoil, she slammed the wadded tissue into her wastebasket. Her gut feeling said Heather was the culprit, but worse, all the forgiveness she'd had for her less than two weeks earlier was absolutely down the drain.

Students began trickling into the room. Pam had questions, and Audra shifted impatiently as she rehashed the instructions before breaking away. "Of all days to be tied up in knots," she muttered, threading through clusters of students as she hurried down West Hall.

That stupid, ugly heart! Why does Heather go out of her way to humiliate me? Clutching her music folder closer to her chest, Audra stared at the floor as she rushed. She didn't like her thoughts. She was falling back into the old pattern, and she didn't want to—no, she *couldn't*—go there.

She slowed just outside the band room. With the hall nearly empty of students, second bell would be ringing any moment. Despite her certainty that Heather drew the heart, she didn't have a smidgeon of proof. Then she jolted. A thought like a fizzle of lightning halted her—*Heather wants me to be outraged over that heart! She enjoys seeing me get angry. Well, not today.*

As second bell rang, she concentrated on the tension in her head, neck, and stomach. She took a deep breath, massaged the back of her neck, and then closed her eyelids and rolled her eyes to relax them. "Forgive me, Lord, for being angry at Heather again. I should pity her—she needs your help," she whispered.

"Are you okay?" Sheldon startled her. Had he heard her whispered prayer?

"This wasn't the way I'd planned to start the morning, but I'm going to be fine." She flashed a confident smile.

Sheldon opened the door for her, and she stood in the back of the room while the morning announcements blared from the intercom. Sheldon would be speaking first, which would give her a few more minutes to relax.

She scanned the sixth-grade intermediate band for Taylor Bailey in the trumpet section. As their principal began his speech urging the students to be diligent in practicing so the academy could have a topnotch music program, one the students could be proud of, Taylor sat, eyes bright, head cocked, listening intently.

Once Sheldon finished, Dann picked up his flute. "Thank you, Mr. Bentley. I feel certain these students will be eager to work at making our music program first-rate." He turned to his students. "Class, I'm an adult, and I'm also your teacher.

I've been playing flute and violin since I was your age, but I still practice my instruments all the time. It's necessary, but it's also something I enjoy. Another teacher here at the academy is also conscientious about practicing her music, and I've asked her to join me today in playing some special music to demonstrate what can be accomplished with practice." He motioned Audra forward.

She knew each child in the room. When she waved, surprise overtook each face. This was their English teacher. Taylor was probably the only one who knew she was also a musician. He peeked around the student next to him, grinned, and gave her a thumbs-up.

After they played "Let It Go" from the movie *Frozen*, Dann asked his students if anyone recognized it. Nearly every hand went up as they correctly identified it.

Audra nodded. He had their attention.

She couldn't watch Taylor while she played, but when they finished the theme to "Pink Panther," the whole class erupted in applause, and she studied him. He had such a joyful countenance, without any guilt or evasiveness—he didn't ornament her window. No need to confront him.

After Dann thanked her and the final applause died, she slipped out of the band room along West Hall. She joyfully considered the student's astonished looks. That had been priceless. Maybe just seeing their English teacher playing the piano would help motivate them, too.

Her steps slowed then as thoughts of Heather crowded in. Pastor Moorehouse had warned her that, even though she'd forgiven Heather, she wouldn't be immune to being angry at her again. That was for sure! But at least, she'd stopped herself before it got out of control, and this time, she wanted to handle it the right way.

Heather surely had no idea Taylor had been caught, but

Audra couldn't do a thing without proof. Still, if it *was* Heather and she did it again, she could end up making a fool of herself, not to mention that Taylor might get dragged back into it. *What on earth can I do?*

Audra entered her room where Pam had everything under control. The students had taken their spelling test and read their library books while she was gone, and Audra handed out sheets of word games to engage their minds during the time she was back in charge.

When the passing bell rang, she started back to the band room and met Taylor on his way to second-period English class. "That was awesome, Miss Knight!" He grinned. Audra held her hand out, palm up, and he slapped it.

Nicole joined Taylor. "That was so cool, Miss Knight. I didn't know you played piano."

Finally, Steven stopped. "I really liked that music, but hey, who's going to teach us English?"

"Miss Gardner will take it until I get back. I'm really glad you all liked the music, but you'd better scoot and get to class."

During second period, they played for the concert band and third period for intermediate orchestra. On her third time meandering along West Hall to her room, she knew what to do about Heather. She almost laughed at the simplicity of it.

She entered her third-period class, greeted her students, and motioned Pam over to her desk. "I have to leave five minutes before the lunch bell rings." Audra handed Pam her keys. "There's something I must take care of. Please lock up before you go to lunch, and I'll see you during fourth period."

Audra left before the bell rang and hurried to the teachers' lunchroom. She pushed her cafeteria tray along the line, and after she picked out her lunch, she stood off to the side. About half the teachers went through the line before Heather came in. Audra intercepted her as she reached the end of the line with her tray. "May I speak with you a minute?"

Heather's eyes fluttered as she momentarily drew back. Then, unsmiling, she followed Audra to an empty table. Audra settled across from her. "I have to ask you to forgive me for something."

Heather's eyebrows shot up as a questioning look crinkled her flawless forehead.

"A month or so ago, I accused you of marking the graffiti around the school. I was upset and embarrassed, but I'm sorry I did it. Will you forgive me?" She kept holding Heather's gaze. Heather didn't answer, but before she could look away, Audra hurried on. "The day before yesterday I caught the boy who was doing it. The issue has been dealt with, and he's very penitent. He won't be doing it again."

While Heather lowered her eyes and rearranged her silverware, Audra unwrapped her chicken salad sandwich and took a bite. Heather stabbed at her salad, but only moved it around the dish.

"It's really been a harrowing few months, and I'm glad it's behind us."

Heather still wouldn't look up. Audra caught herself. She was too close to enjoying seeing Heather fidget.

She opened her carton of milk and poured it into her glass. "I saw you listening yesterday when Dann and I were practicing in the band room. I guess no one ever mentioned what this project we've been working on is all about."

She took another bite of her sandwich, chewed, and swallowed before dabbing her mouth. "Dann was having trouble motivating the kids to practice. He thought if they could see what can be accomplished by spending more time practicing, the bands and orchestras might work harder and sound better, so he asked me to play with him. Sheldon's giving each class a fantastic pep talk, and the students we played for this morning were wonderfully responsive. I sure hope it makes a difference."

Audra finished her sandwich and milk and started on the dish of apple slices. Heather still hadn't touched her food. Audra finished the fruit slices, their crunching accentuating the silence at the table.

Heather wasn't going to respond, but that was all right. Audra could never prove Heather had anything to do with the graffiti. If she did do it, she was getting the message—if she didn't, she was squirming for nothing. Audra picked up her tray. "I'll see you later, Heather. I still have to play three more times." She left Heather with her face turned down.

In the teachers' lounge, Audra relaxed on the couch for ten minutes before heading back to the band room. An incredible sense of lightness lifted her steps.

The seventh-and eighth-grade concert orchestra students were already starting to drift in when she sat at the piano. Dann came over and spoke in a low voice. "I saw you talking to Heather in the lunchroom. She looked like she'd been hit with a two-by-four, and you looked like you were talking to a Sunday school class. Did she do it?"

"Aha!" Audra laughed as she cocked her head to one side and kept her eyes fastened on him. "So, you suspected her, too, huh?" She lowered her gaze, growing serious. "I'll probably never know one hundred percent. She didn't confess and I don't have proof, so that's the end of it. But I don't think it's ever going to happen again."

He started to say something and changed his mind. He shook his head and grinned as he went to his desk and eased his violin out of its case. He called the class to order as Sheldon entered the room.

At the end of that period, only two more performances remained, probably the most important ones as the fifth-grade beginning band and orchestra students came over from the elementary. Dann had dreams of turning them into first-rate musicians by the time they were eighth-graders in his most advanced band and orchestra. Sheldon changed his speech to reflect their moving up to middle school next year and playing with pride in the higher bands and orchestras.

Dann changed his approach also. Since this was her free period, he abandoned the twenty-minute restriction. He emphasized practicing but used the time to instruct these young musicians, also. After each song, he explained different facets of the music. He asked Audra to demonstrate how her accompaniment made the songs he played fuller and richer and had her share how old she was when she started taking piano lessons and what it meant to her.

When the class was nearly finished, lost in thought, she took in the rapt children's faces before her. *Dann got through to them — I can tell by their expressions.* Suddenly, an unexpected sensation crept over her. It was pleasant but almost reverent as it suffused first her mind and then her emotions with awe. *My being here and my music made a difference! He invited me to participate, and this past hour has been more fulfilling than any English class I've ever taught.* She gripped the edge of the piano bench. She couldn't move.

Dann excused the band members to go back to the elementary side and then stood beside the piano. "One more time, and we'll be finished. How are you holding up?"

With the emotion still welling up inside her, she wasn't sure she could answer. She cleared her throat and lifted her gaze. "Dann... I—Thank you for asking me to play with you. Your allowing me to teach music with you will be an experience I'll never forget." She wanted to hug him, but since that would be entirely inappropriate, she clasped her hands in her lap. "You do remember we can't do this for sixth period, don't you? I have to go back for my last class."

"And that's too bad. Do you suppose you could fudge a

few minutes of time? I can keep it shorter than I did for this class, but I know some of the things you said made an impact on those kids. I'd like to repeat it."

Their eyes met and held—like a hug without touching. The door opened, and the beginning orchestra members pushed in amid laughing and giggling and started getting their instruments ready. They both glanced away.

After school, Audra sat with her elbows propped on her desk and her face in her hands. *This day was absolutely incredible.* Odd little bits and pieces of it drifted through her memory— the surprised look on students' faces, the one-sided talk with Heather, the long look from Dann. She sighed. *Somehow, I have to tell him I'm a candidate for cancer surgery. I just have to—but, well, not today.*

Knuckles rapped on her door, and Dann stuck his head in. "Busy?"

"Come on in." She straightened in her seat and ran her hands through her hair. "So, how do you feel the day went overall?"

"Successful. So successful, in fact, I just had to come and tell you Sheldon was quite impressed. Did you know he stayed through two whole performances—the concert band in the morning and concert orchestra this afternoon? He was standing behind you."

"No, actually, I didn't. What did he say?"

"He was there to check how well the students were reacting. He said he was gratified by their responses, and oh yeah, he liked our playing, too." Dann shoved his hands into his pockets. "I'd like to take you out to dinner this evening to express my gratitude—and no fast food."

Almost getting used to the little flushes of warmth he

triggered, she smiled up at him. "I would enjoy that—but all of a sudden, I'm exhausted. I'm going home to take a catnap before my music lesson arrives. I'll be ready any time after five thirty. Some place quiet?"

To her delight, he chose Antonio's, downtown. Each booth was its own dim, private hideaway with its dark-wood paneling, red-checked tablecloth, and outmoded, drippy wax candle in a wine bottle. Before they sat, Audra discretely glanced around. *Good. Nobody I recognize.*

When their wine arrived, he leaned forward, lifting his glass to her. "My appreciation for a job well done."

"Thank you." She leaned toward him and raised her glass to his with a quiet flourish. "May your bands and orchestras excel in every way."

"Now, there's a toast I can drink to!" He clinked his glass against hers, and they each took a sip. "I do appreciate how much you helped me, and I enjoyed every moment. Now we have to see if the results rival what we hoped." He set his glass down and dropped his voice to a whisper. "But, all afternoon I kept wondering, what did you say to Heather?"

"I asked her to forgive me," she whispered back.

"You *what*?"

She continued whispering, "I asked her to forgive me—I was kind of a naughty girl." When he drew back and raised his eyebrows, she let her voice go back to normal. "Heather was pushing on me way back before Kevin's funeral, and things happened so quickly with all that, I guess I never did tell you. I blew up at her and accused her of writing the graffiti."

Dann hunched over the table, tilted his head, and squinted at her. "How did *that* happen?"

"How? Easy. I lost my temper." Taking a deep breath, she studied his face. She wasn't certain she wanted to expose her ugly side, but she needed to explain.

She launched the confrontation with Heather, and when the waiter set hot bread on the table, she continued talking as she sliced it.

He took a piece but paused before buttering it. A little smile worked at his lips. "You really did almost slap her?"

"Dann, I'm not proud of that! I was mortified. I falsely accused her of doing something, and that was wrong. I really *needed* to ask her forgiveness."

His smile widened. "I'm sorry. I know you're serious, but part of me wants to say way to go, girl — Hey, are you blushing?"

She ducked her head. "I am, but thanks for being light-hearted. It makes it easier to confess my misdeeds."

Now, he laughed, a full-throated, all-out laugh. "So, is all that what made you suspect her this morning?"

"Not altogether. She saw us practicing yesterday, and I could tell it made her angry. When I saw that awful heart this morning, I knew it wasn't Taylor, and she was the first one I thought of. When I told her the boy had been caught, the look on her face spoke volumes. If she did it, she knows I know, and like I said earlier, I don't think it's going to happen again. So, case closed."

"Good."

Their salads had been set on the table during their conversation, and they ate those in silence. Next came steaming chicken and spinach ravioli covered in a creamy sauce teasing their taste buds with its garlicky aroma. Their conversation recounted the memorable concert's enjoyable moments.

It was dark when they walked to Audra's back door. The moon, high in the sky, created eerie shadows across the yard. A dog's bark carried in the chilly night air. The kitchen light cast a dim square of light on the patio, and she stopped there. Dann left a little more distance between them than he had the last time they'd stood here, but close enough for her to catch the scent of his aftershave.

He jammed his hands into his pockets and cleared his throat. "Would you have any interest in getting together to play more duets just for fun?"

She gulped. He wasn't asking for help or for a favor. He wanted to play music with her because he enjoyed it. Telling him about the cancer nagged at the back of her mind, and she refused to listen. Yes, she wanted to continue playing duets. The desire was so strong every fiber of her being was screaming at her to tell him yes. "No, no, no!" the voice of reason shouted back. He held her eyes as he had that afternoon, and her resolve suffered a severe crack. She couldn't stop her eyes from lingering on his.

"I'm getting so far behind in grading papers..."

His teeth betrayed a smile even in the dim light. "My project got you behind, so let me help you catch up. I can correct papers for you. There are so many songs we haven't had a chance to play."

Her resolve disintegrated. "I'll have to limit playing to once a week." She fished in her purse for her keys. When she glanced back at him, his smile had morphed into his winsome grin.

"Is it too late to grade some papers now?" he whispered.

She made a pot of coffee. Sitting at the kitchen table, Dann corrected spelling tests, and Audra corrected grammar and punctuation tests.

CHAPTER TWENTY-EIGHT

THE COWARDLY LION ROARS

THE FOLLOWING WEEK A COLD, WINDY RAIN COMBINED WITH snow lingered. Dann thought with the mild winter they'd experienced, spring would just move in calm, warm, and beautiful. Wrong!

On Friday, he stood at the windows in his classroom waiting for Taylor to finish. He could hear improvement in the boy's playing. Beyond the glass, rain pelted down. Spring break would start in a week. Jerold and Vern wanted him to join them on a long bike ride. Even if the weather cleared, Dann wasn't certain he wanted to. He crossed his arms. There was someone else — other plans he was thinking of. A knock brought his attention back.

Heather peeked through the doorway and started to come in. He nearly sprinted across the room to keep her from entering any farther.

"Oh, I didn't know you had a student." She frowned at Taylor. "Can I see you in the hall a minute?"

"Keep on practicing, Taylor." Dann followed and shut the door.

"Spring break's just around the corner, and I was thinking

of having a poker party at my place. Would you be interested?" She moved closer, giving him a flirty smile.

"No," he answered flatly.

"Oh, come on—loosen up. I thought the last one was a lot of fun." She sidled so close to him her breasts nearly brushed his arm.

Up against the door, he couldn't step back. "I'm not interested, Heather." *In poker or you.*

"What's the matter?" she crooned. "We won't be singing 'Auld Lang Syne' at spring break—or maybe you're afraid of me." She dipped her chin and peeked up at him.

Dann exhaled a loud breath. Her attempt at being coy was unconvincing. "Back off, Heather." He flattened himself against the door. Keeping his voice low so Taylor wouldn't hear, when all he wanted was to shout, was becoming a challenge. "You're throwing yourself at me, and I don't like it." His voice modulated to a hoarse whisper. "I don't like you standing this close to me. I don't like you trying to manipulate me. I'm not interested in a poker party, and I'm not interested in dating you." He rested his hand on the door handle, ready to go back inside.

Her smile became a pout. "I'm not trying to manipulate. I'm just trying to be friendly—"

"Read my lips—I'm not interested." When Heather pivoted and started to walk away, he turned the knob and cracked the door open.

She paused and spun back, long hair swinging wildly into her face. "Well," her loud voice reverberated through the hall, "you certainly don't have a problem with Audra coming into your room. You didn't even seem upset when your initials were smeared all over school with hers."

He yanked the door shut again with a *bang*. "That problem's been taken care of. And if I *ever* hear you bring it up again, I'll have you in front of Mr. Bentley before you even know what happened, and we'll talk about a certain red Valentine heart."

Eyes flaring with astonishment, she bolted away and rushed toward her room.

He entered the classroom to Taylor staring at him, but he didn't know what to say to the boy. He jammed his hands into his pockets and stared back at him. *I hope he couldn't understand what I said.*

"Why don't you knock off a little early today?" he said and slouched into his desk chair.

The school week over, Audra sat at her piano as strains from "Autumn Leaves" bathed her with relaxing waves of melody. Her body swayed to the phrasing of the music, rejuvenating mind and emotions. She was happier since her talk with Pastor Moorehouse. When the telephone jangled, she jumped up with a lighthearted air. A thrill shivered through her at Dann's greeting. She hadn't seen him in the past week.

"Just wanted you to know the cowardly lion found his courage today."

She leaned her shoulder against the doorjamb, cradling the receiver to her ear. Her forehead wrinkled. "I'm not sure I know what you mean." Her fingers played with the coiled phone cord.

"I roared at Heather and warned her to back off. Actually, I told her off. I think she got the message."

His words sunk in one by one. "Seriously? You told her off?" Suddenly, she wanted to laugh. Dance. Celebrate. Instead, she pulled a kitchen chair, flopped onto it, and ran a hand through her hair. "Okay — When I confronted Heather, you said, 'way to go, girl.' So, here's back at ya. Atta boy!"

She could envision his face. His eyes would be sparkling and crinkling at the edges. He would toss his head back—and then it came over the line, the same hearty laugh that had overtaken him at Antonio's. "Oh, that's great. Chalk up a gotcha for Aud."

She grinned into the phone. He'd never called her Aud before, and she liked it. When he didn't elaborate details, she decided not to press.

He changed the subject. "I have a couple of questions. First, would you be free to explore some new music for a bit tomorrow afternoon?"

Her heart started beating faster. He hadn't forgotten. "Yes, I'm free after Rosa's lesson."

"Good. The other question is, do you have Easter plans?"

She ignored the voice pestering her to put the brakes on. "Tamina and I will go to church and probably spend the day together, but nothing's set in concrete." She paused as shyness overtook her and her voice lowered. "Would you care to go to church with us?"

He was quiet for such a long time she expected a decline. "If we all go to church together," he finally spoke, "would you both come over to my apartment afterward, and I'll cook?"

Audra released a surprised laugh. "How can I refuse such an offer? Let me check with Tamina, but I'm sure she'll go for it. Can I bring dessert?" She'd make her specialty: apple pie.

Easter morn dawned sunny but March chilly. Easter lilies decorated the front of the church, their heavy scent saturating the sanctuary. Greetings of joy rippled through the clusters of early-arriving worshipers as the music leaders prepared their music.

Buoyant this morning, Audra's lips pursed, and her eyebrows lifted when Dann sat in the pew beside her. It wasn't because of Dann. It was a comment her mother made years before that suddenly popped into her mind, embarrassing her and making her squirm—"Oh, they must be serious—she's bringing him to church." *Good thing Dann can't read my mind!* However, when he enthusiastically joined in the singing, she was certain he had gone to church at some time in his life.

When Audra and Tamina arrived at Dann's just after noon with Audra's apple pie, he ushered them into the living room before he returned to his balcony where he had steaks on the grill.

Furnished in conservative beige and browns, his apartment felt lived in and comfortable. His music stand, buried under a stack of music, stood in one corner, and his violin and flute cases rested on the floor next to it. The living room and dining area flowed in an open space with a counter separating the kitchen. The aroma of baked potatoes permeating the apartment lent a homey feel. An oak table, already set for three, occupied the dining area.

Within a few minutes, they were sitting down to T-bone steaks, baked potatoes with sour cream and bacon bits, and a salad of greens, mandarin oranges, red onion, avocado, and sweet-and-sour dressing, plus warm rolls, and a choice of wines.

"I'm impressed!" Tamina said, shaking her napkin out and placing it over her lap.

"Thanks." He grinned. "Actually, it's the only company meal I know. You want to say grace?"

Tamina gave thanks and Audra squirmed. She had never thought to say a prayer when Dann had eaten with her.

The easy conversation stayed animated and funny as it always was with Tamina. After the table was cleared and the dishwasher running, he taught them to play three-handed crib-bage. At the end of the third game, Audra excused herself to go down the hall.

When she exited the bathroom, she was looking directly into a bedroom. Although the room was dim, she could see there was no bed, only a long table and shelves full of small rail-road cars. She surveyed them and then walked back to the din-ing table.

"Did you build the model train cars?"

"Yeah." He tilted his chair on its back legs and locked his hands behind his head. "That's been my hobby since I was a kid. My layout's still in Skokie at my folks' house. I just keep busy building more cars and doing some landscape stuff occasionally."

"Could we see them?"

He let his chair fall back, led the way down the hall, and flipped the switch, flooding the small museum with light. Three bookshelves housed four shelves each. A passenger train with an orange and black Union Pacific diesel engine took up the length of the top of one bookshelf. All the other shelves held an array of boxcars, coal cars, oil tankers, cattle cars, container cars, flat cars, and cars she couldn't guess the names of. Each car rested on a section of track, and nothing was disorderly. Another bookshelf held several miniature houses, a garage with a mechanic work-ing on a car, a church with a tall steeple, and an assortment of tiny shops and businesses.

"Hopefully, someday I'll have a place where I can set it all up again." A large drawing was tacked to the wall above a work table holding a clutter of tools. He pointed. "This is what I have already." He drew his finger along the upper portion where a mountain, a lake, and several bridges were penciled in. "This is what I envision for all this stuff on the shelves."

"Have you built all these since you've been here?" Tamina bent down to the cars on the bottom shelves.

"Not all of them. I brought a few favorites with me. I didn't do anything on it for a number of years, but since I moved here, I've gotten back into it."

"A great cook and a railroad builder. You've been hiding your talents." Audra laughed, letting her eyes wander over the miniatures and their tiny components.

She had never known a man who could enjoy something other than his job. She thought of her father, married to his job more than to his wife — constantly thinking of ways to earn more money, never smiling, never home. What a contrast. Dann could disconnect from his job. Working on his trains obviously made him happy, gave him something to dream about.

An intense but strange sensation swept over her. She hadn't really noticed until now, but he was different from when she'd first met him. Lately, he didn't seem as hurt...as vulnerable. Actually, he was even different since he'd put Heather in her place — or was she seeing him differently?

She stared at his back as he pointed out the intricate couplers on the cars and how they locked together. He was distancing himself from his past and healing. She wrapped her arms around herself. He was healing, but her life was teetering on a balance beam. And she didn't know on which side she was going to fall off. Maybe the side that would mean a hysterectomy. So, was it so wrong to want to experience life before it passed her by? A lump, so constricting she couldn't swallow it away, formed in her throat, and she returned to the living room to wait for Dann and Tamina.

Eventually, Tamina sat at the other end of the couch. Dann folded himself into the side chair and draped one leg over the arm. "You guys have any plans for the rest of break?"

"Probably same ol', same ol'," Audra answered.

Tamina shook her head, and her hoops jiggled against her neck. "Nothing exciting, that's for sure. Why?" She bent forward, her black eyes searching Dann's face.

"Sometimes I get this urge to do something wild and crazy." He held his eyes on Audra's. "I didn't think of it until a few minutes ago, but what would you think of going to Albuquerque for a couple of days—the three of us?"

"Whoa, that's really over the top!" Tamina leaned closer to them, pushing the sleeves of her sweater to her elbows.

Audra sucked in a quick breath. She certainly hadn't anticipated anything like that! She had never thrown off the traces and done something on a whim. He was smiling at her, still holding her eyes with his. The lump in her throat wasn't going away, but, yes, she wanted to do it. Just to admit she wanted to go was wild and crazy, but she wanted to run away for two glorious days. She wanted to experience life the way she'd just been thinking about. To be free from the worries of waiting for biopsy reports or the possibility of a hysterectomy. To spend two days enjoying something pleasant with Dann, and if Dann asked Tamina along, it would be just what the invitation sounded like—three friends getting away for spring break.

Then, just as suddenly as the first time, she experienced that weird feeling of her father watching her disapprovingly. She ducked her head to hide her consternation.

Of course, he'd disapprove. He always did. She swallowed to hold back a grimace. Dann's invitation was so totally out of the blue, so totally spur-of-the-moment—so totally unlike anything she'd ever done! She didn't care what her father would have thought.

"Oh, I don't have the money to do something so wild and crazy." Tamina shook her head. "Not after dishing out four hundred on my car."

As Audra lowered her face again, her hair fell forward, hiding her face. Disappointment jarred her. *Can't there be a way?* She had deposited her music lesson payments into savings for six years, and most months she added to it from her paycheck. She'd created a fat nest egg because her father had been a stickler for self-sufficiency. She could take both herself and Tamina on a vacation twice as long and not make a dent in it. *So why am I afraid to spend any of it?*

A graphic picture of herself running her fingers through a pile of money intruded. A very uncomfortable thought accused her of being as miserly as her father. She recoiled. That was worse than the specter of her father standing there.

But what if I do get sick and can't work? It's all I'd have to live on. She bit her lip. *God wants me to put my reliance on him, so I must cut myself loose from that money — now. If I don't, it will always be a stumbling block.* She lifted her head and locked eyes with Tamina. "Would you go if I did something wild and crazy and took you?"

"Whoa!" Tamina craned her neck to peer into Audra's face. "Girlfriend, you really want to go!"

"Yes, I think it would be wonderful to get away, don't you?"

"Well, yes, but I don't know when I could pay you back."

"I don't want you to pay me back. I'd like it to be a gift." Audra smiled at her best friend, delight bubbling in her heart.

Tamina's gaze switched from Audra to Dann and back to Audra again. They were both grinning and waiting. "I hardly know what to say, girlfriend, but under those conditions, there's absolutely no reason why I can't go. It would be a hoot, wouldn't it? Okay, let's do it. If nothing else, we can show you our alma mater." She grinned at Dann.

CHAPTER TWENTY-NINE

LANEY'S VISIT

AUDRA TWISTED HER GRIP ON THE STEERING WHEEL. *SHOULD I call Laney and tell her I'm going to Albuquerque? What if something happens — what if there's an accident and Laney doesn't even know I was out of town?* She hadn't talked to Laney for two months. There was no compelling reason to tell her sister her plans, yet the thought wouldn't leave her. At home, she tapped in her sister's number.

"Hi, it's me," she said when Laney answered. "Do you have a minute?"

"Sure. Did you have a nice Easter?"

"Yes. Tamina and I were invited to a friend's house, and he grilled steaks. The three of us decided to take a little trip into Albuquerque for spring break. I called to let you know I'll be gone for a couple of days."

The intense silence on the phone line left Audra wondering if she'd been cut off. "Who's *he*?" Laney finally asked.

"Dann Day, the music director at school. We've gotten acquainted over the last months." Audra let a silence of her own hang in the air. "Are you worried about me going with a man along?"

"Should I be? Or maybe I should ask if he's more than just an acquaintance?"

Audra couldn't keep from smiling. "No on both counts, but don't worry—we're just three friends going to see the sights. I know Father would have totally frowned on the idea, and I probably would have let him talk me out of going—however, I most likely would have inwardly seethed at him, too. Thank goodness, I don't feel angry at him like I used to."

"And Tamina *is* going, right?"

"Right. I just wanted you to know I'll be gone."

"Okay. Well, thanks for letting me know."

Audra hung up and sat at the piano. She called her sister for more than letting her know she was going out of town. She *wanted* Laney to know there was a man involved. *It's almost like I needed her permission.*

The next morning Audra stood at her closet, drumming her fingers on her thighs to the piano part of "Rhapsody In Blue" playing from the living room. She scraped clothes hangers across the rod and pushed school outfits out of the way. *Boy, my wardrobe needs updating.* Spying a mulberry-colored gored skirt and matching sweater, she slid the sweater off its hanger and held it before her at the mirror, turning from side to side. She liked what it did for her figure, but she didn't want flirty.

In the background, "Rhapsody" started playing her favorite passage. Pressing the sweater to her chest, she closed her eyes and waltzed across the room and back. She was in Dann's arms. *Whew. No, I'd better not do flirty.* She tossed the sweater toward her open suitcase and dug in her dresser drawer for the matching scarf with its flashes of chartreuse, navy, and cranberry. It's what made the outfit and highlighted her brown eyes.

She was retrieving the skirt when the doorbell rang. "Coming!" she sang out, stopping to turn down the music. Her hand fixed on the doorknob. "Laney?" Laney never came uninvited, especially at ten in the morning.

"Do you have a few minutes?" Entering, Laney slung her purse off her shoulder and tossed it on the couch.

"Of course. Do you have time for coffee?"

"It's cool this morning—how about a cup of tea?"

"Is there something on your mind?" Audra asked over her shoulder on her way to the kitchen.

Laney took the kitchen chair in front of the windows. "Sort of. You said something yesterday I can't quit thinking about, so I need to talk to you."

As Audra set the teakettle on the stove, Laney's eyes bored into her, intently studying her. Then she shifted her gaze down to her hands, clenching on the table. "Yesterday you said you're not angry with Father the way you used to be. Audie... I always thought you were his favorite and everything went smoothly between the two of you."

Audra rolled her eyes. "Hardly. I held resentment against him for many years. I was hurt because he never gave me any comfort after Mom died. Then I hurt because he wouldn't let me go back to Sunday school. He said we didn't need God, but I did. I only recently discovered how much I need him." She set mugs, teabags, spoons, and sugar on the table and sat back down.

"The real *anger*, though, was because of how he treated you—especially when you came home pregnant with Amanda. I hated the way he yelled at you, but there were so many things I never understood. I never knew why you and Father got so crosswise."

Laney picked up a teabag and put it in her cup. "Audie, I tried *so* hard to please him, but I never measured up. You were only twelve, and I was totally responsible for looking after you, cooking, and keeping the house spotless and keeping up my grades. I thought you should act fifteen like me, but I didn't have the maturity to see why you couldn't. Looking back, I must have been pretty bossy."

The water boiled, and Audra stood and filled their mugs. She was seeing her sister in a different light since she'd forgiven her. "Yes, sometimes you were. But you were the only thing left I had to hang on to, so I just kept trying to do better so you wouldn't be angry like Father was."

Tears welled up in Laney's eyes. "Oh, Audie, I'm sorry. I really am. The thing that got us crosswise was Father began to complain. I didn't cook as good as Mom, I didn't get good grades like you, and I couldn't even play the piano—and that hurt. As hard as I was working, I could never satisfy him." She stirred sugar into her tea and sighed. "I felt worthless. I wanted Mom's comfort so much, but of course, that couldn't happen. I don't remember why I felt I couldn't share with you how stressed I was—maybe I was afraid it would make you sad because you missed Mom so much, too."

Audra took a deep breath assimilating this revelation. *No wonder Laney rebelled.* She reached across the table and clasped her sister's hand. "I never realized you felt worthless. You certainly weren't in my eyes—but I can relate. I often felt small and insignificant when Father was angry. One time I hid in the closet so I couldn't hear him. I wish we could have talked."

"Me, too. After I finally got my life turned around, I thought you didn't want to be around me because I messed up so badly. I don't blame you—I ran off and married Grayson and abandoned you, and when I came back pregnant, things were worse than before. I was so desperate I left again and moved in with Darryl because I thought he had money—what a joke! But I abandoned you again. I was only thinking of myself, and I put you through hell. Oh, Audie, please forgive me. I love you so much."

Tears stung Audra's eyes. She'd already forgiven Laney for

all these things and more. She wasn't going to open old wounds. She moved to the backside of the table and squeezed her arms around Laney. "Laney, I love you, too. You have Andy, now, and Amanda and the boys. I thought you didn't have time for me anymore. I've felt rejected. You're still my big sister, and I do need you."

Laney rose and embraced Audra. The two of them, wedged in between the table and the window, wept on each other's shoulders, and the walls of separation toppled like a line of dominoes.

Still standing in a hug, Audra explained how she had forgiven their father and her.

"Thank you, Audie." Laney eased back, her fingers sliding down Audra's arm to squeeze her hand before releasing her. "Over the years I have come to realize that Father didn't know how to cope with his own grief, let alone how to raise two hurting girls."

"Good insight, Laney. I think you're right."

Laney sat back down. "Well, little sister, now can you tell me something about Dann?" She cocked her head and squinted one eye. "I feel there's a little more to the story."

A smile twitched at the corners of Audra's lips. Sitting, she took a swallow of tea and sighed. "He's a super nice guy. We spent weeks practicing duets and played selections for all his music classes. Sometimes I can't get him out of my mind, but I haven't told him I'm a candidate for cancer—or at least a hysterectomy."

Laney's eyebrows arched. "Are you going to tell him?"

"I'll have to sometime. So far, I haven't ginned up the courage. You must remember I'm a late bloomer at this romance business. In high school, I was never comfortable with boys. Mom warned me that boys could want me to do things I shouldn't do, and I guess I was always scared they might. I didn't even want a boy to kiss me. I think I was afraid I'd end up with all those problems you had with men, and I certainly didn't want a husband like Father. I just shut that part of my life down..." Audra stared at the table.

Laney slid her hand across and covered Audra's. "And now things are changing?"

"Big time." Audra looked at her sister. "I'm experiencing sensations and feelings that surprise me. Part of me doesn't want anything to happen between us because I don't want to break his heart if I get cancer, but the other part wants..."

Laney patted her hand. "I understand perfectly. Just keep a level head going on this trip, okay? I'm glad Tamina's going with you."

"I hope someday you can meet Dann. Marsha's met him."

Laney's eyebrows lifted. "Oh, she did mention seeing you at the restaurant with a dreamy man." She stood up. "Hey, I hate to cut this short, but I've to get going. Amanda's watching the boys, but she has plans with her friends."

They met at the end of the table in another long embrace. "I'm so glad you came, Laney. I feel like a ton of weight has been lifted from me."

"Me, too. Have fun on your trip, and we'll talk when you get back."

When Laney left, Audra went back to the bedroom to finish packing. Briefly, she experienced that odd sensation, again, that there was something inside her wanting to be free, but unable to identify it, she shrugged it off and grinned at Laney's admonition. *Yup, she's acting like my big sister again, and I've never been more grateful.*

CHAPTER THIRTY

SPRING BREAK

COTTON-CANDY CLOUDS DOTTED AN AZURE SKY, A BREEZE SCATtered petals from a flowering plum, and two pigeons pecked at spilled popcorn when Audra exited the car in the motel parking lot and leaned against the side of Dann's Jeep.

Dann slammed his door, stretched, and joined her. His eyes scanned the Sandia Mountains bordering the entire eastern edge of Albuquerque. "How high are they?"

"Mmm, over ten thousand feet."

"And you say the tram goes all the way to the top?"

Tamina clambered from the back seat, pointing, as she stood next to Dann. "Look closely. Can you see the sun glinting on the cables? It doesn't go up to the Crest, but it ends up almost as high in altitude."

Dann laughed. "What are we waiting for? Let's get checked in and be on our way."

Pushed to the window at the rear of the crowded tramcar, Dann tucked Audra in front of him and looked over her shoulder, one hand resting on her waist. While buildings below them diminished to mere dots, his breath warmed her neck as he spoke near her ear. "We must be able to see all the way to Arizona. It's awesome." Then he pointed. "Look! Down to your right. There's a flower blooming in the rocks."

Audra's eyes searched the muted dun of the mountain slope. *Looks about like my life. Dull, monotone, rocky – dead.* Then she spotted the patch of purple verbena stubbornly clinging to the soil next to a boulder. She sucked in a breath.

"Oh, I see it! What a brave little soul—so full of life and blooming gloriously in such an unremarkable environment." She stretched to keep the spot of color in view until the boulder obscured it.

His hand tightened on her waist, and warmth flushed her all over. *Yeah, Laney was right. It's a good thing Tamina's along with us.*

When they stepped out of the gondola at the summit, it was twenty degrees cooler than in town, but they stood on the deck and let the desert beauty below engulf their senses. "I've never stood on top of the world before!" Dann clasped her hand in his. "It's better than any airplane rides I've taken."

For a split second, she wanted to pull away. His breath on her neck, his hand on her waist, had surged a thrill through her in the tramcar. But his simple gesture, now, reminded her she needed to tell him the secret she had bottled up. She'd have to be honest with him, but not now. After they got home. She wasn't going to spoil this vacation. She'd let it be the bright spot in the midst of her drab desert of worry.

She intertwined her fingers with his.

They ate lunch at the tram restaurant and, after the return trip, drove along Central Avenue past UNM, Audra's and Tamina's alma mater with its pueblo-style architecture. They spent the afternoon exploring the antiquated San Felipe de Neri Church and the shops on the plaza of Old Town. Dann held Audra's hand the entire time. Then they spent the evening playing cribbage in Audra and Tamina's motel room until Dann left at ten thirty.

After Audra climbed into bed, Tamina turned on her side, her hand dangling over the edge of the mattress. "It looked like Dann enjoyed holding your hand everywhere we went. Have you changed your mind about getting involved with him?"

Audra stared at the ceiling.

Tamina chuckled. "I don't feel the least bit left out, but I definitely feel like I'm a chaperone."

Audra rolled over on her side. "Girlfriend, to tell you the truth, I'm struggling big time again. I've been almost happy lately, so I wanted to come and spend time with Dann."

Pausing, she pressed out a sheet wrinkle with her fingers. "To be totally honest, I guess I was hoping something like this might happen. But I also thought getting away and doing something so different would give me a chance to relax. Just the opposite is happening."

She scrunched the edge of the sheet in her hand. "I was flooded with warm prickles all day when he held my hand, but it's a jarring reminder that what he doesn't know could hurt him. I'm feeling anxious again. I'm afraid when I tell him he'll say bye-bye, nice knowing you."

"Oh, girl, I'm so sorry. I don't even know what to say."

Audra and Tamina met Dann in the breakfast room the following morning. He was dishing scrambled eggs and bacon while his waffle baked.

"Mmm, the bacon smells delish." After selecting a box of Cheerios and a cherry yogurt, Audra snagged a piece of bacon. Tamina arrived at their table with orange juice, yogurt, and toast.

Dan poured syrup on his waffle and more on his eggs.

"You guys brought coats, didn't you?" He waited for them to nod. "I'm still intrigued by that mountain. I stopped at the desk and found out there's a scenic road up the backside that comes out at the Crest, north of the tram. I'd like to explore a little, but it's bound to be chilly. Interested in checking it out?"

On top of the mountain, a raw March wind buffeted them the moment they stepped out of the Jeep, tangling Audra's hair and sending Tamina's blue knit cap flying into a meadow.

Dann retrieved the hat. "Okay, madam tour guide, what do you suggest now?"

"Tough it out?" Tamina raised a questioning eyebrow to Audra.

Audra shrugged. "It's just wind. Let me stuff my hair inside my jacket."

Dann tucked her hand into his pocket, and they followed the rocky trail along the crest to Kiwanis Point. Wind whistled through paneless window openings in a white rock "cabin" that hugged the edge of the rim overlooking Albuquerque.

As she leaned against the sill to peek out, Dann's arm encircled her waist, and he craned his neck for a better view. "Man, that's one sprawling city down there."

His aftershave was intoxicating, his cheek, brushing her hair, was inches from her face, and his hand was tightening on her side as his body tilted forward. She shivered.

"You cold?"

"A bit." How could she tell him it wasn't the cold making her shiver?

She backed away from the window to Tamina grinning at her. *From the look on her face, she knows what I'm feeling right now.* She glanced at him, still absorbed in the scenery. *His hand was on my waist in the crowded tramcar — but this was different. Was it just an unconscious act? Or...?* He seemed oblivious.

With her hand enclosed in his pocket again, they meandered through an aspen grove before hiking back to the gift shop. Tamina perused a glassed-in case of showy jewelry then glanced around. "This is all new since I was last here. The old gift shop was cramped, but it had some quaint New Mexico souvenirs that would make you laugh—I remember little plastic bags of rocks labeled "rattlesnake eggs" and jackalopes. Those were funny stuffed jackrabbits with antelope horns growing out of their heads. None of that, now."

They dawdled over lunch in the café adjoining the gift shop before heading back down the twisty mountain. Nearing the bottom, Tamina leaned forward in her seat. "Slow down a bit, Dann. There's something along here I want you to see." She pointed. "Over there on the right. See that building down in the trees? All you can see is the brown roof. Turn in there."

Approaching a door set into a wall made entirely of hundreds of old glass bottles mortared together, Audra's eyebrows rose. "Tinker Town. What is it?"

"Come and see." Pulling the door open, Tamina led them along an indoor boardwalk.

Dann strode to a window nearly twenty feet long. "Well, I can see where tinker came from." Behind the glass, lay a miniature western town. Every building was handmade, every person hand-carved. A tiny farrier labored beside his "red-hot" forge preparing a horseshoe, while a few doors down a Navajo craftsman hammered pretend silver into jewelry. Ladies of the night strolled on their balcony above the saloon. Hand-carved horses and wagons occupied every conceivable corner, and thousands of tiny collectibles completed the scene of Western life.

Carrying her jacket, Audra intertwined her fingers with his as they progressed to the next glassed-in scene. "Oh! It's a circus!"

The side of the canvas Big Top was cut back, revealing

hand-carved elephants, lions, and tigers, plus numerous per-formers in three rings. As she pressed closer to the glass, he stepped behind her, resting his hands on her hips, gazing over her shoulder. There was no jacket to camouflage the touch of his hands. She forced herself to breathe. "Do you see the acrobats?" she almost squeaked. "They're on wires, but it looks like they're frozen in space."

Tamina halted next to Audra and pointed. "Look way in the back of the tent—see all the clowns?"

Dann didn't take his hands from Audra's hips but tipped his head, brushing against her hair. "There's my favorite—the horse-drawn wagon carrying the entire circus band."

Audra stared at the bandwagon. *This definitely isn't uncon-scious on his part. But is it wrong? It's taking my breath away. Oh, I have to tell him my problem. But not now, not here. Why do I have to like it?*

For the next hour and a half, they examined all sorts of oddities and antiques—from the clothes once worn by the larg-est man on earth, an eight-foot, three-inch giant from a circus sideshow, to an old sailing cutter dry-docked there after a ten-year voyage around the world. Every time they stopped, Dann stood behind her, resting his hands on her hips.

When they stepped outside again, Tamina prattled on about the exhibits. Audra scarcely noticed. Dann was looking into her eyes, and she couldn't look away.

That evening, they found the barbecue restaurant Audra recalled seeing near the bottom of the tram the day before. It was crowded and noisy, but soon plates of pork ribs, chicken, and sausage, drenched in smoky barbecue sauce, were steaming in front of them. Hot homemade bread and side dishes of pinto beans and coleslaw also crowded the table.

Dann swiped a hunk of sausage through the aromatic

sauce. "This is what the Grove needs—a good barbeque place."

Tamina laughed. "Why don't you open one and add it to your repertoire of many talents?" Then she did a double take.

Seated near them, five men in their late twenties ordered beer and became absorbed in their menus. Their conversation flowed easily, punctuated by laughter.

Audra glanced over at the table while Tamina gawked. Then Audra waved her hand in front of Tamina's intent face until she blinked and looked at her. "Somebody you know?"

"I don't believe it. It's Franklin Perry," Tamina whispered. "I haven't seen him since before I graduated." She began cutting a chicken thigh without looking at it, seeming unable to take her eyes off the table of men.

There was only one black man at the table, and Audra assumed he was Franklin. Nice looking with black-rimmed glasses, a clean-shaven face, and close-cropped hair, he possessed a muscular build.

Two minutes passed before Franklin's gaze lifted beyond his table. Tamina's hand shot up in a not-so-shy wave. The beer in his hand halted halfway to his mouth. His smile disappeared, overtaken by dumbfounded disbelief. After shoving his chair back, he threaded his way over to their table. "Mina! I don't believe it. How are you?"

Audra's head jerked toward Tamina. *I didn't know she went by Mina.*

"I'm great." Tamina folded her hands beneath her chin, a decided excitement in her heightened voice. "Franklin, I'd like you to meet my coworkers Audra Knight and Dann Day—and this is Franklin Perry." She stretched her hand toward Franklin, grinning widely.

Dann stood and shook the younger man's hand, and Franklin shook Audra's hand across the table.

"Sit a minute?" Dann offered, and Franklin pulled out the fourth chair, sliding into it.

"Are you working here in town?" he directed to Tamina.

"No. We came down for spring break. We all teach in Chandler's Grove. What are you up to?"

"I'm a pharmacist finally, for Family Pharm Drug Stores. How long are you here?"

"We're going back tomorrow. We've been bumming around since yesterday. We rode the tram yesterday, and then we drove back up to the Crest today. Dann's quite taken with the mountain."

Franklin grinned at him. "Impressive, huh?"

"I love it. From what I've seen, Albuquerque seems like a nice town."

"I've moved back, and I don't plan to leave." He faced Tamina. "Where are you staying?"

Tamina told him. "It's off I-25. Do you know where it's at?"

Franklin nodded and then glanced over at his friends. The waitress was placing their food on the table. "I've got to get back. We're celebrating a birthday over there. Can I call you?"

"Sure." Tamina smiled.

"What's your room number?"

"One seventeen."

"I'll call you later."

Franklin called as the three of them were watching the news. Tamina's eyes sparkled when she started talking on the phone, and Dann, leaning toward Audra, suggested a visit to the coffee shop. They stayed away for an hour and a half.

Tamina was already under her blanket when Audra returned to their room, so she got ready for bed in the bathroom. She left the bathroom door cracked for a sliver of light and sat on the bed to brush her hair.

"I'm not asleep," Tamina said.

Audra guessed she wanted to talk. "So, where'd you meet him?"

"Here, at school." Tamina sighed. "I was rooming with two other girls. I didn't care much for the one, especially when she started bringing guys in with no warning. One weekend she invited in a bunch of guys and some girls, too. Franklin was one of them. Things started getting a little steamy, and Franklin was embarrassed by it all. He saw I was distressed, too, and asked me if I wanted to get out of there. We sat in an all-night coffee shop until two in the morning just talking.

"The next day I found a cheap boardinghouse room, and he helped me move. We saw each other three times after that, and I guess you'd say I fell head-over-heels. Then he disappeared. I mean, totally disappeared. I never heard from him or saw him again until tonight."

"You never told me that." Audra climbed under her covers. "Did he tell you what happened?"

"He told me right after the last time we saw each other his dad fell off a ladder trying to get on the roof and was really banged up—several broken bones. His dad lived in Silver City, and Franklin left here in the middle of the night expecting to stay the weekend. However, his car broke down, and he didn't have any money. He had brothers and sisters still at home and his dad couldn't work, so he ended up dropping out of school and getting a job to keep things going."

"Didn't he try to get ahold of you?"

"He did. The last time we were together, he told me

employers were starting to look at social media accounts. I was close to entering the job market, and I decided there were a couple of college shenanigans on my site future employers might frown on—"

"You? Guilty of shenanigans?"

Tamina momentarily hid her face with her blanket. "Mmm, yeah. And we'll just let that fade into the dim, distant past, thank you. Nothing shameful, just wild." She flopped over on her back. "Anyway, I immediately deleted my account, effectively cutting him off. I figured he would phone. I didn't count on the boarding house phone number getting lost in the shuffle when his roommate packed up his stuff and sent it to him."

She laid her arm across her forehead and sighed. "He said he was frantic when he couldn't find it. He didn't know the landlady's name or the address, his roomie didn't know me, and he couldn't get back up here to find me. When he finally got back to school, I had graduated and left. I went by Mina all through high school and college—he doesn't even know my real name's Tamina."

"Didn't you try to contact him?"

Tamina turned on her side and let her hand dangle again. "That's where I messed up. After two weeks and he hadn't called, I sort of got in a huff. I had to study for finals, and there were so many guys named Franklin Perry online to sort through, I gave up. I decided if he hadn't called after that long, he wasn't serious. I was disappointed, but I figured it just wasn't meant to be."

"And now you've met up again. Any chance you'll see him?"

"I've been lying here trying to sort it out." She fluffed her pillow and propped herself on an elbow. "He'd like to get together tomorrow. I told him I didn't know what time we are planning to leave or what you two wanted to do. I said I'd check with you."

"So, do you *want* to see him?"

"Yes, very much. But he's settled here, and I'm in the Grove. Maybe I'm getting way ahead of myself, but I don't know if I want a long-distance romance." Tamina picked at a loose thread on her blanket. A long moment passed before she broke the quiet. "Dann didn't say when he wants to leave tomorrow, did he?"

"No, I just assumed it would be some time after breakfast. Why? Do you want to stay over?" A picture of Dann standing with his hands on her hips flashed through her mind. *What if we stayed over?* A familiar sensation tickled through her.

"Franklin said if he could, he'd try to get the day off, but... I'll pay you back if we stay an extra day."

"No, girl, you don't need to. I wouldn't mind staying, either. I'm...I'm—" Audra rolled to face Tamina, supporting herself on her elbow, cupping the side of her face in her hand. "What's happening to us, girlfriend? How long have we both said we are satisfied with being single? Now, all of a sudden, we both have men on our minds. I wasn't looking for romance—"

"Ha! I'd say romance found you." Tamina laughed. "I'd say Dann has something on his mind the way he was acting today."

Audra swallowed. "I know. I hate to think I'm leading him on. I've tried to resist any romantic notions, but, well, I'm losing the battle. Dann gives me tingles big time, and I confess I'm enjoying it... Am I wrong for wanting it?"

Tamina's black eyes gleamed in the dim light. "I hope not, but since you're being honest with me, I'll be honest with you. I know how you feel. I *want* something to happen between me and Franklin. I *want* to feel like I did when I knew him before, but I was just lying here thinking, what if I go head-over-heels again and it turns out he's not in the same place? Or what if my memory of him isn't as accurate as it should be?"

Audra was silent for a moment. "Do you think running into him was just a coincidence? How long has it been since you've seen him? Must be more than four years. This is a big city, what are the chances? Or did God have something to do with it? Pastor Moorehouse keeps talking about letting God lead you, but how do you know if it's God, if it's a coincidence, or if it's just your own desires? I need to know for myself."

Tamina's forehead wrinkled and her lips twisted. "Right now, I have no idea whether it's a coincidence or if it's God, but I want to walk into this with both eyes open. I've been satisfied being single, partly because I haven't seen a man I'd care to spend my life with, but if God brings me a husband, I'll be more than happy to get married. I want God's will, so I want to be cautious. If a man came along and wanted me to compromise myself by doing something I know God says is wrong, I'd *know* God wasn't leading me because God won't lead me to do something his word says is wrong."

"Gotcha, girl." Audra lowered her head back on her pillow. "And I guess if you know in your heart it's not God's will and you go ahead, it probably means it's your own desires talking."

"I think you're right on." Silence settled before Tamina added, "If Franklin can't get the day off, or Dann wants to leave early, we'll just have breakfast together. He's going to call at six forty-five."

"I'll talk to Dann in the morning." Audra closed her eyes. Was Dann God's will for her? She didn't think Dann would ever put her in a compromising position—his hands on her hips aside, he hadn't even tried to kiss her. But she'd never thought to ask God if Dann was his will for her. *What if God said no?*

A strange sensation started at the top of her head and traveled down deep into her body. A fear that God might say no. And she knew by her response she'd let Dann into her heart more than she'd thought. She swallowed hard and folded her hands across her abdomen. *Oh, Lord, I do want your will for my life, but this is all so new. All my life I've made my decisions according to my emotions and desires. Now I've opened myself to Dann without asking you, and, well, I'd feel lost without him in my life. I don't know what your will for me is. Would you please give me a red flag if this isn't what you want for me?*

CHAPTER THIRTY-ONE

A CHANGE OF PLANS

IN THE MORNING, AUDRA WAS STILL IN BED WHEN TAMINA TALKED to Franklin. Once Tamina hung up, Audra called Dann. "I have some news."

"What's up?"

"Franklin got the day off and wants to spend it with Tamina, but the whole thing depends on us spending another day here." She paused, allowing him time to digest it. "If you don't think we should hang around, they'll just go out for breakfast. So, honestly, what do you think?"

"I don't have a problem with it. If Tamina wants to see him after all these years, we ought to let her, huh?" Merriment tinged his voice. "Can you handle paying for her another day?"

"No problem. I guess we can find something to do for the day, can't we?"

"I don't think that will be a problem, either." After a pause, he added, "Why don't you see if they'll have dinner with us this evening?"

At Audra's thumbs-up, Tamina hummed in the background, and then Audra took her turn in the bathroom. After they were both put together, Tamina fished out her signature hoop earrings. They just grazed the collar of her gray corduroy jacket. She gave her pixie haircut one last pat and pulled the bill of her navy-blue knit hat down jauntily above one eye.

Audra sat on the end of the bed and laughed. "Girl, you can always pass for a model, but today, you're a supermodel. Come on, let's wait outside for Franklin."

Spying Franklin's car, Audra grabbed Tamina with a quick hug. "Text Dann if you can join us for dinner. Meet here at six?"

As Tamina sauntered away and slid into Franklin's car, Audra spotted Dann exiting his motel room. Inhaling air bursting with spring and possibilities, she flung her arms wide and allowed herself a little twirl, stopping with a giggle in front of him. "I'm so happy for her. What would you like to do today?"

He caught her hand. "I know you like art galleries, but do you like antique shops?" He grinned at the way she was staring at him. "Yes, I like antique shops, and there's something I'm always on the lookout for."

"I'm game." Seemed some amazing things interested Dann.

They wandered hand-in-hand in and out of antique shops all morning. Just before they broke for lunch, he stopped in front of a booth holding a conglomeration of old tools, oilcans, and license plates. "Well, would you look at that—a Union Pacific 4-8-4."

"What does that mean?"

He picked up the HO gauge steam locomotive from the table and tilted the engine so she could see the side. "See, it has four small wheels up in front so it could turn easier on a curve, then eight large drive wheels and then four more small ones at the back—a pretty popular configuration back then. With the four wheels up in front, it very well could have pulled passenger trains."

The proprietor, a wizened old man, approached. "Are you interested in the locomotive?" he asked in a precise, clipped voice.

"Possibly," Dann said. "I don't see a price on it."

"Just got it in yesterday. I've never had any interest in dealing in toy trains. I couldn't see what anybody saw in them to tell you the truth. Give me old tools any day."

"Does it run?"

"So I assume. Some fellow came in yesterday with some extraordinary tools. He threw the engine into the deal. Didn't seem like it was worth much to him as dirty as he let it get. What will you offer me?"

Delighted, she stood aside as Dann negotiated the price with the shop owner before buying it. "Was that a good deal?" She tucked her hand in the crook of his arm as they left the shop.

"Oh yeah, if he'd known what he had, he could have gotten three times that amount." A sparkle flashed in his eyes. "I don't run steam locomotives on my layout, but I can't resist models of those grand old engines. This will sit on a shelf with the rest of my locomotive collection as a memorial to an era long gone."

Then, with a suggestion and directions from their lunch waiter, they headed to the Rio Grande Nature Center where they stood hand-in-hand behind a cement wall with window cutouts while Canada geese, wood ducks, mallards, and a blue heron enjoyed the pond, unaware they were on display.

As they walked a bike path, she considered her conversation with Tamina. How would she know if God was leading her and Dann together? She stifled a shudder. And how would she tell him a hysterectomy could be in her future? He needed the chance to back out if he wanted to. She studied a flock of birds in the distance. As unpleasant as that conversation might prove to be, avoiding it was not an option. Just not today.

That evening, Audra followed Tamina into a pint-sized

Mexican restaurant and eyed the striped serapes and sombreros hanging on the walls. A pink donkey piñata hung suspended over the cash register. The tantalizing aroma of chile and cheese drifted from the kitchen, and canned mariachi music reverberated through the dining room.

Audra slid into the booth. "Mmm, I'm glad I brought my appetite."

"This is my favorite place in town," Franklin offered, seating himself next to Tamina.

Dann joined Audra. "Looks authentic. So, what did you do all day?"

Tamina and Franklin gazed into each other's eyes until Tamina giggled. "We talked."

A waitress in a blue peasant blouse and colorful fiesta skirt placed chips and salsa on the table and took orders.

Franklin dipped a chip and faced Dann and Audra. "How did you spend the day?"

She dragged a chip through the salsa. "We started antiquing, and Dann dickered for this fabulous model locomotive—"

"You into trains, man?" Franklin broke in.

As he questioned Dann about his hobby, Audra shifted to look at Tamina, who was bouncing in her seat to the blaring trumpets. Audra leaned across the table and hid her mouth behind her hand. "The way you're groovin' it must have been a successful day."

Snapping her fingers to the beat as if playing castanets, Tamina flashed a flirty smile, and her eyebrows hiked twice in rapid succession. Audra laughed. She knew she'd get the rest of the story later.

They continued chatting as they stuffed on enchiladas, chile rellenos, tamales, and the fluffiest fried sopapillas and honey in town. By the time they finished, a line was waiting for a table. They paid and drove back to the motel.

"The night's still young, and I, for one, am reluctant to call it quits." Dann grabbed the back of Franklin's seat. "You know how to play cribbage?"

Franklin glanced over his shoulder. "I've seen it played, but I've never learned it. Is it difficult?"

"Nah, come on in, and we'll try a hand or two." A collective sigh seemed to indicate they were all eager to extend the evening.

They played until midnight around the square table in the girls' room with Franklin sitting on the end of a bed, Dann sitting on a pillow on top of the luggage rack, and the girls taking the two matching chairs. When Franklin finally said he had to get to bed so he could go to work in the morning, it was over.

Tamina grabbed her jacket and walked out to his car with him. Audra picked up the cards and cribbage board, and Dann dragged the table back into the corner and pushed the chairs in place.

He stepped in front of her and held his hands out. "I think I'd better go, too."

"I know." She placed her hands into his. "I don't think I've ever enjoyed anything as much as these last three days. I hate to see it end."

"Me, too." Gently, he pressed his thumb to the back of her hand and looked into her eyes.

Two light taps brushed the door before Tamina came in. She kept her gaze down as she passed by, going directly into the bathroom.

With one last squeeze, he let go of Audra's hands. "I'll go now."

When she finally nestled into bed, snuggling into the crisp sheets, she looked over at Tamina framed by the light from the bathroom. She was lying on her back, one arm resting across her forehead as she stared at the ceiling. A minute passed before she broke the silence. "Thanks for staying over."

"Hey, girlfriend, I'm really glad we could. You were looking good when you left here this morning. Would I be too nosy to ask where you spent the day?"

"At the zoo—and we really did talk all day. We sat and talked. We walked and talked, and we ate and talked. Dann has nothing on Franklin when it comes to talking." Tamina laughed. "It was like we've never been apart, except we've both grown up a lot."

"And you're basking in the afterglow?"

"You've got it, girl. And you?"

"Yeah, me, too."

Driving back to Chandler's Grove Friday, Audra repeatedly replayed the three days. In every scenario, her hand was in Dann's. She was comfortable with it, now, even though she still dreaded having to confess what she'd been keeping from him. She also thought about her savings account becoming an idol.

At her house, he carried her suitcase through the front door and set it down in the living room before stepping in front of her. He had the same expectant, yet hesitant, look on his face. He continued looking into her face, but then all he did was give her upper arms a squeeze. "We made a lot of great memories I'll never forget. I'm so glad we went." He slipped his hands into his pockets and added, "I have to get going, but I'll see you later."

Alone, Audra flopped onto the couch. That look on his face and the way he'd stood close to her had made her think he was going to kiss her goodbye, but he hadn't. *It was like he wanted to and then stopped himself.* After pushing from the couch, she got a drink of water in the kitchen but paused with the glass halfway to her lips. *He does want to kiss me, but he's put a restraint on himself.*

Suddenly an odd thought occurred to her. *What if I tell Dann I might have to have a hysterectomy and he moves on, but then the treatment works? What if I get better, but I've lost him? Oh, dear Lord, what shall I do?* She took a deep breath and let it out. *Lord, if Dann is your will for me but he has a reason why he's hesitating, then I want to wait for him.*

She felt at peace with her decision. She took her suitcase to the bedroom, grabbed her purse and car keys. She made a transaction at her bank and then drove downtown. In the art gallery, she purchased the painting of the boy practicing his violin. She paid the fifteen hundred from her savings. She bought it simply because she wanted Dann to have it. The picture fit him — it *was* him.

CHAPTER THIRTY-TWO

MADDIE AND TAYLOR

As Audra's second-period students bent over their seat-work papers, she opened a window in her stuffy classroom and breathed in the earthy smell of damp soil the breeze brought in, a breeze reminiscent of a crisp wind curling over Sandia Crest. A surge of adrenaline brought it all back—her hand nestled in Dann's jacket pocket, hiking through the aspen hand-in-hand, his hands resting on her hips—*Whoa! Stop right there.*

She spun away from the window and scanned her class. Reality was twenty-five students laboring over a worksheet, not suggestive memories unfit for classroom consumption. She returned to her desk and stacked the eraser-smudged papers from first period, smelling faintly of copier ink. She picked up her red-leaded pencil and began correcting.

Five minutes before the bell should ring, Maddie Lester flipped her paper onto Audra's desk and flounced back to her desk. Without reading any of the answers, Audra knew the girl had an F. She had only completed every other sentence. That seemed too deliberate, too premeditated.

She was a bright girl but still consistently received poor grades. Audra breathed out a frustrated sigh. "Maddie?"

The girl scowled, her shoulders hunching when Audra beckoned her to the front and told her she needed to see her after school.

When Maddie slumped through the door promptly at the end of the day and slouched into a front-row seat, Audra eased into a student desk across the aisle from her. "Maddie, I was looking over your worksheet. Your answers are all correct, and so you could have had a hundred percent on the paper. But you *chose* not to. Is there a reason why?"

The girl pushed her straight brown hair behind her ears and sat stony-faced.

"Maddie, are you having some problems? Maybe with kids at school or even your parents?"

She set her lips tighter.

Audra propped an elbow on the desk and looked into her face. "I'd like to help you if I can."

"You can't help me," Maddie snapped. "Why don't you just send me to the principal's office?"

"Why would you want to get sent to the principal's office?" Puzzled, Audra folded her hands to mask her surprise.

Maddie drew her lips tight again.

"Are you *trying* to get in trouble?"

"Yeah, so what?"

"Why do you want to get in trouble?" Audra fought to keep her voice level and calm.

"Because I hate this school," the girl exploded. Her eyes were flashing. "I don't want to go here. I want to go to my other school where all my friends are. I want to get expelled so my father will have to send me back to my old school."

Audra drew back. "Is that why you dared Taylor to write on my house and here at school?"

"Did he get caught?" Maddie blurted, her eyes still flashing defiantly.

"Yes, he got caught, but—"

"How come *I* didn't get in trouble?"

"Well, Maddie, if you wanted to get in trouble, why didn't you do it yourself?"

Desperation tinged the girl's eyes. "Because I thought I'd be in worse trouble if I got Taylor in trouble, too, and that's what I wanted."

Obviously, the girl was angry at her father. Audra let out a deep breath. She sure could relate. The girl had no idea how many people her plot affected, but no use dragging it all out in the open again.

"Maddie, why does your father want you to go to the academy instead of your old school?"

Maddie shifted and kept her eyes on the desktop. She pushed her hair behind her ears once more. "He keeps saying it's so I can have a good education. But it's because Chandler's Academy is where rich people's kids go and he wants everyone to think he's rich. He doesn't care that I just want to be with my friends."

Mr. Lester in his expensive suit and tie, his mouth grim and set, preoccupied and aloof came to mind. Her father had been the same—a perfectionist you could never please, stern, unsmiling. Were the two men really alike?

Audra sat back in her chair. The girl needed help and counsel, but she could never do it, even if she had the qualification. She'd be too biased against her father.

"Maddie, I'm afraid trying to get yourself into trouble isn't going to solve your problem. I'd like to help you as much as I can, but would you be willing to talk to the school counselor about all this?"

The girl fidgeted in her chair. "I don't know."

"Even if I have to tell Mr. Bentley about everything, he will want to help you, not expel you."

Maddie's body sagged in defeat.

"Would you like me to try to help?"

"I guess so," she finally whispered.

"Maddie," Audra laid her hand on the girl's desk before pushing to her feet, "Monday, we start the state tests. I really hope you'll do your best."

The following day, Audra met with Sheldon Bentley and Karen Ford, the school counselor. Karen would talk with Maddie and take it from there. Audra came away hopeful for Maddie, but when she returned to her classroom, the note on her calendar pad reminded her to make her next doctor appointment, stealing some of her joy.

She'd taken the trip to Albuquerque, hoping for relief from worry over the next biopsy, but she'd found it impossible to put it completely out of her mind. Three months had elapsed since the last progestin injection, and everything was now back in the holding pattern of wait, wait, wait. She made the appointment for April 20, and all the fearful thoughts reared their ugly heads again.

Dann called her on Wednesday evening, and they talked for over an hour. But all the while thoughts were bombarding her mind. *What if the treatment doesn't work? Am I making the right choice by not telling him now?*

She scowled. It would be poor timing to say anything right now, anyway. He was taking his band students to the middle-school competition at Mesa Heights Middle School on Saturday. She didn't want to diminish his zeal by bringing up her problem.

After she spent her time with Rosa and Mrs. Espinosa on Saturday morning, Audra stopped at the grocery store. Dann was coming for dinner after the band competition. She planned to cook, bake, and clean house to keep busy until he arrived. She would serve oven-barbecued pork ribs, baked potatoes, tossed salad, and apple pie. Dann had raved over her apple pie.

When she answered his knock, he looked tired. She definitely wasn't going to spoil the evening with her problems. As he was taking off his jacket, she asked, "Do you want to unwind a few minutes with a glass of wine?"

"That would be great," he called over his shoulder as he threw his jacket on the chair by the piano.

She carried two glasses of rosy-blushed Zinfandel to the living room and slid the drapes shut. He took off his shoes and propped his feet on the coffee table before sipping the wine.

"So, how'd it go?" She perched on the other end of the couch, facing him.

"I think it went really well. I've already seen a change in the students' attitudes. I was satisfied the way the full bands played, and several students who played solos felt they did pretty well, also. After Taylor played his solo, he ran up to me and said, 'Hey, Mr. D, I don't think I made any mistakes!' So, we'll see when the scores come out."

He took another sip of wine. "Taylor's mom was a big help as one of the chaperones. You know, I didn't find out until a week ago that these kids had never gone to a competition. It's been four years since Chandlers' has participated. I couldn't believe it! There were a few cases of nerves, though. My concert first clarinet threw up in the girls' restroom before we played, and one of my drummers was so hyper I wasn't sure if he'd be able to keep a beat or not. I thought his chaperone was going to have to sit on him until we played. But they both came through."

"I'm glad you had the determination to take it on." She smiled at him. "It will be good for the kids and the school."

"Thanks. I'm tired, but it was worth all the work."

As soon as their wine was gone, she stood. "Come on, dinner's waiting in the oven." He followed her into the kitchen and refilled their glasses while she put the meat and potatoes on the table and retrieved the salad and dressing from the refrigerator.

As he cut his baked potato open and spooned sour cream into the cavity, he laughed. "Oh, I almost forgot to tell you — yesterday, I reminded my classes our spring concerts are scheduled for May second and third, and guess what? The sixth-grade band asked if we'd play in the concert. Well, actually, Taylor suggested it first, and the others agreed. So, I put it up for a vote in the other classes, and it was unanimous. The kids want us to play for their parents."

Audra laid her fork on her plate. Across the table, he was waiting for an answer. She cocked her head slightly to one side, letting her gaze hold his. "And you want to do it?" she teased.

He spooned a falling-apart tender pork rib onto his plate. "Of course, silly. Don't you?"

She lifted the dish of meat from him. "Of course, I do. I think it's wonderful that the kids want us. In spite of all his mischief, Taylor's quite a kid, isn't he?"

"Yes, he is. You'll be surprised by how much the kids have improved, but I want to show them off, not us. However, do you think we should go back to practicing on Wednesdays for the next month?"

"How many songs are we going to play?"

"Mmm, what do you think, reruns or a couple of new ones?"

"Maybe a mixture? Do we have time to work up all

new songs?"

"If we practice twice a week." He laughed when she furrowed her forehead. "Hey, don't you miss all that greasy fast food on Wednesday night?"

"All right, twice a week." They didn't need to practice twice a week to have music ready — they *wanted* to. It was going to put her in a time crunch once again, but at least she'd be too busy to dwell on the biopsy.

CHAPTER THIRTY-THREE

BREAKING FREE

AFTER CHURCH ON SUNDAY, AUDRA AND TAMINA SAT EATING peanut butter, banana, and honey sandwiches and iced tea when Dann arrived.

"You're here early," Audra said as he slid into the chair at the end of the table.

"Jerold took his boys with us for the first time. They couldn't go as far."

She set a plate, knife, and glass in front of him and pushed the bread and peanut butter his way.

"Jerold told me there's a cave in the hills out behind the school — you ever been there?"

"I've heard of it, but I've never seen it," she admitted.

"Girl, don't you know that's where teens sneak off to drink beer?" Tamina joshed.

"Well, how do you know? Have *you* been there?" Audra shot back with a grin.

"Not since I was a teenager." Tamina wrinkled her nose, grinning back at her.

"Could you still find it?" Dann loosened the peanut

butter lid.

"Oh sure, it's not hard."

Slapping his sandwich together, he eyed both of them. "Want to go?"

Tamina checked her watch. "I have to be back by four thirty. Franklin will be calling."

Dann raised an eyebrow. "Will we have enough time?"

"Sure, but I'll have to stop by my place and change clothes."

Audra exited Tamina's car in the parking lot reserved for those hiking into the foothills. As she knew he would, Dann refrained from holding her hand in public, so they meandered side by side along the well-worn footpath for nearly a half mile until Tamina pointed. "See where the trail splits? The one on the left takes us to our secret destination."

As the narrower path began gaining altitude, Audra stepped in front of Dann to trek single file behind Tamina. "This seems like a lot of work just to sneak a beer."

"Well said, girl! How many adults do you think climb up here to check on them?" Tamina giggled.

Crossing the rocky bed of a dry arroyo zigzagging down from the top of the mountain, Dann stopped in the middle. "I imagine water tears down here at a pretty good clip when it rains. Kids ever get stranded?"

Tamina stopped to rest. "I've never heard of it happening. Even if you got caught in a cloudburst, when it stopped it would be like turning off a faucet and the arroyo would empty."

"Yeah, all the water would be down in town." Audra laughed.

Tamina took off again with Audra and Dann behind her.

Ten minutes later, Tamina suddenly turned off the trail onto a footpath that climbed sharply, twisting behind an outcropping of rock. Unseen from the main trail below, the cave, little more than a large hole about five feet high and six feet deep, greeted them like a gaping mouth in the side of the mountain.

Tamina panted. "This is it. Was it worth the hike?"

Audra stared at a blackened spot in front of the cave where a campfire had burned. "Did somebody come up here to drink beer at night?"

Dann stood beside her and studied the scorched circle. "Boy, it would be risky going back down that trail in the dark. My guess is somebody hiked up in the daylight and spent the night in the cave." He shot a look at Tamina. "Did you really come up and drink beer?"

"I'm guilty." Tamina laughed. She held her arm in front of her face as if she were fending off expected but deserved blows. "I came up here twice, and I hated beer. If my dad had ever found out, he would've tanned my hide."

He spun to Audra. "And you never did, huh?"

She surveyed the beer cans littering the area, and a few yards away, weathered cans piled in a monument to teen rebellion. Her face flushed. She wasn't sure she'd have come to the cave to drink beer, but she was embarrassed to have them know how dull her teen years had been. "No, I never managed to find my way up here. Would you have made the trip?"

Dann leaned against a ten-foot-high boulder. "Probably. We didn't have a secret place like this. We had to rely on sneaking beer into basement rec rooms when parents were gone."

Finding nothing of interest, other than the cave and the beer cans, they hiked back down. Tamina dropped off Dann and

Audra to walk together to her back door.

He hooked his thumbs into the tops of his jeans pockets. "Do you have to go?"

"I guess I don't have to. Why?" She fished in her pocket for her keys.

"Would you come over to my place for a bit? There's something I'd like to show you."

She paused before putting her key in the lock as the strange sensation of her father watching her gripped her again—his face rigid with his usual reproachful demeanor. And in a flash, she knew why she'd never gone to the cave or why she hadn't wanted a boyfriend. She'd avoided his criticism whenever possible, and like Laney, she'd spent her teen years striving for his approval, unsure she'd gained it. She hated feeling his disapproving eyes. *But why am I still so afraid of his disapproval?* She ducked her chin so Dann wouldn't see her grimace.

Then she shook off those thoughts and traded her house key for her car key. As they returned to the car, their shoulders brushed, calling to mind his hand on her waist as they wandered through Tinker Town. It produced the same inner quiver. After she gulped, she smiled up at Dann. "It sounds like you have a surprise. Throw your bike in the trunk and let's go."

At his apartment, he led her down the hallway to his train room and flipped on the light. The steam engine he'd bought in Albuquerque gleamed atop the bookcase next to the one holding the diesel. He'd cleaned it, placed it on a section of track, and coupled a cattle car, a boxcar, and a caboose behind it.

"Oh, Dann, it's wonderful. I'd love to see all your trains put together." She moved closer to the bookcase, scrutinizing each miniature part of the engine. "How did you ever learn all this?"

"My dad and I learned together. We worked for hours reading and building."

"What does your dad do for a living?"

"He's a stockbroker."

"I hope someday I can meet him." She was genuinely happy for Dann's relationship with his father.

In the living area, Dann stopped in the middle of the room. He jammed his hands into his jeans pockets. "Aud, I'd like your opinion on something. If it were up to me to make a judgment call, I'd say enough time has passed since the initials were taken care of, so we should be free to go out together. What do you think?"

She gawked at him. "Well...I...uh...I guess I hadn't really thought about it." Of course, enough time had passed, but his statement evoked another strong image of her father's judgmental gaze. *Oh, that's ridiculous! He's dead. The only one I must answer to is God, so what's the worst people can say if they see us together — the old maid finally has a boyfriend?* She knew her cheeks colored.

His brow furrowed. "What's the matter? Did I say something wrong?"

A smile tugged at her lips. "No, I just had a stupid thought go through my mind." She shook her head. "Yes, I think enough time has passed. Do you have something in mind?"

"I'd like to be free to say let's run over to Burger Basket and grab a bite."

Old thought patterns die hard, and she hesitated for just a moment. Then she held out her hand to him. "That sounds fun." Her smile widened to a grin.

As they walked to his Jeep, he held her hand for the first time since their return from Albuquerque. She peered out her side window while he drove. How she'd missed that small show of affection. *So, what's this peculiar feeling in my chest, again, like something's trying to struggle free?* Her father's face momentarily glimmered in her mind again. *I was always afraid of his disapproval — Is that why I stuffed all desires for a boyfriend? All hope for marriage? Did I consign them to a locked box in my heart and convince myself it didn't matter if I never married?*

She shot a quick glance at Dann. He was concentrating on the traffic. Lowering her elbow to the armrest, she cupped her chin in her hand and stared out the window. *Dann's shaking that box. All the hopes and dreams I've tried to suffocate want out. They're dying to get out. They're dying for life!*

"What are you thinking about?"

Audra gulped. She couldn't tell him. "Oh, nothing important. Traffic's heavier than usual, isn't it?"

"Seems like it." He slowed to a stop at the intersection.

She turned back to the window. *I want to be with Dann, yet I'm afraid to let people see I like him. It's not just Father's disapproval I'm afraid of—it's everyone's.*

While they were stopped, Dann reached his hand across the console palm up. When she rested her hand in his, he closed his fingers around hers, firm and strong. But she didn't let her gaze remain on him yet. She glanced out the window once more.

Lord, I asked you to give me a red flag if Dann isn't your will for me, and you haven't. I always feel safe with him, and I know we have a clear conscience before you regarding our relationship. I'm almost afraid to ask, but does that mean you approve? And if you approve, I don't need to be afraid of what people think, do I? A smile parted her lips.

"Are you okay?"

She twisted to face him, the smile growing broader. "I am. I really am." She felt like a little key had just unlocked that box.

After they ordered salads, drinks, and an order of fries to share, they saw Taylor Bailey with his parents in a booth against the wall. Taylor beamed when he recognized them, but when he started to get up, his mother restrained him.

"Hey, buddy, are you enjoying your burger?" Dann greeted as he set their tray on a table. He sat in the chair with its back toward Taylor and grinned at Audra. "I hope my judgment call wasn't wrong. Is every kid in school going to know that Mr. D and Miss Knight went out to eat together?" He spoke quietly enough Taylor couldn't hear him.

"I don't know, but our little matchmaker is watching our every move." She dipped three skinny french fries into ketchup and bit the ends off. She felt almost giddy. It no longer mattered what her father might have thought, or schoolkids, either, for that matter. She had broken free from that shackle, and she couldn't wait to see if God would show even more plainly that *he* didn't disapprove. Right now, she didn't care if the whole world thought she was in love with Dann Day.

CHAPTER THIRTY-FOUR

A DRESS AND A PICTURE

AUDRA HELD THE DOOR FOR TAMINA AS THEY ENTERED THE French Pantry with its tempting aromas of quiche and pastries. The restaurant was especially crowded at Saturday noon with dozens of women meeting for luncheon dates. "My treat today," Audra said as they picked out quiche, strawberry-walnut salad, buttery croissants, and iced tea. Carrying trays, she and Tamina negotiated the maze of patrons to a table under a blue umbrella on the front patio.

Tamina hung her purse on the back of her chair. "You said you needed to find a black dress. Why black for spring? That's going to be difficult, you know."

"I know. But Dann asked me to play for the student concerts next month, and I'd like a black dress and shoes." Audra sampled a bite of her salad.

Tamina's head bobbed with an understanding nod. Then lashes down, her long, slender fingers daintily separated her roll. "You'll never guess what Franklin did. He rode his bike on that winding road we drove up to Sandia Crest—all the way to the top." Her hoops swung as she shook her head, her apricot blush enhancing the lovely glow on her face. "I miss him so much—almost wish I could move to Albuquerque."

Absorbing the awe in her voice, Audra savored a bite of the delicate combination of eggs, Swiss cheese, and bacon. *She's in love! And she's sure not afraid to express her feelings. Well, I'm not going to upstage her. I can tell her how my feelings for Dann are changing later. I'll zip my lips on next week's biopsy, too.*

After lunch, they crossed town to the mall. Spring and summer fashions dominated the racks. Color was in; black was out. In the third shop, she found a basic black sheath with flattering princess seams. However, when she sat, the hem crept up to the middle of her thighs. *I'd never be comfortable playing the piano in front of a crowd in that.*

They ended up in a ladies' dress shop Tamina recommended back downtown. They were greeted by a chic black woman with ultra-long red fingernails who obviously recognized Tamina. Audra left them to catch up while she ambled in and out of racks of Easter-egg pastels. She didn't hold out much hope.

"Oooh. I think we found it, girlfriend." Tamina swept a dress off a clearance rack and jiggled it.

The delicate jersey knit hung limply on the hanger. Audra would have passed it by, but Tamina had a sense of fashion she'd never hope to attain.

"You *have* to try it on."

Conceding, Audra ducked into a cramped stall with a full-length mirror on the door. The simple empire-waist dress draped just below her mid-calf. The flared skirt offered a slight swing perfect for sitting at the piano. But… She stared at the expanse of white flesh between the neckline and her throat before she opened the door to Tamina. She whispered, "Tamina, it's *really* low…"

"Girl, you're a woman. You've got more to fill it out than I have, and it's *not* too low. You're just not used to it."

Audra twisted to look at herself in the mirror from all

angles. Was that really her? She did like it.

"Pull your hair up," Tamina suggested, tipping her head. Audra swept her hair up and away from her face. "Think of a string of pearls and your hair up—that would be stunning." Of course, Tamina was right. "That ought to jump-start Mr. Dann." She giggled.

Audra grew fiercely hot. "What makes you think I'm trying to jump-start him?"

Tamina's lips curled into a mischievous smile as she directed a sidelong glance at Audra. "Aren't you?"

Audra sighed. "I wasn't thinking in terms of jump-starting him, but I would like to look a bit more fashionable than plain ol' sixth-grade English teacher in slacks. I'd settle for a 'Hey, you look terrific!' "

A knowing nod bobbed her friend's head. "Should do the trick. Now all you need is some kicky strap shoes."

"With kicky strap shoes, I'd probably kick the end of my toe on the pedal and turn red in the face trying not to howl in pain." They both giggled. "Thanks, but I think I'd better stick to pumps for playing."

Dann was waiting in front of her house when Audra finally arrived home. He sprinted across the lawn and met her at her car as she retrieved her sacks from the back seat.

"Looks like you had fun today." He nodded to the bags.

"I never knew having so much fun could totally wear you out. I'm bushed! I gave a music lesson, went out to lunch, shopped till I was ready to drop, and I'm only now getting home. I'll warn you, there's no dinner cooked."

"Guess we'll wing it, huh? What'd you get?"

"Can it be a surprise?" Clutching the bags in one hand, she unlocked the back door and climbed the steps to the kitchen. "I just got a dress to wear for the concert, but I need something to finish it out. Is that okay?" She didn't wait for an answer but proceeded through the house and chucked the bags on her bed. Coming back into the living room, she wilted onto the couch. "I need to sit a few minutes." When he sat on the other end, she put her head back and closed her eyes. "What did you do all day?"

"Vern, Jerold, and I rode Gravel Pit Road all the way out past the old quarry and on over to the highway and came back in that way."

"That was a pretty good ride, wasn't it?"

"Yes, but we've been talking about a longer ride. They want to ride to Albuquerque right after school is out."

Her eyes flew open. "You're kidding!"

"No. We're planning to leave June 4. The last day of school is May 25. Jerold's going to be tied up over Memorial Day since Francie's parents will be here for a week. Right after that, he's taking the family to the Grand Canyon for Francie's birthday. Vern leaves that week for Montana for the summer, so the fourth's about the only time we can do it."

"Wow. Sounds like an exciting undertaking. I'm envious." She drew herself upright and peered into his face. "This is totally changing the subject—so when's *your* birthday?"

His eyebrows arched with surprise. "March 30."

She calculated for a moment. "March 30! Wasn't that the day we drove back from Albuquerque?" Her forehead furrowed when he nodded. "You mean we drove all that way and you didn't say it was your birthday? Why?"

He shrugged. "I didn't want another birthday. I didn't want to have to say I turned thirty-four."

"Well, you rascal!" She leaned over and punched him in the arm. "You'll never believe what I did on your birthday. Of course, I had no idea it was your birthday, but after we got home that Friday, I went out and bought you a present and put it away. I was going to be all cool and find out when your birthday is and then cook dinner and give you your present, and here your birthday's already past." She laughed. "Well, Plan A didn't work, but I've been dying to give you the present. Sit here, and I'll be right back."

She hurried to the bedroom and drew the painting out from under the bed. She had wrapped it in a sheet to keep the dust off. She eased the sheet off and returned to the living room, calling out. "Close your eyes." She stood in front of him, holding the painting to face him. "Okay, you can open them."

His eyes focused on the painting. "Happy birthday," she whispered, searching his face.

All he could do was stare. His lips parted, but no words came. He slowly stood with his eyes still on the painting as she held it out to him. He took it in his hands, and his gaze moved over every inch of the canvas. He looked at her and then laid the frame on the couch. He enclosed her in his arms and rested his cheek on her head.

"Aud, I don't know what to say — I'm just speechless. Thank you, a thousand times over." He kept his arms around her as his voice softened. "I know how much it cost — it's so — so…"

She moved back only enough to lay a finger against his lips. "Shhh. Remember when you bought the keyboard for Rosa just because you wanted to? That's why I bought this. I love the picture as much as you do and wanted you to have it. That picture — that little boy is you."

"I know. I knew it the moment I first saw it." He ran his hands along her upper arms. "Okay, so when's your birthday?"

"August 3." She settled her hands in his and wished he'd hold her in his arms again. She wished he'd kiss her, but for now, she'd be satisfied with this.

On his way home, Dann relived how it had felt to hold her in his arms. He gave a long sigh. He wasn't sure he'd be able to keep the promise he'd made to himself.

On Sunday night, Audra brushed her hair before settling against her pillow, pulling her knees up, and resting her forehead on them. She and Dann had taken Rosa to the zoo in the afternoon. She'd been comfortable with her hand in his all afternoon, and a couple of times when he looked into her eyes it seemed like time stopped. *But does he love me? Last night, he held me like he does but…*

She tossed her brush in the drawer, crawled under the blankets, and stared at the ceiling. *Sometimes it seems like there's a hurdle that stymies him. I wonder if he still thinks about Gail?*

Her thoughts flitted from the walk at the zoo to Dann leaning closely over her as they peered out a drafty window on the top of a mountain to his hands on her waist at Tinker Town. She'd told God she wanted her relationship with Dann to be his will, but did she really? Did she truly want God's will for her life, or did she want God to do her will? Her heart lurched, and she hid her face under the covers. She'd already crossed a line — she was in love with Dann, and if God were to say no to a deeper relationship with him, her heart would break.

Her body gave an involuntary shiver. Her next biopsy was

only five days away. She was drawing closer to the time when she would be forced to tell Dann what was going on with her. Closer to the time when she would find out whether he would run or stay. Her stomach hardened into a knot. What had started out as happy thoughts had grown depressing, and it was after midnight before she fell asleep.

CHAPTER THIRTY-FIVE

PEARLS OR GOLD?

On Monday morning when Audra woke, her brain froze. She couldn't think of anything except her biopsy on Friday. Swinging her legs out of bed, her whole body felt leaden. She had to strong-arm the desire to dive back under the covers with sheer determination and a quick prayer to show up for work at all.

Before second period started, Taylor stopped at her desk. "Miss Knight?" He handed her a sheet of paper. A perky grin brightened his face below that unruly hair. "Look what I got." He shifted from foot to foot, seemingly having trouble containing his energy. "I finally got my score from when I played my solo in the competitions. I got three ones, and that's the best you can get!"

"Very well played," slanted across the bottom by those perfect three ones, and for the first time that day, she smiled. "How wonderful, Taylor. I'm proud of you."

"I'm sure glad you and Mr. D made me practice every day. I think I really am getting better." He took his paper back then leaned closer over her desk and put his hand to the side of his mouth. "I'm not going to tell anybody I saw you and Mr. D at Burger Basket."

"Well, thank you, Taylor, that's a very mature decision."

He bent closer again. "Mom said I need to respect your privacy." Tipping his head, he peered into her face. "Do you and Mr. D really like each other?"

"Taylor, Taylor, Taylor." She shook her finger at him, pressing her lips together to repress a smile of amusement. "Are you sure you know what it means to respect someone's privacy? Mr. D and I are friends, but that's all you need to know, okay?" Well, maybe she wasn't ready for the *whole* world to know she was in love with Dann.

Disappointment puckered his lips, but those bright eyes regained their sparkle just as quickly. "Okay, but I still won't tell anybody I saw you."

She stifled a laugh. *I needed that. But listen to this boy's romantic notions! A day will probably come when he gets his heart broken by a girl.*

The whole week dragged. By Friday, dread had a firm grip on Audra as she left school at lunchtime. Laney picked her up at one thirty to drive her to the doctor. She turned onto Main Street. "How are you doing, Audie?"

"Okay." The wind sucked her quiet answer out the open window. The rest of the ride was silent.

Audra felt detached. She answered questions from the nurse and Dr. Rhonda with a minimum of words, and during the procedure, her brain darted here and there with inconsequential thoughts. However, the one she especially wanted to ignore repeatedly invaded her mind: *How am I going to tell Dann?* When she finally walked back into the waiting room, Laney opened the exit door, and they left without a word.

"Are you sure you're all right?" Laney asked in the car.

"Yes."

"Do you want to come over for dinner? I can take you home later."

"No, I just want to be alone for a while."

"Audie, you're not all right. What's wrong?"

Her eyes started to sting, and she closed them. "I keep alternating between feeling afraid and resigned. Right now, I feel both. I just don't think it's going to be good news." She faced the window, ending their conversation.

Laney entered the house with her, but Audra remained quiet. "I'm just going to lie down for a bit," she finally said.

She barely responded when Laney hugged her.

Easing back, Laney squeezed her hands. "I'll call you tomorrow."

At eight o'clock, the telephone awakened Audra. Disoriented, she simply blinked at the darkened room for two rings before plodding to the kitchen to answer it. "Audra, this is Dr. Rhonda. I just wanted to check and see how you're doing. Is everything all right?"

"I think so. I was sound asleep, but I think I'm all right."

"You were awfully quiet when you were here. Are you depressed?"

"Yes, I suppose I am. I don't think it's as bad as it was this afternoon, though. It's going to be a long wait."

"I know. I'll call you as soon as I get the results. You be sure and call if the depression doesn't lift."

After Audra hung up, she fixed a can of chicken noodle soup and ate crackers and cheese with it. Then slept until nine fifteen Saturday morning.

Even with all that sleep, she still didn't feel ready to get up, and she didn't feel like pushing herself. She'd already canceled her piano lesson with Rosa and Mrs. Espinosa, the same as she had with her Friday student. She was supposed to take it easy today, so she rolled over and drifted back to sleep.

When she woke again at eleven, she felt much better. Perhaps the depression had merely been a byproduct of all her anxiety plus pushing herself to play duets twice a week. She lounged on the couch reading until two when she couldn't stand the inactivity one more moment. She drove to the mall to look for a necklace to wear with her new black dress.

She wasn't satisfied with anything she found at the jewelry counter in Hudson's, so she sauntered through the mall, unwilling to hurry. She stopped in front of a jewelry store and studied the diamond rings, necklaces, and watches in the window display. Beyond them, a black necklace glowed on a small velveteen bust atop a glass display case. Drawn toward it, she entered the store, and up close beneath the spotlights, the string of black pearls gleamed — gorgeous and expensive.

Further along the counters, a long necklace of several very thin gold strands loosely twisted together into an elegant rope teased her. *Oh, it's beautiful.* She tried to imagine herself in the black dress, sexy strap shoes, and this graceful necklace. She heard Tamina's voice in her mind, "That should jump-start Mr. Dann."

What was she thinking!

"Do you need help, ma'am?"

She backed away from the showcase. "Uh…no. I need more time…" She hastily left the store but settled into a slow walk on her way to the food court. She bought a Coke and sat at an empty corner table. What on earth *had* she been thinking? It was almost like she was trying to compete with Gail and Jasmine.

She nearly choked on her soda. *Is that what this is about?* Dann had said they were both beautiful. Was she subconsciously trying to compete with two faceless ghosts of women? She toyed with the paper from her straw, wrapping it around her finger and then unwrapping it again.

Why was she suddenly trying to remake herself? Was she trying to impress Dann by emulating those women? Did she think she could hold onto him by trying to be glamorous? *Oh, dear Lord, I hope it's not that! I've never been glamorous — I'm too conservative.* She crumpled the straw wrapper. *Just be yourself,* she scolded silently.

The image came back into focus. The black dress with the black pearls and the closed-toe, open-heeled black shoes with back straps she'd chosen as a compromise to plain pumps, and her hair down—even if Tamina thought it would be stunning worn up. She didn't want to force stunning. She wanted to look nice for Dann and professional for the students and parents, but most of all she needed to feel confident in who she was.

She bought the pearls. By then, she'd been on her feet too long.

Since Dann was spending the day with his orchestra students at their competition, he wouldn't arrive for dinner until six. She needed to go home and rest. She'd call out for pizza.

Dann arrived at six fifteen full of enthusiasm. He set his instruments by the piano, came back out to the kitchen, leaned over her as she was preparing the salad, and snatched a tomato slice. "Mmm, smells like pizza. What'd you do all day?"

"Very little. I called off my lessons and took some time out."

He moved to look at her face. "Everything all right?"

She hesitated.

He touched her chin and tipped her face toward his. "What's wrong?"

"I'm just feeling kind of melancholy today. I'll be all right." She turned back to the counter and sliced the cucumber.

He moved behind her and gently placed his hands on her hips. With his face near her ear, his breath was warm on her neck. "Is there anything I can do to help?" he whispered.

She lifted her face toward the ceiling and closed her eyes. Every nerve in her body was reacting. *I can't do this today. He's too close, and all I want is for him to hold me.* She swallowed hard. One little pivot and she would be in his arms. But if she did, she'd cry and end up blubbering and telling him what was going on. *I'm still not ready to share something so personal.*

She slipped away from him and shoved the salad into his hands. "Here, you can put the salad on the table." She rammed the cucumber peelings, tomato stems, and unused romaine leaves into the garbage bag and washed her hands. After she dried them, she swallowed hard again and held her hands out to him. "I guess the thing that will help the most is if you play me some beautiful music."

Her smile, when it came, was a bit lopsided.

On Sunday, Dann didn't come by after church while she and Tamina were eating leftover pizza. Tamina nibbled her pizza crust. "I thought Dann would show, but as long as he's not here, tell me how the biopsy went."

Audra grimaced toward the table. "I'm sorry — I didn't call you, did I? I had some cramping during the procedure, but nothing else. It's just I've been so blasted depressed."

"Worried?"

"More than I want to admit. I wasn't very good company for Dann last night, so I wouldn't blame him if he didn't want to come today. I just don't feel like it's going to be a good report, and it's going to be hellish waiting all week to find out." Pushing her pizza away with one hand, she rested her chin in the other.

"Girl, you *are* depressed. You need to get out and do something to get those miserable stress toxins out of your body. Want to run?"

Audra shook her head. "No, it's too soon, but I'll walk a little way. I think just getting out will do me some good."

They walked westward from Lake Patterson on the path that followed the creek trickling from the pond. The wind was blowing, and Audra twisted her hair into a loose tail before stuffing it inside the back of her jacket. Normally, she didn't like being out in the wind, but today as it buffeted her face, billowed her jacket, and whooshed through the cottonwood branches, it was almost as if God himself was drawing the depression out of her. It felt good.

They walked as far as the fence surrounding the old Chandler homes. The back of Josiah's mansion, as well as the museum housed in Josiah's son's gray, two-story house peeped through the trees.

"Thank you, Dr. Tamina. I do feel better," Audra said, breathing deeply as they returned to the car.

"If you think it would help, would you want to try running again when you're up to it?"

"I should. Let me take it one day at a time, and I'll let you know. Dann and I are practicing twice a week again, and it doesn't leave me much time." As they were getting into the car, Audra noticed Tamina checking her watch. "Is Franklin going to call?"

"Yes. He had today off, so he'll be calling early. He was going out on his bike with a friend, but he said he'd be back by four."

"Does he have any intention of coming to see you?"

Tamina grinned. "He's trying for Memorial Day weekend."

Audra was home only twenty minutes when Dann called. "Hey, where've you been?"

Just the sound of his voice perked her up. "Tamina shooed me out of the house for a walk. Where've you been?"

"Well, I was on my way over to your house this noon when I noticed the tires on the Jeep were almost bald. I got tires, and by the time I got to your place, you were gone. I spent a very boring afternoon. Would you like to do something?"

Audra thought for a moment. "You know what I'd really like to do? Rent an old musical and eat popcorn and apples, but I don't think I have any popcorn."

"I'll pick some up. *My Fair Lady* old enough?"

"I love it." She leaned against the doorframe after she hung up the phone and hugged her arms around herself, comforted by knowing her moodiness hadn't run him off.

CHAPTER THIRTY-SIX

THE HAMMER COMES DOWN

THE SCHOOL WEEK STARTING ON APRIL 23 WAS COMPLETELY ORDI-
nary. Audra thought she'd make it through without giving in to
anxiety, but still, she was grateful when Tamina urged her to try
to run on Tuesday evening. They jogged one minute, then walked
three minutes for four sets. It did help to subdue the stress.

When Dann came on Wednesday, she focused on the music
to keep her calm. After they ate chicken sandwiches at Yellow
Rooster, she suggested they go for a walk. He drove to the east
side of Lake Patterson, and they walked hand-in-hand westward on the trail as the sun sank through pink and gold clouds.
By the time they got back to the car, anxiety was trying to press
in again. Dr. Rhonda would be calling soon, and the hammer
would come down. She couldn't put off telling him much longer.

The call came the next day. When she checked her voicemail
after school, Dr. Rhonda's nurse said, "Please come in tomorrow
after school. Dr. Rhonda has your report."

Audra dialed Patty's number and apologized to her mother
because she'd have to cancel her Friday lesson again. Her throat
was so tight she could barely speak. Then she dialed Tamina. "I
need to run again tonight." Her voice cracked.

"Dr. Rhonda called?"

"Her nurse. All she said was to come in and talk tomorrow afternoon. That's not a good sign. You only have to go in if it's bad news."

"Do you want to run after your lesson?"

"Uh-huh."

"I'll pick you up at five thirty."

Audra hung up. Pensive, she leaned against the kitchen doorjamb out of habit. She'd tried to tell herself the abnormal cells might be gone, but she knew they weren't. It was going to mean a hysterectomy. She rested her head against the cool woodwork, a sense of loss almost overwhelming her. If only Dann were there to hold her in his arms and comfort her, but that wasn't going to happen. The dread over what she feared Dr. Rhonda was going to tell her dropped over her like a suffocating shroud. *Lord, I'm so scared.*

The next afternoon Audra was shown into Dr. Rhonda's consultation office. Sliding into the chair facing her desk, she fumbled her purse to the floor and waited for the doctor to look up. The nurse closed the door with a click.

"How are you today, Audra?" Dr. Rhonda pushed a strand of hair off her face.

Audra studied her face before glancing at the familiar photo of her and her family. She chewed her lip. "To tell you the truth, I'm scared. I don't think you have good news for me."

Her throat closed at the almost imperceptible tightening of the doctor's lips.

"Audra, I wanted very much to buy you some time. I had hoped you would be clear this time, and we could just keep watch every six months." She nodded toward her computer screen. "The biopsy shows abnormal cells still present. There's just no way to know how long before those cells could change, so I think it's time to make a decision." She tapped her pen on her desk pad and took a deep breath. "The general recommendation for this type of hyperplasia is hysterectomy. It's my opinion we've done all we can, and with your risk quotient as high as it is, my advice is you should have the surgery."

Audra stared at the desk in front of her. What she'd dreaded hearing was now reality.

"I don't think you should wait."

When Audra lifted her face, Dr. Rhonda's eyes were tender. "I will be gone for an extended time starting the end of May, and I'd like to see this resolved before I leave. You're thirty-three, which is young for this, but if any of those cells turn cancerous, then your treatment will be radically different. I don't want you to go through that. Do you agree with me?"

"I have to." Audra forced the shaky words out. "I didn't want it to turn out this way, but I'm too scared not to go through with it." She felt far away and detached.

"I was hoping for a better outcome, too. You'll have to make an appointment with a surgeon—no, in fact, I'm going to make the appointment for you now." She buzzed her nurse and wrote something on a pad. The nurse took it and went out again.

Audra squeezed her hands together. "It's rather ironic..." Her voice strained to stay even. "The hardest thing I've struggled with over the last three months is the fact that, after being single all these years, now there's a man in my life..." Her voice trailed off, and a tear slid down her cheek. They both sat without speaking until the nurse returned.

Dr. Rhonda slid an appointment card across the desk toward her. "Dr. Samuels is a very good surgeon. He will see you Wednesday, May 9 at ten o'clock."

She didn't even care if she'd have to take another half day off. She just wanted to escape as quickly as possible.

She drove straight to Tamina's. When Tamina opened the door, Audra didn't wait to be invited in. Clutching Tamina's hand, she propelled the two of them into the living room. Her shimmering tears blurred Tamina's face as she slumped onto the white couch. "I have to have a hysterectomy. Soon." Hunching over, she pressed her elbows to her knees and hid her face in her hands.

Tamina knelt in front of her on the turquoise rug. "Oh, girl!" she whispered. "I've prayed and prayed this wouldn't happen." Tenderly, she wrapped her arms around Audra, and they sobbed together. Tamina held Audra until she calmed. Then she let go and ran to the bathroom, returning with a box of tissues.

"Thanks." Audra released pent-up air. "I'm still numb. It's been an emotional merry-go-round for seven months…it doesn't feel real." She laid her head back on the couch. "I kept trying to convince myself everything was going to be all right, but I knew in my heart it was going to turn out this way." She faced Tamina. "How am I going to tell Dann?"

"What do you mean, how? Can't you just tell him?"

"What do I say? Dann, I'm crazy in love with you, but if you ever get around to asking me to marry you, I won't be able to give you a family?"

Tamina flinched with a quick jerk of her head before contemplating Audra's words for several moments. Then she squeezed Audra's knee. "Are you doubting he's in love with you? Hasn't he given you any indication?"

"He's given me plenty of indications that he likes me, but he's never told me he loves me—he's never kissed me."

While Tamina's lips parted and her eyes widened, Audra closed her eyes. It was almost as embarrassing as confessing she'd never sneaked off to drink beer.

"Oh. I guess I assumed by this time..." She fell silent again.

"I know, it's a little out of the ordinary."

"Do you have any idea what's going on with him?"

Audra sat up, chucked the damp Kleenexes, and riveted her gaze on Tamina's face. "He's been married and he's divorced."

Tamina's eyebrows arched above widening black eyes. "How long have you known?"

"Since Thanksgiving. He was hurt, and now he's being extra cautious. He's healing, and I've decided I can wait for him to finish the process. But well, he wanted a family and his wife refused, and now, if anything comes of our relationship, I'll never give him a family, either. He's being cheated out of something he wants very much." Audra snatched another handful of tissue. "I'm sorry, I thought I was done crying. But I've been grappling with this and wondering if I really do know what God's will is."

Supporting her elbows on her knees, she pressed the tissue against her eyes. "God knows I've fallen in love with Dann. I've told him I want his leading, but I'm still scared I might lose Dann if I tell him I have to have the surgery." Tears were soaking through the tissue.

Tamina pulled more tissue from the box, slid closer, and snugged her arm around Audra's shoulders. "Girlfriend," her voice came whisper soft. "I've watched the relationship between you and Dann go from zero to zing, and I've been excited and happy as it's unfolded. But I didn't know all this other stuff was going on. I hurt because you hurt—go ahead, cry it all out." She pushed another fistful of tissue into Audra's hand and kept her arm around her as fresh sobs shook Audra's whole body.

Audra snuffed and tossed the wad of wet tissue on top of the others. *My face must be a blotchy mess.* She ran her fingers through her hair. "I've just moved from the Big C to the Big H. Just pray God will give me the right words to tell Dann."

"I already have." Tamina grinned, her teeth flashing white. "Are you okay now?"

"Yes." Audra caught Tamina's hand in a heartfelt squeeze. "Thanks for being there for me."

Tamina gave her one last hug. "I was planning to grill a cheese sandwich and open a can of tomato soup. Why don't you stay and have something to eat?"

On Saturday morning, Audra set her coffee cup on the counter and scowled at the calendar hanging next to the telephone. April 28. Anxiety and fear had taken up the whole month, relegating spring to a monotone of drab. After a long talk with Laney, she was surprised by how peaceful she felt. But what was she going to say to Dann?

Sunshine splashed the patio beyond the kitchen windows. *I wish I could spend the whole day with him.* But he was riding with Jerold and Vern getting ready for their Albuquerque trek. Besides, she had to go see Rosa and Mrs. Espinosa. She checked her watch. If she hurried, she would have time to stop by the music store and get them new books.

Rosa played flawlessly, but Mrs. Espinosa's fingers weren't as nimble on sixteenth notes. Audra introduced them to the last two songs in their kindergarten book and showed them the books they would graduate to. Just as they were finishing, Rosa's friend, Sadie, came to the door with Doofus on a leash. Mrs. Espinosa gave Rosa permission to walk with her, and the girl bounded out the door.

"Since the weather is warming up, she needs to be out more," Mrs. Espinosa stated as she settled in her easy chair. "She would spend her whole day at the keyboard if I'd let her."

"I'm glad she went out for a little bit. I wanted to talk to you alone."

"Oh?" Mrs. Espinosa's face seemed less wrinkled with her upward gaze.

"I wanted to tell you I found out I have to have a hysterectomy."

Mrs. Espinosa's mouth pursed as she picked at the arm of her chair.

Audra rushed on, "Things aren't quite right inside, and the doctor wants me to have the surgery before it turns into cancer."

The old woman motioned Audra closer. When Audra dropped to her knees in front of her, Mrs. Espinosa grabbed both of her wrists and gripped them tightly. "You have that operation just as quick as you can. Do you hear me? My granddaughter, Lorraine, didn't have it done fast enough, and she died."

Her black eyes pierced right into Audra's soul, and like a mother's compassion, it was balm to her hurts and fears.

"You are so good to me and Rosa. You're like a daughter to me — better than the only granddaughter I have left, and Rosa loves you very, very much. Don't you go dying on us, you hear?"

Audra gently pried one wrist free and patted her hand. "I still have to see the surgeon, but I'm sure it will be soon. And, Lord willing, I'll come through everything just fine." She rose to go. Would she be this calm when she talked to Dann?

As she left the Espinosa's, her whole inner being seemed to roil with restlessness. She didn't know what she wanted to cook for dinner. She didn't even know if she *wanted* to cook.

Leaving her car in the driveway, she walked to the back-yard. The daffodils had been spent for weeks. Now, the iris shoots were pushing up fat, green buds, getting ready for their annual splash. Spring had passed her by. The restlessness inten-sified as if something inside her wanted to fly away — be free, but she couldn't define what. Perhaps just spring fever.

Dann wouldn't arrive until midafternoon, but she wished she didn't have to wait so long. She didn't know how she was going to tell him about it, but she wanted to be with him. She bolted up the steps to the kitchen, clutched the telephone receiver, and punched in his cell.

Hearing music in the background, she let out a surprised, "Oh! You're home already. I was going to leave a message."

"Got here five minutes ago. What can I do for you?"

"You can take me up to the cave and drink beer with me!" Her hand flew up and covered her mouth. That was the most impulsive, asinine thing she'd ever said. She plopped into a kitchen chair, running her free hand through her hair.

He gave a little laugh. "Did I hear you correctly, or do you want to repeat it?"

"You heard correctly, and I can't believe I said it. No, I can believe it. I don't know why, but something inside me today just wants to…" She paused, fishing for the right word.

"Wants to do something wild and crazy?"

"That'll describe it well enough, I suppose."

"Sounds like an adventure I don't want to miss. How soon do you want to go?"

"Have you had lunch?"

"No."

"I'll pack sandwiches if you bring beer."

When Dann spotted the footpath leading off the main trail, Audra followed him. Winding through desert plants, she stifled a sneeze. Chamisa bushes always made her nose ticklish, and she didn't care for the smell of them, either. When the trail grew rockier with the climb, she was grateful to get away from the stiff grass that sawed at her bare ankles. *Sure glad I'm wearing jeans.*

Stopping where the trail crossed the arroyo, she rested against a boulder taller than herself, panting. "I still say this is a lot of work to sneak a beer."

Dann laughed at her and found another rock to lean on. After a minute, he grabbed her hand. "Come on, the steep part is still ahead."

He hiked faster than Tamina had on this part, and Audra's breath came in gulps. As the footing became more precarious, she tested each step, making certain her sneakers gripped the rocky trail. Finally, they twisted around the last rock outcropping and stood in the small clearing in front of the cave. She kicked two beer cans out of the way before dropping to the hard ground. She leaned back against the tallest boulder. "Guess I need to get a bike and get in shape, huh?"

He slid his daypack off his shoulders and sat beside her. "I'd love it if you got a bike." He took her hand in his. "So, tell me, is there a reason for coming up here to drink beer?"

"Probably." She chewed on her lip and looked off in the distance. "I need to tell you something, but let's eat first. I'm starving."

After unzipping his pack, he handed one tuna sandwich to her and let the other fall into his lap. Next, he opened a can of beer and, after passing it to her, opened one for himself.

She raised her can as if to make a toast but then, without a word, took a swallow. *I don't even like beer.* She ate half her sandwich and more sips of beer in silence.

He kept glancing over at her, but she couldn't look him in the eye. He waited in silence. She took two bites out of the second half of her sandwich and set the beer can on the ground.

"I don't know where to start."

"Well, give me the headlines, and then fill in the details."

She drew her knees close to her body, folded her arms across her knees, and rested her forehead on them, her unfinished sandwich limp in her hand. She didn't speak again for nearly a minute. Finally, turning her face up and looking into his face, she said, "I...have...to have a hysterectomy."

His forehead furrowed, his eyebrows knit together, and his eyes searched her face. But she couldn't read him.

"When?"

"Probably as soon as school lets out. I don't see the surgeon until the ninth of May." She allowed her last piece of sandwich to drop on the ground and put her head on her arms again.

He leaned forward and slipped his arm around her shoulders. "When did you find this out?" His soft breath brushed her ear.

"Yesterday." She sat up straight again and fished in her jeans pocket for a tissue. "I'm sorry. I cried my heart out at Tamina's yesterday, but I thought maybe I could make it through without bawling today." She pressed the tissue to her eyes.

"Hey, it's all right to cry." He pulled her closer to himself until her head rested on his shoulder. Her hand crept up and cupped his other shoulder.

"I've been an emotional wreck for the last couple of weeks, but then you most likely noticed." A short laugh escaped her lips.

"Why didn't you tell me?"

She sighed. "Last August when the doctor first discovered something was wrong—something that could turn into cancer if it wasn't dealt with—I didn't even know you, and then I didn't feel comfortable revealing something so personal. The last several months I've been trying to con myself into believing everything would be okay and I wouldn't have to have the surgery. It's been extremely tough accepting that I'll never have a family." A tear ran down her cheek and splashed on the front of his shirt before she could catch it. She dabbed her eyes. "I'm thirty-three. I always thought I was content being single, but something inside me never gave up hoping someday I'd still be a mother. But now…"

His free arm scooped around her, and he held her tightly. "Oh, Aud, Aud… I'm so sorry." He was still holding her when they heard the crunch of approaching feet on the rocks. She sat up straight beside him and wiped her eyes again. Two teenagers, a boy and a girl, stepped into the clearing.

"Hi." Dann gave them a short wave. "You come up to have a beer, too?"

The girl blushed and jerked away. The boy grabbed her hand. "Come on, let's go up higher," he said.

They exited the clearing and clambered up the rocky path. Dann and Audra laughed once they were out of earshot.

She picked up her can of beer and studied it. The way he held her she knew he was genuinely sorry, not put off. She felt calmer, but there was still something else. "You want to know about the beer?" She tipped the can in front of her. "Asking you to bring me up here to drink beer was totally unplanned, believe me. I was shocked at myself—but as soon as I said it, I knew it's what I needed." She peered off into the distance.

"When I was a teenager, I never, ever rebelled outwardly against my father, even though I wanted to many times. Laney rebelled and had nothing but grief for five years. I never wanted a man like either of the ones who gave Laney trouble, and I surely didn't want a husband like my father." She brought her gaze back at him.

"I've had to struggle the last couple of weeks thinking it unfair how Laney rebelled and has a family, but I didn't rebel and won't have one. If I had defied my father like she did, maybe I'd have a family—but not necessarily happiness."

She shrugged and then traced her finger along the beer can. "When we were up here with Tamina a couple of weeks ago and

I had to admit I'd never been up here, I felt like I'd been cheated out of something everyone else got to do, even if in rebellion. After all these years, I felt left out—sort of like I'd missed a rite of passage. Coming up here today is just acting out what my heart longed to do for years." She pressed her thumb against the side of the aluminum can, denting it. Then she threw it hard. It bounced and plowed across other discarded cans before the cave, coming to rest at the base of the weathered pile that silently declared the rebellion of every teen who made the trip. As the last of the beer spilled from the opening, creating a dark stain on the dry dirt, her final pent-up anger drained away. She gave a little humph. "There. Now I can say, been there, done that."

He drained his can and crushed it with one hand. He flipped it across the clearing, landing it near hers. Then he touched her chin, turning her face toward his, his expression serious. "I'm glad you didn't rebel. If you had a husband and children, I never would've found you."

With little space between their faces, she could have easily touched her lips against his, but she merely tipped her head and rested against his shoulder. *Such precious words. Words of hope.* He wasn't going to walk out, and she'd get through the hysterectomy.

CHAPTER THIRTY-SEVEN

THE CONCERTS AND BEYOND

AUDRA DIDN'T SEE DANN AGAIN UNTIL THE BAND CONCERT Wednesday. Precisely at seven, he picked up his microphone and welcomed parents, families, and friends to the spring concert. The fifth-grade beginning students formed a semicircle in chairs facing their audience, ready and waiting for Dann to pick up his baton.

All three bands played skillfully, each displaying a pleasantly surprising improvement. When the concert band took its bow and the final applause died, Dann faced the bleachers, microphone in hand.

"Thank you. Thank you, very much." He smiled broadly. "I am extremely proud of your students for their hard work and the progress they achieved this year. A month ago, Chandler's middle-school band students attended a competition for the first time in four years, and I'm pleased to announce that, not only did our bands receive good marks, but three students took perfect scores in individual competition—Alice Jackson, Kitty Matthews, and Taylor Bailey."

When Dann signaled with his hand for the three to rise, applause broke out again. Taylor bowed, grinning from ear to ear.

"And now, we have a special treat. Our sixth-grade English teacher, Miss Knight, has been very instrumental this year in motivating our music students to better practice habits. About two months ago, she joined me in playing some duets during class time, and due to a unanimous request from all the students, she is with us again this evening." Dann motioned her to stand, announcing, "Miss Audra Knight!"

Audra stood as welcoming applause rippled across the gym. A smile stretched her lips while she scanned the audience. Tamina sat on the bottom row of bleachers right in the center, flanked by Mrs. Espinosa and Rosa. What a surprise! Tamina hadn't said she was bringing them. And Sheldon Bentley stood at the end of the bleachers, clapping along with everyone else.

When Audra directed her attention to Dann, his eyebrows rose as if it were the first time he'd noticed her dress that evening. She smiled and held his eyes before she sat at the piano.

The Celtic sound of "The Thornbirds" was followed by the quieter, romantic "Annie." The flowing music effortlessly flooded the gym with melodious sound. The applause after their second song echoed loud and sustained. As he motioned her to stand and they took their bow, the students began chanting, "More, more!"

Dann held up his hand for silence and stepped over to Audra with a grin on his face.

" 'Harmonium' or 'Alley Cat'?" he asked.

"How about both? 'Alley Cat' first."

As the applause was dying, he pivoted to the piano, lifting his hand for her to stand. They stood together and took their bow as one last round of applause resounded. Her legs were shaking. She'd never experienced such recognition for her playing, and she felt flushed with excitement.

After he thanked everyone for coming, Rosa darted across the gym floor and stood in front of her. "Oh, Miss Audra, that was soooo beautiful! I want to play the piano like that someday."

Audra spoke softly in her ear. "You just keep practicing the way you have been, and you'll be a wonderful piano player."

Tamina and Mrs. Espinosa joined Rosa, and Tamina hugged Audra. "Hey, girlfriend, awesome performance." She held her hand to the side of her mouth. "I saw Dann's face when you stood up—I told you this dress would electrify him!" She held Audra at arm's length, her eyes bright with glee.

"Don't make me blush." Audra laughed.

When she hugged Mrs. Espinosa, the older lady squeezed her tightly. "What a wonderful, wonderful concert. I want to come again tomorrow night."

Then Audra was aware of students giving Dann high fives or smiling and speaking to him. Now they were approaching her by the piano. Boys and girls from her sixth-grade English classes, plus students she'd had one and two years earlier pressed around her to say how much they enjoyed their music. Knowing these kids appreciated what Dann and she had done made her heart pound with the most amazing sensation.

When everyone started drifting away, Taylor Bailey, who'd been standing off to the side still carrying his trumpet, came and stood in front of her.

She took a deep breath. "Well, Taylor, what do you think?"

He flashed a mischievous grin. "I think I was right. You and Mr. D make beautiful music together."

Audra couldn't help but return his grin as his mother joined them, carrying his trumpet case.

Gripping the case handle in one hand, Joyce Bailey slipped her arm around her son's shoulders. "I certainly enjoyed your music, and I can better understand why Taylor keeps telling me how much he likes to hear you play. He's been working a lot harder on his own music, too."

"I'm proud of his scores at the competition," Audra said,

smiling at Taylor. "Thank you for stopping. I'm glad you enjoyed our music."

"Here—go put your horn away." Mrs. Bailey handed her son his trumpet case. After he walked over to the bleachers, she faced Audra. "Thank you for the way you handled Taylor's problem. Allan and I were speechless when Mr. Bentley told us what he had done. It was quite embarrassing for us. Mr. Bentley explained to us how you and Mr. Day suggested his practicing after school. We are both," she swallowed hard, obviously struggling to speak, "very grateful for the kind, forgiving way you treated Taylor and the whole situation—thank you again."

"You're most welcome," Audra responded, swallowing a lump in her own throat.

After Joyce Bailey walked off, Audra blinked with surprise. With all the cleanup swirling around them, Heather Easton was talking to Dann, and Vern Gilbert was standing next to her. *Dann's smiling, so Heather mustn't have said anything disturbing.* Stepping away from Dann, Heather and Vern approached her. Audra picked up her music and waited.

"Hello, Audra." Heather held out her hand.

Audra clutched her music. *Is her smile for real? Maybe a bit tentative? Her eyes aren't steely. So, do I trust her?* She forced her hand, stiffened by caution, to accept Heather's firm handshake.

"We enjoyed your music. You *do* play very well together."

Relaxing, she let her hand linger a moment in Heather's. "Thank you, Heather. It's nice of you to say so." *Is she conceding the battle? Why is she with Vern? Am I acting like I really forgave her?* She squeezed Heather's hand and allowed a smile to overtake her face. She didn't move her eyes from Heather's until she finally returned a smile that seemed genuine.

"Well, we have to get going. We'll see ya." Slipping her hand around Vern's arm, she started off, her long hair swishing across her back.

Vern glanced over his shoulder and grinned. "It was great." Then he followed Heather's lead.

Audra watched their backs as they walked away. When she turned back, Dann was nearing her. "Was that an apology or what?"

"I'm not sure. It was either an apology, or she wants us to know her attention is on Vern, now." His eyes twinkled as he brought his hand from behind his back and laid a bouquet of pink roses in her arm. "Your first concert deserves more than just applause."

She nestled her face against the soft petals. "Thank you. So much." Their eyes met, communicating a bit more than a present of flowers and a murmured thank you.

Dann cleared his throat. "The janitors are going to dolly the piano back to the band room, and then I can leave. Will you wait for me?"

"Of course."

He clasped her hand as they crossed the dimly lit parking lot toward her car. "Aud, thank you, again. Your music was fantastic as usual, but I also want you to know you look stunning this evening."

So, she looked stunning after all! She gave his hand a squeeze. "Thank you."

Her voice sounded demure, but as she looked up at the stars hanging in the black spring sky, she could see herself bounding across the parking lot in long leaps and pirouettes, her arms flung open with joy. So many unexpected things had happened this evening, but Dann's compliment had set her heart singing.

The orchestra concert the next evening was a repeat performance of the band concert with some minor variations. Audra was prepared for the applause, but an accompanying emotion surprised her. Hard to define, it was as if something inside her was yearning to do more with her music. But where could she find time to do more?

After Rosa told Dann how much she enjoyed the concert, she reminded him that she hadn't seen much of him lately. Dann promised to do something with her as soon as possible, and as soon as Rosa left with Tamina and Mrs. Espinosa, Sheldon Bentley approached.

Dressed in his personal school uniform, white dress shirt, navy dress pants and tie, he beamed like a new father. He hiked his arm over the top of the piano. "I was skeptical when Dann first approached me about playing duets, but I believe this is going to prove a great boon for our music program." He stood straight and shot his hand to Dann. "Thanks, both of you, for a job well done."

"Thank you, sir." Dann pumped Sheldon's hand warmly. "Thank you for giving my idea a chance."

Shaking Audra's hand, he added, "This has been successful beyond my expectations."

"And I thank you for allowing me to be part of it all," she added, still a bit nonplussed over what she was feeling.

After Dann locked the band room, he took her hand in his as they strolled down West Hall to the front doors. "Saturday night I'd like to take you back to Knights & Pawns. Would you wear that gorgeous dress, again?"

She didn't have to think about it. "I'd love to, but will you dress up, too?"

He squeezed her hand. "It's a date."

By six o'clock, tables were already filling quickly at Knights

& Pawns. Conversations buzzed as servers delivered drinks and took orders. Dann lightly touched Audra's elbow as they followed Marsha to a table toward the back of the restaurant. He pulled Audra's chair out and turned to Marsha.

"Something's different. Did you install a new window here?"

She waited for him to sit. "We did. And I thought you might enjoy sitting by it." She handed each of them a menu. "It's dark out there right now, but maybe you can see the new fountain we had installed. Next, we'll be adding flowers in pots and planters, and in a couple more weeks, we'll have tables out there, too."

"That's fantastic, Marsha!" Audra pressed closer to the multipaned window, trying to get a better view of the new patio.

"Thanks." Marsha eyed each of them in turn. "You're all decked out. Are you celebrating something?"

Dann glanced into Audra's eyes a moment, then at Marsha. "Well, part of it is teacher appreciation night. Audra has given a lot of time and talent to helping our music program these last months, and I wanted to take her out to the best restaurant in town to thank her."

"You came to the right place. Enjoy." Marsha returned to the hostess stand, her skirt swishing gracefully as she walked.

After Marsha moved away, Dann observed Vern and Heather three tables over, already eating. He ignored them. *If Audra hasn't noticed them, I won't call attention to them.* He ordered wine.

He leaned back in his chair, let his gaze settle on Audra, and admired her in that knockout dress. Drawing in a silent breath, he drummed his fingers on his leg. *Start a conversation, buddy, before you lose it.* "What did you do all day?"

She unwrapped her silverware and spread her napkin in her lap. "After I went to Rosa's, I frittered the day away. I needed a day off—I didn't even sit down at the piano." A puzzled look passed over her face before she tilted her head in her characteristic way. "If *part* of this is teacher appreciation, what's the other part?"

Enjoying her long-lashed brown eyes as they held his, her pink lips as they curved, and her hair as the ends curled and brushed her shoulders, he leaned forward and placed his hand over hers. "Just because you're on my mind—all the time." *And you have no idea how much.* The long look across the table lingered until the arrival of their wine broke the spell.

Halfway through his salmon and baked potato, he knew the only thing on his mind was holding her in his arms. *And if I cave in, I'll never keep my promise. Change the subject—do something.* He nodded to a point beyond her. "Are you aware Vern and Heather are sitting a few tables behind you?"

"No. Do they seem to be having a good time?"

"Well, Vern's been grinning like a Cheshire cat." Dann took two more bites. "I wonder what would happen if we invited them over for coffee and dessert?" He glanced up to find Audra's eyes wide with surprise.

"Are you serious?"

"Oh, I don't know. It was just a thought." After a pause, he added, "Do you think it would be too awkward?"

She placed her fork on the edge of her plate. "It did sound like she was trying to apologize the other night. I–I guess I've never thought to reach out to her like a friend. Do you suppose Vern sees something in her we haven't seen?" Her voice faltered. "I… suppose we could give her another chance."

He tilted his head to her. "You're sure?"

"I'm sure."

"Okay, let's do it." He put his hand out to catch their waiter's attention and asked him to take a message to Vern. The waiter spoke to Vern, Vern and Heather discussed the question, and Vern smiled back at the waiter and nodded.

"Your friends said they would be delighted to join you," the waiter reported back before walking off.

They finished their meal quickly, and as soon as their waiter removed their plates, Vern and Heather moved over to their table. "You barely caught us with your message. We were just about to leave." Vern slid into a chair, letting Heather pull her own.

"Would you care for dessert and coffee? My treat," Dann invited. Heather and Vern decided to split a piece of carrot cake, Dann and Audra an apple crisp.

"What did you do today?" Audra directed to Heather.

"Vern and I went for a bike ride."

Dann shot a quizzical glance at Vern. They had ridden thirty miles in the morning.

Audra cocked her head toward Heather. "Oh, I didn't know you liked to ride."

"I'm a newbie. Vern wanted me to get a bike so we could ride together. We rode partway around Jeremy Chandler Drive and back to my place." She flashed a smile at Vern.

"I'm a glutton for punishment, huh?" Vern grinned at Dann.

Dann leaned back in his chair, intrigued by the dynamics at the table. Heather seemed to be vacillating between being captivated by Vern and nervously searching for a way to make amends with Audra. *At least I'm off her radar.*

Heather tore her eyes off Vern long enough to lean toward Audra. "I like your dress. Isn't that what you wore for the concert?"

"Yes, and Dann requested I wear it again tonight. Playing at the band concert was the result of some pretty awesome feedback from his students. I'm glad you were there."

A smile tugged at Dann's lips. *Aud's amazing. In complete control — I think Heather knows it, too.*

"We couldn't make it to the orchestra concert. I've been tutoring on Thursday evenings."

He shifted his gaze to Vern. He was eyeing Heather. Something about it made Dann uneasy with his friend.

Their waiter returned with cups, poured coffee, and moments later brought their desserts. Heather divided the piece of cake she was sharing with Vern and passed it to him. She seemed almost giddy. Audra split the apple crisp, handing one dish to Dann. He couldn't miss the twinkle in her eye. *Is she amused?*

When Audra and Dann arrived at her back door, a faint afterglow remained in the darkening sky. A cricket chirped. She breathed in the intoxicating aroma of his aftershave. "Coming in?" she asked.

"Sure." He followed her up the steps. She walked on through to the living room, closed the drapes, and switched on lamps. Dominating the center of the coffee table, his bouquet of roses infused the room with a lovely fragrance.

Kicking her shoes off next to the coffee table, she sat on the couch, drawing her legs up beside her and covering them with her skirt. He took off his tie, slipped his shoes off, dropped onto the couch, and propped his feet on the coffee table.

"You know, I'm glad we asked them over for coffee." She pressed her hand across the smooth knit of her black skirt. "I was pleasantly surprised, but I enjoyed it. Didn't you?"

Dann didn't answer. He put his head back and stared at the ceiling.

"Did you have a problem?" Her head drew back as her eyebrows furrowed. "Maybe we shouldn't have after all."

He tipped his head to her. "No, it's not that at all—my mind just went off in another direction." He closed his eyes as if that would keep her from knowing what he was thinking.

She waited, then finally reached over and jostled his arm. "Anything you can share?"

He opened his eyes again, clasped his hands behind his head, and exhaled. "I was watching Vern and Heather. As far as I know, they've only gone out a couple of times, but he's obviously sweeping her off her feet. I guess I'm a little concerned. Heather seems like she *needs* a man's attention." A small grimace twisted his lips. "I like Vern. But as we've gotten more acquainted, he's boasted of a couple of conquests, so as much as Heather ticked me off, I wouldn't want her to get hurt." He began studying the ceiling again. "I've thought about Tamina, too. Is she in danger of being hurt by Franklin? Is he moving too fast?"

Audra studied his profile. "Well, I don't know about Heather, but I do know Tamina wants God's will in her life. She would be willing to call it off if things started happening she didn't feel were God's will. I admire her. She made me realize that's what I want for my life, too."

He eyed her for a long moment. "I guess if I'd known what God's will was, I wouldn't be where I'm at today. How can you know what God's will is?"

"I'm still working on that myself, but have you ever prayed about it?"

His shoulders sagged. He scowled at his lap before lifting his gaze to her again. "Not really. I've made so many mistakes. Do you think God would even hear me? I'm just trying to get my life back together."

"Are you trying to get yourself all cleaned up so God will accept you?" She whispered it and then held her breath. It was a gutsy question. He didn't move, but she knew he was listening.

"Remember that old song 'Just As I Am Without One Plea'? That's the way we must come to God. We have to say, God, I'm coming to you just the way I am—warts, wounds, scabs, and all, and let God do the forgiving, the healing and the changing. I'm still going through it myself."

He let his head fall on the back of the couch and closed his eyes once more. "I know you're right," he conceded. "I knew all that at one time. How come it's so easy to forget?" He opened his eyes and turned his face to her. "Thanks for reminding me." Then he shifted, gazing at the ceiling once more. "Aud, my past is dead. I don't even go there anymore. I'm ready to move on, but I just can't move as fast as Vern."

"Dann…" Her voice softened. "I don't want you to act like Vern. I want you to be you, and if you're feeling cautious because of what's happened in the past, I can understand and it's okay."

Relief loosened his jaw. He reached over and took her hand and held it. "Do you want to do something tomorrow afternoon?"

"Any suggestions?"

"I guess I wish you did have a bike. I'd suggest we go for a ride and get away from everything."

"You know, ever since I mentioned I should get a bike and get in shape, I've been thinking about buying one. Tamina had me out running a few times lately, and it felt pretty good. But it would be fun for the two of us to ride together, too. Want to help me pick a bike tomorrow?"

CHAPTER THIRTY-EIGHT

A VERY SPECIAL MAN

AUDRA LAY ON DR. SAMUELS'S EXAMINING TABLE, WHITE PAPER crinkling beneath her. Being alone in an examining room was boring. Her thoughts drifted to the new red ten-speed bike waiting in her garage. Dann was planning to skip out of his sixth-period free hour so they could ride to Patterson Lake. Clouds billowing like white cauliflower heads promised a perfect day for riding.

After ten minutes, the doctor breezed in with, "Good afternoon. Your vitals are good. Let's have a quick look." He pressed on her abdomen, explained what the operation would involve, directed her to have blood work done, and scheduled surgery for June 5 at eight thirty a.m.

Driving home, she contemplated the surgery. *Not a very convenient date. But I can't wait until the doctor returns the end of July and start back to work two weeks later. I just want to get it over with.*

She tapped her fingers on the steering wheel. Amazingly, after all the anxiety she'd experienced waiting for the verdict and all the dread she'd gone through over telling Dann, she was now filled with peace.

She didn't return to school after her appointment and used

the time waiting for Dann to catch up on her never-ending pile of paperwork. *Things are different with a man in my life.* In all her years of teaching, she'd never let her paperwork pile up like these last months. Weekends used to crawl by, leaving her eager to be back in the classroom. Now, she lived for the weekends. With less than three weeks of school left, she still had to spend time preparing grades for report cards one last time.

After finishing, she changed into jeans and her red knit polo shirt and secured her hair into a ponytail. She tied a white scarf at its base, letting its tails hang loose.

She was at the sink drinking a glass of water when Dann arrived at the kitchen door dressed in jeans shorts, navy polo, and a Cub's baseball cap. "Need a drink before we leave?"

"Just had one, thanks. So, what did you hear at the doctor's?" He lounged against the counter and crossed his arms.

She studied him over the rim of her glass. His casual stance belied his earnest expression. She lowered the glass. "The surgery's scheduled for the fifth of June."

His eyebrows knit, and his lips tightened, pulling his face into a scowl. "I *knew* that's the way it was going to happen. Of all the rotten luck." His palm whacked the counter.

She flinched as a startled gasp escaped her lips. She moved across the room, nearly upsetting her glass attempting to set it on the table. Her brain froze at his unfamiliar behavior, and she stared at him. "It–it was the only day open. But…"

He jammed his hands into his pockets and let out a sharp breath. His forehead furrowed deeper.

She didn't understand his annoyance. Words suddenly stuck in her throat, like they had for so many years over confrontations. It felt like a dam about to burst. "You don't need to postpone your ride." She forced her voice calm. "Tamina will be here."

"For Pete's sake, I wanted to be there," he snapped.

The dam burst. "Well, it's not my fault that's when they scheduled it!" She backed into the table and clutched the edge of it. His body flattened against the counter as shock drained the color from his face. They both stared, and it seemed time had stopped.

Audra strode across the empty space with her hands stretched toward him. His hands jerked out of his pockets, reaching, and he stepped toward her. "Oh, Dann, I'm so ashamed! Please forgive me?" Her arms circled him, and without any thought to how close she was pressing herself to him, she rested her head on his chest.

"No, it's my fault, Aud. I need *your* forgiveness." He tilted her chin up and kissed her. Their eyes opened at the same time, and his were wide with surprise—or alarm. She wasn't certain which it was, but she knew he hadn't planned to kiss her. He'd let his guard down and acted from what was in his heart as if it were the most natural thing to do. It felt wonderful.

"I forgive you, Dann." She released herself from the embrace she'd caught him in. She wanted to tell him his kiss didn't upset her, but those words wouldn't come.

Keeping his face down, he took a step back and ran his hand through his hair. "I've been looking at the calendar every day since you told me you have to have the surgery. But no matter how I calculated it, I knew it was going to be scheduled during the ride, and I didn't—I *don't*—want it to be that way."

Stepping past her, he gripped the back of a kitchen chair. "I didn't mean to sound angry with you—I'm angry at myself. This surgery's probably the biggest life-changing event you'll ever face, and I'm selfishly thinking of my bike ride." He shook his head. "God has a lot of work to do in me yet, Aud."

She edged next to him and laid her hand over his on the

chair back. "I'm serious, Dann. It's okay if you can't be there. By the time you get back, I'll be over the worst of it."

He exhaled a frustrated puff of air, but he didn't say anything for several moments. "Do you still want to ride over to the lake?" he finally asked.

"Of course, I do," she answered on her way to the door.

She pedaled behind him along the curve of Bend Avenue to the bridge, over the arroyo, and then to the right, past the school grounds. The ride out to the pond gave them both time to reflect, and they remained a bit reserved as they stood side by side while the resident mallards paddled across the water. Even when they ate tacos at El Taco Grande later, they were quieter than usual. She wasn't sure whether it was the surgery date or the kiss.

Audra called Tamina the next afternoon after Mary Lynn's music lesson. "I'd better let you know my surgery is scheduled, and it looks like I'll need somebody to get me to the hospital. June 5, if you can do it."

"Of course, I can! Did you already tell Dann?"

"Yes." She didn't want to talk about what had happened. "He wasn't very happy with the timing, but I'm pretty sure he'll go ahead and go on the ride." She changed the subject then and told Tamina about their encounter with Vern and Heather.

"I can't believe Heather's changed so much." Tamina rushed on, "Oh say, before you hang up — last night, I found out Franklin is coming Memorial Day weekend. He got the whole weekend off."

Audra packed brown-bag lunches for Dann, Rosa, and her-self after they asked Tamina and Kayla to join them on a picnic behind Lake Patterson. Puffy, cotton-candy clouds produced intermittent shade, tempering the agreeable 81 degrees. After eating, the girls energetically explored the area, watched ants going in and out of their hills, climbed on rocks, and pretended they were part of a wagon train while Tamina told them about Franklin's impending visit. Already knowing that news, Audra sat back and listened.

Dann picked up crumb-filled sandwich bags and stuffed them into a paper bag. "Next time you talk to him, tell him if he doesn't mind sleeping on an air mattress, he can bunk with me."

Tamina jerked forward from the rock she was leaning against as her face became animated. Her black eyes widened, and her full lips parted, growing into a smile displaying her even white teeth. "Oh, wow! Thanks—I'll tell him." She settled back as dreamy eyes overtook her surprise. "You two are lucky to be together all the time. I can hardly wait to see him again."

He cleared his throat. "Tamina, can I say something like a brother?"

"Okaaay?" Hesitancy arched one brow, and she squinted at him, waiting for his unsolicited advice.

"When he gets here, it will be a couple of months since you've seen him. Just be careful, will you?"

Audra doubted Dann had ever seen Tamina blush, but their friend's dark skin definitely flared red. When she ducked her head, her straightened pixie haircut provided no cover for her embarrassment. Without answering, she picked up a dry twig and doodled in the dirt for a moment before she lifted her gaze to Audra. "Hey, girl, have you met this guy?" She nodded toward Dann. "He's my big brother, and he's really concerned for me—he's got my back."

Tamina took Kayla home, agreeing to join Dann and Audra at the Espinosa's for hamburgers later. However, when Rosa said, "I don't want to go home yet, Mr. Dann, I want to do something with just you and Miss Audra—pleeeease," the three of them played miniature golf.

Taking bags of hamburgers, fries, and shakes back to Mrs. Espinosa's, they arrived only minutes before Tamina, who brought more laughter and joking than usual to the table. As soon as they ate, Rosa tugged at his hand. "Come on, Mr. Dann. I want to play my new songs for you and Miss Tamina."

Audra braced against the kitchen doorway while he stood over the girl. He was showing as much interest in her music as he had in teaching her how to hold a putter. Did he even realize how much of a need he was filling? It seemed to come so naturally to him. Taylor gravitated toward him, too. Dann would always have children around him. That's just the way he was. Smiling, she went back into the kitchen and began cleaning up.

After Dann pulled into Audra's driveway and killed the motor, she unbuckled her seatbelt. The May evening was balmy, and the scent of fresh-mowed grass drifted through the open window. He had been quiet on the drive home, so she glanced over at him and waited.

"I don't think I'm going to come in tonight—I'm really bushed and…" He fiddled with his keys, then opened his door and came around to hers. He took her hand, but as they walked around to the back door, she felt uncomfortable.

Was he actually too tired? Or was he uneasy about going

in the house tonight since she had run into his arms when he'd kissed her? Maybe the little black dress had something to do with it, too. Her cheeks grew hot. She'd replayed their kiss over and over since it happened. How many times today had she looked at him and hoped tonight would be the night he'd hold her in his arms and kiss her goodnight? She'd thought about it until anticipation filled every fiber of her body.

Well, maybe that would better be defined as desire. Good thing it was dark, and he couldn't see her face. When they reached the back door, he lifted her hand and pressed the backs of her fingers to his lips.

She swallowed hard. *That's as far as he's going to go.* Disappointment left her with a lump in her throat and a lonely feeling. "It was a fun day," was all she could manage.

"It *was* fun. Aud, I always enjoy being with you." His voice was soft. Dropping her hand, he twisted as if to go, but then faced her again. Inching his face closer, he touched his hand to her arm. She lifted her face to him, waiting. Breathing in his aftershave.

He took a deep breath and slowly let it out. "I really must go. I'll see you sometime tomorrow."

Dann hurried to his Jeep. He didn't like how close he'd come to breaking his promise to himself — again.

Audra went up to the kitchen, but because the light was on, she couldn't see out the window as he pulled out. She pressed her fingers to her lips where he had kissed them. She never should have allowed herself to spend the day hoping he would hold her in his arms tonight and kiss her. Now she was frustrated. She walked through the house to her bedroom and switched on the bedside lamp before flopping on the bed.

Dann's reaction to the kiss confirmed he had imposed a restriction on himself. *But why after all these months? Doesn't he ever feel like I do? Doesn't he* want *to kiss me?* A small grimace pulled at the corner of her mouth. *If he doesn't, why did he say I'm on his mind all the time?*

But...what if kissing me is what's really on his mind all the time? What if he wants it even more than I do, to the point where he had to set a boundary for himself? Could his concern for Heather and Tamina stem from having a pretty good idea what Vern and Franklin are thinking about because he's having the same struggle?

She sat up and folded her hands in her lap. *It's not that he doesn't want to kiss me — he's afraid of where it might lead.* "Lord," she whispered, "in all these months, I haven't felt one red flag that you don't want our relationship to grow. I believe you have sent a very special man into my life. Dann respects me, and his desire to protect me is greater than wanting to fulfill his own desires. Lord, please forgive me for being impatient and wanting something he can't yet give me."

Audra put her hands over her cheeks and closed her eyes. "Oh, Dann," she murmured as a wave of affection flowed over her. Her love for him had just gone deeper than she'd ever experienced.

Audra hadn't expected to see Dann in church, but when she passed the offering plate to the woman next to her, she noticed him across the aisle. She caught only a quick glance but enough to see he seemed to be contemplating the Scripture words the music group in front was singing: "Create in me a clean heart—renew a right spirit within me." That was her prayer, too, but seeing him left her elated and having a hard time focusing on the rest of the service.

CHAPTER THIRTY-NINE

HEATHER

A GUST OF WIND, FOLLOWING A BRIEF EVENING SHOWER, SWIRLED rain-fresh air through Audra's open front door. Savoring the fragrance, she let her gaze roam from the piano to the fireplace. *Oh, my poor house. It's been so neglected.* Grasping her floor duster in one hand, she clicked her CD changer on. As "Song Of India" saturated the living room, she began swaying and humming along with the romantic music, the static cloth gliding across her hardwood floor. When the phone rang, she fairly floated to the kitchen. *Can it possibly be Dann?*

"Hey, guess what? I just talked with my dad, and he and my mother are flying out for Memorial Day weekend."

She grinned at the sound of his voice. "Fantastic! I'm excited to meet them. I feel like I already know them."

"That's going to be a busy weekend. I have Franklin staying with me, but since I don't have a bed for them anyway, they're okay with getting a motel room."

"Hmm, I already asked Tamina if she thought they'd be interested in having a cookout while Franklin's here." Audra paused and leaned her duster against the counter. "I wouldn't want to cut into time with your folks, but do you think they'd object to a joint affair?"

"I'll check with them, and we'll have to check with Tamina and see how they feel about it."

Hanging up, she returned to waltzing her duster around her expanse of hardwood, only this time she was swaying in Dann's arms.

On Wednesday, they played duets until six o'clock and sent out for pizza. Plates in hand, they moved to the back patio to enjoy the pleasant May evening. As the sun began creating a rosy sunset and birds twittered their evening song, the strains of Saint-Saens's "The Swan" and Liszt's "Liebestraum" were still running through Audra's mind. "Dann, didn't you say your dad still plays the violin?"

"Uh-huh."

"Do you think he'd have any interest in bringing it along and playing trio with us while they're here?"

He didn't answer immediately. His eyes were trained off in the distance, a small smile working at the edges of his mouth. "You know, Aud," he caught her gaze, "I think he'd be delighted if you asked him."

She froze, pizza slice halfway to her mouth. "You want *me* to ask?"

"Yeah, would you? We could call him right now — would you mind?" He fished his cell phone out. She set her pizza down and twisted her napkin in her hands as he made preliminary conversation with his father. Perching on the edge of her chair, she crumpled the napkin and tossed it beside her plate. A grin widened his face when he handed over the phone.

"Um, hi, this is Audra…"

"Audra, this is David. So, what did you want to ask?"

His voice, mellow and friendly, sent her shoulders relaxing.

Leaning back in her chair, she twirled a strand of hair around a finger. "Would you care to bring your violin and play some trios with us?"

Such a dead silence followed that she held the phone away to check the connection, but then a hearty laugh erupted as if he couldn't contain his joy.

"That would please me no end, young lady! I've heard you're quite accomplished on the piano. You pick the music and let me know so I can practice. I'm already looking forward to it."

After she hung up, a smile lit Dann's face. She held the phone out to him. "You were right. He seemed very happy for the invitation. You seem a bit thrilled yourself."

"Yes, I am," he responded, but before he could add an explanation, his phone rang. Glancing to check the caller, he held a finger up to her, listened a moment, and then pressed the phone against his chest. "It's Vern. Jerold told him the city finished the new bike trail on Canyon Road out to the county road. He and Heather want us to ride it with them on Saturday and then go to Heather's and do burgers."

Wow. Heather's reaching out again? And so soon? Audra nodded her affirmation and picked up what remained of her pizza slice. It was cold, and the grease had congealed. Hours later, she realized she'd never asked why he was so pleased about playing trio.

Audra and Dann met Vern and Heather at Canyon Road Shopping Center. Heather had plaited her hair into a single, thick braid down the middle of her back, and Audra's ponytail stuck through the hole in the back of the baseball cap she usually wore running. Like the men, both she and Heather had water bottles clipped to their bike frames, but neither had felt inclined to invest in bicycle shorts yet.

West on Canyon Road, the houses petered out, giving way to the desert. Yellow sunflowers along the edge of the asphalt trail, scattered yucca, gray rabbitbrush, piñon trees, and tufts of dry grass broke the monotony of dun-brown desert—a stark contrast to the east end of Canyon Road with its springs and ponderosas.

They pedaled two abreast until the bike trail intersected a graveled county road heading south. "End of the line." Dann planted a foot on the asphalt. "If we go on, it'll take us out to the quarry and be hotter than blazes. Are you sure we want to go?"

Heather reached for her water bottle. "I must have been insane to think we could ride at this time of day. I was just thinking ride first and then go back to my place." She guzzled a long drink of water. "I don't want to stay in the desert, but I don't want to go home, either. Anyone know of a cooler place?"

"Probably just a park with a lot of trees." Vern uncapped his bottle before reaching to wipe a drip from her chin. Their eyes met, and then Vern looked away.

"Remember the park we pass when we ride to the quarry from Jerold's?" Dann interrupted. "It's on Third, sort of tucked in with all those nice homes east of Evan's Lane."

"Evan's Lane has lots of trees—and I can show you where my father's old contracting business used to be." Audra chugged tepid water and snapped the lid on her water bottle. For the second time, a sense of pride in her father's accomplishments surprised her. How her attitude was changing!

Even in intermittent shade, heatwaves shimmered over the pavement, and the on-and-off sun beat down. Since Evan's Lane was deserted of cars, Dann moved up beside Audra as they passed a rundown mobile home park on the left. Minutes later, the faint scent of petunias wafted over them, and rows of fruit and shade tree saplings stood at attention before the Flower Pot

Nursery. Sunlight glared off broken windshields and battered car hoods from an auto junkyard on the right before yards of cyclone fencing gave way to an abandoned adobe house with a collapsed roof and several lots of weeds and litter.

She pulled into a dusty area in front of a small building with peeling blue paint. He stopped beside her.

Dirty windows were as forlorn as the sign over the door lettered A & J Construction. The fence hiding the construction yard sagged into tangled grass, emphasizing the neglect.

An immense sadness filled her. "I haven't been out here for years. It *never* looked like this when Father owned it." She had to look away.

"Your father's name was Evan, wasn't it? I thought Evan's Lane was somebody's last name." He paused. "He had a street named after him?" Awe filled his voice.

She gave a half-smile. "Actually, he named it himself. You know, when I was a kid, this seemed so far out in the country."

Dann twirled the pedal of his bike with the toe of his shoe. "Why don't you just remember it the way it used to be?"

"Yeah. It's true—you can never go back. Let's go."

A chapter of her life had just closed.

The temperature rose another two degrees, and the breeze stilled as they pedaled from the construction office to the park. Audra was sweating and knew her face was red by the time they reached their destination. Heather looked overheated, also. Audra laid her bike on the grass and didn't have a chance to sit before Dann snagged her hand.

He let out a loud "Wahoo!" and began running, dragging her along behind him. He ran her directly into the path

317

of an impulse sprinkler, and she shrieked when the cold water smacked her hot skin. He started laughing and towed her through a second and third shower, and she giggled, screeched, and hooted her way across the park before she could pull him into the dry grass.

"Oh, you monster!" She panted, but when she saw a drop of water clinging to the end of his nose, she doubled over howling at the absurd picture they must be presenting.

"Well, I'll bet you're cooler now." His eyes sparkled.

"Well, yeah, because I'm soaked!" She punched his shoulder. "And to think, not too long ago, I couldn't picture you as a rebellious teenager. I'll bet you gave your sister fits, didn't you?"

Dann threw back his head and let out a belly laugh. Water dripped from his nose and chin. "Now you're getting to know the real me." He entwined his fingers in hers, and skirting the sprinklers, they walked back to their bikes.

Vern was standing where a light spray of water could hit him, and Heather was bending over another sprinkler, catching water in her hands and patting it on her face and arms. She watched Audra with wonder on her face.

Audra ran her fingers through her wet ponytail while the men drew two park benches opposite each other. Then the four of them sat and talked under a shady canopy of cottonwood trees. At Dann's suggestion, they pedaled to Heather's where the girls stayed while Dann and Vern biked to the shopping center to get the cars.

Audra followed Heather into her hot, stuffy apartment, grateful when she switched the air conditioner on. "Would you like a soda or iced tea?"

"Iced tea, I think. I'm parched, but at least my clothes are dry now." She tossed her hat on the couch and stood in the kitchen doorway. The living arrangement of her apartment mirrored Dann's, except the furniture was blue instead of beige. Not a thing seemed out of place.

Heather handed her a cold, bottled tea and walked into the living room with her soda. She motioned Audra to the couch and sank into the easy chair, setting her soda on a coaster on the end table.

"I was watching you at the park. How did you manage not to get angry when Dann got you all wet? I would have been livid if Vern dragged me through the sprinklers."

Audra shrugged. "I guess I really didn't see anything to get angry about—I wasn't going to melt. Anyway, the surprise of it struck me as funny. Why would you have felt angry?"

"My first thought would have been, Oh, I'm going to get dirty!" she answered in a prissy, little-girl voice. "My mother instilled the idea in me from a very young age that little girls don't get dirty. I guess I still think that way." She slid her shoes off and set them side by side next to her chair, lining the toes up perfectly, and then eased the elastic band off her braid and began to work her hair free. "The bike ride was hot, but I enjoyed it. I guess I was kind of surprised you agreed to go with us, though." She shifted her gaze off down the hallway.

"You know, it took you and Dann and Vern all saying something tough to me to make me realize I was acting like a snot." She faced Audra. "When you asked me to forgive you a few weeks ago, it had a bigger impact than you'll ever know, but now I must ask you to forgive me for acting like a stupid idiot."

Audra opened her mouth to comment and decided against it. She tipped the tea to her lips, instead.

Heather sighed. "I had a really good job in Minneapolis, but I got tired of my mother running my life. She couldn't see anything good about any guy I ever liked. I haven't held onto a guy from the time I was seventeen and fell madly in love with a boy in my chemistry class. My best friend deliberately stole him away. My mother drove the rest away—or at least I've always blamed her. When I got here to the academy, I was out from under her thumb, and there was Dann as big as life. I couldn't resist making a play for him, but..." She shrugged. "I couldn't even flirt successfully. Let me get my comb. I'll be right back."

Audra remained on the couch. The day had taken an unexpected turn. Why was Heather telling her all this?

Heather returned from the bathroom already working her comb through her long hair. When she finished, she swished her hair back and forth and let it fall behind her, and then held her eyes on Audra. "Forgive me for obsessing over Dann and for being jealous of you. When you smiled at him, there he was falling all over himself to be nice to you, and I wanted him to act that way toward me."

"Well, it wasn't exactly like—"

"And I was angry over the music because I knew I could never compete."

"Well, I do forgive you, Heather." Audra's hot hand stroked the cool droplets of condensation forming on the side of her bottle. Why had Heather just spilled her guts? She'd never seen Heather with anyone who might be considered a friend. Audra reached back and undid her ponytail. Her hair had to be a mess after running through the sprinklers. She shook it out to give herself more time to think. "Heather, we sort of got off on the wrong foot. Can we put it behind us and agree not to bring it up again and start over?"

"I'd like that."

"Would you care to do something with Tamina and me sometime?"

"Sure. How'd you get to be such good friends with her, since she works on the elementary side of the academy?"

"I went up to her in the gym on her first day at the academy and started talking to her, and we just meshed."

"Just like you tried to do with me."

"Yes." Audra smiled at her, and Heather returned it.

They finished their drinks, and Heather excused herself to the kitchen to slice tomatoes while Audra scanned the titles on her easy-listening CD collection. When Dann and Vern clattered on the balcony outside the door, Heather let them in.

Dann grinned, handing Audra her purse. "I thought you might need this."

"You're right about that." She made a quick exit to the bathroom. Bending over, she let her hair fall forward and combed through it vigorously before giving it a shake and letting it fall back on her shoulders. She applied fresh pink lipstick and rejoined the others, feeling very good.

After nine, Audra opened the back door of the garage, and Dann wheeled her bicycle in and parked it. "Come in for a while?"

"Only for a little bit. I need some ice water. Those hamburgers made me thirsty." He followed her up to the kitchen. "I sure hope you weren't upset when I dragged you through the sprinklers." He set two glasses on the counter. "That was total impulse, and I didn't think about ruining your hair."

She retrieved ice from the freezer. "No, silly, I thought it was funny. The hair recovered."

"Heather seemed shocked."

"Oh, she was. She really expected me to get angry, but it opened a wonderful conversation while you guys were gone."

He cocked his eyebrow. "Oh yeah? About what?" He ran water over the ice in the glasses. She carried hers to the living room where she closed drapes, flipped on lights, and then sat on the couch. She waited for him to sit with her. "Well, she confided some things that aren't necessary to go into. She realizes she did some things wrong, and basically, we mended fences and agreed to let bygones be bygones."

"As simple as that?"

"As simple as that."

Dann drank from his glass and set it on a coaster. He leaned back and clasped her hand. "Aud, you constantly amaze me."

She shifted to look him in the face. "Why? What did I do?"

"I guess you were just being you, but you always have wisdom for these kinds of situations."

"Well, if there's any wisdom, I don't think it comes from me, but I will agree there have been a lot of situations this year." She took a sip of her water and set her glass beside his. "As I think back," she hugged her arms around herself thoughtfully, "some of the situations were difficult and I didn't like them, but you know what? Every one of them brought me closer to God. Sometimes I can hardly believe the way God's changed me over this school year."

Dann reached over and took her hand. "He's been working on me, too."

His soft words still hanging between them, they sat side by side in a comfortable silence until they had finished their ice water. Then he stood, set his glass on the coaster, and pulled her to her feet.

"I really need to go." He pressed the backs of her fingers to his lips the way he had the last time he'd said goodnight. Looking into her face, he let his eyes linger on hers.

She was content with that.

CHAPTER FORTY

END OF SCHOOL VISITORS

THE MEMORIAL DAY WEEKEND MARKING THE END OF SCHOOL was almost upon them. Audra sat at the kitchen table with a glass of iced tea, working on grades on Sunday afternoon. After she finished Maddie Lester's, she straightened her legs, slid down in her chair, and whooshed out a long breath. Maddie was going to pass sixth-grade English with a D+.

She'd had a touching talk with the girl a week earlier, and Maddie had confided that her parents were getting a divorce. She was going to have to leave her friends, after all, and move to Virginia with her mother. Her mother had already warned her that she'd have to repeat sixth grade if she failed anything. During their talk, Audra found out it was Maddie Heather had been tutoring. Maybe Heather was a more compassionate teacher than she'd given her credit for. Audra chewed her lip. *I wonder if any of these situations have brought Heather closer to God?*

Audra arranged the reports she'd read and snapped her briefcase shut. *Come on, Dann. I'm hungry.* She almost laughed when, as though on cue, the back door rattled and Dann clomped up to the kitchen and stuck his head in. "Chicken delivery!" He set the sack on the table.

"Hey — good timing!" She undid a corner of the bag and inhaled the aroma of deep-fried chicken. "Mmm, smells good. Just have a few more reports to read tomorrow, and I'll be done." She began setting the table.

He clunked two glasses on the table. "I had a lot of time on my hands this afternoon, and I got to thinking. School gets out at noon on Friday, so why don't you go with me to pick up my folks? We could leave as soon as school's out, drive down to Albuquerque and spend the afternoon, have dinner and pick my mom and dad up at the airport at eight thirty."

The expectant look in his gray eyes reminded her of their trip to Albuquerque with Tamina. She dearly wanted to tell him she'd go. Instead, she sighed. "I still have Patty's music lesson that afternoon." She didn't even try to keep the disappointment out of her voice.

"Could you cancel?"

She studied his face. It was tempting. She'd always reserved cancelations for emergency situations, but right now, she wanted to go with him more than she wanted to give the music lesson. That was a surprising admission. *Does falling in love make you do out-of-character things?*

More than just the desire to go with Dann tugged at her. He was asking her to be there with him when he met his parents. He wanted her there beside him and knowing that was almost as good as a goodnight kiss. She took a breath and let it out. "I really want to go, but I've canceled Patty so many times for doctor appointments…"

His eyes lowered, and his mouth gave a quick little twitch. When he glanced up, he covered her hand with his. His eyes were soft. Compassionate. "It's okay. I just thought leaving early would give us some extra time together. I suppose we can leave as soon as you're finished and still get to the airport on time."

Her throat tightened. He had never looked at her in quite that way before, and she'd never experienced more of a desire to lean across the table and kiss him.

He removed his hand, reached into the bag of chicken, and began dividing it out. She slowly dragged her portion in front of herself. But she couldn't eat. She was having a hard time getting past the desire to kiss him.

Audra splatted a chunk of margarine into the frying pan and listened to it sizzle. Frustration had settled in, and it didn't want to budge. *I want to leave for Albuquerque at noon with Dann on Friday. He wants me there.* She broke two eggs into the pan and stirred them. The whole time Jason had played his lesson, she'd tried to finagle a way to make it happen. No flash of lightning lit her brain with a solution. She dumped grated cheese on the eggs, and the phone rang. She shoved the pan off the burner and stepped to the phone.

"Hi. This is Loreen," Patty's mom said. "I thought I'd better let you know we're going out of town for the long weekend, so Patty won't be here for her lesson. Actually, I've needed to talk to you for a while. Her dad and I have noticed she seems to be losing interest in playing the piano. Does it appear that way to you?"

Guilt zinged her chest. "Well, somewhat, yes, but I was afraid it was because I had to cancel her so many times—"

"Oh no, it's not that at all. She's got it in her head she wants to take a jazz dance class with her friends." Loreen paused, then added, "I don't feel inclined to force her to take piano if she's not interested, so I'll tell you what—Friday's the end of school and a natural time to make the break. I'll tell her she can quit."

Audra stared at the phone in her hand after the woman hung up, vacillating between elation and shock. She'd just lost a hundred dollars a month in addition to the hundred she'd lost when Kevin died. *But I can go with Dann.*

She didn't care that her eggs were cold. She punched in his number. "I can go, Dann. I can go when school lets out Friday."

The temperature in Albuquerque topped out at 91 degrees, the heat rising in waves around the frantic, Friday-afternoon traffic ushering in the holiday weekend. Even as they sat in the Mexican restaurant Franklin had taken them to, a din of laughter and merriment swelled above the clatter of dishes and normal noise. Summer had unofficially begun.

"So, what did you think of the aquarium?" Dann dipped a tortilla chip into the dish of spicy salsa.

"Smaller than I expected, but interesting, Actually, I think I had more fun at the mall. I like your taste in women's clothes."

"Thanks. I've never gotten to do that before, and I enjoyed it." He dipped another chip, tapping off the excess before reaching it across the table and holding it before her mouth. "Will you wear it sometime this weekend?"

The spices exploded over her tongue, and she giggled at his delightful show of affection. After the aquarium, they'd gone to the mall because it would be a cool place to walk. Dann spied the light-blue denim dress with delicate, pale-blue flowers in the boutique window and urged her to try it on. The princess-cut bodice buttoned down the front, with a sweetheart neck and a mid-calf full skirt. He gave her a wolf whistle and a grin and insisted on buying. She bought a pair of beige toe-ring sandals to accompany it. They were pretty close to kicky strap shoes.

"I'll make a time to wear it. I just don't know which day, yet. Thank you again for buying it. I consider it something very special."

"*You're* special, Aud." Their eyes met and held a little bit longer than usual.

She picked up her fork and relished the beef enchilada drenched in red chile and cheese the waiter had set in front of her. "Dann, what do your folks know about me?"

He lowered his fork to his plate. "Why?"

"Well, I'm looking forward to meeting them, but all of a sudden, I have butterflies."

"Well, I told them about the duets and the concerts."

She scooped some guacamole. "Do they know we've been spending time together?"

"If they're reading between the lines, they've probably figured it out. Aud?" He waited for her to look up at him. "Just be your wonderful self, and you won't have a thing to worry about."

She smiled. *I sure hope I can trust you on that.*

The plane landed at the Southwest-style Albuquerque Sunport at 8:34, right on time. Wheeled suitcases clacked on tile floors, people scurried in multiple directions, and the smell of leather luggage, perfume, and airport Mexican food melded together as they rode the escalator to the third level and found the passenger greeting area.

She shivered as he held her hand while they waited for his parents to enter the waiting area. Holding hands was going to send a clear message right up front, but he seemed comfortable with it.

"I see them coming." He gave her hand a squeeze.

Even if she hadn't seen their picture, she would have known them. David Day was the only man carrying a violin case and a carry-on bag. As they came closer, she knew what Dann was going to look like in twenty years. A more mature version of his son, David Day had the same gray eyes and straight brows, but gray hair showed at his temples.

His mother was shorter than Audra had imagined her, and a little plumper, but very attractive. Her salt-and-pepper hair was layered in the back and beauty-shop perfect.

Dann dropped Audra's hand to embrace both of his parents and inquired about their flight.

His father set his violin case and the carry-on on the floor. "And this must be Audra." Eyes sparkling, just like Dann's, he extended a hand to her. "David Day. We've heard a lot about you." He moved his hand to his wife's arm. "My wife, Janna."

Audra took the hand Janna extended and covered it with her other hand. She returned their smiles. "I've been looking forward to meeting both of you."

On the return trip, Audra and Janna sat in the Jeep's back seat, chatting nonstop for the hour and a half ride home. Dann and his father were caught up in their own discussion. Audra found herself totally at ease, but one thought kept intruding: *Do they know I'll be having surgery in mere days?*

After they carried all the bags into the motel, David asked Audra, "When are we going to play this music together? I can hardly wait."

She shifted her gaze to Dann on the end of a bed. "Do you have plans for tomorrow?"

"Nothing concrete. Are you going to Rosa's?"

"I was planning on it." She faced David and Janna. "I give music lessons to a little friend of mine and her great-grandmother on Saturday mornings. Would you like to come for lunch, and then we can play in the afternoon?"

They were agreeable. They visited until ten o'clock before Dann and Audra drove to Tamina's.

Franklin had been there for thirty minutes. He and Tamina were sitting at her kitchen table, talking over decaf coffee and fresh-baked chocolate chip cookies. "Come on in and join us," Tamina invited. "The coffee's still hot. I was expecting you to show up any time now."

When they were still talking at two a.m., Dann yawned and said they needed to get going. Franklin stood and stretched. "Give me directions to your place, and I'll be right behind you, bro."

Audra had an hour after she got home from Mrs. Espinosa's to finish preparing the chicken Caesar salads and set the table. She was putting the last of the grapes on the fruit plate when Dann maneuvered the Cherokee into the driveway. She set the plate on the table and dried her hands. She had butterflies again. *What if they don't care for chicken Caesar salad? Oh good, they're coming to the back door.*

Climbing the steps from the landing, the trio entered the kitchen. Janna gave Audra a hug. "My, what an exquisite kitchen! I would just love to have my kitchen table by a window overlooking the yard. My only window's over the sink."

David gave Audra's arm a squeeze. "And just look at this beautiful luncheon table she's set." He stopped in front of the table. Then he held up his violin case. "Where do you want me to put this?"

Audra nodded toward the piano room. "In there — Dann can show you." She silently breathed out and let the tension drain from her shoulders. They were just as unpretentious today as they had been on the drive from the airport. "Did Dann give you the grand tour?" she asked when the men returned to the kitchen.

"He came over to the motel for breakfast, then took us out to the academy and around for a bit," his mother answered.

"That's a nice little school you have, but Dann said he'd save the rest until you're with us. And say, that's an impressive piano in there." David snatched a grape from the fruit plate.

"David, mind your manners," Janna scolded.

Dann was leaning against the counter. He hadn't said a word since he'd entered the house, but a broad grin crinkled his face during their interchange. "Do you want some help with drinks?"

"Sure. We have iced tea, water, or coffee." Everyone agreed to the iced tea. As Audra set salads on the table, she observed Janna's brow lift when Dann went to the correct cupboard for glasses and filled them with ice and tea. *Is she curious how Dann knows my kitchen? I think she wants to know more than Dann's told her.*

After they ate, Janna brought dishes for Audra to put into the dishwasher while the two men began tuning their instruments.

"It's good to see Dann happy again." Janna grew quiet as if covering a faux pas.

"He really was happy when he heard you were coming this weekend." Audra was reasonably sure that wasn't what Janna referred to. *Do I tell her I know what Dann went through?*

In the piano room, Dann and his father sat in folding chairs next to the piano while Janna took the pecan chair. After an hour and a half, she was still as attentive as when they had first started. Finishing a song, David laid his bow on the music stand, handed his violin to Janna, and pulled Dann to his feet. "Ah, son, it's been a long time. You'll never know how much I've missed playing with you. Welcome back!" He gathered Dann into a bear hug.

Audra's eyes widened. That was unexpected. After his father released him, Dann laid his bow on top of his father's bow on the music stand and handed Audra his violin.

"I've missed it, too, Dad. Please forgive me." He embraced his father.

David's eyes were shiny when he stepped back and took a handkerchief from his hip pocket. At the piano, he rested his hand on Audra's shoulder. "And you, my dear young lady, play beautifully. You made me the happiest man in the world when you asked me to bring my violin."

Audra reached across herself and laid her hand atop of his. "Thank you." But *what* was happening?

In the corner of the room, David opened his violin case, removed two dog-eared, smudged sheets, and placed them on the music stand. He handed Dann his bow, and they retrieved their instruments. From the nod of his head and the slight lift of his lip, Audra knew Dann recognized the papers. Without a word, he and his father played an exquisitely sweet duet, each unfamiliar refrain piercing Audra's heart.

When both musicians stilled and the last notes faded to breathless silence, Janna crossed behind the piano and kissed Dann's cheek. "Thank you, son. That was just as beautiful as when you and Davene first played it for me. Audra," she turned, "Dann composed that so he and Davene could play it on my birthday when they were in high school."

Dann hugged his mother and then sat on the piano bench next to Audra. He lowered his face, and Audra had no idea what he was thinking.

Audra slid her hand over his. "That was wonderful — absolutely beautiful."

After everyone had regained their composure, David's enthusiastic air returned. "Dann said there was a lake around here he was going to take us to — what'd you call it, Lake Patterson?"

"Well," Audra laughed, "I'll warn you, Lake Michigan it isn't! Let's go out for a while and stretch our legs."

David and Janna laughed as they stood at the edge of the pond. "Our bathtub is larger than this."

Dann scuffed the toe of his sneaker. "I know, but when this is all you have, you learn to love it. Do you want to take a walk around it?"

"Lead the way. You two can probably walk farther and faster than we can."

Dann grasped Audra's hand, and setting out ahead of his parents, they walked in silence for a number of yards before she slowed their pace. "Earlier I sort of got the idea something might have happened between you and your dad at some time. Is that why you wanted *me* to ask him to bring his violin?"

He gave her a sheepish grin. "No. There was never anything between us. It was more than that. We haven't played together since I got married. Gail always complained when we played together, and so we quit. I never realized how much that must have hurt him, but when you suggested he bring his violin, I knew it would mean the world to him to have *you* ask him — like a new beginning." He grimaced and shook his head. "Aud, the more I get away from the past, the more I realize how little sense I had."

"Have you asked God to forgive you?"

"Over and over."

"Well, he has — just believe it and forgive yourself, too. God has redeemed the time that was lost for you."

Squeezing his hand, she smiled at him. He appeared to consider her words and then lifted her hand and touched it to his lips. He twisted to see if his parents were still coming. David and Janna hadn't missed his gesture, and David gave him a thumbs-up.

In the hot sun, it didn't take long for them to retreat to

Dann's apartment. Dann took his parents to his train room. While she stood to the side, joy overwhelmed Audra's heart as she watched his mom and dad lovingly ooh and ahh over his new additions. With expert hands, David uncoupled the Union Pacific steam locomotive and inspected it end to end. "It's going to get more and more difficult to find these babies. You were lucky."

In the living room, Janna stopped in front of the boy practicing his violin, now hanging above his music stand. "Dann, where did you get this picture?"

"Aud gave it to me for my birthday." Dann unboxed the cribbage board and set it on the table.

"It sure reminds me of when you were young." Hands clasped behind her, Janna continued studying the canvas. While Janna's gaze traveled from Dann to Audra and back to the picture again, Audra busied herself removing the cards from their box. If Janna hadn't been reading between the lines before, she was getting a headline. Tipping her head enough to hide a smile, Audra savored the warmth spreading through her. She liked Janna.

They played cribbage until heading to Knights & Pawns for dinner. While they were waiting for their wine, Janna nodded toward Audra's dress. "That is very becoming. Blue is a good color for you."

"Thank you." She smoothed her hand across the soft cotton. *I was afraid she'd think it was too low cut.*

"Stunning, isn't it? I picked it out and bought it," Dann volunteered.

Audra swallowed as Janna glanced over at Dann. She wished he hadn't said that. Her father would never have allowed a boyfriend to give her such an expensive, personal gift. *What will Janna say?*

Laughing, Janna laid her hand on his arm. "Well, I'm glad

you have such good taste."

Audra sat back in her chair, folded her hands, and rested them against her lips. *She accepts me – just the way I am.* A smile tugged at her hidden mouth. *I tried so hard to please Father and never felt I measured up. I was always striving to please – Laney, teachers, professors – everyone. I even doubted Dann would want me as a woman. But Janna accepts me. I do measure up.*

"I remember the first time I picked out something for your mother." David leaned forward, speaking directly into Audra's face. "It was the most awful shade of green you ever saw. She never did wear it."

Janna giggled. "That was right after we were engaged. It was a scarf." She looked into Audra's face, also.

Audra laughed at the story, but a lump formed in her throat. Something was welling up in her she didn't comprehend. "Excuse me a minute. I have to run the ladies' room."

She stared at her reflection in the glaring mirror. *I do measure up.* A rippling sensation fluttered at her throat. It slid off her shoulders like a worn-out, ragged garment. It slithered down her body and crumpled on the floor at her feet. It was the old Audra. She blinked at her image, then grinned. *I do measure up!* Halleluiah would have burst from her lips, but another woman walked in, and she stifled it. Head held high, she strode back to the table with a spring in her step.

Night lighting illuminated the parking lot when they parked at his parents' motel room. Dann's father leaned forward, supporting his hand on the back of Audra's seat. "It's been rather a long day for Mama and me, so why don't the two of you run on and spend some time?"

Dann didn't hesitate to say, "Okay, we'll see you in the morning."

Audra twisted and touched his hand. "Will you be going to church with us in the morning?"

David jerked his head to look at Janna's face. The silence that followed seemed to spell surprise. Janna recovered first. "How nice that you're going to church, Dann. What time?"

Embarrassment pursed Dann's lips, and he only peeked at Audra out of the corner of his eye. "Umm, I can pick you up at nine thirty."

They went to Tamina's again. While Dann told Franklin the plans for his upcoming bike ride, Tamina scooted next to Audra. "I haven't seen that dress before. Is it new?"

"Dann bought it." She pretended to ignore Tamina's raised eyebrows and the way her mouth formed an *O*. She studied Dann. There'd been a not-so-subtle change in him since his parents arrived. Perhaps that hurdle he couldn't seem to get past wasn't quite as high anymore.

After church, Tamina stood beside Janna at Audra's kitchen windows. David, Dann, and Franklin were standing around the grill as Audra approached them.

Janna craned her neck. "She's wearing that lovely dress Dann bought her again."

Tamina peered out the window. Carrying the pork tenderloins on a cookie sheet, Audra paused as though asking who was in charge of grilling. David took the meat and busied himself with seasoning it. Then Dann offered her a sip of his iced tea and said something that made her smile.

"I still can't get over the change in Dann." Janna turned from the window while Tamina began setting plates on the table.

"Oh yeah? What sort of change?"

Janna opened a drawer and began counting out silverware. "Oh, he was so sad and withdrawn for a couple of years, but now —" She shifted to the window again. "Well, he certainly seems taken with Audra. From what you've observed, do you think they're in love?"

Tamina chuckled. "If they're not in love, they're in a whole lot of like!"

An anxious look twisted Janna's face. "Does Audra know what he's gone through?"

"Hmm, I think she knows a whole lot more than she's ever told me, but she seems to be all right with it."

A slight relaxing loosened Janna's shoulders. Relief smoothed her face. Audra's sandals slapped the steps toward the kitchen door, and both women returned to finishing the table.

The table cleared, Audra tossed a deck of cards toward Dann before sitting next to him. "Okay, men against the women." She pulled the cribbage board from its box. The afternoon was whiled away at the game until Franklin and Tamina excused themselves in favor of a movie. After they left, Janna pushed the jumble of cards toward Dann. "They are a nice young couple. Does he come to see Tamina often?"

Dann raked the cards to himself. "This is the first time he's been here."

"Oh, I thought you'd known him for a long time. If this is the first time he's been here, how'd you meet him?"

He grinned at his mother. "Tamina, Audra, and I spent a few days in Albuquerque together. Tamina introduced us then."

"Oh." Janna furrowed her brow, but she let the matter drop.

Audra peeked up at Dann. *Is Dann teasing her, or is he trying to tell her something without telling her?*

"Well, is there any chance of playing some more music?" David broke in, rubbing his hands together. "I twisted Dann's arm to stop and get his instruments after church so the two of you could play some of your concert music for us, and I brought my violin again, too."

"Oh, you did, huh?" Audra laughed, cocking her head toward David. "I guess if you want the full treatment, we'd better pull another chair over for you."

Dann carried a pecan chair from the living room and placed it next to the one by the piano. They started with the flute. David smiled and nodded appreciatively from "Let It Go" all the way through "Badinerie." Janna kept time with her foot. When they were ready to start "Harmonium," Dann grinned. "Hang on to your hats, folks—here we go!" He winked at Audra. "Hit it, baby!"

Audra almost started laughing. Dann certainly hadn't said *that* to her when they played the concerts! They launched the Celtic beat with more enthusiasm than they'd ever played before. When they finished, David threw back his head and laughed with hearty delight, and Audra joined him.

"Is that what you said to her when you played at school?" Janna joked.

"What—you don't think it would've been appropriate?" Dann mocked surprise, and they all laughed.

Something *had* happened to him with the arrival of his parents. Audra didn't know what it was, but he was making her feel vibrantly alive. And it was so freeing knowing she was accepted by his fun-loving parents.

After the concert music, David joined for several songs from their wedding collection book. Audra tipped her watch. "Do you realize it's almost eight o'clock? This is wonderful and I'm sure we could keep it up all night, but my stomach is starting to let me know lunch was a long time ago. Maybe we should stop and get something to eat."

"Oh, Audra, don't go to any trouble," Janna rose as if

to help.

"No trouble at all." Audra sliced the leftover tenderloin into paper-thin rounds, which they nibbled on along with cottage cheese with pineapple and Ritz crackers. As they sat around the table, Dann reminisced about childhood days, and she propped her chin in her palm, listening with fascination.

They spent Memorial Day in Santa Fe showing David and Janna the sights before driving back to Albuquerque on Tuesday morning. They'd been on the road an hour when Audra leaned over toward Janna. "Did Dann tell you I will be having surgery next week?" she asked in a low voice.

Janna's eyebrows lifted. "No! I hope it's nothing serious."

"I have to have a hysterectomy."

The older woman's eyebrows knit together, and her lips pursed. Audra was certain thoughts were racing through her head. Finally, Janna faced Audra. "I'm sorry to hear it. I feel— well, rather shocked. Weren't you?"

"At first, yes. It all started last August and took until the end of last month for all the tests to be run and the doctor finally to tell me it had to be done. That was pure torture, and I was a nervous wreck waiting. The longer it dragged on, the worse it got, and I was resigned by the end. But I'm too much at risk not to go through with it." Audra sighed.

Janna clasped her hand. "I had it done close to ten years ago, but for a different reason, I'm sure, and of course, I'd had my children." She slowly shook her head. "I don't know what I would have done if I'd had to have it done before I had my babies." Lowering her gaze, she squeezed Audra's hand.

Audra studied Janna's profile. Her information had impacted Janna, and a rush of sympathy hit Audra. Janna had studied her and Dann all weekend, piecing little scraps of information together. Had she allowed herself to skip ahead in time and imagine the possibility of a wedding? Of grandchildren? Wouldn't that be the natural thing for a mother who wanted her son to be happy to do? It had seemed only fair to tell her, but now, Audra hurt as much as when she'd first found out herself. They rode in silence for nearly ten minutes, each lost in their own thoughts until David twisted backward in his seat.

"You gals are awfully quiet back there. Everything all right?" When he saw his wife's hand over Audra's, he just smiled and resumed talking with Dann.

Brunch at the motel dining room where they had stayed in March was long and leisurely, and they lingered over coffee as they crammed in the last bit of visiting possible. When they stood together at the final point before David and Janna had to make their way through airport security, David set his violin and the carry-on bag on the floor and swallowed Dann in his bear-hug embrace. Janna hugged Audra and then kissed her lightly on her lips.

"Thank you for everything, Audra." When she drew back, they looked into each other's eyes. It was a look that can pass between two women without need for words. It was a look that conveyed comprehension of what was really going on in spite of everything left unsaid over the weekend. They understood each other. Audra was confident Janna knew she was in love with her son.

Janna tugged her close again and whispered into her ear, "Please have Dann call us after the surgery and tell us how everything went."

"I will." Audra felt tears stinging her eyes. She loved Janna for who she was, but she couldn't help wondering what it would be like if her own mother were still alive.

While Dann hugged his mother, David put his arm around Audra's shoulders and drew her to his side. "Well, young lady, when you come to see us be sure and bring your piano."

Audra laughed. She reached up then and kissed his cheek. "I want you to know, David, you have a wonderful son, and I wish I could have had a relationship with my father the way the two of you have."

David stood taller and cleared his throat. "Well, thank you, Audra. Thank you for everything this weekend. I enjoyed every moment." The final goodbyes said, David picked up the two bags, and they walked to wait their turn at the security gate.

Audra knocked on Tamina's door when they arrived back in Chandler's Grove that afternoon. "We said we'd call, but we just happened to be in the neighborhood. Are we interrupting anything?"

"Not at all. We've been waiting for you. We were hoping you'd join us in a game of miniature golf."

Audra enjoyed the game, but she studied Dann every chance she got. She couldn't wait to be alone with him and see what he had to say about the weekend. Would these changes translate into a goodnight kiss?

They ate salads at The Yellow Rooster before driving Franklin and Tamina back to her apartment where they made their farewells. The last thing Dann said to Franklin was, "I have your phone number — I'll call you when I get to Albuquerque."

Home again, Audra collapsed on the couch. Dann let his head fall back and closed his eyes. The urge to snuggle up close to him and have him put his arms around her was strong, but she refrained. She only moved close enough to place her hand in his. "I'm glad your mom and dad came. I felt totally at ease with them." But that only halfway expressed the connection she'd felt.

Dann opened his eyes and rubbed his thumb across the back of her hand. "Aud, right now, I don't even have words to tell you how wonderful this weekend was for me. I knew you'd hit it off with my folks, but to watch it happen! And to see the joy on Dad's face when we all played was more gratifying than any other time he and I played together."

He was thoughtful for a minute. "You know, this weekend I think I got rid of another bag of trash I've been carrying around. Having you here with me and Mom and Dad was like hitting the reset button. I felt free — like I haven't felt in years." He lifted her hand to his lips and kissed the backs of her fingers.

"But I need to get going. The air mattress is still in the middle of the floor, and the bathroom looks like a couple of bachelors used it all weekend." He kissed the backs of her fingers, again.

After he left, she sat in the wheat-colored chair, rested her elbows on her knees, and dropped her chin into her hands. She couldn't decide whether she was elated or disappointed. The weekend had been tremendous, and yes, there was a big change in Dann, but… She stood, held her hands with the palms up, and spoke to the ceiling. "Am I going to have to *ask* him when he's going to kiss me?"

CHAPTER FORTY-ONE

LUNCH WITH HEATHER

AFTER AUDRA INFORMED JANNA OF HER UPCOMING SURGERY, SHE found it difficult to get it out of her mind again. When she awoke on Friday morning, she stayed in bed another thirty minutes. Random thoughts flitted through her head until one landed and wouldn't fly away again. *It's the first of June already, and in four days, I'll be at the hospital.* She swung her legs out of bed and headed for the shower. She didn't want to think of that now. She was meeting Tamina and Heather for lunch, and she'd told Dann she'd cook tonight. She'd rather think about that.

She picked Tamina up just before noon, and they met Heather at The French Pantry only a block from Heather's apartment. After ordering quiche, salad, and lemonade, Heather asked, "What did you guys do over the holiday weekend?"

"My boyfriend came in from Albuquerque," Tamina said.

The waitress set their lemonades and salads on the table. Audra tore the paper from her straw and watched Tamina, glowing as she acknowledged Franklin as her boyfriend. She sampled her salad. "Dann's mom and dad flew in from Chicago, and we had a pretty busy weekend. What about you?"

"Oh, Vern and I went to Albuquerque," she answered off-handedly. "We had a blast."

Dann's remark about Vern's conquests came to mind, and somehow Audra didn't feel happy for Heather the way she did for Tamina—but then maybe she was jumping to the wrong conclusion. She shouldn't judge. Maybe it was as innocent as her trip with Dann. Well, maybe, but something inside wasn't buying it. She shot a quick glance at Tamina, whose lips had pressed tight.

"Did you do all the tourist things?" Audra picked a pecan and a slice of tart strawberry from her salad that puckered her mouth.

"No. We spent most of our time at the hotel casino. I came home with two fifty more than I left with." She tore the paper from her straw and plunged it into her lemonade. "I'm flying to Minneapolis a week from Sunday. Vern's driving me to Albuquerque to catch my plane. He's going to Montana for the summer, and then in August, he's going to drive over to Minneapolis and pick me up and drive me back here." She lowered her eyes and started picking at her salad with her fork. "He wants me to move in with him when we get back."

The waitress set a slice of quiche in front of each of them as Audra and Tamina exchanged glances. Heather kept her face turned down, and Audra studied her across the table. She didn't feel shocked over Vern suggesting the arrangement, but she was surprised at Heather. Heather had latched onto Vern within weeks after Dann told her off. A knot began forming in the pit of Audra's stomach. *Is Vern toying with her?* Audra slid her fork under a bite of quiche, but she couldn't make herself put it in her mouth. She set it back on her plate.

"Are you considering it?"

Heather lifted her face. Her eyes grew hard. "Why not?"

"God says it's not right!" Tamina blurted.

Heather grimaced. "That's your opinion—not mine." She frowned at Audra. "Why are you concerned about me all of a sudden? You sound like my mother."

Sadness engulfed Audra. The old Heather had resurfaced. She had baited them in order to tell them her news. She *wanted* them to know.

Heather laughed. "Hey, I told you I was a stupid jerk for obsessing over Dann. Well, I'm over him now. When you get to know Vern, he's really a neat guy, and I'm not going to lose another man because you think I should be a Goody Two Shoes." Her eyes were bright, the old defiance tautening her lips and lifting her jaw.

Audra wanted to reach out to warn her, but before she could even formulate how she would say such a thing, Tamina asked, "What do your parents think of it?"

Heather glared at her. "Who says I'm going to tell them? I'm a big girl now. I can make my own decisions. Hey, I thought you guys wanted to be friends."

With her throat tight, Audra had to force herself to keep her voice even. "I do, Heather, but will you listen for a minute? As a friend, I'd like to ask you to think your plans over very carefully. Please? Tamina's right. Living together isn't what God wants for us. I don't mean to sound self-righteous but rebelling against God's word will only bring trouble. I know. I've seen too many people I love hurt by rebellion."

Heather's face dropped into a pout. She stabbed at her quiche. "Don't you think that's a little harsh?"

They lapsed into silence, and when they got up to pay, three half-eaten plates of quiche remained on the table.

Out on the sidewalk, Audra touched Heather's arm. "I'm sorry, Heather. I don't want us to get off on the wrong foot again, but I also don't want to see you get hurt. I guess I'm old-fashioned. I believe a couple should be married before living together. Tamina does, too. If you ever want to know how I came to that decision, I'll be glad to talk to you. I still want to be your friend."

A cold sheen froze Heather's blue eyes. "Don't bother worrying about me." She stalked toward her car without saying goodbye.

Audra's chest was heavy. *Maybe I said too much, but I hope she's not flirting with disaster.*

When she and Dann were sitting on the patio, she told him about it. "I think I was probably a little naïve to think that when she asked me to forgive her that her basic nature had changed. She still seems to have the attitude she's going to get whatever she wants."

Audra paused and shook her head. "I feel sorry for her. She's headstrong, and I don't know if she'll listen. I'm not sure she'll even give Tamina or me an opening to say anything more. She told me she'd never held onto a man, and the way she said it led me to believe she wasn't sleeping around, so is she so desperate now that she'd compromise her integrity to keep Vern? Or is she simply afraid of being manipulative again and can't discern when she should say no?"

She shook her head once more. "Am I living in the wrong era? I don't seem to understand the moral code of the times. I think she's headed for trouble."

He intertwined his fingers with hers. "You're an innocent, Aud. Sleeping together is pretty much the norm now. So is living together—people don't seem to see anything wrong with it anymore. Maybe, in her own mind, she really does believe it's all right. You're right, though, she could be headed for trouble, and you may have to help her pick up the pieces somewhere down the line." He ran his hand through his hair. "I wish Vern would show some restraint. If she's as inexperienced as you think, he might be taking advantage of her, but..." His voice faded. "Come on," he squeezed her hand, "let's go out to the lake and watch the sun go down."

CHAPTER FORTY-TWO

PRE-OP JITTERS

WHEN AUDRA WOKE UP ON SATURDAY MORNING SHE WISHED SHE could roll over and go back to sleep. *I'm not even out of bed yet, and I'm depressed.* She threw the sheet back and sat on the edge of the bed. *Today and tomorrow — that's all the time left before Dann leaves on his ride, and while he's here, I want to be with him. Tuesday will come whether I'm ready or not.*

She forced herself to take her shower. She didn't even want to go see Rosa and her grandmother. Her other piano students were taking the summer off, but Mrs. Espinosa had so little else to occupy her time that she wanted to continue through the summer. Audra would have made an excuse to call it off today, but Rosa would be celebrating her birthday while she was recuperating from surgery. She had to take her present to her today.

While Rosa and her grandmother played their lessons, the aroma of cooking pinto beans drifted into the cramped living room. *I hope they have more than beans and tortillas to eat.*

After Mrs. Espinosa played and went to stir the beans, Audra called Rosa back to the living room. Long wisps of soft black hair escaped her braids and drooped about her face. *I should offer to stay and brush her hair, but...* She reached her hand to the girl. "I have to cancel our lessons for a couple of Saturdays, sweetie. I'm going to have an operation, and I'll need time to get healed up…" Just saying the words took effort.

Rosa's eyes widened, and throwing her arms around Audra's neck, she silently clung to her. Audra's eyes stung at the child's sweetly innocent hug.

As she returned from the kitchen, a tired sigh fell from Mrs. Espinosa's lips as she sank into her easy chair. Audra caressed Rosa's hair away from her face and handed her a package. "Also, I'm not going to be able to come over on your birthday this year, and so I brought your present today. Nine years old! I can hardly believe it."

Pulling her hand, Rosa led her to plunk on the couch beside her and tore open the pink-striped paper. She giggled as she pulled out two shorts outfits, one pink and one yellow, and a grin spread across her face at the other gift nestled below. "Oh, Miss Audra—a new Barbie doll with outfits for her, too. Oh, thank you very much!"

Audra accepted another hug from the child but felt detached. She drove home wearing melancholy like a gray dress. Dann's car was parked in front of her house, and she ran to the backyard to find him sitting on the patio.

The joy of seeing him buoyed her, but not enough to erase the cloud of depression shrouding her. "Didn't you ride this morning?"

"No, Francie's folks left this morning, but we decided to take the weekend off to rest up for Monday." He motioned her to sit beside him and took her hand. "I was hoping we could do something. Would you like to go for a bike ride?"

She ducked her head. "I think I'd rather just walk." *I need my hand in yours. I need to draw strength from your touch. I need to feel close to you today.* "Is that all right with you? We should grab a sandwich before we do anything."

After lunch, she snuggled her hand in his as they walked

east on Bend to merge with the bike trail following Jeremy Chandler Drive along the arroyo. A block from Tamina's, he said, "Do you want to invite Tamina to walk along?"

Audra shook her head. "I don't want to share you today."

Giving an understanding nod, he intertwined their fingers.

When they reached the bike path, what conversation they'd had stopped, and they walked in silence. Bikers whizzed past them, and sweaty, panting runners left them behind. Even an elderly couple outpaced them. Everyone on the path was animated and energetic, but she couldn't catch the spirit of it. She wanted time to stand still so she could simply enjoy having her hand in his. They walked for another ten minutes until they came to a series of park benches facing the cottonwoods surrounding the Academy. They chose one and sat.

"Are you excited for your ride to start?" She finally broke the long silence.

He let out a long breath. "Yes and no. I was excited when we first planned this, but—" He bent and picked up a rock near his foot. Standing, he threw it as hard as he could, and it landed in a patch of weeds on the other side of the arroyo. "Are you sure you don't want me to stay home?" He turned and studied her before he sat again.

She didn't answer for a moment. "Well, it's not that I don't want you with me, but you've trained hard for this. I don't want you to get this close and then miss it. I really think you should go. I'll be all right—honest."

"You're a hundred-percent sure?"

"A hundred percent."

"Do you think if we got the Jeep and took in a movie, it would cheer you up?"

She rested her head against his shoulder. "Possibly, but only if you hold my hand the whole time."

He offered her his hand. "Come on. I can handle that."

Audra awoke on Sunday morning with the same heavy feeling weighing her down. It wasn't any different from the depression she'd gone through when she'd first found out she needed the surgery. *Dann will be leaving in the morning.*

Yesterday she'd urged him to go ahead with the ride, but how much of that was only bravado? She wasn't one-hundred-percent sure this morning. There was no problem with going to the hospital with Tamina. It wasn't that—it was just, well, she *did* want Dann with her. At the same time, she didn't want him to miss this experience. She couldn't ask him to change his plans and stay home. *Oh, God, I need strength not to be jealous of his decision.*

Something somewhere between apprehension and dread weighed on her all through church. When they filed out, she told Pastor Moorehouse about the upcoming surgery, and then she found herself standing in front of the church with Dann and Tamina. They were both looking at her. *Do they realize how emotionally frayed I am?* She wanted the day to slow down. She wanted to push the inevitable back.

"What do you say we stop at the store and get some steaks, and I'll throw them on your grill?" Dann offered.

She smiled. "That would be nice." Yesterday she hadn't wanted to share him with Tamina. Today she needed her. If anything could keep the day out of the pits, it would be her.

Audra laughed and joked along with them while they ate T-bone steaks, bagged salad, rolls, and store-bought pumpkin pie, but it seemed like she was outside of herself watching somebody else. She tried to maintain the gaiety while they played cribbage, but as the afternoon wore on, the façade slipped. Surely, Dann and Tamina knew it, too.

The day dragged. At seven, Audra suggested they go out

to Lake Patterson and watch the sunset. He held her hand as they walked into the sun.

They hadn't gone very far when Tamina shifted her gaze across Audra to Dann. "Hey, big brother, yesterday I found out Franklin has Sunday and Monday, the seventeenth and eighteenth, off this month, and he wants me to come to Albuquerque. You have any problem with that?"

A grin flashed across Dann's lips. "Depends on who you're staying with," he teased.

"He has a cousin there. She has a husband and four kids, and she said I could stay with them."

"Then go for it."

Tamina peered into Audra's face, waiting for a comment. When Audra didn't respond, a worried little frown tugged at Tamina's lips.

Dusk was fading to darkness when they returned to Audra's. Tamina left immediately, and Dann followed Audra into the kitchen.

She leaned against the counter, inundated by sadness. "That steak was a long time ago. Would you like a sandwich?" Every movement was like walking through water.

"Sure. I'll need something before bedtime."

"Peanut butter sandwich?"

"Perfect. Let me help."

She brought out bread and peanut butter while he set the table. She grew even more remote while they ate. It was an almost-silent meal. They cleared the table without a word. After she closed the dishwasher, he stepped in front of her, gripping her upper arms. "You're having a hard time, aren't you?"

"Yes, I am." She was afraid to put her arms around him because she'd cry but putting her arms around him was exactly what she wanted to do. Even if there was still a hurdle he couldn't get over, she wanted his arms around her. Even if he wasn't ready to tell her he loved her, she wanted him to hold her close, but she didn't want to cry. She kept her eyes down. "I thought I was doing okay, but it's been really hard for me to deal with it today."

"Do you want me to stay home?"

"No." But she did. She really did.

"What part's bothering you?" His arms encircled her, nestling her closer.

"It's not the surgery itself." She drew back, tilting her face at him. "It's... it's all the other stuff—everything I'm going to lose. I wish I didn't have to go through with it."

He lightly touched her cheek. "I want you to have the surgery, Aud. If you don't have it, and later you develop cancer... I don't know what I'd do if I lost you."

His finger traced the curve of her jawline, his gaze melding with hers. She'd never experienced such tenderness. He embraced her even closer to himself. She knew it was coming, and when he kissed her, she yielded to him and slid her arms around him. However, she didn't want just a sip—she wanted to drown in the delicious sensation. When he eased back, she lifted her hands, drew his face close to hers again, and pressed her lips against his. There was some fire in this kiss, and when she met his eyes, no alarm lingered there. His eyes were soft.

"I–I think I'd better get going before I can't," he whispered into her ear. "I'll see you as soon as I get back."

She tipped her face up to his, and their lips met for one last, lingering kiss before he pulled away and found his way down to the landing and out the back door.

Audra stood in the middle of the kitchen floor as he went down the steps. She continued to stare even after the door closed. "Oh my! That was bold of me. That was really bold." She started laughing as she danced to the living room, dropped in the wheat-colored chair, and hugged her arms around herself. "He kissed me. He *finally* kissed me — and oh my goodness, did I kiss him back!"

Not an ounce of depression remained in her. She was going to get through the surgery just fine.

CHAPTER FORTY-THREE

DANN'S RIDE

DANN WOKE A FEW MINUTES BEFORE HIS ALARM WENT OFF, A WAR raging within him. To go or not to go. He hadn't slept well. He kept waking with thoughts of Audra. She had assured him over and over that she wanted him to ride, but it seemed his very soul was being shredded. Ride or stay with Audra? He wanted one as badly as the other, and he had to decide. He lay in bed for ten minutes after the alarm. Finally, he got up, shaved, and procrastinated in a long shower. He had been anticipating this trip for months. He should be revved up and ready to go. He vaguely felt like there was another person in his body urging him toward an obligation he would just as soon back out of.

He smoothed sunscreen across his face and arms and massaged it in before pulling on his red and yellow biking shorts and matching shirt. He walked into the kitchen but didn't feel like eating and stalled in the middle of the floor. Random thoughts assailed him before he mixed a protein drink and forced it down. His body was going through the motions of getting ready, but his mind was still negotiating.

Grabbing his bottles of water, he put five of them in his daypack by the door and the other one next to it. In the kitchen, he peeled a banana. He stood at the living room window eating and staring out at nothing. He was back at the evening before, holding Audra in his arms, experiencing her lips against his. *She wanted those kisses as much as I did.* He couldn't forget how wonderful he'd felt. He jumped when the telephone rang.

"Hey, man, you're late!" Jerold's voice irritated Dann.

He tilted his watch. He'd totally lost track of time.

"I'll be there in a couple of minutes." Hanging up, he picked up his pack, helmet, sunglasses, and water bottle and left.

Dann fell in behind Vern and Jerold along Jeremy Chandler Drive to catch the highway south to Albuquerque. Once they were out on the highway beyond the old abandoned drive-in-movie and riding by the gray rock mesas, the heaviness would lift. It didn't.

He rode for another hour, trying to evade the nagging questions at the corners of his mind: Why hadn't he given up the trip? If he really wanted to be with Audra, why didn't he go back? He tried to ignore them and followed the leader. They refused to be ignored. They were demanding answers, and he didn't have any.

God, why am I riding away when my heart wants to be with Audra? What's keeping me from turning around? He kept on pedaling.

He thought about the night before. All day he had known he was going to kiss her. He had known because he had finally come to the place where he wanted her to know he was in love with her.

All right, God, what is keeping me from turning around? Once again, he allowed his thoughts to linger on the evening before. He wanted her to know he loved her, but when it came right down to it, he hadn't been able to say it last night. Something had stopped him. He kept on pedaling.

On their first date when he had taken her home after they went to the art galleries, he wanted to kiss her then. He almost had. What had stopped him? He knew the answer—he had kissed Gail on their first date. He had rushed into it and look what it had gotten him. So, he'd gone home that night and promised himself he wasn't going to kiss Audra for six months. He wanted to know her — to become best friends with her first.

In hindsight, kissing Gail first had distracted him from finding out who she really was, and if he had truly known who she was, he wouldn't have married her. He didn't want to make the same mistake twice.

They started up a grade. It wasn't steep, but it made him work harder. He kept pedaling behind Vern. Did Vern really like Heather or was she just another conquest? He thought about Heather and her desire to keep Vern at all cost... even if it meant moving in with him.

Audra's face floated before him. *Aud's a woman of integrity. She possesses more character, wisdom, and patience in her little finger than Heather, Gail, and Jasmine combined.* It hadn't taken him six months to figure that out. It was why he had fallen in love with her. Why he hadn't felt it necessary to wait one more month to kiss her. He knew her, and she certainly had become his best friend. *God, what a blessing she is.*

The thought startled him. *A blessing? From you, God?*

Audra claimed she wanted God's will for her life. Was Audra God's will for *his* life? Mulling the question over, he continued pedaling.

He had more questions now than when he'd started. *Oh, God, I need answers.*

At noon, Jerold halted on the side of the road. Dann grabbed two peanut butter sandwiches out of his pack and wolfed them down. He followed that with a protein bar and a sports drink. He hadn't realized he was so hungry. He ignored the banter between Jerold and Vern.

"You're worn out?" Jerold asked.

"No, I just have some things on my mind. I'm ready

whenever you are." He drained the last of his third water bottle and clipped a fresh one onto the bike frame.

He could turn back now. This would be a good place, and it would be easy. No, it wouldn't. He still didn't have his answers. If he loved Audra so much, why was he running away? Why hadn't he called off the trip and stayed with her? If he couldn't go back and tell her he loved her, he had to know why.

Oh, please, God, I need answers. He put his helmet back on before mounting his bike to fall in behind Vern.

Heatwaves were dancing above the asphalt and over the rough brown terrain, but he kept on pedaling. Ahead, rock formations rose like a fleet of desert battleships, but his mind wondered how God spoke to people when they had questions like his. In one of his sermons, Pastor Moorehouse said God spoke through his word, but he didn't have a Bible here. He wouldn't know where to look anyway. He'd have to rely on God speaking some other way. *God, please speak to me.* He kept pedaling.

A little after one o'clock, he was fast approaching the point of no return. If God didn't speak to him soon… Another hill. He leaned into his pedaling harder.

What's the matter, God? Do you think I'm afraid of making a commitment? He winced. That probably wasn't the way to speak to God. *Forgive me, but you know I made a commitment to Gail and I meant it. She was the one who didn't keep the promise. She was the one who betrayed me. You know I forgave her — but she hurt me. She hurt me, God!*

He wanted to lie down and beat his fist on the ground, but he couldn't. He had to keep pedaling. Vern was thirty yards in front of him now.

A short way on down the road the answer came. It came just as a silent knowing within, but he understood with his whole being. It came with such clarity that he answered aloud. "You're right, God. I'm afraid of being hurt again. I'm running away because I'm afraid of being hurt." *Oh, that was awesome!*

Without warning, he saw Gail in his mind—aloof, distant, self-absorbed. The hindsight factor was at work again. Suddenly he knew without a doubt that if he'd gotten to know her, if he had honestly admitted to himself how self-centered she was instead of being distracted by sweet kisses, he never would have married her.

His dad had tried to tell him he was making a mistake, and he'd refused to listen. *God, I was a rebel. My own rebellion caused me to get hurt, and instead of letting it go, I've hung on to my hurt like some kid's dirty thumb-sucking blanket. I've dragged it along with me for such a long time that it's filled me with fear.*

Then, like a breath of fresh air, Audra's words came back to him. "We have to say, 'God, I'm coming to you just the way I am—warts, wounds, scabs, and all, and let God do the forgiving, the healing, and the changing.' "

Dann smiled to himself. *Well, God, here I am. I've got every one of those. Would you please forgive me? I'm ready for you to create that new heart in me I heard about a few Sundays ago.*

On the day Audra told him the date for her surgery, they had spoken careless words. She had been the first to run into his arms and ask him to forgive her. Once she'd said, "If you're feeling cautious because of what's happened in the past, I can understand, and it's okay." How relieved he'd felt!

Suddenly, like the first ray of sunshine piercing the dark and bringing light, understanding dawned on him—she'd done those things because she loved him. She had even been willing to go through the surgery alone because she'd wanted him to experience this ride—because she wasn't self-centered. She loved him.

She forgave her father because she didn't want to carry a burden of anger any longer. She couldn't bear to reprimand Taylor harshly, and she hadn't even been able to hold onto her anger at Heather because something replaced her anger with love. She would never intentionally hurt him. He was certain of that. He would always be safe with her. The fear began to melt.

So, am I willing to sit around a motel swimming pool tomorrow while she's in surgery? Will I be content to lie around tomorrow resting up for the ride back while she grieves over not ever being able to have a baby?

Then his heart lurched. She wasn't grieving because she would never have a baby—she was grieving because she loved him and she wouldn't be having *his* baby! He winced like he had a rock in the pit of his stomach. *You jerk — you stupid jerk! That's what she was trying to tell you last night! God, forgive me for being insensitive. I have to turn around — now!*

He hadn't realized how much he'd slowed his pace. Vern was nearly fifty yards in front of him. He forced his legs to pump faster, faster. His muscles burned. Vern was forty yards ahead. He kept pushing. Thirty yards. He lifted the whistle on the lanyard around his neck to his lips and gave a shrill blast. Vern and Jerold pulled to the right immediately. Dann was panting when he wheeled up next to them.

"I'm turning around. I've got to go back."

"Why? Something wrong? You feel all right?" Jerold grasped Dann's shoulder as his brow wrinkled.

"I'm all right." Dann unbuckled his helmet and wiped the sweat off his face with his shirt. "I have to go back and be with Audra. She wanted me to ride, but I should have called it off. I have to be with her at the hospital. You guys go on without me."

"Man, you've got a five-hour ride back." Vern squirted water into his mouth and over his face.

"I know. Longer than you guys have, but I have to do it."

"Here." Jerold handed him a water bottle. "For some reason, I stuck an extra in this morning. You might need it."

"Thanks." Dann swigged a long drink and stuck the bottle

in his pack. He rummaged another peanut butter sandwich from his pack to eat on the way. He'd ride an hour and then stop for another snack. It was going to be a long ride, but at least he was going toward, not running from.

As he rode, he thought about Audra. He hummed music they played. He remembered the day they had gone to the cave, and the horrible, momentary fear he'd felt when she said it was difficult for her to tell him what she had to say. For just an instant, he'd been afraid she was going to say she didn't want to see him anymore. Hearing she had to have the surgery had been almost a relief.

It meant so much to him when she asked if his dad would care to bring his violin because she wasn't like Gail. The elation he'd experienced when the three of them played together came back to mind. Seeing how she related to his parents had freed him from a whole lot of emotional clutter.

At three fifteen, he rested for twenty minutes, but there was no shade. He ate another protein bar and the banana in his pack that was growing soft and brown, drank another sports drink, and thought about Audra. At five, he rested for another thirty minutes in a sliver of shade under a billboard, leaning back against his daypack. He probably wasn't in quite as good shape as he'd thought.

He arrived at a filling station and food mart on the outskirts of Chandler's Grove at ten till seven. His hands were trembling from hunger. After chugging a bottle of water, he sat in a booth and ate two hot dogs, a bag of chips, and drank a quart carton of chocolate milk. Retrieving his cell phone from the depths of his pack, he called Audra. No answer. He tried her cell. Unavailable. Almost an hour later, he rolled up to Jerold's and put his bike in the back of his Cherokee. He quickly told Francie, lest she wonder where his Jeep went.

Ten minutes later, he dropped his pack and helmet on his kitchen floor and called Audra. Still no answer on either phone.

His muscles were screaming. He took a couple aspirin with two full glasses of water, held his head under the cold-water tap, and dried off on the kitchen hand towel and then called Tamina. She wasn't home, either. He was too exhausted to think where they might be. He'd lie on the couch and try again in half an hour.

He fell asleep wondering if he would have gotten the answer to his question as plainly if he'd stayed home. Sometime after midnight, he woke up, drank more water, stumbled into the bedroom, set the alarm, and fell asleep again on top of the bed, still in his clothes.

The next morning, he found Tamina in the surgery waiting room at Kirkwood Memorial Hospital. A half-dozen people with bored faces sat around her. She was reading a magazine and paid no attention when he claimed the chair next to her.

"Did they already take her in?" he asked, leaning toward her.

She snapped the magazine shut. Her eyes widened. "How did you get here?"

He grinned. "I turned around and came back. I had to be here. I guess they took her in already?"

"They took her into pre-op fifteen minutes ago. They're going to come out and get me in a few minutes, and I'll go in and sit with her. She can have two people in there, so you can go in, too."

He hesitated. His knee was bouncing a staccato beat, feeling like he was about to crawl out of his skin. *I've got to see her alone before they wheel her off—I have to.* He stood and took three paces away, and then back. He cleared his throat. "Umm, do you mind if I go in alone for a few minutes?"

Tamina lifted an eyebrow. "Of course not. She's going to be pretty happy to see you."

"How was she doing when you brought her in?" He sat back down and grasped the armrests.

"Sort of quiet. I'm sure she was missing you. You must have been missing her, too, huh?"

"There's an understatement! That was the longest day of my life."

An overweight nurse in baggy scrubs stepped into the room. "Audra Knight's friend can come in now."

Tamina crossed the room, with him close behind her. "This is Audra's friend, Dann. He's going to go in first, and I'll come in a few minutes," she explained.

The nurse shrugged and nodded for Dann to follow. She led him through the double doors into the pre-op area and opened the curtain to Audra's cubicle. "Do you want the curtain closed?"

"Please." The bed was cranked up to a forty-five-degree angle. Even in a white hospital gown and no makeup, Audra was beautiful, and he'd never once told her so. As he rounded the end of the bed, her hand was already reaching toward him as if she were expecting him.

She grabbed the rail and pulled herself forward. "You came."

"I came." Stretching over the low bedrail, he kissed her. "I've been going nuts—I couldn't get ahold of you."

She touched his cheek. "Tamina and I went to a movie, and my cell died—Oh, Dann." She frowned, studying his face. "You're sunburned. How far did you go?"

"Over halfway." Her hand was cool on his face. "Just far enough for God to knock me on the head with a two-by-four."

"Any lumps?"

He grinned. "Quite a few, I'd say." He stroked her cheek. "Actually, I think he had to do heart surgery." He smiled and kissed her again. "Aud, I—"

A nurse in blue scrubs flipped the curtain open. "Just need to check your breakfast, here." She inspected the IV needle in Audra's hand and her glucose bag before she left.

"Aud, I wanted—"

The curtain flipped open again. "I need your signature on these consent forms." The rotund nurse shoved a clipboard in front of Audra.

After Audra signed and she left, he stepped close to the bed again and took her hand. "I don't know how much time I have, but I have to say something before they wheel you off. I'm not afraid any longer. I know God sent you to me. I love you more than words can say. Will you marry me?"

His eyes were so soft, so unguarded. It seemed they were caressing her very soul, and Audra knew with all certainty what God's will was. She lifted his hand to her lips and kissed it. "I love you, too, Dann. Yes, I'll marry you."

He leaned over the rail and tenderly kissed her.

The curtain grated on its track again as the nurse in blue scrubs reentered. "I have to get your vitals." She took Audra's blood pressure and checked her temperature and pulse. "Hmmm, pulse is just a little fast."

"Must be that last kiss." Audra giggled. "He just proposed to me."

The nurse entered the information on the bedside computer and then arched one eyebrow at him. "Well, I don't think we've ever had that happen in pre-op before." She laughed. "Congratulations!"

"Thanks." He grinned. She walked out.

"There's one more thing you must know before you go in."

He bent closer, holding her hand again. "There won't be any babies, and that's perfectly all right because I know God will bless us in many other ways."

As tears blurred her eyes, he grabbed a tissue from the box on the table beside the bed and caught them as they slid down her cheeks.

"Oh, Dann, you don't know how much that means to me." Their eyes locked, a silent communication of a love they both knew would endure.

"Do you want Tamina to come in?" he finally asked.

Minutes later, Tamina squinted one eye at Audra. "From the grins on your faces, I'd say something's going on. So, what's happening?"

Audra reached up and stroked his face. "We're getting married." Awe filled her voice.

"Girlfriend, that's wonderful!" Tamina rushed to Audra's side, and leaning over the rail, she hugged her and kissed her cheek. "I'm thrilled for both of you." Straightening, she wagged a finger at him. "You asked her to marry you right here in the hospital? Is that romantic or what!" She rounded to the other side of the bed and hugged him, too. "She doesn't need me to sit with her — you have it all under control. I'll see you in the waiting room." She flashed one last grin.

"Hey, Tamina!" he called to her back. "When you talk to Franklin, tell him I didn't make it to Albuquerque."

Audra's eyes didn't leave Dann's face as peace swaddled her. *He loves me. I will never, ever doubt that. Lord, make me a wife worthy of his love.* A new sensation shivered down her back. *I'm an inexperienced thirty-three-year-old virgin — what will it be like?* She touched his face, again. "I never dreamed I'd be going into the operating room with such anticipation. I'm excited for what's on the other side. Please hold my hand and tell me about your ride so I can settle down."

"Well, I can't tell you much about the scenery, because all I saw was you."

The nurse in the blue scrubs came in. "I'm going to put a mild sedative in your IV to start relaxing you."

Within seconds, Audra could feel it starting to take effect. There was one more thing she wanted to say before her tongue would no longer behave. "Dann, your mom asked that you call her when it's over. Tell her I said everything she suspected when she was here is very, very true."

CHAPTER FORTY-FOUR

RECUPERATING

As groggy as she was, Audra was grateful Dann stayed at her bedside all day and into Tuesday evening. She was sitting up when he entered her room at noon the next day, carrying a cyclamen plant covered in pink blossoms. He set the plant on her bedside table before he kissed her and stroked her cheek. "You look considerably better this morn. Are you feeling better?"

"I was awake several times in the night, and I won't be going very far or fast today. But I do feel better than when you left last night." She touched a rosy petal then gave him a peck of a kiss. "Thank you. I love cyclamen—they're so cheery. Did you call your folks back?"

"Uh-huh. They were sorry they missed my call last night, but they were glad to hear all went well. It was a fun conversation. Dad answered, so I told him you are doing well. But then I said, 'Dad, I'd like you to sell some stock for me.' He said, 'Okay. How much?' I said, 'Enough to invest in diamonds.' " Dann started laughing. "I'm sure, for a minute, he thought I'd fallen for some get-rich-quick scheme. He got quiet and said, 'Where are you going to invest in diamonds?' I told him, 'At a jewelry store, Dad. I need to buy some wedding rings.' Oh, man, Aud, I wish I could have seen his face right then! He let out this loud

'Hallelujah,' and he was laughing."

"Ohhhh, don't make me laugh!" She winced. "Dann, you're such a tease." *Diamonds*! She hadn't even thought about a ring, let alone diamonds. She reached over and took his hand in both of hers.

"He called Mom to the phone then. I had to lead her on a little, too. I told her your surgery went fine, and that you had asked me to give her this cryptic little message—that what she had suspected while she was here is very true. So, I asked her, 'Whatever did you suspect?' Without missing a beat, she said, 'I suspected the two of you were in love. Was I right or was I wrong?' So, I told her, 'A funny thing happened on the way to the operating room. I asked her to marry me.' First, she squealed, and then she just kept saying, 'That's wonderful,' over and over."

He stood there grinning, his eyes sparkling. "I called Davene, too. She can't wait to meet you." Pulling her closer, he kissed her. "They're all happy for us, Aud, and they send you their love. Somehow, I don't think they were as surprised as Evan and Marsha and Laney and Andy were last night when we told them."

Audra caressed the side of his face. "Your mother is very perceptive. I knew she knew. I have to get up and walk my laps. Come with me?"

After Audra's discharge Thursday evening, Tamina spent the night. On Friday, Audra spent the day on the couch with her pillow, and Dann and Tamina pampered her. The doorbell rang at one o'clock, and Tamina ushered in Pastor Moorehouse. He shook her hand and then Dann's before crossing the room to Audra. "Well, young lady, they kicked you out of the hospital in fine time, didn't they? I called the hospital last evening once I got back from my meeting in Sacramento and you'd already been discharged, so I assumed you must be doing well."

"I am. Dann keeps bootin' me off the couch and making me walk, and I feel a little stronger each time we go out in the backyard."

"Good for you." Pastor Moorehouse nodded toward Dann and Tamina. "It looks like you have a couple of good nurses here."

"They're the best." Audra smiled up at Dann.

Dann grinned and cleared his throat, motioning toward the pecan chair to the left of the couch. "Won't you have a seat, Pastor?"

"Actually, I can't stay. I have two other hospital calls to make, but I just wanted to check in on Audra, here, and make sure everything's all right."

As she eased her feet off the couch and pushed herself to a sitting position, Dann gave her a nod. "Do you want to tell him?"

Pastor glanced at Tamina, who was grinning at them. "Maybe I do need to sit down."

"Pastor, things have changed a little since I talked to you on Sunday." Audra couldn't keep from grinning. "Dann and I want to get married. You're the first one to know since we told our families." She paused. It still seemed incredible. She was certain joy was oozing out of every pore. "We haven't set a date — well, we haven't had a chance to make any plans yet, but we wanted you to know."

"Ah, fresh off the press, is it? Well, when you are back on your feet, the two of you come in and see me." He shot his hand out to Dann. "I hope you'll be open to some pastoral counsel?"

Dann shook the pastor's hand. "We certainly will."

Pastor Moorehouse motioned for Tamina to move closer, and with the four of them holding hands, he prayed for Audra's continued healing and for a blessing on her and Dann as they began to move forward in their plans to wed.

On his way to the door, he nodded toward the piano on the other end of the room. "Yes, you told me you play piano. May I call on you sometime to play at church?"

"Call on both of them, Pastor," Tamina broke in. "Dann plays violin and flute, and they play some pretty awesome duets together."

"Oh, really? Well, we'll talk about that soon." He gave them all a smile and made his exit.

After their third trek around the backyard, Audra headed for the couch for a short rest. The doorbell rang, and Lucy Sanders stood there, holding a plate of peanut butter cookies. Handing the cookies to Tamina, she darted to the couch. Her dyed-red hair bounced as she shook her head at Audra. "Oh, my dear, I saw you come home last night. You were walking so slow, and your young man was carrying a suitcase—and then I saw you out walking today in your housecoat. I thought you must have been in the hospital, so I baked you some cookies. Are you doing all right?"

"Thank you for your concern, Lucy. I'm just fine." Lucy was on a fishing expedition, so Audra changed the subject. "Have you met my friend, Tamina York? This is my neighbor, Lucy Sanders." Then she lifted her hand toward Dann. "And this is my *fiancé*, Dann Day."

Lucy's eyebrows arched. The news would be halfway down the block within thirty minutes, but Audra did enjoy rolling that word *fiancé* off her tongue.

"Well, congratulations." Lucy extended her hand to Dann. "I've seen you coming so often with your violin and flute. I just love to sit outside and listen to the two of you play."

"Thank you." Reticence guarded his face as he accepted the offered hand.

Lucy continued to stand there, but the silence grew until she finally said, "Well, you probably need to rest, so I'll run on.

If you need anything, let me know."

"Thanks, Lucy, but Tamina and Dann have everything under control. Thanks again for the cookies. We'll have them for dessert this evening."

As soon as the door closed, Dann asked, "Does she watch everything you do?"

"Lucy Loose Lips sees everything and tells everything." Audra giggled. "Haven't you noticed I always close the drapes as soon as we come in?"

Dann and Tamina joined her laughter.

On Saturday morning, the aroma of French toast still wafted through the kitchen as Audra swirled the last of her coffee in her cup. "You guys are spoiling me. But thanks. I'm feeling better with each day." She stood to put her cup in the dishwasher when the doorbell rang. "I'll get it."

"Well, hi," she greeted Vern and Heather. Vern was carrying a grocery-store bouquet of flowers.

"We thought we'd stop by and see how the invalid is doing." He held the flowers toward Audra. "You have a vase for these?" White chrysanthemums, pink daisies, and burgundy-and-white alstroemeria peeked out of the cellophane wrapper.

Dann and Tamina entered from the kitchen. "Tamina, I think there might be a vase on one of the top shelves in the hall linen closet." Gesturing to the other end of the room, Audra headed for the couch. "Come on in and sit down."

Audra curiously eyed Heather as she slid into one of the matching side chairs. Vern took the other. Heather seemed a bit reserved. *I wonder if she's still planning to move in with him?* "Everything go okay?" Vern leaned closer, supporting his elbows on his knees.

"Pretty good. I'm doing a lot of resting, and when I'm not, I'm eating and walking. It will be awhile before I'm riding my bike, though."

"I didn't realize you'd had surgery until Vern got back from his ride to Albuquerque." A hesitancy softened Heather's voice. "I hope it wasn't anything serious."

"I had to have a hysterectomy."

Heather's eyes popped open, but she hastily lowered her gaze to the floor. "Oh, I didn't know. I'm sorry —"

"What time did you and Jerold get to Albuquerque on Monday?" Dann deftly turned the conversation away from Heather.

"I guess it was around five. What time did you get back here?"

"It was eight o'clock before I got to the apartment after picking up the Jeep. That afternoon heat was grueling. I had to stop a couple of times, and I was probably a little dehydrated when I got to town."

Tamina returned with the bouquet in a vase and set it on the coffee table next to Dann's cyclamen. She sat in the wheat-colored chair and studied Heather's downcast face.

"What did you do while Vern was gone?" Audra asked, trying to draw Heather back into the conversation.

Heather glanced up at Audra and promptly glanced down again. "I...umm...I did some packing."

Vern hopped back into the conversation. "Heather's lease is up the first of July. We decided there's no sense both of us paying rent all summer while we're gone, so we're moving her stuff over to my place before she leaves."

Heather glanced at Vern, but she wasn't smiling. Her face went white, and she didn't add anything. Everything grew quiet and awkward.

"Would you guys like some coffee? I think there might be some soda, too." Tamina started to rise.

Vern checked his watch. "No thanks. We have a load of boxes in the car now, and we still have another load to get before lunch." When he stood, Dann got up from the end of the couch and, with a nod, motioned Vern toward the front door. They went out.

Heather moved over to the couch. "I didn't mean to pry, asking about your surgery." She focused on her hands. "A hysterectomy was entirely unexpected. I hope that wasn't too hurtful of me."

"No, it wasn't. Dann and I have both come to terms with it."

Heather's face twisted with puzzlement before she finally met Audra's steady gaze.

"Heather, Dann asked me to marry him. We haven't had a chance to plan anything, but I'm glad I had a chance to tell you before you left."

Heather sucked in a breath. "I'm glad for you both. I really am." But her eyes were sad.

"What are you going to do all summer?"

"My grandmother has a friend with an eleven-year-old grandson who needs tutoring over the summer, and I said I'd take it on. I don't know what else I'll do. My folks will spend the summer at their lake cabin, but it's too boring there. I'll just join them on a couple of weekends." She shrugged and lifted her heavy, blond hair off her neck. Another awkward silence stretched between them.

She's got Vern, but she still seems lonely. Audra didn't know what else to say.

Heather stood. "I guess I'd better go. Vern will be waiting." She forced a smile at both Audra and Tamina. "You guys have a nice summer."

"You, too, Heather. Thanks again for the flowers. Give me

a call when you get back?"

"I'll do that." She let herself out.

As soon as Vern's car pulled away, Tamina moved over next to Audra on the couch. "That girl's hurtin', don't you know?"

"I know."

The kitchen door opened, and Dann stomped through to the living room. He stood at the front window without speaking, his hands jammed into the pockets of his jeans shorts.

"What happened out there?"

He sagged onto the pecan chair at the end of the couch. "I told him I was disappointed he was going through with this living together stuff. He just blew me off and said Heather was putting the pressure on. Somehow, I don't think that's the way it is, but then he said, '*You* know what she's like,' and that put enough doubt in my mind that I wasn't sure. I told him to have a nice summer and I'd see him when he gets back, and I went out in the backyard to cool off." He eyed Audra then Tamina. "Do you think she's the one putting the pressure on?"

The women passed glances between them. Audra spoke first. "I don't think so. I think she's having second thoughts. I'll bet living together is in direct conflict with her upbringing, because when we went to lunch, she said she wouldn't tell her parents."

"I agree, I think she's having a big attack of conscience. Maybe we should pray for her over summer."

"Maybe we should." Dann nodded, and they sat for several more minutes in silence.

After lunch, Audra settled on the couch with a paperback. Tamina began cleaning house and doing Audra's laundry while

Dann went out to mow the lawn. The front door was open just wide enough that she heard him call out, "Hey, buddy, what's up?" to someone. She crossed to the front window. Taylor was at the end of the driveway, one foot on the curb balancing his bike. Another boy was with him. She went to the door and opened it wider.

"Hi, Miss Knight," he waved. "This is my cousin, Josh. I'm spending the day with him."

"Hi, Josh," she waved back. Yes, she had seen him in the neighborhood before.

"Are you sick?" Taylor called out.

"No, I had an operation. I'm getting better now."

"Is that why you're mowing the grass, Mr. D?"

Dann chuckled. "Yeah, I'm sort of helping out."

Tamina came and stood in the doorway next to Audra. "Hey, Taylor. I thought I recognized your voice."

"Miss York! What are you doing here?"

"I'm helping Miss Knight out, too."

"My three most favorite teachers. I don't believe it." He slapped the side of his head with the flat of his hand. "Hey, Mr. D, do you need any help?"

Dann rubbed his chin. "Well, I still have to mow the back. Do you want to trim around the edges?"

"Oh, sure." Taylor dropped his bike onto the driveway behind Dann's Cherokee. Josh followed suit, and both boys trailed Dann to the backyard. "Bye, Miss Knight—Miss York. Hope you get better fast, Miss Knight."

Thirty minutes later, Dann grabbed three sodas from the refrigerator and headed to the backyard. Audra gave them another ten minutes alone and then went out to take her walk. She had a feeling there were always going to be kids in their house.

She ordered pizza from Canyon Road House for dinner to

thank Tamina for all her help. Shortly after Tamina left, Laney, Andy, Jon, and Jonah brought a roast beef, potatoes, gravy, and carrots and put them in the refrigerator. They stayed until after eight.

Audra stretched back out on the couch once silence settled in. "Oh, I'm tired."

Dann's forehead furrowed. "You didn't overdo it, did you? I wasn't expecting a constant stream of people all day." He sat on the floor beside her.

"I wasn't, either, but I'll be all right after a good night's sleep. It's just, well, I was looking forward to a nice quiet evening with just the two of us."

"I was, too. Tomorrow. We'll have tomorrow. Do you want me to come and fix breakfast?"

"No, I can handle a bowl of cereal. You go on to church."

"Okay." He kissed her three times before he got up to leave.

"Lock up for me, will you, please?"

CHAPTER FORTY-FIVE

VISION FOR THE FUTURE

By Sunday morning, Audra couldn't face sitting around in her robe another day. She showered, put on shorts and a yellow polo shirt, applied her makeup, and brushed her hair out. No more ponytail, either.

After making her bed, she sat at the piano and ad-libbed chords for the song "Give Thanks With A Grateful Heart." It had been running through her mind all morning. She sang it through, but after the words stopped, the music kept flowing—arpeggios of joyous sound up and down the keyboard, until she felt like she couldn't hold another ounce of happiness.

Dann would arrive momentarily, so she moved to the couch. She was still sitting there at quarter till twelve, and he hadn't arrived. She stretched out on her side on the couch and put her arm under her head. The feeling of elation was still there, but she wondered where he could be. At noon, she moved to the front window. She stood there another five minutes before he pulled into the driveway. She had the front door open before he was out of the car.

He entered the house carrying a large white sack, and the aroma told her immediately he had stopped at Burger Basket.

"Well, look at you up and dressed. You look great."

"Thanks. I feel great, too." As soon as he placed the bag on the kitchen table and turned back toward her, she reached up and slid her arms around his neck and kissed him until he answered by sliding his arms around her back and drawing her close.

"Mmm, that's nice to come home to," he murmured into her ear.

She rested her head on his chest and then tipped her face up at him. "I was sitting at the piano this morning, and all of a sudden, I was just overcome with awe. I don't know which struck me more, the fact that I'm going to be your wife or that you're going to be my husband. I vividly remember you asking me to marry you, and I vividly remember saying I would. But ever since those words were spoken, either I was totally groggy, there was a bedrail between us, or there was an audience of people in and out. All I've wanted to do all week is to tell you I love you, I love you, I love you, and so I will. I love you, I love you, I love you."

"That's not a bit different from what I experienced." He smoothed a stray hair off her face. "I love you, I love you, I love you, too." He drew her into a kiss reminiscent of the one before he left on his bike ride.

Still in his embrace, she snuggled closer. "When I was sitting on the couch waiting for you, some questions were going through my mind."

"Such as?"

"Well, two major ones. Are we ready to set a date, and where will we live?"

"Valid questions. Where do you want to start?"

"I don't care. You pick."

He released her and stepped across to the calendar hanging on the cupboard above the telephone. He lifted it off its nail, pushed the bag of hamburgers out of the way, and laid the calendar flat on the table. "I have to admit, I've already checked the calendar because I was curious, but what do you think? Do you want to wait awhile or plan on soon? Please be truthful, because I don't want to pressure you."

Audra studied him. She had fallen in love with him long before he kissed her, but she knew his kisses were awakening things in her she'd never experienced before. Things she liked. Would she be able to show the same restraint he'd shown over the months, or would it be possible she'd be the one to cause them to go too far by waiting too long? She pressed her lips together as she pondered. "How soon is soon?"

"If we want a honeymoon, it would have to be before we start back to work on the eighth of August."

Her mouth flew open. "Oh my!" she gasped. *And he thought Franklin and Vern were moving too fast!* That thought slightly amused her, but with Dann's face so serious, she wasn't certain he'd appreciate the humor. "That would make it soon, wouldn't it?" she said, suddenly comprehending the reality of how soon "soon" was.

"If we didn't go on a honeymoon, there'd be Labor Day weekend or Thanksgiving or Christmas break. We'd have more time then, but it would sure limit where we went. Or we could wait until next summer."

Audra shook her head. She didn't like that choice at all. She eased out a kitchen chair and sat. "This is making my head swim!"

He settled into a chair facing her, his forearms resting on his thighs, his fingers laced. "Is a honeymoon important to you?"

She searched his eyes. "I don't think we'd want just a quick weekend and then have to go right back to work, would we?"

His breath let go in a release of relief. "No, I don't think we would."

"If it were soon, what do you see as viable?"

Dann rotated the calendar where they could both see it. "The doctor said six weeks until your checkup, and this Tuesday will mark a week. Count one, two, three," he ran his finger down the weeks, and then flipping the page, "four, five, six—that takes it to the eighteenth of July." He moved his finger down one more line. "The end of the next week—say, Friday the twenty-seventh, would give us eleven days before we'd have to be at work."

Time wise, that could work, but her mind was having a difficult time adjusting. It was an enormous transition from just finding out they were getting married to stepping off into that place of no return in a few short weeks. On the other hand, she didn't want to wait a long time, either. She gulped. *What if I'm not completely healed by then? How will we get everything arranged on such short notice? We're not making a mistake, are we?*

Dann took her hand. "Do you need to think about it?"

She gripped his hand tightly and whispered, "I don't know."

"Would it help if we talked to Pastor Moorehouse?"

She slid onto his lap ran her hand through the side of his hair. "Oh, Dann, I'm sure it would. If he doesn't think we'd be rushing things, I wouldn't have a qualm about going ahead the end of July, but if he thinks it's too soon—"

"Then we make Plan B. I'll talk to him tomorrow." He took advantage of her closeness and kissed her again.

She reluctantly relocated to the other chair. *Six weeks seems so short, but what's going on inside of me is going to make it one long wait.*

He nudged the bag of hamburgers back across the table. "You do realize lunch is totally cold, don't you?" He slid a hamburger with wilted lettuce hanging out the edge and a tray of limp fries over to her. "Oh, by the way—I was late getting here because I stopped by and talked to Jake at the bike shop. He said if I want the job, he'll pay me twenty bucks for each bicycle I assemble. No set hours and not much pay, but I can't sit around doing nothing all summer. I can start tomorrow."

On Wednesday afternoon, Audra led Dann to the side entrance to Pastor Moorehouse's office. Pastor's secretary invited them to take a seat and pointed them to a coffee carafe spilling its aroma into the waiting area. They declined the coffee, and she clutched Dann's hand when they sat.

"You have both our papers?" She peeked across at him. He nodded and lifted the manila folder in his hand. *Of course, he has them. He wouldn't forget them any more than he would have forgotten to explain our time constraints to Pastor.* She sagged into the chair with nubby upholstery. *Describing Dann's strengths was a thought-provoking assignment, but I wonder what he wrote about me? Wouldn't it be interesting to know!*

Pastor Moorehouse sat at his desk with the two papers in front of him. He put his glasses on and began to read. Audra licked her lips and glanced at Dann. He was hunched forward in his chair, his eye fastened on Pastor. *Did I portray Dann as strong and steady as he really is? What if Pastor doesn't think we're ready?*

Pastor took his glasses off and held the papers in his hands. "Dann and Audra, I have given marriage counseling to many, many couples, but few have the understanding of each other that you two already possess. I think if young couples, who think they are ready for marriage, looked for as many of the inner qualities that the two of you see in each other, there'd be a lot less divorce."

His chair squeaked when he leaned back. "Dann, you told me that, for you to have a honeymoon before you start back to teaching, you have to get married at the end of July. Audra, I can understand how you would feel this is rushing things, but time notwithstanding, let me encourage you on a couple of points." He edged forward again and laid the papers on his desk. "I feel a honeymoon is an important part of the marriage process. It doesn't have to be elaborate, but a time to get away from family and friends to be by yourselves—to express yourselves to each other.

"These papers I gave you are the first assignment in my marriage counseling course. Nine more lessons are designed to explore every aspect of marriage, answer your questions, and prepare you to enter into marriage with confidence. If you choose to get married in July, we'll have to double up on some of them, but I don't see that as a problem."

He tapped the papers in front of him. "When a couple fills out this first assignment, I can usually tell with a fair amount of certainty whether or not they are ready to be married. I don't see any reason for you to have a prolonged engagement. By the time you finish the counseling, I'm certain you will be ready in July."

He picked up the papers and stood up. "I seldom let couples see each other's papers, as they are often superficial and shallow. However, yours are both rich and uplifting, and I want you each to read what the other wrote." He came around the desk and handed them each a paper and then returned to his chair. "You both said you believe this is God's will, but there's another common thread I hope you'll catch."

As she read, she could feel tears welling up. She glanced up at Pastor Moorehouse, and he already had a handful of tissues to pass to her.

He waited until they finished reading and looked into each other's eyes. He nodded as if he knew they'd caught it.

"Pastor," she dabbed at her eyes, "I told Dann that if you thought we were ready and not rushing it, I'd have no qualms about July. What you've said has laid my fears to rest." She turned to Dann. "I'm ready to marry you in July." Then she smiled at him. "Did I ever tell you how much I love the sparkle in your eyes?"

He grinned back at her. "I think I just read that some-where," he answered, offering her his hand to stand to make their goodbyes to Pastor Moorehouse.

After they left the church office, they walked hand-in-hand toward the Cherokee. Dann gave her an extra squeeze. "Do you know who we need to tell?"

"Who?"

"Mrs. Espinosa and Rosa."

"Oh my goodness, yes! This week has been such a three-ring circus I didn't even think. Let's go home so I can lie down for a little bit and then go visit them."

He sat on the floor next to her when she stretched out on her side on the couch with one arm under her head. She ran her fingers through the side of his hair. "You asked me to marry you a week ago and I thought that was the happiest day of my life, but I think I'm even happier today. What you wrote on your paper was absolutely lovely. I want to keep it forever."

"Please keep them both. I really had to fight to keep from getting teary-eyed myself. Thank you for what you wrote, too — it was as beautiful as you, Aud."

They sat and studied each other for several long moments.

"Do you know what touched me the most?" She caressed his smooth cheek with her hand. "Where you wrote that you feel totally safe in my love — "

"I do, Aud, and you said the same thing in your paper. It was the common thread, wasn't it?"

"Yes, but do you know how I came to that place? It was because you didn't kiss me." She watched Dann's eyebrow arch. "Oh, there were times when kissing me was all I wanted, and sometimes when you walked me to the door you'd hesitate, and I'd think maybe you were going to—and then you didn't. It took me a while to realize you'd put a constraint on yourself, a limit to protect—well, both of us. I began to see how strong you are, how much self-control you have, and I not only felt safe, I began to feel secure that you did love me even if you couldn't demonstrate it."

Dann ducked his head. When he met her eyes again, he said, "God is good, Aud. All along I thought not kissing you for a season was just something I had to do for myself to ensure I wouldn't make another mistake—and you don't know how often I struggled with it. I wanted to kiss you and hold you close to me all the time, but I think maybe God was directing me when I wasn't even aware of it. He knew your needs, too."

A smile lifted her lips. "Every day I see more and more how God takes care of me—us." She ran her fingers through his hair once more. "Dann…where do you want to live?"

He smiled back at her. "That was your second question the other day, and we never answered it, did we?" He swept his hand through the air, indicating the room. "I like this house, and it's perfect for your piano. I think I'd like to start out here, but someday, I'd like a place where I can set up my trains."

She rested her hand on his arm. "Would you do me a favor? Please go down in the basement for me. The light switch is next to the kitchen door. There's another light switch on the wall next to the furnace. Just go down and tell me what you see."

His eyebrows knit, but he stood without saying anything.

The kitchen door opened and closed. His feet clattered down the steps to the landing, but the sound faded as he descended the basement steps then died away. She could see it in her mind. He would see the furnace first, and then the washer and dryer on the other wall and the water heater to the left of them. He'd notice the gray metal shelves holding the laundry supplies and a few things stored there. If he were paying attention, he might even notice the clothesline just on the other side of the furnace, stretched from a post to the opposite wall. By now, he would have flipped the switch by the furnace. He'd be walking back, back, back into the empty space.

She waited. He was coming back up the steps. She heard the kitchen door close softly. He came and sat on the floor beside her again.

"Did you see the trains?"

He had the same look on his face as when she gave him the picture for his birthday, except, this time, tears were in his eyes. He didn't fight it. "I saw them, Aud." He wiped his eyes on his shirtsleeve. "I looked down those steps every time I came in the back door, but *my* trains in *your* basement never entered my head. But when we're married... Oh, wow!" His eyes flashed sparkles through new tears. "It'll be ideal—and you can help me build my dream."

She touched the side of his face. "Do you have any idea how rare a full basement is in this part of the country? Most homes are built on a slab, but the people who built this house came out from the Midwest and thought they'd never get along without their basement. They went to the extra expense to have it dug, even though my father thought they were crazy—and then they never used it except to accumulate junk. Little did I know, when I bought this house, it was waiting just for you."

He crossed his arms over his knees and rested his head on them. She let her fingers rest on his shoulder. "Dann...there's one more thing..." He turned his face to her, lifting his eyebrow. "I have some money I want your dad to invest for us." He kept looking at her without speaking. "It's about thirty thousand dollars."

He dropped his head back onto his arms across his knees, hiding his expression. "Aud," he lifted his head and smoothed his hand over her brow and the side of her face, "that's your money."

"No, my darling, it has to be *our* money. I started saving it before I began trusting the Lord, when I thought I was responsible for doing everything for myself. Remember when we went to Albuquerque and I paid for Tamina? In a flash, the Lord showed me I had a miserly, proud attitude toward that money and I had to let go of my hold on it."

"Is that where you got the money for my picture?"

She grinned. "Well, it is, but I bought it for you because I was already madly in love with you and I wanted you to have it. I want your dad to invest the money for us until the Lord tells us what to do with it."

His eyes were sparkling. "I think being married to you is going to be the greatest adventure of my life."

"Oh, I hope so." She leaned closer, giving him a kiss. "Are you ready to go tell Mrs. Espinosa?"

A NOTE FROM THE AUTHOR

Dear Reader,

Thank you for reading my debut novel, *Audra – Dying for Life*. I hope you enjoyed reading it as much as I enjoyed writing it. Please do take time to write a review on Amazon for me.

The idea for this story came to me in a dream. The circumstances were a bit different—a teacher stood at her blackboard, embarrassed by her initials written there connected to another teacher. Yes, I really do dream dreams that have a plot to them! The dream evolved into graffiti written on Audra's house, but that was the beginning. I praise the Lord for sparking my imagination.

However, when *Audra – Dying for Life* came to an end, I had as many questions as you may have had. What happened to Tamina, Heather, Mrs. Espinosa, and Rosa? That naturally led into the next book, *Audra – Life Transformed*. But to learn more about *Audra – Life Transformed*, please visit Carol's Book Spot – Stories for Women About Women at www.caroljnelson.com.

Happy reading, Carol